THE GREAT MODERN AMERICAN STORIES

THE
GREAT MODERN
AMERICAN STORIES

AN ANTHOLOGY

COMPILED AND EDITED
WITH AN INTRODUCTION

BY

WILLIAM DEAN HOWELLS

NEW YORK
BONI AND LIVERIGHT
1921

Printed in the United States of America

CONTENTS

A REMINISCENT INTRODUCTION

William Dean Howells

My reading has always been so much my living that I cannot separate them, and I should not like to part my remembrance of *My Double; and How He Undid Me* from my sense of convalescence on the sick bed where I first read it in Columbus, Ohio, and laughed myself back into health over it. I discovered in it the dear and delightful author of it, and felt as if I had invented Edward Everett Hale long before I knew him by name, for in those days *The Atlantic Monthly,* where I first read it, never gave the names of its contributors, such being its sacred *Blackwood Magazine* tradition. My first reading of the story was the first of many readings of it and laughings over it with all the friends who then inhabited Columbus to the sum of the little city's population of 20,000. These were all people of my own age, say of twenty or twenty-one, and my partners, both sexes, in the awful joy of Miss Prescott's (not yet Mrs. Spofford's) tremendous story of *Circumstance,* still unsurpassed of its kind. We thrilled over it severally and collectively (the whole 20,000 of us), and are still ready to swear it unsurpassed, though we are now over seventy or eighty years old and 200,000 in number.

It wanted at least two generations to freeze our young blood with Mrs. Perkins Gilman's story of *The Yellow Wall Paper,* which Horace Scudder (then of *The Atlantic*) said in refusing it that it was so terribly good that it ought never to be printed. But terrible and too wholly dire as it was, I could not rest until I had corrupted the editor of *The New England Magazine* into publishing it. Now that I have got it into my collection here, I shiver over it as much as I did when I first read it in manuscript, though I agree with the editor of *The Atlantic* of the time that it was too terribly good to be printed.

In a far zigzag of time and kind from this awful study of
incipient madness is *A Passionate Pilgrim,* which I had the
privilege of accepting from Henry James in the earliest years
of my long *Atlantic* editorship. I had the privilege of accepting many more famous things of his, but "young" as this
story is in many ways, it is of a life, a feeling, a color, and
above all a prompt distinctness, altogether absent from his
later, and, if one will, more masterly work. In fact it is of
a masterliness which its maturer author might deny but would
not forbid, his young editor affirming. The American character studied in it is American to the last degree, and as
sharply distinct from the English, as the fervidest American could wish, and it is of the greater interest because the
young author's Americanism eventuated, after many long
years of English sojourn, in his renouncing his American
citizenship and becoming an English subject. Every reader
will have his, or her, feeling as to the biographical fact, but
I think no one can deny the genuine passion of this most
passionate pilgrim, or the pathos of his experience. It is an
intense piece of American fiction, such as the author has
never since surpassed.

The three great artists, working always in simple and
native stuff, whom I have almost inevitably grouped together in the order of my acquaintance with their stories, are
collectively, if not severally, without equal among their contemporaries in their order of fiction. I like the beautiful
art, the gentle nature-love and the delicate humor of Sarah
Orne Jewett because I knew it first as the very junior editor
whom it first came to in settled form, but I do not know that
I value it more than the stories of Mrs. Wilkins Freeman or
the stories of Miss Alice Brown, which I knew with the rest
of the public when they began to appear in response to other
editorial welcome. I think *The Revolt of Mother* had the
widest and warmest welcome from the whole English-read-
ing world; Miss Brown's story here is fairly suggestive of her
far-reaching study of New England life; and very possibly
it is because of my earlier liking for Sarah Orne Jewett's
story that I like it most. She is less dramatic in the piece
chosen than the others; the story is scarcely more than a

placid and whimsical study of scene and character; it was
hard to find any story of hers that was more than a study,
but how preciously richer than a story this study is!

I had a like difficulty in getting a story from Charles
Warren Stoddard's *South Sea Idyls,* for when I came to renew my friendship with them, I found *A Prodigal in Tahiti*
the only one among those delicious sketches which was like a
story, and this was scarcely like a story at all. Half my
life it had been a delight to me, and I was not going to
forego it because it was a bit of autobiography and not a
dramatic invention. My situation would have been the joy
of Stoddard himself, and if there are smiles in heaven, where
he has been these half dozen years, he must be looking down
with a characteristic pleasure in the dilemma of the earliest
editor of a study which refused to be quite a story. He must
be generously sharing with that editor the delight of the
"detonating boot" which he wore in the dusty walks to the
joy of the gentle Tahitian crowds following him in his famine
around their island from breakfastless morn till supperless
eve.

I think Aldrich came after Stoddard's sketch with his
unique invention of *Marjorie Daw* and I am sure of the succession of *Mademoiselle Zabriski* following that, and which
I reproduce here, not as the better but the best his publishers
can allow his latest editor who was his earliest. *Mademoiselle
Zabriski* is not only the next cleverest thing of Aldrich's
after *Marjorie Daw,* but is notable for being one of those
feats of fact in which nature sometimes imitates art, as I
personally learned from an experience behind the scenes of
a country circus where I was once presented to an amiable
clown who said he liked my books, and then presented me to
his son newly alighted from the trapeze. I viewed the youth
with the surprise of a spectator who had just seen him in
flying skirts and now beheld him in succinct tights. "But—
but," I faltered, and "Oh, yes," his father interjected, "You
thought he was a girl. Well, the public likes them better as
girls," and I was aware of standing in the presence of one
who might well have been *Mademoiselle Zabriski,* but had
not quite the artistic touch of Aldrich in his realization. Some

day I hope to tell the pleasant tale of my relation with Aldrich as a most favored and desired contributor with the young under-editor, and all our joyous lunching and joking together in the rivalry of our new-married housekeeping; but this is not yet the time or place. I can only affirm it one of the happiest things I remember.

With Miss Edith Wyatt's story I had the same sort of difficulty in finding anything definitely dramatic among her studies of Chicago life, as I had in finding a story among Stoddard's *South Sea Idyls.* She called them *Every One His Own Way,* perhaps because she could not think of a more distinctive name for them. But they were all exquisite things, most artistic and most realistic things, delicate portraits of life worthy of equal place with the stories and studies of those unrivalled sisters three, Miss Jewett, and Mrs. Wilkins Freeman and Miss Alice Brown whom I have put here in their rare succession.

If I am required to say why I have chosen from Mrs. Edith Wharton's many minor masterpieces *The Mission of Jane,* I should be defied in vain unless I were suffered to say that it was the instant delight of the whole family who read it together and cherished it thereafter as one of the most precious jewels of remembrance. Even this would appear no sufficient reason save to such elect as could rejoice in the portrayal of the perfect and entire dullness of Jane and her equally dull admirer. It is truly an unsurpassed piece of art, worthy of like rank with the best things in our wonder-book of good things here, though there is nothing better here than the episode of *Aunt Sanna Terry,* which a beneficent chance vouchsafed to one of us in the very unexpected pages of *The Southern Workman* where the humor of Miss Dashiell had lavished it on that organ of Hampton Institute. There is, to my thinking, no superior to it in the whole range of colored character, as the mastery of the South which knows it best has portrayed it in *Uncle Remus,* and Mark Twain and Mr. Cable's very varied and exquisitely rendered shades and differences of the race unsurpassedly known to him.

Not yet to turn aside to these greater names, I must ask

the reader to share my pleasure in Miss Virginia Tracy's
delightful tale of *The Lotus Eaters* where they sit famishing at the lunch table in the absence of the retarded alimony
of the hostess. There is never so good talk as that of players
off the stage, however they fail on it, and the climax of the
hostess's announcement to the lovers among the clothes-lines
on the roof that "the alimony has come" is something unrivalled in the strokes of tragi-comedy or comi-tragedy.

I could not read Mr. Cable's most touching story of *Jean-
ah Poquelin* without hearing the voice of Mark Twain in
reading its most dramatic phrases with his tragic pleasure
in the old Negro-trader's concealment of his leper-brother in
defiance of the authorities proposing to run a street through
his property, in the interest of public improvement. His
glorious defiance of "Strit shall not pass!" sounds in my
ears yet, as Clemens pronounced it; and in its other kind I
hear him read *The Tar Baby* as he heard the colored fablers
of his Missouri childhood tell it. His own earliest and last-
ingest masterpiece, *The Jumping Frog,* I never heard him
read among the other masterpieces of his which he delighted
to give with that unequalled dramatic authority of his, but
many a time I heard him tell the story of its publication by
his fellow Californian who first brought it out in New York
when they had both ceased from the Pacific Slope and transferred themselves to these Atlantic shores. It was supposed
to have enriched the publishers in the same measure that it
impoverished the author, but this may have been one of those
imaginary experiences in which his varied life abounded.
It did not affect the unequalled quality of the great story
itself which remains one of the most stupendous of his inventions. It won that English renown which others of his
great things enjoyed before their home-acceptance, and it
lost nothing in hearing "Tom Brown" of Rugby speaking of
it at Lowell's table as *The Leapin' Frog* instead of *The
Jumping Frog,* though the loving misnomer hurt the American ear.

Clemens was by all odds the best reader I ever heard,
whether he read his own things or others' things, and he
sang with as great feeling the Negro spirituals of the Jubilee

Singers when they first made their way North. He told the stories of Uncle Remus in his native speech. How Joel Chandler Harris might have interpreted them I cannot venture to say. From an almost inarticulate meeting with him at Boston I have the impression of a transcendent bashfulness in which we made no way with him in any hospitable endeavor and he left us with the remembrance of nothing more distinctive than a meeting at his publisher's, who was also mine; but I could imagine all delightful things in him if once I could get beyond that insuperable diffidence of his.

The *Son of the Middle Border* is represented here by an early favorite of mine in *The Return of the Private* which remembers all the simple pathos of the home-coming of those Civil War veterans when they returned to their corn-fields from their battle-fields. Hamlin Garland has done many other beautiful and manly things, but no homely things more beautiful and manly or more characteristic of his art; and I think Mr. Ambrose Bierce has done nothing more imaginative than *An Occurence at Owl Creek Bridge,* where he carries further the sort of post-mortem consciousness which Tolstoy and Turgenev were the first to imagine. It is very excellent work, and is all the more interesting in the expression of Confederate feeling, which is less known to fiction than Union feeling in the war dear alike to North and South.

The plain poetry, tending to the plain wierdness of Mr. Theodore Dreiser's story of *The Lost Phœbe* is of a quality that I find in almost nothing else of anyone else. The tenderness of the plainest of Lincoln's plain people whom God seemed to him to have made mainly in our nearer Middle West is expressed incomparably in the delusion of the old widower who believes that his wife returns to him as the phantom he can make no other see. The local conditioning is studied with the same fidelity that keeps the older New England alive in the art of those Sisters Three whom I have grouped together and am never tired of praising. There is a "touch of nature beyond the reach of art" in the crazy custom of the old wanderer who throws his stick before him in his search for his "lost Phœbe" sure that he will find her beside it when he comes up to it.

One does not escape that choice of *The Outcasts of Poker Flat* which so many have made before me as more representative of Bret Harte's most characteristic work. Why we do not choose *The Luck of Roaring Camp,* the thing that first won him world-wide recognition, or some other thing, like *Tennessee's Partner,* I cannot say; I only know that *The Outcasts of Poker Flat* offers itself at the hands of general preference. Perhaps it has been chosen because of the characterization of the gentleman-gambler whom the keenest critic among Harte's contemporary Californians regarded as his strongest suit. Certainly he has done nothing better in his best sort than "Mr. John Oakhurst, Gambler."

With the like perversity of editors, I have chosen one of the shipwrecks dear to Frank Stockton's whimsical humor, and not the unique triumph which all the rest of the world likes best in *The Lady and the Tiger.* But I shall always believe that a large minority of his lovers will be with me in my choice of *The Christmas Wreck,* though to be sure there is *The Wreck of the Thomas Hike.* His fine spirit is subtly with us in the far range of its numberless caprices and inventions, though eternity seems the richer and time the poorer in his going from us. If his fame seems in a momentary abeyance it is because this sort of eclipse must come to all. We must remember that it is the shadow of our little moon that now and again blots the sun, though I cannot specify personally any renown which has come between us and Stockton's beloved name.

In this collection there is nothing humaner or more humane than Mr. George Ade's quite perfect study of real life, *Effie Whittlesy.* It is a contribution to American fiction of a value far beyond most American novels; and the American small town which has often shrunken into the American City lives again here in its characteristic personality. It is a thing which I have read unnumbered times to myself and to those I love best, but I am still in doubt whether the admirable Effie or the excellent Ed Wallace is more my friend. I have so much affection for them both that I have a sincere regard for Mrs. Wallace, though she somewhat tardily wins it. The story is the best in the volume *In Babel,* where the Chicago-West, which so incomparably burlesques itself in the famous *Fables,* studies its likeness in the art of a master, as it does in Mr. Henry B. Fuller's *Striking an Average.* This is not only good Chicago, but is good native American—not too fine in the youth intending municipal politics in his own interest—and is good Irish-American in the clever, handsome Irish girl who means to help him up with the help of her efficient political father, already at the top in municipal politics. It is all very lightly and persuasively done, not only in the youth's society mother, but in the girl's mother and their unforced friendliness. The girl's superiority to the youth is never rubbed into the reader, who is not made to do more than share the young American's own sense of it.

I think that probably more interesting people, especially interesting women, have a greater devotion for Mrs. Wynne's romance of *The Little Room* than for any like story—if there is any other like story. It first appeared in *Harper's Magazine* some thirty years ago, and it has never since disappeared, though evanescence is the prime motive of it. I myself was one of the many editors of the collections which contain it; and I put it in one of my first volumes of those *Harper Novelettes* which it was another's happy thought to suggest the republication of in kindred groups. It remains forever a question whether *The Little Room* was a habitable chamber, or a mere closet without valuable character; the sequel to it which the author wrote has not seemed to explain or enhance its interest in this editor's view. But no such difference of opinion can affect its weird charm; it must remain forever a triumph of the imagination, an unending tease of the curiosity, though this is a quite inadequate expression of its peculiar charm. It may or may not add to its appeal that there is an architectural plagiarism of its motive in the beautiful house which Henry VIII built for Anne Boleyn at Southampton. From the street you see a window which opens to no room within. If you doubt of Mrs. Wynne's Little Room yon can go there and verify it.

PUBLISHER'S NOTE

References for the Study of the Short Story

Those who wish to study the short story beyond the material afforded in the present volume will find the following references helpful:

For American literature in general three of the best short accounts are: *A History of American Literature,* by Fred Lewis Pattee (Silver, Burdett & Co., 1896); *A History of American Literature,* by William Peterfield Trent (D. Appleton & Co., 1903); and *American Literature,* by Alphonso G. Newcomer (Scott, Foresman & Co., 1901). For a more extended treatment the three-volume *Cambridge History of American Literature* (G. P. Putnam's Sons, 1917-1918-1920) is the most thorough work. This is edited by William P. Trent, John Erskine, Stuart P. Sherman and Carl Van Doren, and the chapters are written by specialists, but in a way to interest the general reader. Particular chapters are referred to farther on. For an extended treatment of one period of American literature Fred Lewis Pattee's *A History of American Literature Since 1870* (The Century Co., 1915) is invaluable. A stimulating little work along critical lines is *The Spirit of American Literature,* by John Albert Macy (Boni & Liveright, 1913: The Modern Library).

For a study of the short story in general an excellent approach is through the collection, edited by Alexander Jessup and Henry Seidel Canby, *The Book of the Short Story* (D. Appleton & Co., 1903), which shows the evolution of the short story from about 2500 B. C. through 1890 by its eighteen representative stories from various literatures. An introduction of twenty-eight pages traces the development of the short story under the headings, *The Short Story and the Tales, The Short Story and the Novel,* and *The Rise of the Short Story.* This was the pioneer collection of short stories from various literatures, to show the development of the form. The *List of Representative Tales and Short Stories* included directs the student to further reading. Four years after the appearance of the book edited by Jessup and Canby, Brander Matthews put out a collection along similar lines, *The Short Story* (American Book Co., 1907).

The most comprehensive collection of purely American short stories is *The American Short Story: Examples Showing its Development* (Allyn & Bacon: Boston, 1920), which contains seventy-three stories ranging in date from 1788 to 1920. This is the largest collection of short stories in one volume yet made. As a guide to more extended reading there is included a list of over thirty-five hundred American short stories and short story collections. A much smaller undertaking is *American Short Stories,* edited by Charles Sears Baldwin (Longmans, Green & Co., 1904), which contains fifteen stories ranging in date from 1819 to 1897. An interesting introduction of thirty-five pages is marred by many errors, including wrong dates and misstatements of fact. Apart from its many mistakes the book is good as far as it goes. A collection of American short stories in a special field is *The Best American Humorous Short Stories* (Boni & Liveright, 1920), edited by Alexander Jessup. The volume contains eighteen stories ranging in date from 1839 to 1914, and an interesting introduction of twenty-six pages. Bret Harte, Stockton, Bunner, and O. Henry are among the authors represented. A series of ten small volumes, *Stories by American Authors,* edited anonymously (Charles Scribner's Sons, 1884-88) contains fifty-eight stories. The selection in no way represents American literature adequately, since neither Irving, Poe, Hawthorne nor Bret Harte are included, nor does it contain any stories written after 1885.

Those who wish to read some of the best short stories in French literature will find forty-four of them in the series of six small volumes, *Little French Masterpieces,* edited by

Alexander Jessup (G. P. Putnam's Sons, 1903). The
authors represented are Mérimée, Flaubert, Gautier, Daudet,
Maupassant and Balzac. Each volume has an introduction
by a distinguished critic; especially valuable for the student of the short story are the *Essays on Maupassant*, by
Arthur Symons; and Balzac, by Ferdinand Brumetiére.
In the latter a differentiation is made for the first time
between the French forms of fiction, the nouvelle, the conte
and the roman. The translation is by George Burnham
Ives. A remarkably comprehensive and incisively critical
work is *A Century of French Fiction*, by Benjamin W. Wells
(Dodd, Mead & Co., 1898). The three essays on the various
aspects of Balzac, and those on Mérimée, Gautier, Flaubert,
Daudet, and Maupassant will be found the most interesting
of its seventeen chapters to the student of the short story.
A single-volume collection of twenty-two stories is *The
Great Modern French Stories: A Chronological Anthology*,
edited by Willard Huntington Wright (Boni & Liveright,
1917). It contains a valuable introduction of forty-two
pages.

Among the purely critical volumes dealing with the short
story, in addition to the collections containing critical
matter mentioned above, is *A Study of the Short Story*, by
Henry Seidel Canby (Henry Holt & Co., 1913). This
volume contains eleven short stories, all from English and
American literature, but the critical portion of the book so
far outweighs the collection in importance that it is mentioned here rather than with the collections. The introduction of seventy-eight pages is divided into sixteen chapters.
Another excellent volume dealing critically with the subject is *A Handbook of Story Writing* (Dodd, Mead & Co.,
1917). This treats the short story from a technical stand-
point. A somewhat more advanced treatment of the
subject is *The Art and the Business of Story Writing*, by
Walter B. Pitkin (The Macmillan Co., 1912). *The
Philosophy of the Short Story*, by Brander Matthews
(Longmans, Green & Co., 1901; republished with revision
from *The Saturday Review*, 1884) was the first American
treatment of the short story as a separate form of fiction.

It said explicitly what Poe had hinted at in his review of *Hawthorne's Twice-Told Tales* in 1842 and in his essay on the *Philosophy of Composition* (1846). The chapter on *The Short Story* (republished from *The Atlantic Monthly,* August, 1902) in Bliss Perry's, *A Study of Prose Fiction* (Houghton, Mifflin Co., 1902) is interesting, as is Clayton Hamilton's *Structure of the Short Story,* in his book, *A Manual of the Art of Fiction* (Doubleday, Page & Co., 1908). William Dean Howells' chapter on *Some Anomalies of the Short Story* (reprinted from *The North American Review,* October, 1901) in his *Literature and Life* (Harper & Bros., 1902) is decidedly stimulating.

For the American short story the chapters in *The Cambridge History of American Literature,* Volume II (G. P. Putnam's Sons, 1918) on *Hawthorne,* by John Erskine; *Poe,* by Killis Campbell; *Magazines, Annuals and Gift-Books, 1783-1850,* by William B. Cairns; and *The Short Story,* by Fred Lewis Pattee, are all valuable. The chapter on *The Triumph of the Short Story* in *Patte's History of American Literature Since 1870* (The Century Co., 1915) is a comprehensive survey from Bret Harte almost down to date. John Erskine's *Leading American Novelists* (Henry Holt & Co., 1910) is especially interesting to the student of the short story for its chapters on *Hawthorne and Bret Harte.* William Crary Brownell's *American Prose Masters* (Charles Scribner's Sons, 1909) is a notable work of criticism of six great American authors. The chapters on *Hawthorne, Poe* and *Henry James* will attract the short-story investigator. Then there is *Hawthorne and the Short Story,* by Walter Morris Harte (University of California: Berkeley, 1900), the introduction by Alexander Jessup to his collection, *The American Short Story* (Allyn & Bacon, 1920), already mentioned, and Charles Sears Baldwin's introduction to his *American Short Stories* (Longmans, Green & Co., 1904), also referred to above. The chapters in Henry Siedel Canby's *A Study of the Short Story* (Henry Holt & Co., 1913) entitled *Poe, and the Further Development of the Romantic Short Story, Nathaniel Hawthorne, America in the Midcentury, Bret Harte, The Local Colorists,* and *The*

Deepening of the Short Story: Henry James, will all be found extremely interesting, as will this writer's chapters on *Edgar Allan Poe, Nathaniel Hawthorne, The Midcentury in America* and *The Americans from Bret Harte to the Nineties*, in his larger book, *The Short Story in English* (Henry Holt & Co., 1909).

The most comprehensive treatment of the short story in any one literature is Henry Seidel Canby's *The Short Story in English* (Henry Holt & Co., 1909). Until recently there has been no comprehensive or entirely satisfactory collection showing the development of the English short story. *The Great Modern English Stories*, compiled and edited, with an introduction by Edward J. O'Brien (Boni & Liveright, 1919) is an interesting and valuable collection containing twenty-eight stories all of which were written within the last forty years. Mr. O'Brien stresses the point that the short story is not a characteristic English form. In this same *Great Modern Short Story Series* will appear in 1920, *The Great Modern German Stories*, compiled and edited with an introduction by Ludwig Lewisohn, *The Great Modern Scandinavian Stories*, compiled and edited with an introduction by Edwin Bjorkman, and *The Great Modern Italian Stories*, compiled and edited with an introduction by Arturo Giovannitti.

The two volumes already mentioned by Blanche Colton Williams and Walter B. Pitkin, although chiefly technical treatments of the subject, also go into what may be termed the "practical" side to a certain extent. Other volumes dealing with this, including such aspects as popularity, marketing, etc., are J. Berg Esenwein's *Writing the Short Story* (Hinds, Noble & Eldredge, 1909), *The Contemporary Short Story*, by Harry T. Baker (D. C. Heath & Co., 1916), and *Where and How to Sell MSS; a Descriptive Directory for Writers*, edited by William B. McFourtie (Home Correspondence School: Springfield, Mass., 1919).

Edward J. O'Brien's annual volumes, of which the latest at this writing is *The Best Short Stories of 1919* (Small, Maynard & Co.), keep the student of the subject up-to-date. Besides reprinting a selection of the best stories by American authors that have appeared in American magazines each year, these volumes contain a list of a larger number of the best short stories, a list of the best story collections of the year, and other valuable matter.

CHARLES STEWART RIVERS.

MY DOUBLE; AND HOW HE UNDID ME *

By Edward Everett Hale

IT is not often that I trouble the readers of the *Atlantic Monthly*. I should not trouble them now, but for the importunities of my wife, who "feels to insist" that a duty to society is unfulfilled, till I have told why I had to have a double, and how he undid me. She is sure, she says, that intelligent persons cannot understand that pressure upon public servants which alone drives any man into the employment of a double. And while I fear she thinks, at the bottom of her heart, that my fortunes will never be remade, she has a faint hope, that, as another Rasselas, I may teach a lesson to future publics, from which they may profit, though we die. Owing to the behavior of my double, or, if you please, to that public pressure which compelled me to employ him, I have plenty of leisure to write this communication.

I am, or rather was, a minister of the Sandemanian connection. I was settled in the active, wide-awake town of Naguadavick, on one of the finest water-powers in Maine. We used to call it a Western town in the heart of civilization of New England. A charming place it was and is. A spirited, brave young parish had I; and it seemed as if we might have all "the joy of eventful living" to our hearts' content.

Alas! how little we knew on the day of my ordination, and in those halcyon moments of our first housekeeping! To be the confidential friend in a hundred families in the town— cutting the social trifle, as my friend Haliburton says, "from the top of the whipped-syllabub to the bottom of the sponge-

---

* Permission of Little, Brown & Co., and Ellen Day Hale.

3

cake, which is the foundation"; to keep abreast of the thought of the age in one's study, and to do one's best on Sunday to interweave that thought with the active life of an active town, and to inspirit both and make both infinite by glimpses of the Eternal Glory, seemed such an exquisite fore-look into one's life! Enough to do, and all so real and so grand! If this vision could only have lasted!

The truth is, that this vision was not in itself a delusion, nor, indeed, half bright enough. If one could only have been left to do his own business, the vision would have accomp-lished itself and brought out new paraheliacal visions, each as bright as the original. The misery was and is, as we found out, I and Polly, before long, that, besides the vision, and besides the usual human and finite failures in life (such as breaking the old pitcher that came over in the *May-flower,* and putting into the fire the alpenstock with which her father climbed Mont Blanc)—besides these, I say, (imitating the style of Robinson Crusoe) there were pitch-forked in on us a great rowen-heap of humbugs, handed down from some unknown seed-time, in which we were expected, and I chiefly, to fulfill certain public functions before the community, of the character of those fulfilled by the third row of supernumeraries who stand behind the Sepoys in the spectacle of the *Cataract of the Ganges.* They were the duties, in a word, which one performs as member of one or another social class or subdivision, wholly distinct from what one does as A by himself A. What invisible power put these functions on me, it would be very hard to tell. But such power there was and is. And I had not been at work a year before I found I was living two lives for two sets of people, one real and one merely functional—one my parish, whom I loved, and the other a vague public, for whom I did not care two straws. All this was in a vague notion, which every-body had and has, that this second life would eventually bring out some great results, unknown at present, to some-body somewhere.

Crazed by this duality of life, I first read Dr. Wigan on the *Duality of the Brain,* hoping that I could train one side of my head to do these outside jobs, and the other to do my intimate and real duties. For Richard Greenough once told me that, in studying for the statue of Franklin, he found that the left side of the great man's face was philosophic and reflective, and the right side funny and smiling. If you will go and look at the bronze statue, you will find he has repeated this observation there for posterity. The eastern profile is the portrait of the statesman Franklin, the western of Poor Richard. But Dr. Wigan does not go into these niceties of this subject, and I failed. It was then, that, on my wife's suggestion, I resolved to look out for a Double.

I was, at first, singularly successful. We happened to be recreating at Stafford Springs that summer. We rode out one day, for one of the relaxations of that watering-place, to the great Monsonpon House. We were passing through one of the large halls, when my destiny was fulfilled! I saw my man!

He was not shaven. He had on no spectacles. He was dressed in a green baize roundabout and faded blue overalls, worn sadly at the knee. But I saw at once that he was of my height, five feet four and a half. He had black hair, worn off by his hat. So have and have not I. He stooped in walking. So do I. His hands were large, and mine. And —choicest gift of Fate in all—he had, not "a strawberry-mark on his left arm," but a cut from a juvenile brickbat over his right eye, slightly affecting the play of that eyebrow. Reader, so have I! My fate was sealed!

A word with Mr. Holly, one of the inspectors, settled the whole thing. It proved that this Dennis Shea was a harmless, amiable fellow, one of the class known as shiftless, who had sealed his fate by marrying a dumb wife, who was at that moment ironing in the laundry. Before I left Stafford, I had hired both for five years. We had applied to Judge Pynchon, then the probate judge at Springfield, to change the name of Dennis Shea to Frederic Ingham. We had explained to the Judge, what was the precise truth, that an eccentric gentleman wished to adopt Dennis under this new name into his family. It never occurred to him that Dennis might be more than fourteen years old. And thus, to shorten this preface, when we returned at night to my parsonage at

Naguadavick, there entered Mrs. Ingham, her new dumb laundress, myself, who am Mr. Frederic Ingham, and my double, who was Mr. Frederic Ingham by as good right as I.

Oh, the fun we had the next morning in shaving his beard to my pattern, cutting his hair to match mine, and teaching him how to wear and how to take off gold-bowed spectacles! Really, they were electro-plate, and the glass was plain (for the poor fellow's eyes were excellent). Then in four successive afternoons I taught him four speeches. I had found these would be quite enough for the supernumerary-Sepoy line of life, and it was well for me they were. For though he was good-natured, he was very shiftless, and it was, as our national proverb says, "like pulling teeth" to teach him. But at the end of the next week he could say, with quite my easy and frisky air:

1. "Very well, thank you. And you?" This for an answer to casual salutations.

2. "I am very glad you liked it."

3. "There has been so much said, and, on the whole, so well said, that I will not occupy the time."

4. "I agree, in general, with my friend the other side of the room."

At first I had a feeling that I was going to be at great cost for clothing him. But it proved, of course, at once, that, whenever he was out, I should be at home. And I went, during the bright period of his success, to so few of those awful pageants which require a black dress-coat and what the ungodly call, after Mr. Dickens, a white choker, that in the happy retreat of my own dressing-gowns and jackets my days went by as happily and cheaply as those of another Thalaba. And Polly declares there was never a year when the tailoring cost so little. He lived (Dennis, not Thalaba) in his wife's room over the kitchen. He had orders never to show himself at that window. When he appeared in the front of the house, I retired to my sanctissimum and my dressing-gown. In short, the Dutchman and his wife, in the old weather-box, had not less to do with each other than he and I. He made the furnace-fire and split the wood before daylight; then he went to sleep again, and slept late; then came for orders, with a red silk bandanna tied round his head, with his over-alls on, and his dress-coat and spectacles off. If we hap-pened to be interrupted, no one guessed that he was Frederic Ingham as well as I; and, in the neighborhood, there grew up an impression that the minister's Irishman worked day-times in the factory village at New Coventry. After I had given him his orders, I never saw him till the next day.

I launched him by sending him to a meeting of the En-lightenment Board. The Enlightenment Board consists of seventy-four members, of whom sixty-seven are necessary to form a quorum. One becomes a member under the regu-lations laid down in old Judge Dudley's will. I became one by being ordained pastor of a church in Naguadavick. You see you cannot help yourself, if you would. At this particular time we had had four successive meetings, averaging four hours each—wholly occupied in whipping in a quorum. At the first only eleven men were present; at the next, by force of three circulars, twenty-seven; at the third, thanks to two days' canvassing by Auchmuty and myself begging men to come, we had sixty. Half the others were in Europe. But without a quorum we could do nothing. All the rest of us waited grimly for our four hours, and adjourned without any action. At the fourth meeting we had flagged and only got fifty-nine together. But on the first appearance of my double —whom I sent on this fatal Monday to the fifth meeting— he was the *sixty-seventh* man who entered the room. He was greeted with a storm of applause! The poor fellow had missed his way—read the street signs ill through his spectacles (very ill, in fact, without them)—and had not dared to inquire. He entered the room, finding the presi-dent and secretary holding to their chairs two judges of the Supreme Court, who were also members *ex officio,* and were begging leave to go away. On his entrance all was changed. *Presto,* the by-laws were amended, and the Western prop-erty was given away. Nobody stopped to converse with him. He voted, as I had charged him to do, in every instance, with the minority. I won new laurels as a man of sense, though a little unpunctual—and Dennis, *alias* Ingham, returned to the parsonage, astonished to see with how little wisdom the world is governed. He cut a few of my parishioners in the street; but he had his glasses off, and I am known to be near-sighted. Eventually he recognized them more readily than I.

I "set him again" at the exhibition of the New Coventry Academy; and here he undertook a "speaking part"—as, in my boyish, worldly days, I remember the bills used to say of Mlle. Céleste. We are all trustees of the New Coventry Academy; and there has lately been "a good deal of feeling" because the Sandemanian trustees did not regularly attend the exhibitions. It has been intimated, indeed, that the Sandemanians are leaning towards Free-Will, and that we have, therefore, neglected these semi-annual exhibitions, while there is no doubt that Auchmuty last year went to Commencement at Waterville. Now the head master at New Coventry is a real good fellow, who knows a Sanskrit root when he sees it, and often cracks etymologies with me, so that, in strictness, I ought to go to their exhibitions. But think, reader, of sitting through three long July days in that Academy chapel, following the programme from

TUESDAY MORNING. *English Composition.* "SUNSHINE." Miss Jones.

round to

Trio on Three Pianos. Duet from the Opera of "MIDSHIPMAN EASY." *Marryatt.*

coming in at nine, Thursday evening! Think of this, reader, for men who know the world is trying to go backward, and who would give their lives if they could help it on! Well! The double had succeeded so well at the Board, that I sent him to the Academy. (Shade of Plato, pardon!) He arrived early on Tuesday, when, indeed, few but mothers and clergymen are generally expected, and returned in the evening to us, covered with honors. He had dined at the right hand of the chairman, and spoke in high terms of the repast. The chairman had expressed his interest in the French conversation. "I am very glad you liked it," said Dennis; and the poor chairman, abashed, supposed the ac-cent had been wrong. At the end of the day, the gentlemen present had been called upon for speeches—the Rev. Frederic

Ingham first, as it happened; upon which Dennis had risen, and had said, "There has been so much said, and, on the whole, so well said, that I will not occupy the time." The girls were delighted because Dr. Dabney, the year before, had given them at this occasion a scolding on impropriety of behavior at lyceum lectures. They all declared Mr. Ingham was a love,—and *so* handsome! (Dennis is good-looking.) Three of them, with arms behind the others' waists, followed him up to the wagon he rode home in; and a little girl with a blue sash had been sent to give him a rosebud. After this *début* in speaking, he went to the exhibition for two days more, to the mutual satisfaction of all concerned. Indeed, Polly reported that he had pronounced the trustees' dinners of a higher grade than those of the parsonage. When the next term began, I found six of the Academy girls had obtained permission to come across the river and attend our church. But this arrangement did not long continue.

After this he went to several Commencements for me, and ate the dinners provided; he sat through three of our Quarterly Conventions for me, always voting judiciously, by the simple rule mentioned above, of siding with the minority. And I, meanwhile, who had before been losing caste among my friends, as holding myself aloof from the associations of the body, began to rise in everybody's favor. "Ingham's a good fellow—always on hand"; "never talks much—but does the right thing at the right time"; "is not as unpunctual as he used to be—he comes early, and sits through to the end." "He has got over his old talkative habit, too. I spoke to a friend of his about it once; and I think Ingham took it kindly," etc., etc.

This voting power of Dennis was particularly valuable at the quarterly meetings of the Proprietors of the Naguadavick Ferry. My wife inherited from her father some shares in that enterprise, which is not yet fully developed, though it doubtless will become a very valuable property. The law of Maine then forbade stockholders to appear by proxy at such meetings. Polly disliked to go, not being, in fact, a "hens'-rights hen," and transferred her stock to me. I, after going once, disliked it more than she. But Dennis went to the next

meeting and liked it very much. He said the armchairs were
good, the collation good, and the free rides to stockholders
pleasant. He was a little frightened when they first took
him upon one of the ferry-boats, but after two or three
quarterly meetings he became quite brave.

Thus far I never had any difficulty with him. Indeed,
being of that type which is called shiftless, he was only too
happy to be told daily what to do, and to be charged not to
be forthputting or in any way original in his discharge of that
duty. He learned, however, to discriminate between the lines
of his life, and very much preferred these stockholders' meetings and trustees' dinners and Commencement collations to
another set of occasions, from which he used to beg off most
piteously. Our excellent brother, Dr. Fillmore, had taken
a notion at this time that our Sandemanian churches needed
more expression of mutual sympathy. He insisted upon it
that we were remiss. He said, that, if the Bishop came to
preach at Naguadavick, all the Episcopal clergy of the
neighborhood were present; if Dr. Pond came, all the Congregational clergymen turned out to hear him; if Dr. Nichols,
all the Unitarians; and he thought we owed it to each other,
that, whenever there was an occasional service at a Sandemanian church, the other brethren should all, if possible, attend. "It looked well," if nothing more. Now this really
meant that I had not been to hear one of Dr. Fillmore's
lectures on the *Ethnology of Religion.* He forgot that he
did not hear one of my course on the "Sandemanianism of
Anselm." But I felt badly when he said it; and afterwards
I always made Dennis go to hear all the brethren preach,
when I was not preaching myself. This was what he took
exception to—the only thing, as I said, which he ever
did except to. Now came the advantage of his long morning-
nap, and of the green tea with which Polly supplied the
kitchen. But he would plead, so humbly, to be let off, only
from one or two! I never excepted him, howewer. I knew
the lectures were of value, and I thought it best he should
be able to keep the connection.

Polly is more rash than I am, as the reader has observed
in the outset of this memoir. She risked Dennis one night

under the eyes of her own sex. Governor Gorges had always
been very kind to us; and when he gave his great annual party
to the town, asked us. I confess I hated to go. I was deep in
the new volume of Pfeiffer's *Mystics,* which Haliburton
had just sent me from Boston. "But how rude," said Polly,
"not to return the Governor's civility and Mrs. Gorges's, when
they will be sure to ask why you are away!" Still I demurred, and at last she, with the wit of Eve and of Semiramis
conjoined, let me off by saying, that if I would go in with her,
and sustain the initial conversations with the Governor and
the ladies staying there, she would risk Dennis for the rest
of the evening. And that was just what we did. She took
Dennis in training all that afternoon, instructed him in
fashionable conversation, cautioned him against the tempta-
tions of the supper-table—and at nine in the evening he drove
us all down in the carry-all. I made the grand star-*entrée*
with Polly and the pretty Walton girls, who were staying with
us. We had put Dennis into a great rough top-coat, without
his glasses—and the girls never dreamed, in the darkness, of
looking at him. He sat in the carriage, at the door, while we
entered. I did the agreeable to Mrs. Gorges, was introduced
to her niece, Miss Fernanda—I complimented Judge Jeffries
on his decision in the great case of D'Aulnay *vs.* Laconia
Mining Co.—I stepped into the dressing-room for a moment—
stepped out for another—walked home, after a nod with
Dennis, and tying the horse to a pump—and while I walked
home, Mr. Frederic Ingham, my double, stepped in through
the library into the Gorges's grand saloon.

Oh! Polly died of laughing as she told me of it at midnight!
And even here, where I have to teach my hands to hew the
beech for stakes to fence our cave, she dies of laughing as
she recalls it—and says that single occasion was worth all
we have paid for it. Gallant Eve that she is! She joined
Dennis at the library door, and in an instant presented him
to Dr. Ochterlong, from Baltimore, who was on a visit in
town, and was talking with her, as Dennis came in. "Mr.
Ingham would like to hear what you were telling us about
your success among the German population." And Dennis
bowed and said, in spite of a scowl from Polly, "I'm very

glad you liked it." But Mr. Ochterlong did not observe, and plunged into the tide of explanation—Dennis listening like a prime-minister, and bowing like a mandarin—which is, I suppose, the same thing. Polly declared it was just like Haliburton's Latin conversation with the Hungarian minister, of which he is very fond of telling. *"Quæne sit historia Reformationis in Ungariâ?"* quoth Haliburton, after some thought. And his *confrère* replied gallantly, *"In seculo decimo tertio,"* etc.; and from *decimo tertio** to the nineteenth century and a half lasted till the oysters came. So was it that before Dr. Ochterlong came to the "success," or near it, Governor Gorges came to Dennis and asked him to hand Mrs. Jeffries down to supper, a request which he heard with great joy.

Polly was skipping round the room, I guess, gay as a lark. Auchmuty came to her "in pity for poor Ingham," who was so bored by the stupid pundit—and Auchmuty could not understand why I stood it so long. But when Dennis took Mrs. Jeffries down, Polly could not resist standing near them. He was a little flustered, till the sight of the eatables and drinkables gave him the same Mercian courage which it gave Diggory. A little excited then, he attempted one or two of his speeches to the Judge's lady. But little he knew how hard it was to get in even a *promptu* there edgewise. "Very well, I thank you," said he, after the eating elements were adjusted; "and you?" And then did not he have to hear about the mumps, and the measles, and arnica, and belladonna, and camomile-flower, and dodecathem, till she changed oysters for salad—and then about the old practice and the new, and what her sister said, and what her sister's friend said, and what the physician to her sister's friend said, and then what was said by the brother of the sister of the physician of the friend of her sister, exactly as if it had been in Ollendorff? There was a moment's pause, as she declined champagne. "I am very glad you liked it," said Dennis again, which he never should have said but to one who complimented a ser-

---

* Which means, "In the thirteenth century," my dear little bell-and-coral reader. You have rightly guessed that the question means, "What is the history of the Reformation in Hungary?"

mon. "Oh! you are so sharp, Mr. Ingham! No! I never
drink any wine at all—except sometimes in summer a little
currant spirits from our own currants, you know. My own
mother—that is, I call her my own mother, because, you
know, I do not remember," etc.; till they came to the candied
orange at the end of the feast, when Dennis, rather confused,
thought he must say something, and tried No. 4—"I agree,
in general, with my friend, the other side of the room"—
which he never should have said but at a public meeting.
But Mrs. Jeffries, who never listens expecting to understand,
caught him up instantly with, "Well, I'm sure my husband
returns the compliment; he always agrees with you—
though we do worship with the Methodists—but you know,
Mr. Ingham," etc., till the move was made upstairs; and as
Dennis led her through the hall, he was scarcely understood
by any but Polly, as he said, "There has been so much said,
and, on the whole, so well said, that I will not occupy the
time."

His great resource the rest of the evening was standing in
the library, carrying on animated conversations with one and
another in much the same way. Polly had initiated him in
the mysteries of a discovery of mine, that it is not necessary
to finish your sentences in a crowd, but by a sort of mumble,
omitting sibilants and dentals. This, indeed, if your words
fail you, answers even in public extempore speech—but better
where other talking is going on. Thus, "We missed you at
the Natural History Society, Ingham." Ingham replies, "I
am very gligloglum, that is, that you were mmmmm." By
gradually dropping the voice, the interlocutor is compelled to
supply the answer. "Mrs. Ingham, I hope your friend
Augusta is better." Augusta has not been ill. Polly cannot
think of explaining, however, and answers, "Thank you,
Ma'am; she is very rearason wewahwewoh," in lower and
lower tones. And Mrs. Throckmorton, who forgot the subject of which she spoke as soon as she asked the question, is
quite satisfied. Dennis could see into the card-room, and
came to Polly to ask if he might not go and play all-fours.
But, of course, she sternly refused. At midnight they came
home delighted, Polly, as I said, wild to tell me the story of

victory; only both the pretty Walton girls said, "Cousin Frederic, you did not come near me all the evening."

We always called him Dennis at home, for convenience, though his real name was Frederic Ingham, as I have explained. When the election-day came round, however, I found that by some accident there was only one Frederic Ingham's name on the voting-list; and, as I was quite busy that day in writing some foreign letters to Halle, I thought I would forego my privilege of suffrage, and stay quietly at home, telling Dennis that he might use the record on the voting-list and vote. I gave him a ticket, which I told him he might use, if he liked to. That was that very sharp election in Maine which the readers of the *Atlantic* so well remember, and it had been intimated in public that the ministers would do well not to appear at the polls. Of course, after that, we had to appear by self or proxy. Still, Naguadavick was not then a city, and this standing in a double queue at town meeting several hours to vote was a bore of the first water; and so, when I found that there was but one Frederic Ingham on the list, and that one of us must give up, I staid at home and finished the letters (which, indeed, procured for Fothergill his coveted appointment of Professor of Astronomy at Leavenworth), and I gave Dennis, as we called him, the chance. Something in the matter gave a good deal of popularity to the Frederic Ingham name; and at the adjourned election, next week, Frederic Ingham was chosen to the legislature. Whether this was I or Dennis, I never really knew. My friends seemed to think it was I; but I felt, that, as Dennis had done the popular thing, he was entitled to the honor; so I sent him to Augusta when the time came, and he took the oaths. And a very valuable member he made. They appointed him on the Committee on Parishes; but I wrote a letter for him, resigning, on the ground that he took an interest in our claim to the stumpage in the minister's sixteenths of Gore A, next No. 7, in the 10th Range. He never made any speeches, and always voted with the minority, which was what he was sent to do. He made me and himself a great many good friends, some of whom I did not afterwards recognize as quickly as Dennis did my parishioners. On one or two occasions, when there was wood to saw at home, I kept him at home; but I took those occasions to go to Augusta myself. Finding myself often in his vacant seat at these times, I watched the proceedings with a good deal of care; and once was so much excited that I delivered my somewhat celebrated speech on the Central School-District question, a speech of which the State of Maine printed some extra copies. I believe there is no formal rule permitting strangers to speak, but no one objected.

Dennis himself, as I said, never spoke at all. But our experience this session led me to think, that, if by some such "general understanding" as the reports speak of in legislation daily, every member of Congress might leave a double to sit through those deadly sessions and answer to roll-calls and do the legitimate party-voting, which appears stereotyped in the regular list of Ashe, Bocock, Black, etc., we should gain decidedly in working-power. As things stand, the saddest state prison I ever visit is that Representatives' Chamber in Washington. If a man leaves for an hour, twenty "correspondents" may be howling, "Where was Mr. Pendergrast when the Oregon bill passed?" And if poor Pendergrast stays there! Certainly, the worst use you can make of a man is to put him in prison!

I know, indeed, that public men of the highest rank have resorted to this expedient long ago. Dumas's novel of *The Iron Mask* turns on the brutal imprisonment of Louis the Fourteenth's double. There seems little doubt, in our own history, that it was the real General Pierce who shed tears when the delegates from Lawrence explained to him the sufferings of the people there—and only General Pierce's double who had given the orders for the assault on that town, which was invaded the next day. My charming friend George Withers, has, I am almost sure, a double who preaches his afternoon sermons for him. This is the reason that the theology often varies so from that of the forenoon. But that double is almost as charming as the original. Some of the most well-defined men who stand out most prominently on the background of history, are in this way stereoscopic men who owe their distinct relief to the slight differences between the doubles. All this I know. My present suggestion is simply the great extension of the system, so that all public machine-work may be done by it.

But I see I loiter on my story, which is rushing to the plunge. Let me stop an instant more, however, to recall, were it only to myself, that charming year while all was yet well. After the double had become a matter of course for nearly twelve months before he undid me, what a year it was! Full of active life, full of happy love, of the hardest work, of the sweetest sleep, and the fulfillment of so many of the fresh aspirations and dreams of boyhood! Dennis went to every school-committee meeting, and sat through all those late wranglings which used to keep me up till midnight and awake till morning. He attended all the lectures to which foreign exiles sent me tickets begging me to come for the love of Heaven and of Bohemia. He accepted and used all the tickets for charity concerts which were sent to me. He appeared everywhere where it was specially desirable that "our denomination," or "our party," or "our class," or "our family," or "our street," or "our town," or "our county," or "our State," should be fully represented. And I fell back to that charming life which in boyhood one dreams of, when he supposes he shall do his own duty and make his own sacrifices, without being tied up with those of other people. My rusty Sanskrit, Arabic, Hebrew, Greek, Latin, French, Italian, Spanish, German and English began to take polish. Heavens! how little I had done with them while I attended to my *public* duties! My calls on my parishioners became the friendly, frequent, homelike sociabilities they were meant to be, instead of the hard work of a man goaded to desperation by the sight of his lists of arrears. And preaching— what a luxury preaching was when I had on Sunday the whole result of an individual, personal week, from which to speak to a people whom all that week I had been meeting as hand-to-hand friend! I never tired on Sunday, and was in condition to leave the sermon at home, if I chose, and preach it extempore, as all men should do always. Indeed, I wonder, when I think that a sensible people like ours—really more attached to their clergy than they were in the lost days when

the Mathers and Nortons were noblemen—should choose to
neutralize so much of their ministers' lives, and destroy so
much of their early training, by this undefined passion for
seeing them in public. It springs from our balancing of
sects. If a spirited Episcopalian takes an interest in the
alms-house, and is put on the Poor Board, every other denomination must have a minister there, lest the poor-house
be changed into St. Paul's Cathedral. If a Sandemanian is
chosen president of the Young Men's Library, there must
be a Methodist vice-president and a Baptist secretary. And
if a Universalist Sunday-School Convention collects five hundred delegates, the next Congregationalist Sabbath-School
Conference must be as large, "lest 'they'—whoever 'they' may
be—should think 'we'—whoever 'we' may be—are going
down."

Freed from these necessities, that happy year, I began to
know my wife by sight. We saw each other sometimes. In
those long mornings, when Dennis was in the study explaining
to map-peddlers that I had eleven maps of Jerusalem already,
and to school-book agents that I would see them hanged
before I would be bribed to introduce their text-books into the
schools, she and I were at work together—as in those old
dreamy days and in these of our log-cabin again. But all
this could not last—and at length poor Dennis, my double,
over-tasked in turn, undid me.

It was thus it happened: There is an excellent fellow,
once a minister—I will call him Isaacs—who deserves well
of the world till he dies and after, because he once, in a
real exigency, did the right thing in the right way, at the
right time, as no other man could do it. In the world's great
football match, the ball by chance found him loitering on
the outside of the field; he closed with it, "camped" it,
charged it home—yes, right through the other side—not disturbed, not frightened by his own success—and breathless
found himself a great man, as the Great Delta rang applause.
But he did not find himself a rich man; and the football has
never come to his way again. From that moment to this
moment he has been of no use, that one can see, at all. Still,
for that great act we speak of Isaacs gratefully and remember

him kindly; and he forges on, hoping to meet the football somewhere again. In the vague hope, he had arranged a "movement" for a general organization of the human family into debating clubs, county societies, state unions, etc., with a view of inducing all children to take hold of the handles of their knives and forks, instead of the metal. Children have bad habits in that way. The movement, of course, was absurd; but we all did our best to forward, not it, but him. It came time for the annual county-meeting on this subject to be held at Naguadavick. Isaacs came round— good fellow!—to arrange for it; got the town-hall, got the Governor to preside (the saint!—he ought to have triplet doubles provided him by law), and then came to get me to speak. "No," I said, "I would not speak, if ten Governors presided. I do not believe in the enterprise. If I spoke, it should be to say children should take hold of the prongs of the forks and the blades of the knives. I would subscribe ten dollars, but I would not speak a mill." So poor Isaacs went his way sadly, to coax Auchmuty to speak, and Delafield. I went out. Not long after, he came back, and told Polly that they had promised to speak, the Governor would speak, and he himself would close with the quarterly report, and some interesting anecdotes regarding Miss Biffin's way of handling her knife and Mr. Nellis's way of footing his fork. "Now if Mr. Ingham will only come and sit on the platform, he need not say one word; but it will show well in the paper—it will show that the Sandemanians take as much interest in the movement as the Armenians or the Mesopotamians, and will be a great favor to me." Polly, good soul! was tempted, and she promised. She knew Mrs. Isaacs was starving and the babies, she knew Dennis was at home—and she promised! Night came, and I returned. I heard her story. I was sorry. I doubted. But Polly had promised to beg me, and I dared all. I told Dennis to hold his peace, under all circumstances, and sent him down.

It was not half an hour more before he returned, wild with excitement—in a perfect Irish fury—which it was long be-

fore I understood. But I knew at once that he had undone
me!

What happened was this: The audience got together, attracted by Governor Gorges's name. There were a thousand
people. Poor Gorges was late from Augusta. They became
impatient. He came in direct from the train at last, really
ignorant of the object of the meeting. He opened it in the
fewest possible words, and said other gentlemen were present
who would entertain them better than he. The audience were
disappointed, but waited. The Governor, prompted by
Isaacs, said, "The Honorable Mr. Delafield will address
you." Delafield had forgotten the knives and forks, and was
playing Ruy Lopez opening at the chess-club. "The Rev.
Mr. Auchmuty will address you." Auchmuty had promised
to speak late, and was at the school-committee. "I see Dr.
Stearns in the hall; perhaps he will say a word." Dr. Stearns
said he had come to listen and not to speak. The Governor
and Isaacs whispered. The Governor looked at Dennis, who
was resplendent on the platform; but Isaacs, to give him his
due, shook his head. But the look was enough. A miserable
lad, ill-bred, who had once been in Boston, thought it would
sound well to call for me, and peeped out, "Ingham!" A few
more wretches cried, "Ingham! Ingham!" Still Isaacs was
firm, but the Governor anxious, indeed, to prevent a row.
knew I would say something, and said, "Our friend Mr.
Ingham is always prepared—and though we had not relied
upon him, he will say a word, perhaps." Applause followed,
which turned Dennis's head. He rose, fluttered, and tried
No. 3: "There has been so much said, and, on the whole,
so well said, that I will not longer occupy the time!" and
sat down, looking for his hat; for things seemed squally. But
the people cried, "Go on! go on!" and some applauded.
Dennis, still confused, but flattered by the applause, to which
neither he nor I are used, rose again, and this time tried No.
2: "I am very glad you liked it!" in a sonorous, clear de-
livery. My best friends stared. All the people who did not
know me personally yelled with delight at the aspect of the
evening; the Governor was beside himself, and poor Isaacs
thought he was undone! Alas, it was I!   A boy in the

gallery cried in a loud tone, "It's all an infernal humbug," just as Dennis, waving his hand, commanded silence, and tried No. 4: "I agree, in general, with by friend the other side of the room." The poor Governor doubted his senses, and crossed to stop him—not in time, however. The same gallery-boy shouted, "How's your mother?" and Dennis, now completely lost, tried as his last shot No. 1, vainly: "Very well, thank you; and you?"

I think I must have been undone already. But Dennis, like another Lockhard, chose "to make sicker." The audience rose in a whirl of amazement, rage and sorrow. Some other impertinence aimed at Dennis broke all restraint, and in pure Irish he delivered himself of an address to the gallery, inviting any person who wished to fight to come down and do so—stating that they were all dogs and cowards and the sons of dogs and cowards and that he would take any five of them single-handed. "Shure, I have said all his Riverence and the Misthress bade me say," cried he, in defiance; and seizing the Governor's cane from his hand brandished it, quarter-staff fashion, above his head. He was, indeed, got from the hall only with the greatest difficulty by the Governor, the city marshal, who had been called in, and the superintendent of my Sunday-School.

The universal impression, of course, was, that the Rev. Frederic Ingham had lost all command of himself in some of those haunts of intoxication which for fifteen years I have been laboring to destroy. Till this moment, indeed, that is the impression in Naguadavick. This number of the *Atlantic* will relieve from it a hundred friends of mine who have been sadly wounded by that notion now for years;—but I shall not be likely ever to show my head there again.

No! My double has undone me.

We left town at seven the next morning. I came to No. 9, in the Third Range, and settled on the Minister's Lot. In the new towns in Maine, the first settled minister has a gift of a hundred acres of land. I am the first settled minister in No. 9. My wife and little Paulina are my parish. We raise corn enough to live on in summer. We kill bear's meat enough to carbonize it in winter. I work on steadily on my

Traces of Sandemanianism in the Sixth and Seventh Centuries, which I hope to persuade Phillips, Sampson & Co. to publish next year. We are very happy, but the world thinks we are undone.

CIRCUMSTANCE *

By Harriet Prescott Spofford

SHE had remained, during all that day, with a sick neighbor—those eastern wilds of Maine in that epoch frequently making neighbors and miles synonymous—and so busy had she been with care and sympathy that she did not at first observe the approaching night. But finally the level rays, reddening the snow, threw their gleam upon the wall, and, hastily donning cloak and hood, she bade her friends farewell and sallied forth on her return. Home lay some three miles distant, across a copse, a meadow, and a piece of woods—the woods being a fringe on the skirts of the great forests that stretch far away into the North. That home was one of a dozen log-houses lying a few furlongs apart from each other, with their half-cleared demesnes separating them at the rear from a wilderness untrodden save by stealthy native or deadly panther tribes.

She was in a nowise exalted frame of spirit—on the contrary, rather depressed by the pain she had witnessed and the fatigue she had endured; but in certain temperaments such a condition throws open the mental pores, so to speak, and renders one receptive of every influence. Through the little copse she walked slowly, with her cloak folded about her, lingering to imbibe the sense of shelter, the sunset filtered in purple through the mist of woven spray and twig, the companionship of growth not sufficiently dense to band against her the sweet home-feeling of a young and tender winter wood. It was therefore just on the edge of the evening that she emerged from the place and began to cross the meadowland. At one hand lay the forest to which her path wound;

---

* Permission of the author.

at the other the evening star hung over a tide of failing orange that slowly slipped down the earth's broad side to sadden other hemispheres with sweet regret. Walking rapidly now, and with her eyes wide-open, she distinctly saw in the air before her what was not there a moment ago, a winding-sheet —cold, white, and ghastly, waved by the likeness of four wan hands—that rose with a long inflation and fell in rigid folds, while a voice, shaping itself from the hollowness above, spectral and melancholy, sighed, "The Lord have mercy on the people! The Lord have mercy on the people!" Three times the sheet with its corpse-covering outline waved beneath the pale hands, and the voice, awful in its solemn and mysterious depth, sighed, "The Lord have mercy on the people!" Then all was gone, the place was clear again, the gray sky was obstructed by no deathly blot; she looked about her, shook her shoulders decidedly, and, pulling on her hood, went forward once more.

She might have been a little frightened by such an apparition if she had led a life of less reality than frontier settlers are apt to lead; but dealing with hard fact does not engender a flimsy habit of mind, and this woman was too sincere and earnest in her character, and too happy in her situation to be thrown by antagonism merely upon superstitious fancies and chimeras of the second-sight. She did not even believe herself subject to an hallucination, but smiled simply, a little vexed that her thought could have framed such a glamour from the day's occurrences, and not sorry to lift the bough of the warder of the woods and enter and disappear in their sombre path. If she had been imaginative, she would have hesitated at her first step into a region whose dangers were not visionary; but I suppose that the thought of a little child at home would conquer that propensity in the most habituated. So, biting a bit of spicy birch, she went along. Now and then she came to a gap where the trees had been partially felled, and here she found that the lingering twilight was explained by that peculiar and perhaps electric film which sometimes sheathes the sky in diffused light for very many hours before a brilliant aurora. Suddenly, a swift shadow, like the fabulous flying-dragon, writhed through the air be-

fore her, and she felt herself instantly seized and borne
aloft. It was that wild beast—the most savage and serpentine and subtle and fearless of our latitudes—known by
hunters as the Indian Devil, and he held her in his clutches
on the broad floor of a swinging fir-bough. His long sharp
claws were caught in her clothing, he worried them saga-
ciously a little, then, finding that ineffectual to free them, he
commenced licking her bare white arm with his rasping
tongue and pouring over her the wide streams of his hot,
fetid breath. So quick had this flashing action been that the
woman had had no time for alarm, moreover, she was not
of the screaming kind; but now, as she felt him endeavoring
to disentangle his claws, and the horrid sense of her fate
smote her, and she saw instinctively the fierce plunge of those
weapons, the long strips of living flesh torn from her bones,
the agony, the quivering disgust—itself a worse agony—
while by her side and holding her in his great lithe embrace the monster crouched, his white tusks whetting and
gnashing, his eyes glaring through all the darkness like balls
of fire—a shriek that rang in every forest hollow, that
startled every winter-housed thing, that stirred and woke
the last needle of the tasselled pines, tore through her lips.
A moment afterward, the beast left the arm, once white, now
crimson, and looked up alertly.

She did not think at this instant to call upon God. She
called upon her husband. It seemed to her that she had but
one friend in the world—that was he; and again the cry,
loud, clear, prolonged, echoed through the woods. It was not
the shriek that disturbed the creature at his relish; he was
not born in the woods to be scared of an owl, you know—
what then? It must have been the echo, most musical, most
resonant, repeated and yet repeated, dying with long sighs
of sweet sound, vibrated from rock to river and back again
from depth to depth of cave and cliff. Her thought flew after
it; she knew, that, even if her husband heard it, he yet could
not reach her in time; she saw that while the beast listened
he would not gnaw,—and this she *felt* directly, when the
rough, sharp, and multiplied stings of his tongue retouched
her arm. Again her lips opened by instinct, but the sound

that issued thence came by reason. She had heard that music charmed wild beasts—just this point between life and death intensified every faculty—and when she opened her lips the third time it was not for shrieking, but for singing.

A little thread of melody stole out, a rill of tremulous motion; it was the cradle-song with which she rocked her baby—how could she sing that? And then she remembered the baby sleeping rosily on the long settee before the fire; the father cleaning his gun, with one foot on the green wooden rundle; the merry light from the chimney dancing out and through the room, on the rafters of the ceiling with their tassels of onions and herbs, on the log walls painted with lichens and festooned with apples, on the king's-arm slung across the shelf with the old pirate's-cutlass, on the snow-pile of the bed, and on the great brass clock,—dancing, too, and lingering on the baby, with his fringed gentian eyes, his chubby fists clenched on the pillow, and his fine breezy hair fanning with the motion of his father's foot. All this struck her in one, and made a sob of her breath, and she ceased.

Immediately the long red tongue was thrust forth again. Before it touched, a song sprang to her lips, a wild sea-song, such as some sailor might be singing far out on track-less blue water that night, the shrouds whistling with frost and the sheets glued in ice—a song with the wind in its burden and the spray in its chorus. The monster raised his head and flared the fiery eyeballs upon her, then fretted the imprisoned claws a moment and was quiet; only the breath like the vapor from some hell-pit still swathed her. Her voice, at first faint and fearful, gradually lost its quaver, grew under her control and subject to her modulation; it rose on long swells, it fell in subtile cadences, now and then its tones pealed out like bells from distant belfries on fresh sonorous mornings. She sung the song through, and, wondering lest his name of Indian Devil were not his true name, and if he would not detect her, she repeated it. Once or twice now, indeed, the beast stirred uneasily, turned, and made the bough sway at his movement. As she ended, he snapped his jaws together, and tore away the fettered member, curling it

under him with a snarl,—when she burst into the gayest reel
himself from birch and cherry-wood; how many a time she
had heard her husband play it on the homely fiddle made by
himself from birch and cherry-wood; how many a time she
had seen it danced on the floor of their one room, to the patter
of wooden clogs and the rustle of homespun petticoat; how
many a time she had danced it herself;—and did she not
remember once, as they joined clasps for right-hands-round,
how it had lent its gay, bright measure to her life? And
here she was singing it alone, in the forest, at midnight, to a
wild beast! As she sent her voice trilling up and down its
quick oscillations between joy and pain, the creature who
grasped her uncurled his paw and scratched the bark from
the bough; she must vary the spell, and her voice spun leap-
ing along the projecting points of tune of a hornpipe. Still
singing, she felt herself twisted about with a low growl and
a lifting of the red lip from the glittering teeth; she broke
the hornpipe's thread, and commenced unravelling a lighter,
livelier thing, an Irish jig. Up and down and round about
her voice flew, the beast threw back his head so that the
diabolical face fronted hers, and the torrent of his breath
prepared her for his feast as the anaconda slimes his prey.
Frantically she darted from tune to tune; his restless movements followed her. She tired herself with dancing and
vivid national airs, growing feverish and singing spasmodi-
cally as she felt her horrid tomb yawning wider. Touching
in this manner all the slogan and keen clan cries, the beast
moved again, but only to lay the disengaged paw across her
with heavy satisfaction. She did not dare to pause; through
the clear cold air, the frosty starlight, she sang. If there
were yet any tremor in the tone, it was not fear—she had
learned the secret of sound at last; nor could it be chill—
far too high a fervor throbbed her pulses; it was nothing but
the thought of the log-house and of what might be passing
within it. She fancied the baby stirring in his sleep and
moving his pretty lips—her husband rising and opening the
door, looking out after her, and wondering at her absence.
She fancied the light pouring through the chink and then shut
in again with all the safety and comfort and joy, her husband

taking down the fiddle and playing lightly with his head inclined, playing while she sang, while she sang for her life
to an Indian Devil. Then she knew he was fumbling for
and finding some shining fragment and scoring it down the
yellowing hair, and unconsciously her voice forsook the wild
war-tunes and drifted into the half-gay, half-melancholy
Rosin the Bow.

Suddenly she woke pierced with a pang, and the daggered
tooth penetrating her flesh—dreaming of safety, she had
ceased singing and lost it. The beast had regained the use
of all his limbs, and now, standing and raising his back,
bristling and foaming, with sounds that would have been
like hisses but for their deep and fearful sonority, he withdrew step by step toward the trunk of the tree, still with his
flaming balls upon her. She was all at once free, on one end
of the bough, twenty feet from the ground. She did not
measure the distance, but rose to drop herself down, careless
of any death, so that it were not this. Instantly, as if he
scanned her thoughts, the creature bounded forward with a
yell and caught her again in his dreadful hold. It might
be that he was not greatly famished; for, as she suddenly
flung up her voice again, he settled himself composedly on the
bough, still clasping her with invincible pressure to his
rough, ravenous breast, and listening in a fascination to the
sad, strange U-la-lu that now moaned forth in loud, hollow
tones above him. He half closed his eyes, and sleepily re-
opened and shut them again.

What rending pains were close at hand! Death! and
what a death! worse than any other that is to be named!
Water, be it cold or warm, that which buoys up blue ice-
fields, or which bathes tropical coasts with currents of balmy
bliss, is yet a gentle conqueror, kisses as it kills, and draws
you down gently through darkening fathoms to its heart.
Death at the sword is the festival of trumpet anl bugle and
banner, with glory ringing out around you and distant hearts
thrilling through yours. No gnawing disease can bring such
hideous end as this; for that is a fiend bred of your own
flesh, and this—is it a fiend, this living lump of appetites?
What dread comes with the thought of perishing in flames!

but fire, let it leap and hiss never so hotly, is something too remote, too alien, to inspire us with such loathly horror as a wild beast; if it have a life, that life is too utterly beyond our comprehension. Fire is not half ourselves; as it devours, arouses neither hatred nor disgust; is not to be known by the strength of our lower natures let loose; does not drip our blood into our faces from foaming chaps, nor mouth nor snarl above us with vitality. Let us be ended by fire, and we are ashes, for the winds to bear, the leaves to cover; let us be ended by wild beasts, and the base, cursed thing howls with us forever through the forest. All this she felt as she charmed him, and what force it lent to her song God knows. If her voice should fail! If the damp and cold should give her any fatal hoarseness! If all the silent powers of the forest did not conspire to help her! The dark, hollow night rose indifferently over her; the wide, cold air breathed rudely past her, lifted her wet hair and blew it down again; the great boughs swung with a ponderous strength, now and then clashed their iron lengths together and shook off a sparkle of icy spears or some long-lain weight of snow from their heavy shadows. The green depths were utterly cold and silent and stern. These beautiful haunts that all the summer were hers and rejoiced to share with her their bounty, these heavens that had yielded their largess, these stems that had thrust their blossoms into her hands, all these friends of three moons ago forgot her now and knew her no longer.

Feeling her desolation, wild, melancholy, forsaken songs rose thereon from that frightful aerie—weeping, wailing tunes, that sob among the people from age to age, and overflow with otherwise unexpressed sadness—all rude, mournful ballads—old tearful strains, that Shakspeare heard the vagrants sing, and that rise and fall like the wind and tide—sailor-songs, to be heard only in lone mid-watches beneath the moon and stars—ghastly rhyming romances, such as that famous one of the *Lady Margaret,* when

> She slipped on her gown of green
>   A piece below the knee,—
> And 'twas all a long, cold winter's night
>   A dead corse followed she.

Still the beast lay with closed eyes, yet never relaxing his grasp. Once a half-whine of enjoyment escaped him,—he fawned his fearful head upon her; once he scored her cheek with his tongue: savage caresses that hurt like wounds. How weary she was! and yet how terribly awake! How fuller and fuller of dismay grew the knowledge that she was only prolonging her anguish and playing with death! How appalling the thought that with her voice ceased her existence! Yet she could not sing forever; her throat was dry and hard, her very breath was a pain, her mouth was hotter than any dessert-worn pilgrim's—if she could but drop upon her burning tongue one atom of the ice that glittered about her!—but both of her arms were pinioned in the giant's vice. She remembered the winding-sheet, and for the first time in her life shivered with spiritual fear. Was it hers? She asked herself, as she sang, what sins she had committed, what life she had led, to find her punishment so soon and in these pangs, and then she sought eagerly for some reason why her husband was not up and abroad to find her. He failed her —her one sole hope in life—and without being aware of it her voice forsook the songs of suffering and sorrow for old Covenanting hymns,—hymns with which her mother had lulled her, which the class-leader pitched in the chimney-corners—grand and sweet Methodist hymns, brimming with melody and with all fantastic involutions of tune to suit that ecstatic worship, hymns full of the beauty of holiness, steadfast, relying, sanctified by the salvation they had lent to those in worse extremity than hers, for they had found themselves in the grasp of hell, while she was but in the jaws of death. Out of this strange music, peculiar to one character of faith, and than which there is none more beautiful in its degree nor owning a more potent sway of sound, her voice soared into the glorified chants of churches. What to her was death by cold or famine or wild beasts? "Though He slay me, yet will I trust in Him," she sang. High and clear through the frore fair night, the level moonbeams splintering in the wood, the scarce glints of stars in the shadowy roof of branches, these sacred anthems rose—rose as a hope from despair, as some snowy spray of flower-bells from

blackest mould. Was she not in God's hands? Did not
the world swing at His will? If this were in His great plan
of Providence, was it not best, and should she not accept
it?

"He is the Lord our God; His judgments are in all the
earth."

Oh, sublime faith of our fathers, where utter self-sacrifice
alone was true love, the fragrance of whose unrequired sub-
jection was pleasant as that of golden censers swung in
purple-vapored chancels!

Never ceasing in the rhythm of her thoughts, articulated
in music as they thronged, the memory of her first communion flashed over her. Again she was in that distant place
on that sweet spring morning. Again the congregation rustled
out, and the few remained, and she trembled to find herself
among them. How well she remembered the devout, quiet
faces, too accustomed to the sacred feast to glow with their
inner joy, how well the snowy linen at the altar, the silver
vessels slowly and silently shifting, and as the cup approached and passed, how the sense of delicious perfume
stole in and heightened the transport of her prayer, and she
had seemed, looking up through the windows where the sky
soared blue in constant freshness, to feel all heaven's balms
dripping from the portals, and to scent the lilies of eternal
peace! Perhaps another would not have felt so much
ecstasy as satisfaction on that occasion; but it is a true, if a
later disciple, who had said, "The Lord bestoweth his blessings there, where he findeth the vessels empty." "And does
it need the walls of a church to renew my communion?" she
asked. "Does not every moment stand a temple four-square
to God? And in that morning, with its buoyant sunlight,
was I any dearer to the Heart of the World than now?" "My
beloved is mine, and I am his," she sang over and over again,
with all varied inflection and profuse tune. How gently all
the winter-wrapt things bent toward her then! Into what relation with her had they grown! How this common dependence was the spell of their intimacy! How at one with
Nature had she become! How all the night and the silence
and the forest seemed to hold its breath, and to send its

to dwell in the tents of wickedness!" And as the broad rays here and there broke through the dense covert of shade and lay in rivers of lustre on crystal sheathing and frozen fretting of trunk and limb and on the great spaces of refraction, they builded up visibly that house, the shining city on the hill; and singing, "Beautiful for situation, the joy of the whole earth, is Mount Zion, on the sides of the North, the city of the Great King," her vision climbed to that higher picture where the angel shows the dazzling thing, the holy Jerusalem descending out of heaven from God, with its splendid battlements and gates of pearls, and its foundations —the eleventh a jacinth, the twelfth an amethyst—with its great white throne, and the rainbow round about it, in sight like unto an emerald—"And there shall be no night there, for the Lord God giveth them light," she sang.

What whisper of dawn now rustled through the wilderness? How the night was passing! And still the beast crouched upon the bough, changing only the posture of his head that again he might command her with those charmed eyes. Half their fire was gone—she could almost have released herself from his custody—yet, had she stirred, no one knows what malevolent instinct might have dominated anew. But of that she did not dream; long ago stripped of any expectation, she was experiencing in her divine rapture how mystically true it is that "he that dwelleth in the secret place of the Most High shall abide under the shadow of the Almighty."

Slow clarion cries now wound from the distance as the cocks caught the intelligence of day and reëchoed it faintly from farm to farm—sleepy sentinels of night, sounding the foe's invasion, and translating that dim intuition to ringing notes of warning. Still she chanted on. A remote crash of brushwood told of some other beast on his depredations, or some night-belated traveller groping his way through the narrow path. Still she chanted on. The far, faint echoes of the chanticleers died into distance, the crashing of the branches grew nearer. No wild beast that, but a man's step, a man's form in the moonlight, stalwart and strong, on one arm slept a little child, in the other hand he held his gun. Still she chanted on.

soul up to God in her singing! It was no longer despond
ency, that singing. It was neither prayer nor petition. She
had left imploring "How long wilt Thou forget me, O
Lord?," "Lighten mine eyes, lest I sleep the sleep of death,"
"For in death there is no remembrance of Thee," with
countless other such fragments of supplication. She cried
rather, "Yea, though I walk through the valley of the
shadow of death, I will fear no evil, for Thou art with me;
Thy rod and Thy staff, they comfort me"; and lingered, and
repeated, and sang again, "I shall be satisfied, when I awake,
with Thy likeness."

Then she thought of the Great Deliverance, when He drew
her up out of many waters, and the flashing old psalm pealed
forth triumphantly:

> The Lord descended from above, and bow'd the heavens hie:
> And underneath his feet he cast the darkness of the skie.
> On cherubs and on cherubins full royally he road:
> And on the wings of all the winds came flying all abroad.

She forgot how recently, and with what a strange pity for
her own shapeless form that was to be, she quaintly sung

> Oh, lovely appearance of death!
> What sight upon earth is so fair?
> Not all the gay pageants that breathe
> Can with a dead body compare!

She remembered instead, "In Thy presence is fulness of joy;
at Thy right hand there are pleasures forevermore"; and,
"God will redeem my soul from the power of the grave: for
He shall receive me"; "He will swallow up death in victory."
Not once now did she say, "Lord how long wilt Thou look
on? Rescue my soul from their destructions, my darling
from the lions," for she knew that "the young lions roar
after their prey and seek their meat from God." "O Lord,
Thou preservest man and beast!" she said.

She had no comfort or consolation in this season, such as
sustained the Christian martyrs in the amphitheatre. She
was not dying for her faith, there were no palms in heaven
for her to wave—but how many a time had she declared,
"I had rather be a doorkeeper in the house of my God, than

Perhaps, when her husband last looked forth, he was half ashamed to find what a fear he felt for her. He knew she would never leave the child so long but for some direst need, —and yet he may have laughed at himself, as he lifted and wrapped it with awkward care, and, loading his gun and strapping on his horn, opened the door again and closed it behind him, going out and plunging into the darkness and dangers of the forest. He was more singularly alarmed than he would have been willing to acknowledge; as he had sat with his bow hovering over the strings, he had half believed to hear her voice mingling gayly with the instrument, till he paused and listened if she were not about to lift the latch and enter. As he drew nearer the heart of the forest, that intimation of melody seemed to grow more actual, to take body and breath, to come and go on long swells and ebbs of the night-breeze, to increase with tune and words, till a strange, shrill singing grew even clearer, and, as he stepped into an open space of moonbeams, far up in the branches, rocked by the wind, and singing, "How beautiful upon the mountains are the feet of him that bringeth good tidings, that publisheth peace," he saw his wife—his wife—but, great God in heaven! how? Some mad exclamation escaped him, but without diverting her. The child knew the singing voice, though never heard before in that unearthly key, and turned toward it through the veiling dreams. With a celerity almost instantaneous, it lay, in the twinkling of an eye, on the ground at the father's feet, while his gun was raised to his shoulder and levelled at the monster covering his wife with shaggy form and flaming gaze—his wife so ghastly white, so rigid, so stained with blood, her eyes so fixedly bent above, and her lips, that had indurated into the chiselled pallor of marble, parted only with that flood of solemn song.

I do not know if it were the mother-instinct that for a moment lowered her eyes—those eyes, so lately riveted on heaven, now suddenly seeing all life-long bliss possible. A thrill of joy pierced and shivered through her like a weapon, her voice trembled in its course, her glance lost its steady strength, fever-flushes chased each other over her face, yet she never once ceased chanting. She was quite aware that if her husband shot now the ball must pierce her body before reaching any vital part of the beast—and yet better that death, by his hand, than the other. But this her husband also knew, and he remained motionless, just covering the creature with the sight. He dared not fire lest some wound not mortal should break the spell exercised by her voice, and the beast, enraged with pain, should rend her in atoms; moreover, the light was too uncertain for his aim. So he waited. Now and then he examined his gun to see if the damp were injuring its charge, now and then he wiped the great drops from his forehead. Again the cocks crowed with the passing hour—the last time they were heard on that night. Cheerful home sound then, how full of safety and all comfort and rest it seemed! What sweet morning incidents of sparkling fire and sunshine, of gay household bustle, shining dresser, and cooing baby, of steaming cattle in the yard, and brimming milk-pails at the door! What pleasant voices, what laughter, what security! And here—

Now as she sang on in the slow, endless, infinite moments, the fervent vision of God's peace was gone. Just as the grave had lost its sting, she was snatched back again into the arms of earthly hope. In vain she tried to sing, "There remaineth a rest for the people of God"—her eyes trembled on her husband's, and she could think only of him, and of the child, and of happiness that yet might be, but with what a dreadful gulf of doubt between! She shuddered now in the suspense; all calm forsook her; she was tortured with dissolving heats or frozen with icy blasts; her face contracted, growing small and pinched; her voice was hoarse and sharp—every tone cut like a knife—the notes became heavy to lift—withheld by some hostile pressure—impossible. One gasp, a convulsive effort, and there was silence—she had lost her voice.

The beast made a sluggish movement—stretched and fawned like one awakening—then, as if he would have yet more of the enchantment, stirred her slightly with his muzzle. As he did so a sidelong hint of the man standing below with the raised gun smote him; he sprung round furiously, and, seizing his prey, was about to leap into some unknown airy den of the top-most branches now waving to the slow dawn. The late moon had rounded through the sky so that her gleam at last fell full upon the bough with fairy frosting; the wintry morning light did not yet penetrate the gloom. The woman, suspended in mid-air an instant, cast only one agonized glance beneath, but across and through it, ere the lids could fall, shot a withering sheet of flame—a rifle-crack, half heard, was lost in the terrible yell of desperation that bounded after it and filled her ears with savage echoes, and in the wide arc of some eternal descent she was falling—but the beast fell under her.

I think that the moment following must have been too sacred for us, and perhaps the three have no special interest again till they issue from the shadows of the wilderness upon the white hills that skirt their home. The father carries the child hushed again to slumber, the mother follows with no such feeble step as might be anticipated, and as they slowly climb the steep under the clear gray sky and the paling morning star, she stops to gather a spray of the red-rose berries or a feathey tuft of dead grasses for the chimney-piece of the log-house, or a handful of brown ones for the child's play,—and of these quiet, happy folk you would scarcely dream how lately they had stolen from under the banner and encampment of the great King Death. The husband proceeds a step or two in advance; the wife lingers over a singular foot-print in the snow, stoops and examines it, then looks up with a hurried word. Her husband stands alone on the hill, his arms folded across the babe, his gun fallen—stands defined against the pallid sky like a bronze. What is there in their home, lying below and yellowing in the light, to fix him with such a stare? She springs to his side. There is no home there. The log-house, the barns, the neighboring farms, the fences, are all blotted out and mingled in one smoking ruin. Desolation and death were indeed there, and beneficence and life in the forest. Tomahawk and scalping-knife, descending during that night, had left behind them only this work of their accomplished hatred and one subtle foot-print in the snow.

For the rest—the world was all before them, where to choose.

THE CELEBRATED JUMPING FROG OF CALAVERAS COUNTY *

By Mark Twain

IN compliance with the request of a friend of mine, who wrote me from the East, I called on good-natured, garrulous old Simon Wheeler, and inquired after my friend's friend, *Leonidas W.* Smiley, as requested to do, and I hereunto append the result. I have a lurking suspicion that *Leonidas W.* Smiley is a myth; that my friend never knew such a personage; and that he only conjectured that, if I asked old Wheeler about him, it would remind him of his infamous *Jim* Smiley, and he would go to work and bore me nearly to death with some infernal reminiscence of him as long and tedious as it should be useless to me. If that was the design, it certainly succeeded.

I found Simon Wheeler dozing comfortably by the barroom stove of the old, dilapidated tavern in the ancient mining camp of Angel's, and I noticed that he was fat and baldheaded, and had an expression of winning gentleness and simplicity upon his tranquil countenance. He roused up and gave me good-day. I told him a friend of mine had commissioned me to make some inquiries about a cherished companion of his boyhood named *Leonidas W.* Smiley—*Rev. Leonidas W.* Smiley—a young minister of the Gospel, who he had heard was at one time a resident of Angel's Camp. I added, that, if Mr. Wheeler could tell me anything about this Rev. Leonidas W. Smiley, I would feel under many obligations to him.

Simon Wheeler backed me into a corner and blockaded me there with his chair, and then sat me down and reeled off the monotonous narrative which follows this paragraph. He never smiled, he never frowned, he never changed his voice

---

* From the collected works of Mark Twain, published by Harper & Brothers.

from the gentle-flowing key to which he tuned the initial
sentence, he never betrayed the slightest suspicion of enthusiasm; but all through the interminable narrative there ran
a vein of impressive earnestness and sincerity, which showed
me plainly that, so far from his imagining that there was
anything ridiculous or funny about his story, he regarded it
as a really important matter, and admitted its two heroes
as men of transcendent genius in *finesse.* To me, the
spectacle of a man drifting serenely along through such a
queer yarn without ever smiling, was exquisitely absurd. As
I said before, I asked him to tell me what he knew of Rev.
Leonidas W. Smiley, and he replied as follows. I let him
go on in his own way, and never interrupted him once:

There was a feller here once by the name of *Jim* Smiley,
in the winter of '49—or maybe it was the spring of '50—I
don't recollect exactly, somehow, though what makes me
think it was one or the other is because I remember the big
flume wasn't finished when he first came to the camp; but
anyway, he was the curiousest man about always betting on
anything that turned up you ever see, if he could get anybody to bet on the other side; and if he couldn't, he'd change
sides. Any way that suited the other man would suit him—
any way just so's he got a bet, *he* was satisfied. But still he
was lucky, uncommon lucky—he most always come out winner. He was always ready and laying for a chance; there
couldn't be no solit'ry thing mentioned but that feller'd offer
to bet on it, and take any side you please, as I was just telling you. If there was a horse-race, you'd find him flush, or
you'd find him busted at the end of it; if there was a dog-
fight, he'd bet on it; if there was a cat-fight, he'd bet on it;
if there was a chicken-fight, he'd bet on it; why, if there
was two birds setting on a fence, he would bet you which
one would fly first; or if there was a camp-meeting, he would
be there reg'lar, to bet on Parson Walker, which he judged
to be the best exhorter about here, and so he was, too, and a
good man. If he even seen a straddle-bug start to go any-
wheres, he would bet you how long it would take him to get
wherever he was going to, and if you took him up, he would
foller that straddle-bug to Mexico but what he would find

out where he was bound for and how long he was on the road. Lots of the boys here has seen that Smiley, and can tell you about him. Why, it never made no difference to *him*—he would bet on *any*thing—the dangdest feller. Parson Walker's wife laid very sick once, for a good while, and it seemed as if they warn't going to save her; but one morning he came in, and Smiley asked how she was, and he said she was considerable better—thank the Lord for his inf'nit mercy—and coming on so smart that, with the blessing of Prov'dence, she'd get well yet; and Smiley, before he thought, says, "Well, I'll risk two-and-a-half that she don't, anyway."

Thish-yer Smiley had a mare—the boys called her the fifteen-minute nag, but that was only in fun, you know, because, of course, she was faster than that—and he used to win money on that horse, for all she was so slow and always had the asthma, or the distemper, or the consumption, or something of that kind. They used to give her two or three hundred yards start, and then pass her under way; but always at the fag-end of the race she'd get excited and desperate-like, and come cavorting and straddling up, and scattering her legs around limber, sometimes in the air, and sometimes out to one side amongst the fences, and kicking up m-o-r-e dust, and raising m-o-r-e racket with her coughing and sneezing and blowing her nose—and always fetch up at the stand just about a neck ahead, as near as you could cipher it down.

And he had a little small bull pup, that to look at him you'd think he wan't worth a cent but to set around and look ornery and lay for a chance to steal something. But as soon as money was up on him, he was a different dog; his under-jaw'd begin to stick out like the fo'castle of a steamboat, and his teeth would uncover, and shine savage like the furnaces. And a dog might tackle him, and bully-rag him, and bite him, and throw him over his shoulder two or three times, and Andrew Jackson—which was the name of the pup —Andrew Jackson would never let on but what *he* was satisfied, and hadn't expected nothing else—and the bets being doubled and doubled on the other side all the time, till the money was all up; and then all of a sudden he would grab that other dog jest by the j'int of his hind leg and freeze to it—not claw, you understand, but only jest grip and hang on till they throwed up the sponge, if it was a year. Smiley always come out winner on that pup, till he harnessed a dog once that didn't have no hind legs, because they'd been sawed off by a circular saw, and when the thing had gone along far enough, and the money was all up, and he come to make a snatch for his pet holt, he saw in a minute how he'd been imposed on, and how the other dog had him in the door, so to speak, and he 'peared surprised, and then he looked sorter discouraged-like, and didn't try no more to win the fight, and so he got shucked out bad. He give Smiley a look, as much to say his heart was broke and it was *his* fault for putting up a dog that hadn't no hind legs for him to take holt of, which was his main dependence in a fight, and then he limped off a piece and laid down and died. It was a good pup, was that Andrew Jackson, and would have made a name for hisself if he'd lived, for the stuff was in him, and he had genius—I know it, because he hadn't no opportunities to speak of, and it don't stand to reason that a dog could make such a fight as he could under them circumstances, if he hadn't no talent. It always makes me feel sorry when I think of that last fight of his'n, and the way it turned out.

Well, thish-yer Smiley had rat-tarriers, and chicken-cocks, and tom-cats, and all them kind of things, till you couldn't rest, and you couldn't fetch nothing for him to bet on but he'd match you. He ketched a frog one day, and took him home, and said he cal'klated to edercate him; and so he never done nothing for these three months but set in his back yard and learn that frog to jump. And you bet you he *did* learn him, too. He'd give him a little punch behind, and the next minute you'd see that frog whirling in the air like a doughnut—see him turn one summerset, or maybe a couple, if he got a good start, and come down flat-footed and all right, like a cat. He got him up so in the matter of catch-ing flies, and kept him in practice so constant, that he'd nail a fly every time as far as he could see him. Smiley said all a frog wanted was education, and he could do most anything—and I believe him. Why, I've seen him set Dan'l Webster down here on this floor—Dan'l Webster was the name of the frog—and sing out, "Flies, Dan'l, flies!" and quicker'n you could wink, he'd spring straight up, and snake a fly off'n the counter there, and flop down on the floor again as solid as a gob of mud, and fall to scratching the side of his head with his hind foot as indifferent as if he hadn't no idea he's been doin' any more'n any frog might do. You never see a frog so modest and straight-for'ard as he was, for all he was so gifted. And when it come to fair and square jumping on the dead level, he could get over more ground at one straddle than any animal of his breed you ever see. Jumping on a dead level was his strong suit, you understand; and when it come to that, Smiley would ante up money on him as long as he had a red. Smiley was monstrous proud of his frog, and well he might be, for fellers that had traveled and been everywhere all said he laid over any frog that ever *they* see.

Well, Smiley kept the beast in a little lattice box, and he used to fetch him downtown sometimes and lay for a bet. One day a feller—a stranger in the camp, he was—come across him with his box, and says:

"What might it be that you've got in the box?"

And Smiley says, sorter indifferent like, "It might be a parrot, or it might be a canary, maybe, but it ain't—it's only just a frog."

An' the feller took it, and looked at it careful, and turned it round this way and that, and says, "H'm—so 'tis. Well, what's *he* good for?"

"Well," Smiley says, easy and careless, "He's good enough for *one* thing, I should judge—he can outjump ary frog in Calaveras county."

The feller took the box again, and took another long, particular look, and give it back to Smiley, and says, very deliberate, "Well, I don't see no p'ints about that frog that's any better'n any other frog."

"Maybe you don't," Smiley says. "Maybe you understand frogs, and maybe you don't understand 'em; maybe you've had experience, and maybe you ain't only a amature, as it were. Anyways, I've got *my* opinion, and I'll risk forty dollars that he can outjump any frog in Calaveras county."

And the feller studied a minute, and then says, kinder sad like, "Well, I'm only a stranger here, and I ain't got no frog; but if I had a frog, I'd bet you."

And then Smiley says, "That's all right—that's all right —if you'll hold my box a minute, I'll go and get you a frog." And so the feller took the box, and put up his forty dollars along with Smiley's, and set down to wait.

So he set there a good while thinking and thinking to hisself, and then he got the frog out and prized his mouth open and took a teaspoon and filled him full of quail shot— filled him pretty near up to his chin—and set him on the floor. Smiley he went to the swamp and slopped around in the mud for a long time, and finally he ketched a frog, and fetched him in, and give him to this feller, and says:

"Now, if you're ready, set him alongside of Dan'l, with his fore-paws just even with Dan'l, and I'll give the word." Then he says, "One—two—three—jump!" and him and the feller touched up the frogs from behind, and the new frog hopped off, but Dan'l give a heave, and hysted up his shoulders—so—like a Frenchman, but it wasn't no use—he couldn't budge; he was planted as solid as an anvil, and he couldn't no more stir than if he was anchored out. Smiley was a good deal surprised, and he was disgusted too, but he didn't have no idea what the matter was, of course.

The feller took the money and started away; and when he was going out at the door, he sorter jerked his thumb over his shoulder—this way—at Dan'l, and says again, very deliberate, "Well, *I* don't see no p'ints about that frog that's any better'n any other frog."

Smiley he stood scratching his head and looking down at Dan'l a long time, and at last he says, "I do wonder what in the nation that frog throw'd off for—I wonder if there ain't something the matter with him—he 'pears to look mighty baggy, somehow." And he ketched Dan'l by the nap of the neck, and lifted him up and says, "Why, blame my cats, if he don't weight five pounds!" and turned him upside down, and he belched out a double handful of shot. And then he see how it was, and he was the maddest man—he set the frog down and took out after that feller, but he never ketched him. And—

(Here Simon Wheeler heard his name called from the front yard, and got up to see what was wanted.) And turning to me as he moved away, he said: "Just set where you are, stranger, and rest easy—I ain't going to be gone a second."

But, by your leave, I did not think that a continuation of the history of the enterprising vagabond *Jim* Smiley would be likely to afford me much information concerning the Rev. *Leonidas W.* Smiley, and so I started away.

At the door I met the sociable Wheeler returning, and he buttonholed me and recommended:

"Well, thish-yer Smiley had a yeller one-eyed cow that didn't have no tail, only jest a short stump like a bannanner, and—"

"Oh, hang Smiley and his afflicted cow!" I muttered, good-naturedly, and bidding the old gentleman good-day, I departed.

A PASSIONATE PILGRIM *

By Henry James

I

INTENDING to sail for America in the early part of June, I determined to spend the interval of six weeks in England, of which I had dreamed much but as yet knew nothing. I had formed in Italy and France a resolute preference for old inns, deeming that what they sometimes cost the ungratified body they repay the delighted mind. On my arrival in London, therefore, I lodged at a certain antique hostelry far to the east of Temple Bar, deep in what I used to denominate the Johnsonian city. Here, on the first evening of my stay, I descended to the little coffee-room and bespoke my dinner of the genius of decorum, in the person of the solitary waiter. No sooner had I crossed the threshold of this apartment than I felt I had mown the first swath in my golden-ripe crop of British "impressions." The coffee-room of the Red-Lion, like so many other places and things I was destined to see in England, seemed to have been waiting for long years, with just that sturdy sufferance of time written on its visage, for me to come and gaze, ravished but unamazed.

The latent preparedness of the American mind for even the most delectable features of English life is a fact which I fairly probed to its depths. The roots of it are so deeply buried in the virgin soil of our primary culture, that, without some great upheaval of experience, it would be hard to say exactly when and where and how it begins. It makes an American's enjoyment of England an emotion more fatal and sacred than his enjoyment, say, of Italy or Spain. I had seen

* By permission of, and by special arrangement with, Houghton Mifflin Company, the authorized publishers; and by permission of Henry James.

the coffee-room of the Red-Lion years ago, at home—at Sara-in Smollett, and Boswell. It was small, and subdivided into six small compartments by a series of perpendicular screens of mahogany, something higher than a man's stature, furnished on either side with a narrow uncushioned ledge, denominated in ancient Britain a seat. In each of the little dining-boxes thus immutably constituted was a small table, which in crowded seasons was expected to accommodate the several agents of a fourtold British hungriness. . . . On the floor was a Turkey carpet—as old as the mahogany, almost, as the Bank of England, as the Queen—into which the waiter in his lonely revolutions had trodden so many massive soot-flakes and drops of overflowing beer, that the glowing looms of Smyrna would certainly not have recognized it. To say that I ordered my dinner of this superior being would be altogether to misrepresent the process, owing to which, having dreamed of lamb and spinach, and a charlotte-russe, I sat down in penitence to a mutton-chop and a rice pudding. Bracing my feet against the cross-beam of my little oaken table, I opposed to the mahogany partition behind me that vigorous dorsal resistance which expresses the old-English idea of repose. The sturdy screen refused even to creak; but my poor Yankee joints made up the deficiency. While I was waiting for my chop there came into the room a person whom I took to be my sole fellow-lodger. He seemed, like myself, to have submitted to proposals for dinner; the table on the other side of my partition had been prepared to receive him. He walked up to the fire, exposed his back to it, consulted his watch, and looked apparently out of the window, but really at me. He was a man of something less than middle age and more than middle stature, though indeed you would have called him neither young nor tall. He was chiefly remarkable for his exaggerated leanness. His hair, very thin on the summit of his head, was dark, short, and fine. His eye was of a pale, turbid gray, unsuited, perhaps, to his dark hair and brow, but not altogether out of harmony with his colorless, bilious complexion. His nose was aquiline and delicate; beneath it hung a thin, comely, dark mustache. His mouth and chin were meagre and uncertain of

outline; not vulgar, perhaps, but weak. A cold, fatal, gentle-
manly weakness, indeed, seemed expressed in his attenuated
person. His eyes was restless and deprecating; his whole
physiognomy, his manner of shifting his weight from foot to
foot, the spiritless droop of his head, told of exhausted purpose, of a will relaxed. His dress was neat and careful, with
an air of half-mourning. I made up my mind on three
points: he was unmarried, he was ill, he was not an Englishman. The waiter approached him, and they murmured momentarily in barely audible tones. I heard the words "claret,"
"sherry," with a tentative, inflection, and finally "beer," with
a gentle affirmative. Perhaps he was a Russian in reduced
circumstances; he reminded me of a certain type of Russian which I had met on the Continent. While I was weighing this hypothesis—for you see I was interested—there appeared a short, brisk man with reddish-brown hair, a vulgar
nose, a sharp blue eye, and a red beard, confined to his lower
jaw and chin. My impecunious Russian was still standing on
the rug with his mild gaze bent on vacancy; the other marched
up to him, and with his umbrella gave him a playful poke in
the concave frontage of his melancholy waistcoat. "A penny-
ha'penny for your thoughts!" said the new-comer.

His companion uttered an exclamation, stared, then laid
his two hands on the other's shoulders. . . . As my
neighbors proceeded to dine, I became conscious that,
through no indiscretion of my own a large portion of their
conversation made its way over the top of our dividing
partition and mingled its savor with that of my simple repast. The two voices were pitched in an unforgotten key,
and equally native to our Cisatlantic air; they seemed to
fall upon the muffled medium of surrounding parlance as the
rattle of pease on the face of a drum. They were American, however, with a difference; and I had no hesitation in
assigning the lighter and softer of the two to the pale, thin
gentleman, whom I decidedly preferred to his comrade. The
latter began to question him about his voyage.

"Horrible, horrible! I was deadly sick from the hour we
left New York."

. . . .

There was a pause; after which: "You're the same cheerful old boy, Searle. Going to die to-morrow, eh?"

"I almost wish I were."

"You're not in love with England, then? I've heard people say at home that you dressed and talked and acted like an Englishman. But I know Englishmen, and I know you. You're not one of them, Searle, not you. You'll go under here, sir; you'll go under as sure as my name is Simmons."

Following this, I heard a sudden clatter, as of the dropping of a knife and fork. "Well, you're a delicate sort of creature, Simmons! I have been wandering about all day in this accursed city, ready to cry with home-sickness and heart-sickness and every possible sort of sickness, and thinking, in the absence of anything better, of meeting you here this evening, and of your uttering some syllable of cheer and comfort, and giving me some feeble ray of hope. Go under? Am I not under now? I can't sink lower, except to sink into my grave!"

Mr. Simmons seems to have staggered a moment under this outbreak of passion. But the next, "Don't cry, Searle," I heard him say. "Remember the waiter. I've grown Englishman enough for that. For heaven's sake, don't let us have any feelings. Feelings will do nothing for you here. It's best to come to the point. Tell me in three words what you expect of me."

I heard another movement, as if poor Searle had collapsed in his chair. "Upon my word, Simmons, you are inconceivable. You got my letter?"

"Yes, I got your letter. I was never sorrier to get anything in my life."

At this declaration Mr. Searle rattled out an oath, which it was well perhaps that I but partially heard. "John Simmons," he cried, "what devil possesses you? Are you going to betray me here in a foreign land, to turn out a false friend, a heartless rogue?"

"Go on, sir," said sturdy Simmons. . . . "I don't want to say anything to make you feel sore. I pity you.

But you must allow me to say that you have acted like a blasted fool!"

Mr. Searle seemed to have made an effort to compose himself. "Be so good as to tell me what was the meaning of your letter."

"I was a fool, myself, to have written that letter. It came of my infernal meddlesome benevolence. I had much better have let you alone. To tell you the plain truth, I never was so horrified in my life as when I found that on the strength of that letter you had come out here to seek your fortune."

"What did you expect me to do?"

"I expected you to wait patiently till I had made further inquiries and had written to you again."

"You have made further inquiries now?"

"Inquiries! I have made assaults."

"And you find I have no claim?"

"No claim to call a claim. It looked at first as if you had a very pretty one. I confess the idea took hold of me—"

.   .   .   .

"I'll have some brandy. Come, Searle," he resumed, "don't challenge me to the arts of debate, or I'll settle right down on you. Benevolence, as I say, was part of it. The reflection that if I put the thing through it would be a very pretty feather in my cap and a very pretty penny in my purse was part of it. And the satisfaction of seeing a poor nobody of a Yankee walk right into an old English estate was a good deal of it. Upon my word, Searle, when I think of it, I wish with all my heart that, erratic genius as you are, you had a claim, for the very beauty of it! I should hardly care what you did with the confounded property when you got it. I could leave you alone to turn it into Yankee notions—into ducks and drakes, as they call it here. I should like to see you stamping over it and kicking up its sacred dust in their very faces!"

"You don't know me, Simmons!" said Searle, for all response to this untender benediction.

"I should be very glad to think I didn't, Searle.

It seems your brother George, some twenty years ago, put

forth a feeler. So you are not to have the glory of even frightening them."

"I never frightened any one," said Searle. "I shouldn't begin at this time of day. I should approach the subject like a gentleman."

"Well, if you want very much to do something like a gentleman, you've got a capital chance. Take your dissappointment like a gentleman."

I had finished my dinner, and I had become keenly interested in poor Mr. Searle's mysterious claim; so interested that it was vexatious to hear his emotions reflected in his voice without noting them in his face. I left my place, went over to the fire, took up the evening paper, and established a post of observation behind it.

Lawyer Simmons was in the act of choosing a soft chop from the dish—an act accompanied by a great deal of prying and poking with his own personal fork. My disillusioned compatriot had pushed away his plate; he sat with his elbows on the table, gloomily nursing his head with his hands. His companion stared at him a moment, I fancied half tenderly; I am not sure whether it was pity or whether it was beer and brandy.

. . . .

Searle disgustedly gave his plate another push. "Anything may happen, now!" he said. "I don't care a straw."

"You ought to care. Have another chop and you *will* care. Have some brandy. Take my advice!"

Searle from between his two hands looked at him. "I have had enough of your advice!" he said.

"A little more," said Simmons, mildly; "I sha'n't trouble you again. What do you mean to do?"

. . . .

"I won't go home! I have crossed the ocean for the last time."

"What is the matter? Are you afraid?"

"Yes, I'm afraid! 'I thank thee, Jew, for teaching me that word!'"

"You're more afraid to go than to stay?"

"I sha'n't stay. I shall die."

"O, are you sure of that?"

"One can always be sure of that."

Mr. Simmons started and stared: his mild cynic had turned grim stoic. "Upon my soul," he said, "one would think that Death had named the day!"

"We have named it, between us."

This was too much even for Mr. Simmons's easy morality. "I say, Searle," he cried, "I'm not more of a stickler than the next man, but if you are going to blaspheme, I shall wash my hands of you. If you'll consent to return home with me by the steamer of the 23d, I'll pay your passage down. More than that, I'll pay your wine bill."

Searle meditated. "I believe I never willed anything in my life," he said; "but I feel sure that I have willed this, that I stay here till I take my leave for a newer world than that poor old New World of ours. . . . I have about my person some forty pounds' worth of British gold and the same amount, say, of Yankee vitality. They'll last me out together! After they are gone, I shall lay my head in some English churchyard, beside some ivied tower, beneath an English yew."

.   .   .   .

They had risen to their feet. Simmons had put on his overcoat; he stood polishing his rusty black hat with his napkin. "Do you mean to go down to the place?" he asked.

"Possibly. I have dreamed of it so much I should like to see it."

"Shall you call on Mr. Searle?"

"Heaven forbid!"

"Something has just occurred to me," Simmons pursued, with an unhandsome grin, as if Mephistopheles were playing at malice. "There's a Miss Searle, the old man's sister."

"Well?" said the other, frowning.

"Well, sir, suppose, instead of dying, you should marry!"

Mr. Searle frowned in silence. Simmons gave him a tap on the stomach. "Line those ribs a bit first!" The poor gentleman blushed crimson and his eyes filled with tears.

"You *are* a coarse brute," he said. The scene was pathetic.

The next morning, not finding the innocent object of my benevolent curiosity in the coffee-room, I learned from the waiter that he had ordered breakfast in bed. Into this asylum I was not yet prepared to pursue him. I spent the morning running about London, chiefly on business, but snatching by the way many a vivid impression of its huge metropolitan interest. Beneath the sullen black and gray of that hoary civic world the hungry American mind detects the magic colors of association. As the afternoon approached, however, my impatient heart began to babble of green fields; it was of English meadows I had chiefly dreamed. Thinking over the suburban lions, I fixed upon Hampton Court. The day was the more propitious that it yielded just that dim, subaqueous light which sleeps so fondly upon the English landscape.

At the end of an hour I found myself wandering through the multitudinous rooms of the great palace. They follow each other in infinite succession, with no great variety of interest or aspect, but with a sort of regal monotony, and a fine specific flavor. They are most exactly of their various times. You pass from great painted and panelled bed-chambers and closets, ante-rooms, drawing-rooms, council-rooms, through king's suite, queen's suite, and prince's suite, until you feel as if you were strolling through the appointed hours and stages of some decorous monarchical day. On one side are the old monumental upholsteries, the vast cold tarnished beds and canopies, with the circumference of disapparelled royalty attested by a gilded balustrade, and the great carved and yawning chimney-places, where dukes-in-waiting may have warmed their weary heels; on the other side, in deep recesses, the immense windows, the framed and draped embrasures where the sovereign whispered and favorites smiled, looking out on the terraced gardens and the misty glades of Bushey Park. The dark walls are gravely decorated by innumerable dark portraits of persons attached to court and state, more especially with various members of the Dutch-looking *entourage* of William of Orange, the restorer of the palace; with good store, too, of the lily-bosomed models of

Lely and Kneller. The whole tone of this long-drawn interior is immensely sombre, prosaic, and sad. The tints of all things have sunk to a cold and melancholy brown, and the great palatial void seems to hold no stouter tenantry than a sort of pungent odorous chill. I seemed to be the only visitor. I held ungrudged communion with the formal genius of the spot. Poor mortalized kings! ineffective lure of royalty! This, or something like it, was the murmured burden of my musings. They were interrupted suddenly by my coming upon a person standing in devout contemplation before a simpering countess of Sir Peter Lely's creation. On hearing my footstep this person turned his head, and I recognized my fellow-lodger at the Red-Lion. I was apparently recognized as well; I detected an air of overture in his glance. In a few moments, seeing I had a catalogue, he asked the name of the portrait. On my ascertaining it, he inquired, timidly, how I liked the lady.

"Well," said I, not quite timidly enough, perhaps, "I confess she seems to me rather a light piece of work."

He remained silent, and a little abashed, I think. As we strolled away he stole a sidelong glance of farewell at his leering shepherdess. To speak with him face to face was to feel keenly that he was weak and interesting. We talked of our inn, of London, of the palace; he uttered his mind freely, but he seemed to struggle with a weight of deprsssion. It was a simple mind enough, with no great culture, I fancied, but with a certain appealing native grace. I foresaw that I should find him a true American, full of that perplexing interfusion of refinement and crudity which marks the American mind. His perceptions, I divined, were delicate; his opinions, possibly gross. On my telling him that I too was an American, he stopped short and seemed overcome with emotion: then silently passing his arm into my own, he suffered me to lead him through the rest of the palace and down into the gardens. A vast gravelled platform stretches itself before the basement of the palace, taking the afternoon sun. A portion of the edifice is reserved as a series of private apartments, occupied by state pensioners, reduced gentlewomen in receipt of the Queen's bounty, and other deserving persons. Many of these apartments have their little private gardens; and here and there, between their verdure-coated walls, you catch a glimpse of these dim horticultural closets. My companion and I took many a turn up and down this spacious level, looking down on the antique geometry of the lower garden and on the stoutly woven tapestry of vine and blossom which muffles the foundations of the huge red pile. . . . There are few sensations so exquisite in life as to stand with a companion in a foreign land and inhale to the depths of your consciousness the alien savor of the air and the tonic picturesqueness of things. This common relish of local color makes comrades of strangers. My companion seemed oppressed with vague amazement. He stared and lingered and scanned the scene with a gentle scowl. His enjoyment appeared to give him pain. I proposed, at last, that we should dine in the neighborhood and take a late train to town. We made our way out of the gardens into the adjoining village, where we found an excellent inn. Mr. Searle sat down to table with small apparent interest in the repast, but gradually warming to his work, he declared at the end of half an hour that for the first time in a month he felt an appetite.

"You're an invalid?" I said.

"Yes," he answered. "A hopeless one!"

The little village of Hampton Court stands clustered about the broad entrance of Bushey Park. After we had dined we lounged along into the hazy vista of the great avenue of horse-chestnuts. There is a rare emotion, familiar to every intelligent traveller, in which the mind, with a great passionate throb, achieves a magical synthesis of its impressions. You feel England; you feel Italy. The reflection for the moment has an extraordinary poignancy. I had known it from time to time in Italy, and had opened my soul to it as to the spirit of the Lord. Since my arrival in England I had been waiting for it to come. A bottle of excellent Burgundy at dinner had perhaps unlocked to it the gates of sense; it came now with a conquering tread. Just the scene around me was the England of my visions. Over against us, amid the deep-hued bloom of its ordered gardens, the dark red palace, with its formal copings and its vacant windows, seemed to tell of a proud and splendid past; the little village nestling between park and palace, around a patch of turfy common, with its tavern of gentility, its ivy-towered church, its parsonage, retained to my modernized fancy the lurking semblance of a feudal hamlet. . . .

"Well," I said to my friend, "I think there is no mistake about this being England. We may like it or not, it's positive! No more dense and stubborn fact ever settled down on an expectant tourist. It brings my heart into my throat."

Searle was silent. I looked at him; he was looking up at the sky, as if he were watching some visible descent of the elements. "On me too," he said, "it's settling down!" Then with a forced smile: "Heaven give me strength to bear it!"

. . . .

"You have the advantage over me," my companion resumed, after a pause, "in coming to all this with an educated eye. You already know the old. I have never known it but by report. I have always fancied I should like it. In a small way at home, you know, I have tried to stick to the old. I must be a conservative by nature. People at home—a few people—used to call me a snob."

"I don't believe you were a snob," I cried. "You look too amiable."

He smiled sadly. "There it is," he said. "It's the old story! I'm amiable! I know what that means! I was too great a fool to be even a snob! If I had been I should probably have come abroad earlier in life—before—before—" He paused, and his head dropped sadly on his breast.

The bottle of Bergundy had loosened his tongue. I felt that my learning his story was merely a question of time. Something told me that I had gained his confidence and he would unfold himself. "Before you lost your health," I said.

"Before I lost my health," he answered. "And my property—the little I had. And my ambition. And my self-esteem."

"Come!" I said. "You shall get them all back. This tonic English climate will wind you up in a month.

And with the return of health, all the rest will return."

.   .   .   .

Just at this moment there came cantering down the shallow glade of the avenue a young girl on a fine black horse—one of those lovely budding gentlewomen, perfectly mounted and equipped, who form to American eyes the sweetest incident of English scenery. She had distanced her servant, and, as she came abreast of us, turned slightly in her saddle and looked back at him. In the movement she dropped her whip. Drawing in her horse, she cast upon the ground a glance of maidenly alarm. "This is something better than a Lely," I said. Searle hastened forward, picked up the whip, and removing his hat with an air of great devotion, presented it to the young girl. Fluttered and blushing, she reached forward, took it with softly murmured gratitude, and the next moment was bounding over the elastic turf. Searle stood watching her; the servant, as he passed us, touched his hat. When Searle turned toward me again, I saw that his face was glowing with a violent blush. "I doubt of your having come abroad too late!" I said, laughing.

A short distance from where we had stopped was an old stone bench. We went and sat down on it and watched the light mist turning to sullen gold in the rays of the evening sun. "We ought to be thinking of the train back to London, I suppose," I said at last.

"O, hang the train!" said Searle.

"Willingly! There could be no better spot than this to feel the magic of an English twilight." So we lingered, and the twilight lingered around us—a light and not a darkness. As we sat, there came trudging along the road an individual whom, from afar, I recognized as a member of the genus "tramp." I had read of the British tramp, but I had never yet encountered him, and I brought my historic consciousness to bear upon the present specimen. As he approached us he slackened pace and finally halted, touching his cap. He was a man of middle age, clad in a greasy bonnet, with greasy ear-locks depending from its sides. Round his neck was a grimy red scarf, tucked into his waistcoat; his coat and trousers had a remote affinity with those of a reduced hostler.

In one hand he had a stick; on his arm he bore a tattered basket, with a handful of withered green stuff in the bottom. His face was pale, haggard, and degraded beyond description—a singular mixture of brutality and *finesse*. He had a history. From what height had he fallen, from what depth had he risen? Never was a form of rascally beggarhood more complete. There was a merciless fixedness of outline about him which filled me with a kind of awe. I felt as if I were in the presence of a personage—an artist in vagrancy.

"For God's sake, gentlemen," he said, in that raucous tone of weather-beaten poverty suggestive of chronic sore-throat exacerbated by perpetual gin, "for God's sake, gentlemen, have pity on a poor fern-collector!"—turning up his stale dandelions. "Food hasn't passed my lips, gentlemen, in the last three days."

We gaped responsive, in the precious pity of guileless Yankeeism. "I wonder," thought I, "if half a crown would be enough?" And our fasting botanist went limping away through the park with a mystery of satirical gratitude superadded to his general mystery.

"I feel as if I had seen my *doppel-ganger,*" said Searle. "He reminds me of myself. What am I but a tramp?"

Upon this hint I spoke. "What are you, my friend?" I asked. "Who are you?"

A sudden blush rose to his pale face, so that I feared I had offended him. He poked a moment at the sod with the point of his umbrella, before answering. "Who am I?" he said at last. "My name is Clement Searle. I was born in New York. I have lived in New York. What am I? That's easily told. Nothing! I assure you, nothing."

"A very good fellow, apparently," I protested.

"A very good fellow! Ah, there it is! You've said more than you mean. It's by having been a very good fellow all my days that I've come to this. I have drifted through life. I'm a failure, sir—a failure as hopeless and helpless as any that ever swallowed up the slender investments of the widow and the orphan. I don't pay five cents on the dollar. Of what I was to begin with no memory remains. I have been ebbing away, from the start, in a steady current which, at

forty, has left this arid sand-bank behind. To begin with,
certainly, I was not a fountain of wisdom. All the more
reason for a definite channel—for will and purpose and
direction. I walked by chance and sympathy and sentiment.
Take a turn through New York and you'll find my tattered
sympathies and sentiments dangling on every bush and fluttering in every breeze; the men to whom I lent money, the
women to whom I made love, the friends I trusted, the dreams
I cherished, the poisonous fumes of pleasure, amid which
nothing was sweet or precious but the manhood they stifled!
It was my fault that I believed in pleasure here below. I
believe in it still, but as I believe in God and not in man!
I believed in eating your cake and having it. I respected
Pleasure, and she made a fool of me. Other men, treating her
like the arrant strumpet she is, enjoyed her for the hour, but
kept their good manners for plain-faced Business, with the
larger dowry, to whom they are now lawfully married. My
taste was to be delicate; well, perhaps I was so! I had a
little money; it went the way of my little wit. Here in my
pocket I have forty pounds of it left. The only thing I have
to show for my money and my wit is a little volume of verses,
printed at my own expense, in which fifteen years ago I
made bold to sing the charms of love and idleness. Six
months since I got hold of the volume; it reads like the
poetry of fifty years ago. The form is incredible. I hadn't
seen Hampton Court then. When I was thirty I married.
It was a sad mistake, but a generous one. The young girl
was poor and obscure, but beautiful and proud. I fancied
she would make an incomparable woman. It was a sad
mistake! She died at the end of three years, leaving no
children. . . . I have always fancied that I was meant
for a gentler world. Before heaven, sir—whoever you are—
I'm in practice so absurdly tender-hearted that I can afford
to say it,—I came into the world an aristocrat. I was
born with a soul for the picturesque. It condemns me, I
confess; but in a measure, too, it absolves me. I found it
nowhere. I found a world all hard lines and harsh lights,
without shade, without composition, as they say of pictures,
without the lovely mystery of color. To furnish color, I

melted down the very substance of my own soul. I went about with my brush, touching up and toning down; a very pretty chiaroscuro you'll find in my track! Sitting here, in this old park, in this old land, I feel—I feel that I hover on the misty verge of what might have been! I should have been born here and not there; here my vulgar idleness would have been—don't laugh now!—would have been elegant leisure. How it was that I never came abroad is more than I can say. It might have cut the knot; but the knot was too tight. I was always unwell or in debt or entangled. Besides, I had a horror of the sea—with reason, heaven knows. A year ago I was reminded of the existence of an old claim to a portion of an English estate, cherished off and on by various members of my family for the past eighty years. It's undeniably slender and desperately hard to define. I am by no means sure that to this hour I have mastered it. . . . A couple of months since there came out here on business of his own a sort of half-friend of mine, a sharp New York lawyer, an extremely common fellow, but a man with an eye for the weak point and the strong point. It was with him yesterday that you saw me dining. He undertook, as he expressed it, to 'nose round' and see if anything could be made of this pretended right. The matter had never seriously been taken up. A month later I got a letter from Simmons, assuring me that things looked mighty well, that he should be vastly amazed if I hadn't a case. I took fire in a humid sort of way; I acted, for the first time in my life—I sailed for England. I have been here three days: it seems three months. After keeping me waiting for thirty-six hours, last evening my precious Simmons makes his appearance and informs me, with his mouth full of mutton, that I was a blasted fool to have taken him at his word; that he had been precipitate; that I had been precipitate; that my claim was moonshine; and that I must do penance and take a ticket for another fortnight of seasickness in his agreeable society. . . . Poor Simmons! I forgave him with all my heart. But for him I shouldn't be sitting in this place, in this air, with these thoughts. This is a world I could have loved. There's a great fitness in its having been kept for the last. After this nothing would have been tolerable. I shall now have a month of it, I hope, and I shall not have a chance to be disenchanted. There's one thing!", and here, pausing, he laid his hand on mine; I rose and stood before him, "I wish it were possible you should be with me to the end."

"I promise you," I said, "to leave you only at your own request. But it must be on condition of your omitting from your conversation this intolerable flavor of mortality. The end! Perhaps it's the beginning." . . . "Get well, and the rest will take care of itself. I'm interested in your claim.

. . . .

What is the estimated value of your interest?"

"We were instructed from the first to accept a compromise. Compared with the whole property, our utmost right is extremely small. Simmons talked of eighty-five thousand dollars. Why eighty-five I'm sure I don't know. Don't beguile me into figures."

"Allow me one more question. Who is actually in possession?"

"A certain Mr. Richard Searle. I know nothing about him."

"He is in some way related to you?"

"Our great-grandfathers were half-brothers. What does that make?"

"Twentieth cousins, say. And where does your twentieth cousin live?"

"At Lockley Park, Herefordshire."

I pondered awhile. "I'm interested in you, Mr. Searle," I said. "In your story, in your title, such as it is, and in this Lockley Park, Herefordshire. Suppose we go down and see it."

He rose to his feet with a certain alertness. "I shall make a sound man of him, yet," I said to myself.

"I shouldn't have the heart," he said, "to accomplish the melancholy pilgrimage alone. But with you I'll go anywhere."

On our return to London we determined to spend three days there together, and then go into the country. We felt to excellent purpose the sombre charm of London, the mighty mother-city of our mighty race, the great distributing heart of our traditional life. Certain London characteristics—monuments, relics, hints of history, local moods and memories—are more deeply suggestive to an American soul than anything else in Europe. With an equal attentive piety my friend and I glanced at these things. Their influence on Searle was deep and singular. His observation I soon perceived to be extremely acute. His almost passionate relish for the old, the artificial, and social, wellnigh extinct from its long inanition, began now to tremble and thrill with a tardy vitality. I watched in silent wonderment this strange metaphysical renascence.

Between the fair boundaries of the counties of Hereford and Worcester rise in a long undulation the sloping pastures of the Malvern Hills. Consulting a big red book on the castles and manors of England, we found Lockley Park to be seated near the base of this grassy range—though in what county I forget. In the pages of this genial volume, Lockley Park and its appurtenances made a very handsome figure. We took up our abode at a certain little wayside inn, at which in the days of leisure the coach must have stopped for lunch, and burnished pewters of rustic ale been tenderly exalted to "outsides" athirst with breezy progression. Here we stopped, for sheer admiration of its steep thatched roof, its latticed windows, and its homely porch. We allowed a couple of days to elapse in vague, undirected strolls and sweet sentimental observance of the land, before we prepared to execute the especial purpose of our journey. This admirable region is a compendium of the general physiognomy of England. The noble friendliness of the scenery, its subtle old-friendliness, the magical familiarity of multitudinous details, appealed to us at every step and at every glance. Deep in our souls a natural affection answered. The whole land, in the full, warm rains of the last of April, had burst into sudden perfect spring. The dark walls of the hedge-rows had turned into blooming screens; the sodden verdure of lawn and meadow was streaked with a ranker freshness. We went forth without loss of time for a long walk on the hills. Reaching their summits, you find half

England unrolled at your feet. A dozen broad counties, within the vast range of your vision, commingle with their green exhalations. Closely beneath us lay the dark, rich flats of hedgy Worcestershire and the copse-checkered slopes of rolling Hereford, white with the blossom of apples. At widely opposite points of the large expanse two great cathedral towers rise sharply, taking the light, from the settled shadow of their circling towns—the light, the ineffable English light! "Out of England," cried Searle, "it's but a garish world!"

The whole vast sweep of our surrounding prospect lay answering in a myriad fleeting shades the cloudy process of the tremendous sky. The English heaven is a fit antithesis to the complex English earth. We possess in America the infinite beauty of the blue; England possesses the splendor of combined and animated clouds. Over against us, from our station on the hills, we saw them piled and dissolved, compacted and shifted, blotting the azure with sullen rain spots, stretching, breeze-fretted, into dappled fields of gray, burst into a storm of light or melting into a drizzle of silver. We made our way along the rounded summits of these well-grazed heights—mild, breezy inland downs—and descended through long-drawn slopes of fields, green to cottage doors, to where a rural village beckoned us from its seat among the meadows. Close behind it, I admit, the railway shoots fiercely from its tunnel in the hills; and yet there broods upon this charming hamlet an old-time quietude and privacy, which seems to make it a violation of confidence to tell its name so far away. We struck through a narrow lane, a green lane, dim with its height of hedges; it led us to a superb old farmhouse, now jostled by the multiplied lanes and roads which have curtailed its ancient appanage. . . . Passing out upon the high-road, we came to the common browsing-patch, the "village green" of the tales of our youth. Nothing was wanting: the shaggy, mouse-colored donkey, nosing the turf with his mild and huge proboscis; the geese; the old woman—*the* old woman, in person, with her red cloak and her black bonnet, frilled about the face and double-frilled beside her decent, placid cheeks; the towering ploughman with his white smock-frock, puckered on chest and back, his short corduroys, his mighty calves, his big, red, rural face. We greeted these things as children greet the loved pictures in a story-book, lost and mourned and found again. It was marvellous how well we knew them. Beside the road we saw a ploughboy straddle, whistling, on a stile. Gainsborough might have painted him. Beyond the stile, across the level velvet of a meadow, a footpath lay, like a thread of darker woof. We followed it from field to field and from stile to stile. It was the way to church. At the church we finally arrived, lost in its rook-haunted churchyard, hidden from the workday world by the broad stillness of pastures—a gray, gray tower, a huge black yew, a cluster of village graves, with crooked headstones in grassy, low relief. The whole scene was deeply ecclesiastical. My companion was overcome.

"You must bury me here," he cried. "It's the first church I have seen in my life. How it makes a Sunday where it stands!"

The next day we saw a church of statelier proportions. We walked over to Worcester, through such a mist of local color, that I felt like one of Smollett's pedestrian heroes, faring tavenward for a night of adventures. As we neared the provincial city we saw the steepled mass of the cathedral, long and high, rise far into the cloud-freckled blue. And as we came nearer still, we stopped on the bridge and viewed the solid minister reflected in the yellow Severn. . . . On the third morning we betook ourselves to Lockley Park, having learned that the greater part of it was open to visitors, and that, indeed, on application, the house was occasionally shown.

Within its broad enclosure many a declining spur of the great hills melted into parklike slopes and dells. A long avenue wound and circled from the outermost gate through an untrimmed woodland, whence you glanced at further slopes and glades and copses and bosky recesses—at everything except the limits of the place. It was as free and wild and untended as the villa of an Italian prince; and I have never seen the stern English fact of property put on such an air of innocence. The weather had just become perfect; it was one of the dozen exquisite days of the English year— days stamped with refinement of purity unknown in more liberal climes. It was as if the mellow brightness, as tender as that of the primroses which starred the dark waysides like petals wind-scattered over beds of moss, had been meted out to us by the cubic foot, tempered, refined, recorded! From this external region we passed into the heart of the park, through a second lodge-gate, with weather-worn gild-ing on its twisted bars, to the smooth slopes where the great trees stood singly and the tame deer browsed along the bed of a woodland stream. Hence, before us, we perceived the dark Elizabethan manor among its blooming parterres and ter-races.

"Here you can wander all day," I said to Searle, "like a proscribed and exiled prince, hovering about the dominion of the usurper."

"To think," he answered, "of people having enjoyed this all these years! I know what I am—what might I have been? What does all this make of you?"

"That it makes you happy," I said, "I should hesitate to believe. But it's hard to suppose that such a place has not some beneficent action of its own."

"What a perfect scene and background it forms!" Searle went on. "What legends, what histories it knows! My heart is breaking with unutterable visions. There's Tennyson's *Talking Oak*. What summer days one could spend here! How I could lounge my bit of life away on this shady stretch of turf! Haven't I some maiden-cousin in yon moated grange who would give me kind leave?" And then turning almost fiercely upon me: "Why did you bring me here? Why did you drag me into this torment of vain regrets?"

At this moment there passed near us a servant who had emerged from the gardens of the great house. I hailed him and inquired whether we should be likely to gain admittance. He answered that Mr. Searle was away from home, and that he thought it probable the housekeeper would consent to do the honors of the mansion. I passed my arm into Searle's. "Come," I said. "Drain the cup, bitter-sweet though it be.

We shall go in." We passed another lodge-gate and entered
the gardens. The house was an admirable specimen of complete Elizabethan, a multitudinous cluster of gables and
porches, oriels and turrets, screens of ivy and pinnacles of
slate. Two broad terraces commanded the great wooded
horizon of the adjacent domain. Our summons was answered
by the butler in person, solemn and *tout de noir habillé*. He
repeated the statement that Mr. Searle was away from home,
and that he would present our petition to the housekeeper.
We would be so good, however, as to give him our cards.
This request, following so directly on the assertion that Mr.
Searle was absent, seemed to my companion not distinctly
pertinent. "Surely not for the housekeeper," he said.

The butler gave a deferential cough. "Miss Searle is at
home."

"Yours alone will suffice," said Searle. I took out a card
and pencil, and wrote beneath my name, *New York*. Standing with the pencil in my hand I felt a sudden impulse.
Without in the least weighing proprieties or results, I yielded
to it. I added above my name, *Mr. Clement Searle*. What
would come of it?

Before many minutes the housekeeper attended us—a
fresh rosy little old woman in a dowdy clean cap and a
scanty calico gown; an exquisite specimen of refined and
venerable servility. She had the accent of the country, but
the manners of the house. Under her guidance we passed
through a dozen apartments, duly stocked with old pictures,
old tapestry, old carvings, old armor, with all the constituent
properties of an English manor. The pictures were especially valuable. The two Vandykes, the trio of rosy
Rubenses, the sole and sombre Rembrandt, glowed with
conscious authenticity. A Claude, a Murillo, a Greuze, and
a Gainsborough hung gracious in their chosen places. Searle
strolled about silent, pale, and grave, with bloodshot eyes and
lips compressed. He uttered no comment and asked no
question. Missing him, at last, from my side, I retraced my
steps and found him in a room we had just left, on a tarnished silken divan, with his face buried in his hands. Before him, ranged on an antique buffet, was a magnificent col-

lection of old Italian majolica; huge platters radiant with their steady colors, jugs and vases nobly bellied and embossed. There came to me, as I looked, a sudden vision of the young English gentleman, who eighty years ago had travelled by slow stages to Italy and been waited on at his inn by persuasive toymen. "What is it, Searle?" I asked. "Are you unwell?"

He uncovered his haggard face and showed a burning blush. Then smiling in hot irony: "A memory of the past! I was thinking of a china vase that used to stand on the parlor mantel-shelf while I was a boy, with the portrait of General Jackson painted on one side and a bunch of flowers on the other. How long do you suppose that majolica has been in the family?"

"A long time probably. It was brought hither in the last century, into old, old England, out of old, old Italy, by some old young buck of this excellent house with a taste for *chinoiseries*. Here it has stood for a hundred years, keeping its clear, firm hues in this aristocratic twilight."

Searle sprang to his feet. "I say," he cried, "in heaven's name take me away! I can't stand this. Before I know it I shall do something I shall be ashamed of. I shall steal one of their d—d majolicas. I shall proclaim my identity and assert my rights! I shall go blubbering to Miss Searle and ask her in pity's name to keep me here for a month!"

If poor Searle could ever have been said to look "dangerous" he looked so now. I began to regret my officious presentation of his name, and prepared without delay to lead him out of the house. We overtook the housekeeper in the last room of the suite, a small, unused boudoir, over the chimney-piece of which hung a noble portrait of a young man in a powdered wig and a brocaded waistcoat. I was immediately struck with his resemblance to my companion.

"This is Mr. Clement Searle, Mr. Searle's great-uncle, by Sir Joshua Reynolds," quoth the housekeeper. "He died young, poor gentleman. He perished at sea, going to America."

"He's the young buck," I said, "who brought the majolica out of Italy."

"Indeed, sir, I believe he did," said the housekeeper, staring.

"He's the image of you, Searle," I murmured.

"He's wonderfully like the gentleman, saving his presence," said the housekeeper.

My friend stood gazing. "Clement Searle—at sea—going to America—" he muttered. Then harshly, to the housekeeper, "Why the deuce did he go to America?"

"Why, indeed, sir? You may well ask. I believe he had kinsfolk there. It was for them to come to him."

Searle broke into a laugh. "It was for them to have come to him! Well, well," he said, fixing his eyes on the little old woman, "they have come to him at last!"

She blushed like a wrinkled rose-leaf. "Indeed, sir," she said, "I verily believe that you are one of *us!*"

"My name is the name of that lovely youth," Searle went on. "Kinsman, I salute you! Attend!" And he grasped me by the arm. "I have an idea! He perished at sea. His spirit came ashore and wandered forlorn till it got lodgment again in my poor body. In my poor body it has lived, homesick, these forty years, shaking its rickety cage, urging me, stupid, to carry it back to the scenes of its youth. And I never knew what was the matter with me! Let me exhale my spirit here!"

The housekeeper essayed a timorous smile. The scene was embarrassing. My confusion was not allayed when I suddenly perceived in the doorway the figure of a lady. "Miss Searle!" whispered the housekeeper. My first impression of Miss Searle was that she was neither young nor beautiful. She stood with a timid air on the threshold, pale, trying to smile, and twirling my card in her fingers. I immediately bowed. Searle, I think, gazed marvelling.

"If I am not mistaken," said the lady, "one of you gentlemen is Mr. Clement Searle."

"My friend is Mr. Clement Searle," I replied. "Allow me to add that I alone am responsible for your having received his name."

"I should have been sorry not to receive it," said Miss

Searle, beginning to blush. "Your being from America has led me to—to interrupt you."

"The interruption, madam, has been on our part. And with just that excuse—that we are from America."

Miss Searle, while I spoke, had fixed her eyes on my friend, as he stood silent beneath Sir Joshua's portrait. The housekeeper, amazed and mystified, took a liberty. "Heaven preserve us, Miss! It's your great-uncle's picture come to life."

"I'm not mistaken, then," said Miss Searle. "We are distantly related." She had the aspect of an extremely modest woman. She was evidently embarrassed at having to proceed unassisted in her overture. Searle eyed her with gentle wonder from head to foot. I fancied I read his thoughts. This, then, was Miss Searle, his maiden-cousin, prospective heiress of these manorial acres and treasures. She was a person of about thirty-three years of age, taller than most women, with health and strength in the rounded amplitude of her shape. She had a small blue eye, a massive chignon of yellow hair, and a mouth at once broad and comely. She was dressed in a lustreless black satin gown, with a short train. Around her neck she wore a blue silk handkerchief, and over this handkerchief, in many convolutions, a string of amber beads. Her appearance was singular; she was large, yet not imposing; girlish, yet mature. Her glance and accent, in addressing us, were simple, too simple. Searle, I think, had been fancying some proud cold beauty of five-and-twenty; he was relieved at finding the lady timid and plain. His person was suddenly illumined with an old disused gallantry.

"We are distant cousins, I believe. I am happy to claim a relationship which you are so good as to remember. I had not in the least counted on your doing so."

"Perhaps I have done wrong," and Miss Searle blushed anew and smiled. "But I have always known of there being people of our blood in America, and I have often wondered and asked about them; without learning much, however. To-day, when this card was brought me and I knew of a Clement Searle wandering about the house like a stranger, I felt as if I ought to do something. I hardly knew what! My brother is in London. I have done what I think he would have done. Welcome, as a cousin." And with a gesture at once frank and shy, she put out her hand.

"I'm welcome indeed," said Searle, taking it, "if he would have done it half as graciously."

"You've seen the show," Miss Searle went on. "Perhaps now you'll have some lunch." We followed her into a small breakfast-room, where a deep bay-window opened on the mossy flags of the great terrace. Here, for some moments, she remained silent and shy, in the manner of a person resting from a great effort. Searle, too, was formal and reticent, so that I had to busy myself with providing small-talk. It was of course easy to descant on the beauties of park and mansion. Meanwhile I observed our hostess. She had small beauty and scanty grace; her dress was out of taste and out of season; yet she pleased me well. There was about her a sturdy sweetness, a homely flavor of the sequestered *châtelaine* of feudal days. To be so simple amid this massive luxury, so mellow and yet so fresh, so modest and yet so placid, told of just the spacious leisure in which I had fancied human life to be steeped in many a park-circled home. Miss Searle was to the *Belle au Bois Dormant* what a fact is to a fairy-tale— an interpretation to a myth. We, on our side, were to our hostess objects of no light scrutiny. The best possible English breeding still marvels visibly at the native American. Miss Searle's wonderment was guileless enough to have been more overt and yet inoffensive; there was no taint of offence indeed in her utterance of the unvarying amenity that she had met an American family on the Lake of Como whom she would have almost taken to be English.

"If I lived here," I said, "I think I should hardly need to go away, even to the Lake of Como."

"You might perhaps get tired of it. And then the Lake of Como! If I could only go abroad again!"

"You have been but once?"

"Only once. Three years ago my brother took me to Switzerland. We thought it extremely beautiful. Except for this journey, I have always lived here. Here I was born.

It's a dear old place, indeed, and I know it well. Sometimes I fancy I'm a little tired." And on my asking her how she spent her time and what society she saw, "It's extremely quiet," she went on, proceeding by short steps and simple statements, in the manner of a person summoned for the first time to define her situation and enumerate the elements of her life. "We see very few people. I don't think there are many nice people hereabouts. At least we don't know them. Our own family is very small. My brother cares for little else but riding and books. He had a great sorrow ten years ago. He lost his wife and his only son, a dear little boy, who would have succeeded him in the estates. Do you know that I'm likely to have them now? Poor me! Since his loss my brother has preferred to be quite alone. I'm sorry he's away. But you must wait till he comes back. I expect him in a day or two." She talked more and more, with a rambling earnest vapidity, about her circumstances, her solitude, her bad eyes, so that she couldn't read, her flowers, her ferns, her dogs, and the curate, recently inducted by her brother and warranted sound orthodox, who had lately begun to light his altar candles; pausing every now and then to blush in self surprise, and yet moving steadily from point to point in the deepening excitement of temptation and occasion. Of all the old things I had seen in England, this mind of Miss Searle's seemed to me the oldest, the quaintest, the most ripely verdant; so fenced and protected by convention and precedent and usage; so passive and mild and docile. I felt as if I were talking with a potential heroine of Miss Burney. As she talked, she rested her dull, kind eyes upon her kinsman with a sort of fascinated stare. At last, "Did you mean to go away," she demanded, "without asking for us?"

"I had thought it over, Miss Searle, and had determined not to trouble you. You have shown me how unfriendly I should have been."

"But you knew of the place being ours and of our relationship?"

"Just so. It was because of these things that I came down

here—because of them, almost, that I came to England. I have always liked to think of them."

"You merely wished to look, then? We don't pretend to be much to look at."

"You don't know what you are, Miss Searle," said my friend, gravely.

"You like the old place, then?"

Searle looked at her in silence. "If I could only tell you," he said at last.

"Do tell me! You must come and stay with us."

Searle began to laugh. "Take care, take care," he cried. "I should surprise you. At least I should bore you. I should never leave you."

"O, you'd get homesick for America!"

At this Searle laughed the more. "By the way," he cried to me, "tell Miss Searle about America!" And he stepped through the window out upon the terrace, followed by two beautiful dogs, a pointer and a young stag-hound, who from the moment we came in had established the fondest relation with him. Miss Searle looked at him as he went, with a certain tender wonder in her eye. I read in her glance, methought, that she was interested. I suddenly recalled the last words I had heard spoken by my friend's adviser in London: "Instead of dying you'd better marry." If Miss Searle could be gently manipulated. O for a certain divine tact! Something assured me that her heart was virgin soil; that sentiment had never bloomed there. If I could but sow the seed! There lurked within her the perfect image of one of the patient wives of old.

"He has lost his heart to England," I said. "He ought to have been borne here."

"And yet," said Miss Searle, "he's not in the least an Englishman."

"How do you know that?"

"I hardly know how. I never talked with a foreigner before; but he looks and talks as I have fancied foreigners."

"Yes, he's foreign enough!"

"Is he married?"

"He's a widower—without children."

"Has he property?"

"Very little.

"But enough to travel?"

I meditated. "He has not expected to travel far," I said at last. "You know he's in poor health."

"Poor gentleman! So I fancied."

"He's better, though, than he thinks. He came here because he wanted to see your place before he dies."

"Poor fellow!" And I fancied I perceived in her eye the lustre of a rising tear. "And he was going off without my seeing him?"

"He's a modest man, you see."

"He's very much of a gentleman."

"Assuredly!"

At this moment we heard on the terrace a loud, harsh cry. "It's the great peacock!" said Miss Searle, stepping to the window and passing out. I followed her. Below us on the terrace, leaning on the parapet, stood our friend, with his arm round the neck of the pointer. Before him, on the grand walk, strutted a splendid peacock, with ruffled neck and expanded tail. The other dog had apparently indulged in a momentary attempt to abash the gorgeous fowl, but at Searle's voice he had bounded back to the terrace and leaped upon the parapet, where he now stood licking his new friend's face. The scene had a beautiful old-time air: the peacock flaunting in the foreground, like the very genius of antique gardenry; the broad terrace, which flattered an innate taste of mine for all deserted promenades to which people may have adjourned from formal dinners, to drink coffee in old Sèvres, and where the stiff brocade of women's dresses may have rustled autumnal leaves; and far around us, with one leafy circle melting into another, the timbered acres of the park. "The very beasts have made him welcome," I said, as we rejoined our companion.

"The peacock has done for you, Mr. Searle," said his cousin, "what he does only for very great people. A year ago there came here a duchess to see my brother. I don't think that since then he has spread his tail as wide for any one else by a dozen feathers."

"It's not alone the peacock," said Searle. "Just now there came slipping across my path a little green lizard, the first I ever saw, the lizard of literature! And if you have a ghost, broad daylight though it be, I expect to see him here. Do you know the annals of your house, Miss Searle?"

"O dear, no! You must ask my brother for all those things."

"You ought to have a book full of legends and traditions. You ought to have loves and murders and mysteries by the roomful. I count upon it."

"O Mr. Searle. We have always been a very well-behaved family. Nothing out of the way has ever happened, I think."

"Nothing out of the way? O horrors! We have done better than that in America. Why, I myself!"—and he gazed at her a moment with a gleam of malice, and then broke into a laugh. "Suppose I should turn out a better Searle than you? Better than you, nursed here in romance and pictur- esqueness. Come, don't disappoint me. You have some his- tory among you all, you have some poetry. I have been famished all my days for these things. Do yo understand? Ah, you can't understand! Tell me something! When I think of what must have happened here! when I think of the lovers who must have strolled on this terrace and wan- dered through those glades! of all the figures and passions and purposes that must have haunted these walls! of the births, the deaths, the joys and sufferings, the young hopes and the old regrets, the intense experience—" And here he faltered a moment, with the increase of his vehemence. The gleam in his eye, which I have called a gleam of malice, had settled into a deep, unnatural light. I began to fear he had become over-excited. But he went on with redoubled pas- sion. "To see it all evoked before me," he cried, "if the Devil alone could do it, I'd make a bargain with the Devil! O Miss Searle, I'm a most unhappy man!"

"O dear, O dear!" said Miss Searle.

"Look at that window, that blessed oriel!" And he pointed to a small, protruding casement above us, relieved against the purple brick-work, framed in chiselled stone, and curtained with ivy.

"It's my room," said Miss Searle.

"Of course it's a woman's room. Think of the forgotten loveliness which has peeped from that window; think of the old-time women's lives which have known chiefly that outlook on this bosky world. O gentle cousins! And you, Miss Searle, you're one of them yet." And he marched towards her and took her great white hand. She surrendered it, blushing to her eyes, and pressing the other hand to her breast. "You're a woman of the past. You're nobly simple. It has been a romance to see you. It doesn't matter what I say to you. You didn't know me yesterday, you'll not know me to-morrow. Let me to-day do a mad, sweet thing. Let me fancy you the soul of all the dead women who have trod these terrace-flags, which lie here like sepulchral tablets in the pavement of a church. Let me say I worship you!" And he raised her hand to his lips. She gently withdrew it, and for a moment averted her face. Meeting her eyes for the next moment, I saw that they were filled with tears. *The Belle au Bois Dormant* was awake.

There followed an embarrassed pause. An issue was suddenly presented by the appearance of the butler bearing a letter. "A telegram, Miss," he said.

"Dear me!" cried Miss Searle, "I can't open a telegram. Cousin, help me."

Searle took the missive, opened it, and read aloud. "I shall be home to dinner. Keep the American."

II

"Keep the American!" Miss Searle, in compliance with the injunction conveyed in her brother's telegram (with something certainly of telegraphic curtness), lost no time in expressing the pleasure it would give her to have my companion remain. "Really you must," she said; and forthwith repaired to the housekeeper, to give orders for the preparation of a room.

"How in the world," asked Searle, "did he know of my being here?"

"He learned, probably," I expounded, "from his solicitor of the visit of your friend Simmons. Simmons and the solicitor must have had another interview since your arrival in England. Simmons, for reasons of his own, has communicated to the solicitor your journey to this neighborhood, and Mr. Searle, learning this, has immediately taken for granted that you have formally presented youself to his sister. He's hospitably inclined, and he wishes her to do the proper thing by you. More perhaps! I have my little theory that he is the very Phœnix of usurpers, that his nobler sense has been captivated by the exposition of the men of law, and that he means gracefully to surrender you your fractional interest in the estate."

"I give it up!" said my friend, musing. "Come what come will!"

"You of course," said Miss Searle, reappearing and turning to me, "are included in my brother's invitation. I have bespoken your lodging as well. Your luggage shall immediately be sent for."

It was arranged that I in person should be driven over to our little inn, and that I should return with our effects in time to meet Mr. Searle at dinner. On my arrival, several hours later, I was immediately conducted to my room. The servant pointed out to me that it communicated by a door and a private passage with that of my companion. I made my way along this passage—a low, narrow corridor, with a long latticed casement, through which there streamed, upon a series of grotesquely sculptured oaken closets and cupboards, the lurid animating glow of the western sun—knocked at his door, and, getting no answer, opened it. In an arm-chair by the open window sat my friend, sleeping with arms and legs relaxed and head placidly reverted. It was a great relief to find him resting from his rhapsodies, and I watched him for some moments before waking him. There was a faint glow of color in his cheek and a light parting of his lips, as in a smile; something nearer to mental soundness than I had yet seen in him. It was almost happiness, it was almost health. I laid my hand on his arm and gently shook it. He opened his eyes, gazed at me a moment, vaguely recognizing me, then closed them again. "Let me dream, let me dream!" he said.

"What are you dreaming about?"

A moment passed before his answer came. "About a tall woman in a quaint black dress, with yellow hair, and a sweet, sweet smile, and a soft, low, delicious voice! I'm in love with her."

"It's better to see her," I said, "than to dream about her. Get up and dress, and we shall go down to dinner and meet her."

"Dinner—dinner—" And he gradually opened his eyes again. "Yes, upon my word, I shall dine!"

"You're a well man!" I said, as he rose to his feet. "You'll live to bury Mr. Simmons." He had spent the hours of my absence, he told me, with Miss Searle. They had strolled together over the park and through the gardens and greenhouses. "You must already be intimate!" I said, smiling.

"She is intimate with me," he answered. "Heaven knows what rigmarole I've treated her to!" They had parted an hour ago, since when, he believed, her brother had arrived.

The slow-fading twilight still abode in the great drawing-room as we entered it. The housekeeper had told us that this apartment was rarely used, there being a smaller and more convenient one for the same needs. It seemed now, however, to be occupied in my comrade's honor. At the farther end of it, rising to the roof, like a ducal tomb in a cathedral, was a great chimney-piece of chiselled white marble, yellowed by time, in which a light fire was crackling. Before the fire stood a small short man with his hands behind him; near him stood Miss Searle, so transformed by her dress that at first I scarcely knew her. There was in our entrance and reception something profoundly chilling and solemn. We moved in silence up the long room. Mr. Searle advanced slowly a dozen steps to meet us. His sister stood motionless. I was conscious of her masking her visage with a large white tinselled fan, and of her eyes, grave and expanded, watching us intently over the top of it. The master of Lockley Park grasped in silence the proffered hand of his kinsman, and eyed him from head to foot, suppressing, I think, a start of surprise at his resemblance to Sir Joshua's portrait. "This is a happy day!" he said And then turning to me with a bow, "My cousin's friend is my friend." Miss Searle lowered her fan.

The first thing that struck me in Mr. Searle's appearance was his short and meagre stature, which was less by half a head than that of his sister. The second was the preternatural redness of his hair and beard. They intermingled over his ears and surrounded his head like a huge lurid nimbus. His face was pale and attenuated, like the face of a scholar, a dilettante, a man who lives in a library, bending over books and prints and medals. At a distance it had an oddly innocent and youthful look; but on a nearer view it revealed a number of finely etched and scratched wrinkles, of a singularly aged and cunning effect. It was the complexion of a man of sixty. His nose was arched and delicate, identical almost with the nose of my friend. In harmony with the effect of his hair was that of his eyes, which were large and deep-set, with a sort of vulpine keenness and redness, but full of temper and spirit. Imagine this physiognomy—grave and solemn in aspect, grotesquely solemn, almost, in spite of the bushy brightness in which it was encased—set in motion by a smile which seemed to whisper terribly, "I am *the* smile, the sole and official, the grin to command," and you will have an imperfect notion of the remarkable presence of our host; something better worth seeing and knowing, I fancied as I covertly scrutinized him, than anything our excursion had yet introduced us to. Of how thoroughly I had entered into sympathy with my companion and how effectually I had associated my sensibilities with his, I had small suspicion until, within the short five minutes which preceded the announcement of dinner, I distinctly perceived him place himself, morally speaking, on the defensive. To neither of us was Mr. Searle, as the Italians would say, sympathetic. I might have fancied from her attitude that Miss Searle apprehended our thoughts. A signal change had been wrought in her since the morning, during the hour, indeed (as I read in the light of the wondering glance he cast at her) that had elapsed since her parting with her cousin. She had not yet recovered from some great agitation. Her face was pale and her eyes red with weeping. These tragic betrayals gave an unexpected dignity to her aspect, which was further enhanced by the rare picturesqueness of her dress.

Whether it was taste or whether it was accident, I know not; but Miss Searle, as she stood there, half in the cool twlight, half in the arrested glow of the fire as it spent itself in the vastness of its marble cave, was a figure for a cunning painter. She was dressed in the faded splendor of a beautiful tissue of combined and blended silk and crape of a tender sea-green color, festooned and garnished and puffed into a massive *bouillonnement;* a piece of millinery, which, though it must have witnessed a number of stately dinners, preserved still an air of admirable elegance. Over her white shoulders she wore an ancient web of the most precious and venerable lace, and about her rounded throat a necklace of heavy pearls. I went with her in to dinner, and Mr. Searle, following with my friend, took his arm (as the latter afterwards told me) and pretended sportively to conduct him. As dinner proceeded, the feeling grew within me that a drama had begun to be played in which the three persons before me were actors, each of a most exacting part. The part of my friend, however, seemed the most heavily charged, and I was filled with a strong desire that he should summon his shadowy faculties to obey his shadowy will. The poor fellow sat playing solemnly at self-esteem. With Miss Searle, credulous, passive, and pitying, he had finally flung aside all vanity and propriety, and shown her the bottom of his fantastic heart. But with our host there might be no talking of nonsense nor taking of liberties; there and then, if ever, sat a double-distilled conservative, breathing the fumes of hereditary privilege and security. For an hour, then, I saw my poor friend turn faithfully about to speak graciously of barren things. He was to prove himself a sound American, so that his relish of this elder world might seem purely disinterested. What his kinsman had expected to find him, I know not; but with all his finely adjusted urbanity, he was unable to repress a shade of annoyance at finding him likely to speak graciously at all. Mr. Searle was not the man to show his hand, but I think his best card had been a certain implicit confidence that this exotic parasite would hardly have good manners.

Our host, with great decency, led the conversation to America, talking of it rather as if it were some fabled planet, alien to the British orbit, lately proclaimed indeed to have the proportion of atmospheric gases required to support animal life, but not, save under cover of a liberal afterthought, to be admitted into one's regular conception of things. I, for my part, felt nothing but regret that the spheric smoothness of his universe should be strained to cracking by the intrusion of our square shoulders.

"I knew in a general way," said Mr. Searle, "of my having relations in America; but you know one hardly realizes those things. I could hardly more have imagined people of our blood there, than I could have imagined being there myself. There was a man I knew at college, a very odd fellow, a nice fellow too; he and I were rather cronies; I think he afterwards went to America; to the Argentine Republic, I believe. Do you know the Argentine Republic? What an extraordinary name, by the way! And then, you know, there was that great-uncle of mine whom Sir Joshua painted. He went to America, but he never got there. He was lost at sea. You look enough like him to have one fancy he *did* get there, and that he has lived along till now. If you are he, you've not done a wise thing to show yourself here. He left a bad name behind him. There's a ghost who comes sobbing about the house every now and then, the ghost of one against whom he wrought a great evil!"

"O brother!" cried Miss Searle, in simple horror.

"Of course you know nothing of such things," said Mr. Searle. "You're too sound a sleeper to hear the sobbing of ghosts."

"I'm sure I should like immensely to hear the sobbing of a ghost!" said my friend, with the light of his previous eagerness playing up into his eyes. "Why does it sob? Unfold the wondrous tale."

Mr. Searle eyed his audience for a moment gaugingly; and then, as the French say, *se receuillit,* as if he were measuring his own imaginative force.

He wished to do justice to his theme. With the five fingernails of his left hand nervously playing against the tinkling

crystal of his wineglass, and his bright eye telling of a glee-
ful sense that, small and grotesque as he sat there, he was
for the moment profoundly impressive, he distilled into our
untutored minds the sombre legend of his house. "Mr.
Clement Searle, from all I gather, was a young man of great
talent but a weak disposition. His mother was left a widow
early in life, with two sons, of whom he was the older and
the more promising. She educated him with the utmost fondness and care. Of course, when he came to manhood she
wished him to marry well. His means were quite sufficient
to enable him to overlook the want of means in his wife; and
Mrs. Searle selected a young lady who possessed, as she con-
ceived, every good gift save a fortune—a fine, proud, handsome girl, the daughter of an old friend—an old lover, I
fancy, of her own. Clement, however, as it appeared, had
either chosen otherwise or was as yet unprepared to choose.
The young lady discharged upon him in vain the battery of
her attractions; in vain his mother urged her cause. Clement
remained cold, insensible, inflexible. Mrs. Searle possessed
a native force of which in its feminine branch the family
seems to have lost the trick. A proud, passionate, imperious
woman, she had had great cares and a number of law-suits;
they had given her a great will. She suspected that her son's
affections were lodged elsewhere, and lodged amiss. Irritated
by his stubborn defiance of her wishes, she persisted in her
urgency. The more she watched him the more she believed
that he loved in secret. If he loved in secret, of course he
loved beneath him. He went about sombre, sullen, and pre-
occupied. At last, with the fatal indiscretion of an angry
woman, she threatened to bring the young lady of her choice
—who, by the way, seems to have been no shrinking blossom
—to stay in the house. A stormy scene was the result. He
threatened that if she did so, he would leave the country and
sail for America. She probably disbelieved him; she knew
him to be weak, but she overrated his weakness. At all
events, the fair rejected arrived and Clement departed. On
a dark December day he took ship at Southampton. The
two women, desperate with rage and sorrow, sat alone in this
great house, mingling their tears and imprecations. A fort-

night later, on Christmas eve, in the midst of a great snow-storm, long famous in the country, there came to them a mighty quickening of their bitterness. A young woman, soaked and chilled by the storm, gained entrance to the house and made her way into the presence of the mistress and her guest. She poured out her tale. She was a poor curate's daughter of Hereford. Clement Searle had loved her; loved her all too well. She had been turned out in wrath from her father's house. His mother, at least, might pity her; if not for herself, then for the child she was soon to bring forth. The poor girl had been a second time too trustful. The women, in scorn, in horror, with blows, possibly, turned her forth again into the storm. In the storm she wandered, and in the deep snow she died. Her lover, as you know, perished in that hard winter weather at sea; the news came to his mother late, but soon enough. We are haunted by the curate's daughter!"

There was a pause of some moments. "Ah, well we may be!" said Miss Searle, with a great pity.

Searle blazed up into enthusiasm. "Of course you know," —and suddenly he began to blush violently,—"I should be sorry to claim any identity with my faithless namesake, poor fellow. But I shall be hugely tickled if this poor ghost should be deceived by my resemblance and mistake me for her cruel lover. She's welcome to the comfort of it. What one can do in the case I shall be glad to do. But can a ghost haunt a ghost? I *am* a ghost!"

Mr. Searle stared a moment, and then smiling superbly: "I could almost believe you are!" he said.

"O brother—cousin!" cried Miss Searle, with the gentlest, yet most appealing dignity, "how can you talk so horribly?"

This horrible talk, however, evidently possessed a potent magic for my friend; and his imagination, chilled for a while by the frigid contact of his kinsman, began to glow again with its earlier fire. From this moment he ceased to steer his cockle-shell, to care what he said or how he said it, so long as he expressed his passionate satisfaction in the scene about him. As he talked I ceased even mentally to protest. I have wondered since that I should not have resented the exhibition of so rank and florid an egotism. But a great frankness for the time makes its own law, and a great passion its own channel. There was, moreover, an immense sweetness in the manner of my friend's speech. Free alike from either adulation or envy, the very soul of it was a divine apprehension, an imaginative mastery, free as the flight of Ariel, of the poetry of his companion's situation and of the contrasted prosiness of their attitude.

"How does the look of age come?" he demanded, at dessert. "Does it come of itself, unobserved, unrecorded, unmeasured? Or do you woo it and set baits and traps for it, and watch it like the dawning brownness of a meerschaum pipe, and nail it down when it appears, just where it peeps out, and light a votive taper beneath it and give thanks to it daily? Or do you forbid it and fight it and resist it, and yet feel it settling and deepening about you, as irrestible as fate?"

"What the deuce is the man talking about?" said the smile of our host.

"I found a gray hair this morning," said Miss Searle.

"Good heavens! I hope you respected it," cried Searle.

"I look at it for a long time in my little glass," said his cousin, simply.

"Miss Searle, for many years to come, can afford to be amused at gray hairs," I said.

"Ten years hence I shall be forty-three," she answered.

"That's my age," said Searle. "If I had only come here ten years ago! I should have had more time to enjoy the feast, but I should have had less of an appetite. I needed to get famished for it."

"Why did you wait for the starving point?" asked Mr. Searle. "To think of these ten years that we might have been enjoying you!" And at the thought of these wasted ten years Mr. Searle broke into a violent nervous laugh.

"I always had a notion,—a stupid, vulgar notion, if there ever was one,—that to come abroad properly one ought to have a pot of money. My pot was too nearly empty. At last I came with my empty pot!"

Mr. Searle coughed with an air of hesitation. "You're a —you're in limited circumstances?"

My friend apparently was vastly tickled to have his bleak situation called by so soft a name. "Limited circumstances!" he cried with a long, light laugh; "I'm in no circumstances at all!"

"Upon my word!" murmured Mr. Searle, with an air of being divided between his sense of the indecency and his sense of the rarity of a gentleman taking just that tone about his affairs. "Well—well—well!" he added, in a voice which might have meant everything or nothing; and proceeded, with a twinkle in his eye, to finish a glass of wine. His sparkling eye, as he drank, encountered mine over the top of his glass, and, for a moment, we exchanged a long deep glance—a glance so keen as to leave a slight embarrassment on the face of each. "And you," said Mr. Searle, by way of carrying it off, "how about your circumstances?"

"O, his," said my friend, "his are unlimited! He could buy up Lockley Park!" He had drunk, I think, a rather greater number of glasses of port—I admit that the port was infinitely drinkable—than was to have been desired in the interest of perfect self-control. He was rapidly drifting beyond any tacit dissuasion of mine. A certain feverish harshness in his glance and voice warned me that to attempt to direct him would simply irritate him. As we rose from the table he caught my troubled look. Passing his arm for a moment into mine, "This is the great night!" he whispered. "The night of fatality, the night of destiny!"

Mr. Searle had caused the whole lower region of the house to be thrown open and a multitude of lights to be placed in convenient and effective positions. Such a marshalled wealth of ancient candlesticks and flambeaux I had never beheld. Niched against the dark panelling, casting great luminous circles upon the pendent stiffness of sombre tapestries, enhancing and completing with admirable effect the vastness and mystery of the ancient house, they seemed to people the great rooms, as our little group passed slowly from one to another, with a dim, expectant presence. We had a delightful hour of it. Mr. Searle at once assumed the part of cice-

rone, and—I had not hitherto done him justice—Mr. Searle
became agreeble. While I lingered behind with Miss Searle,
he walked in advance with his kinsman. It was as if he had
said, "Well, if you want the old place, you shall have it—
metaphysically!" To speak vulgarly, he rubbed it in. Carrying a great silver candlestick in his left hand, he raised it
and lowered it and cast the light hither and thither, upon
pictures and hangings and bits of carving and a hundred
lurking architectural treasures. Mr. Searle knew his house.
He hinted at innumerable traditions and memories, and
evoked with a very pretty wit the figures of its earlier occu-
pants. He told a dozen anecdotes with an almost reverential
gravity and neatness. His companion attended, with a sort
of brooding intelligence. Miss Searle and I, meanwhile,
were not wholly silent.

"I suppose that by this time," I said, "you and your cousin
are almost old friends."

She trifled a moment with her fan, and then raising her
homely candid gaze: "Old friends, and at the same time
strangely new! My cousin,—my cousin,"—and her voice
lingered on the word,—"it seems so strange to call him my
cousin, after thinking these many years that I had no cousin!
He's a most singular man."

"It's not so much he as his circumstances that are singular," I ventured to say.

"I'm so sorry for his circumstances. I wish I could help
him in some way. He interests me so much." And here
Miss Searle gave a rich, mellow sigh. "I wish I had known
him a long time ago. He told me that he is but the shadow
of what he was."

I wondered whether Searle had been consciously playing
upon the fancy of this gentle creature. If he had, I believed
he had gained his point. But in fact his position had become to my sense so charged with opposing forces, that I
hardly ventured wholly to rejoice. "His better self just now,"
I said, "seems again to be taking shape. It will have been a
good deed on your part, Miss Searle, if you help to restore
him to soundness and serenity."

"Ah, what can I do?"

"Be a friend to him. Let him like you, let him love you! You see in him now, doubtless, much to pity and to wonder at. But let him simply enjoy awhile the grateful sense of your nearness and dearness. He will be a better and stronger man for it, and then you can love him, you can respect him without restriction."

Miss Searle listened with a puzzled tenderness of gaze. "It's a hard part for poor me to play!"

Her almost infantine gentleness left me no choice but to be absolutely frank. "Did you ever play any part at all?" I asked.

Her eyes met mine, wonderingly; she blushed, as with a sudden sense of my meaning. "Never! I think I have hardly lived."

"You've begun now, perhaps. You have begun to care for something outside the narrow circle of habit and duty. (Excuse me if I am rather too outspoken: you know I'm a foreigner.) It's a great moment: I wish you joy."

"I could almost fancy you are laughing at me. I feel more trouble than joy."

"Why do you feel trouble?"

She paused with her eyes fixed on our two companions. "My cousin's arrival," she said at last, "is a great disturbance."

"You mean that you did wrong in recognizing him? In that case the fault is mine. He had no intention of giving you the opportunity."

"I did wrong, after a fashion! But I can't find it in my heart to regret it. I never shall regret it! I did what I thought proper. Heaven forgive me!"

"Heaven bless you, Miss Searle! Is any harm to come of it? I did the evil; let me bear the brunt!"

She shook her head gravely. "You don't know my brother!"

"The sooner I do know him, then, the better!" And hereupon I felt a dull irritation which had been gathering force for more than an hour explode into sudden wrath. "What on earth is your brother?" I demanded. She turned away. "Are you afraid of him?" I asked.

She gave me a tearful sidelong glace. "He's looking **at** me!" she murmured.

I look at him. He was standing with his back to us, holding a large Venetian hand-mirror, framed in rococo silver, which he had taken from a shelf of antiquities, in just such a position that he caught the reflection of his sister's person. Shall I confess it? Something in this performance so tickled my sense of the picturesque, that it was with a sort of blunted anger that I muttered, "The sneak!" Yet I felt passion enough to urge me forward. It seemed to me that by implication I, too, was being covertly watched. I should not be watched for nothing! "Miss Searle," I said, insisting upon her attention, "promise me something."

She turned upon me with a start and the glance of one appealing from some great pain. "O, don't ask me!" she cried. It was as if she were standing on the verge of some sudden lapse of familiar ground and had been summoned to make a leap. I felt that retreat was impossible, and that it was the greater kindness to beckon her forward.

"Promise me," I repeated.

Still with her eyes she protested. "O, dreadful day!" she cried, at last.

"Promise me to let him speak to you, if he should ask you, any wish you may suspect on your brother's part notwithstanding."

She colored deeply. "You mean," she said, "you mean that he—has something particular to say."

"Something most particular!"

"Poor cousin!"

I gave her a deeply questioning look. "Well, poor cousin! But promise me."

"I promise," she said, and moved away across the long room and out of the door.

"You're in time to hear the most delightful story!" said my friend, as I rejoined the two gentlemen. They were standing before an old sombre portrait of a lady in the dress of Queen Anne's time, with her ill-painted flesh-tints showing livid in the candlelight against her dark drapery and background. "This is Mistress Margaret Searle,—a sort of

Beatrix Esmond,—who did as she pleased. She married a paltry Frenchman, a penniless fiddler, in the teeth of her whole family. Fair Margaret, my compliments! Upon my soul, she looks like Miss Searle! Pray go on. What came of it all?"

Mr. Searle looked at his kinsman for a moment with an air of distaste for his boisterous homage, and of pity for his crude imagination. Then resuming, with a very effective dryness of tone: "I found a year ago, in a box of very old papers, a letter from Mistress Margaret to Cynthia Searle, her elder sister. It was dated from Paris and dreadfully ill-spelled. It contained a most passionate appeal for—a— for pecuniary assistance. She had just been confined, she was starving, and neglected by her husband; she cursed the day she left England. It was a most dismal effusion. I never heard that she found means to return."

"So much for marrying a Frenchman!" I said, sententiously.

Mr. Searle was silent for some moments. "This was the first," he said, finally," and the last of the family who has been so d—d un-English!"

"Does Miss Searle know her history?" asked my friend, staring at the rounded whiteness of the lady's heavy cheek.

"Miss Searle knows nothing!" said our host, with zeal.

This utterance seemed to kindle in my friend a generous opposing zeal. "She shall know at least the tale of Mistress Margaret," he cried, and walked rapidly away in search of her.

Mr. Searle and I pursued our march through the lighted rooms. "You've found a cousin," I said, "with a vengeance."

"Ah, a vengeance?" said my host, stiffly.

"I mean that he takes as keen an interest in your annals and possessions as yourself."

"O, exactly so!" and Mr. Searle burst into resounding laughter. "He tells me," he resumed, in a moment, "that he is an invalid. I should never have fancied it."

"Within the past few hours," I said, "he's a changed man.

Your place and your kindness have refreshed him immensely."

Mr. Searle uttered the little shapeless ejaculation with which many an Englishman is apt to announce the concussion of any especial courtesy of speech. He bent his eyes on the floor frowningly, and then, to my surprise, he suddenly stopped and looked at me with a penetrating eye. "I'm an honest man!" he said. I was quite prepared to assent; but he went on, with a sort of fury of frankness, as if it was the first time in his life that he had been prompted to expound himself, as if the process was mightily unpleasant to him and he was hurrying through it as a task. "An honest man, mind you! I know nothing about Mr. Clement Searle! I never expected to see him. He has been to me a—a—" And here Mr. Searle paused to select a word which should vividly enough express what, for good or for ill, his kinsman had been to him. "He has been to me an *amazement!* I have no doubt he is a most amiable man! You'll not deny, however, that he's a very odd style of person. I'm sorry he's ill! I'm sorry he's poor! He's my fiftieth cousin! Well and good! I'm an honest man. He shall not have it to say that he was not received at my house."

"He, too, thank heaven! is an honest man!" I said, smiling.

"Why the deuce, then," cried Mr. Searle, turning almost fiercely upon me, "has he established this underhand claim to my property?"

This startling utterance flashed backward a gleam of light upon the demeanor of our host and the suppressed agitation of his sister. In an instant the jealous soul of the unhappy gentleman revealed itself. For a moment I was so amazed and scandalized at the directness of his attack that I lacked words to respond. As soon as he had spoken, Mr. Searle appeared to feel that he had struck too hard a blow. "Excuse me, sir," he hurried on, "if I speak of this matter with heat. But I have seldom suffered so grievous a shock as on learning, as I learned this morning from my solicitor, the monstrous proceedings of Mr. Clement Searle. Great heaven, sir, for what does the man take me? He pretends to the Lord knows what fantastic passion for my place. Let him respect it, then. Let him, with his tawdry parade of imagination, imagine a tithe of what I feel. I love my estate; it's my passion, my life, myself! Am I to make a great hole in it for a beggarly foreigner, a man without means, without proof, a stranger, an adventurer, a Bohemian? I thought America boasted that she had land for all men! Upon my soul, sir, I have never been so shocked in my life."

I paused for some moments before speaking, to allow his passion fully to expend itself and to flicker up again if it chose; for on my own part it seemed well that I should answer him once for all. "Your really absurd apprehensions, Mr. Searle," I said at last, "your terrors, I may call them, have fairly overmastered your common-sense. You are attacking a man of straw, a creature of base illusion; though I'm sadly afraid you have wounded a man of spirit and of conscience. Either my friend has no valid claim on your estate, in which case your agitation is superfluous; or he *has* a valid claim—"

Mr. Searle seized my arm and glared at me, as I may say; his pale face paler still with the horror of my suggestion, his great keen eyes flashing, and his flamboyant hair erect and quivering.

"A valid claim!" he whispered. "Let him try it!"

We had emerged into the great hall of the mansion and stood facing the main doorway. The door stood open into the porch, through whose stone archway I saw the garden glittering in the blue light of a full moon. As Mr. Searle uttered the words I have just repeated, I beheld my companion come slowly up into the porch from without, bareheaded, bright in the outer moonlight, dark then in the shadow of the archway, and bright again in the lamplight on the threshold of the hall. As he crossed the threshold the butler made his appearance at the head of the staircase on our left, faltered visibly a moment on seeing Mr. Searle; but then, perceiving my friend, he gravely descended. He bore in his hand a small plated salver. On the salver, gleaming in the light of the suspended lamp, lay a folded note. Clement Searle came forward, staring a little and startled, I think, by some fine sense of a near explosion. The butler applied the match. He advanced toward my friend, extending salver and note. Mr. Searle made a movement as if to spring forward, but controlled himself. "Tottenham!" he shouted, in a strident voice.

"Yes, sir!" said Tottenham, halting.

"Stand where you are. For whom is that note?"

"For Mr. Clement Searle," said the butler, staring straight before him as if to discredit a suspicion of his having read the direction.

"Who gave it to you?"

"Mrs. Horridge, sir." (The housekeeper.)

"Who gave it Mrs. Horridge?"

There was on Tottenham's part just an infinitesimal pause before replying.

"My dear sir," broke in Searle, completely sobered by the sense of violated courtesy, "is n't that rather my business?"

"What happens in my house is my business; and mighty strange things seem to be happening." Mr. Searle had become exasperated to that point that, a rare thing for an Englishman, he compromised himself before a servant.

"Bring me the note!" he cried. The butler obeyed.

"Really, this is too much!" cried my companion, affronted and helpless.

I was disgusted. Before Mr. Searle had time to take the note, I possessed myself of it. "If you have no regard for your sister," I said, " let a stranger, at least, act for her." And I tore the disputed thing into a dozen pieces.

"In the name of decency," cried Searle, "what does this horrid business mean?"

Mr. Searle was about to break out upon him; but at this moment his sister appeared on the staircase, summoned evidently by our high-pitched and angry voices. She had exchanged her dinner-dress for a dark dressing-gown, removed her ornaments, and begun to disarrange her hair, a heavy tress of which escaped from the comb. She hurried downward, with a pale, questioning face. Feeling distinctly that, for ourselves, immediate departure was in the air, and divining Mr. Tottenham to be a butler of remarkable intuitions and extreme celerity, I seized the opportunity to request him, *sotto voce,* to send a carriage to the door without delay. "And put up our things," I added.

Our host rushed at his sister and seized the white wrist which escaped from the loose sleeve of her dress. "What was in that note?" he demanded.

Miss Searle looked first at its scattered fragments and then at her cousin. "Did you read it?" she asked.

"No, but I thank you for it!" said Searle.

Her eyes for an instant communed brightly with his own; then she transferred them to her brother's face, where the light went out of them and left a dull, sad patience. An inexorable patience he seemed to find it: he flushed crimson with rage and the sense of his unhandsomeness, and flung her away. "You're a child," he cried. "Go to bed."

In poor Searle's face as well the gathered serenity was twisted into a sickened frown, and the reflected brightness of his happy day turned to blank confusion. "Have I been dealing these three hours with a madman?" he asked plaintively.

"A madman, yes, if you will! A man mad with the love of his home and the sense of its stability. I have held my tongue till now, but you have been too much for me. Who are you, what are you? From what paradise of fools do you come, that you fancy I shall cut off a piece of my land, my home, my heart, to toss to you? Forsooth, I shall share my land with you? Prove your infernal claim! There is n't *that* in it!" And he kicked one of the bits of paper on the floor.

Searle received this broadside gaping. Then turning away, he went and seated himself on a bench against the wall and rubbed his forehead amazedly. I looked at my watch, and listened for the wheels of our carriage.

Mr. Searle went on. "Was n't it enough that you should have practiced against my property? Need you have come into my very house to practice against my sister?"

Searle put his two hands to his face. "Oh, oh, oh!" he softly roared.

Miss Searle crossed rapidly and dropped on her knees at his side.

"Go to bed, you fool!" shrieked her brother.

"Dear cousin," said Miss Searle, "it's cruel that you are to have to think of us so!"

"O, I shall think of you!" he said. And he laid a hand on her head.

"I believe you have done nothing wrong!" she murmured.

"I've done what I could," her brother pursued. "But it's arrant folly to pretend to friendship when this abomination lies between us. You were welcome to my meat and my wine, but I wonder you could swallow them. The sight spoiled my appetite!" cried the furious little man, with a laugh. "Proceed with your case! My people in London are instructed and prepared."

"I have a fancy," I said to Searle, "that your case has vastly improved since you gave it up."

"Oho! you don't feign ignorance, then?" and he shook his flaming *chevelure* at me. "It is very kind of you to give it up!" And he laughed resoundingly. "Perhaps you will also give up my sister!"

Searle sat in his chair in a species of collapse, staring at his adversary. "O miserable man!" he moaned at last. "I fancied we had become such friends!"

"Boh! you imbecile!" cried our host.

Searle seemed not to hear him. "Am I seriously expected," he pursued, slowly and painfully, "am I seriously expected—to—to sit here and defend myself—to prove I have done nothing wrong? Think what you please." And he rose, with an effort, to his feet. "I know what *you* think!" he added, to Miss Searle.

The carriage wheels resounded on the gravel, and at the same moment the footman descended with our two portmanteaus. Mr. Tottenham followed him with our hats and coats.

"Good God!" cried Mr. Searle; "you are not going away!" This ejaculation, under the circumstances, had a grand comicality which prompted me to violent laughter. "Bless my soul!" he added, "of course you are going."

"It's perhaps well," said Miss Searle, with a great effort,

inexpressibly touching in one for whom great efforts were visibly new and strange, "that I should tell you what my poor little note contained."

"That matter of your note, madam," said her brother, "you and I will settle together!"

"Let me imagine its contents," said Searle.

"Ah! they have been too much imagined!" she answered simply. "It was only a word of warning. I knew something painful was coming."

Searle took his seat. "The pains and the pleasures of this day," he said to his kinsman, "I shall equally never forget. Knowing you," and he offered his hand to Miss Searle, "has been the pleasure of pleasures. I hoped something more was to come of it."

"A deal too much has come of it!" cried our host, irrepressibly.

Searle looked at him mildly, almost benignantly, from head to foot; and then closing his eyes with an air of sudden physical distress: "I'm afraid so! I can't stand more of this." I gave him my arm, and crossed the threshold. As we passed out I heard Miss Searle burst into a torrent of sobs.

"We shall hear from each other yet, I take it!" cried her brother, harassing our retreat.

Searle stopped and turned round on him sharply, almost fiercely. "O ridiculous man!" he cried.

"Do you mean to say you shall not prosecute?" screamed the other. "I shall force you to prosecute! I shall drag you into court, and you shall be beaten—beaten—beaten!" And this soft vocable continued to ring in our ears as we drove away.

We drove, of course, to the little wayside inn whence we had departed in the morning so unencumbered, in all broad England, with either enemies or friends. My companion, as the carriage rolled along, seemed utterly overwhelmed and exhausted. "What a dream!" he murmured stupidly. "What an awakening! What a long, long day! What a hideous scene! Poor me! Poor woman!" When we had resumed possession of our two little neighboring rooms, I asked him if Miss Searle's note had been the result of anything that had passed between them on his going to rejoin her. "I found her on the terrace, he said, "walking a restless walk in the moonlight. I was greatly excited; I hardly know what I said. I asked her, I think, if she knew the story of Margaret Searle. She seemed frightened and troubled, and she used just the words her brother had used, 'I know nothing.' For the moment, somehow, I felt as a man drunk. I stood before her and told her, with great emphasis, how sweet Margaret Searle had married a beggarly foreigner, in obedience to her heart and in defiance of her family. As I talked the sheeted moonlight seemed to close about us, and we stood in a dream, in a solitiude, in a romance. She grew younger, fairer, more gracious. I trembled with a divine loquacity. Before I knew it I had gone far. I was taking her hand and calling her 'Margaret!' She had said that it was impossible; that she could do nothing; that she was a fool, a child, a slave. Then, with a sudden huge conviction, I spoke of my claim against the estate. 'It exists, then,' she said. 'It exists,' I answered, 'but I have foregone it. Be generous! Pay it from your heart!' For an instant her face was radiant. 'If I marry you,' she cried, 'it will repair the trouble.' 'In our marriage,' I affirmed, 'the trouble will melt away like a raindrop in the ocean.' 'Our marriage!' she repeated, wonderingly; and the deep, deep ring of her voice seemed to shatter the crystal walls of our illusion. 'I must think, I must think!' she said; and she hurried away with her face in her hands. I walked up and down the terrace for some moments, and then came in and met you. This is the only witchcraft I have used!"

The poor fellow was at once so excited and so exhausted by the day's events that I fancied he would get little sleep. Conscious, on my own part, of a stubborn wakefulness, I but partly undressed, set my fire a-blazing, and sat down to do some writing. I heard the great clock in the little parlor below strike twelve, one, half-past one. Just as the vibration of this last stroke was dying on the air the door of communication into Searle's room was flung open, and my companion stood on the threshold, pale as a corpse, in his nightshirt, standing like a phantom against the darkness behind him. "Look at me!" he said, in a low voice, "touch me, embrace, me, revere me! You see a man who has seen a ghost!"

"Great heaven, what do you mean?"

"Write it down!" he went on. "There, take your pen. Put it into dreadful words. Make it of all ghost-stories the ghostliest, the truest! How do I look? Am I human? Am I pale? Am I red? Am I speaking English? A ghost, sir! Do you understand?"

I confess, there came upon me, by contact, a great supernatural shock. I shall always feel that I, too, have seen a ghost. My first movement—I can't smile at it even now—was to spring to the door, close it with a great blow, and then turn the key upon the gaping blackness from which Searle had emerged. I seized his two hands; they were wet with perspiration. I pushed my chair to the fire and forced him to sit down in it. I kneeled down before him and held his hands as firmly as possible. They trembled and quivered; his eyes were fixed, save that the pupil dilated and contracted with extraordinary force. I asked no questions, but waited with my heart in my throat. At last he spoke. "I'm not frightened, but I'm—O *excited!* This is life! This is living! My nerves—my heart—my brain! They are throbbing with the wildness of a myriad lives! Do you feel it? Do you tingle? Are you hot! Are you cold? Hold me tight—tight—tight! I shall tremble away into waves—waves—waves, and know the universe and approach my Maker!" He paused a moment and then went on: "A woman—as clear as that candle—no, far clearer! In a blue dress, with a black mantle on her head, and a little black muff. Young, dreadfully pretty, pale and ill, with the sadness of all the women who ever loved and suffered pleading and accusing in her dead dark eyes. God knows I never did any such thing! But she took me for my elder, for the other Clement. She came to me here as she would have come to me there. She wrung her hands and spoke to me. 'Marry me!' she moaned; 'marry me and right me!'

I sat up in bed just as I sit here, looked at her, heard her—heard her voice melt away, watched her figure fade away. Heaven and earth! Here I am!"

I made no attempt either to explain my friend's vision or to discredit it. It is enough that I felt for the hour the irresistible contagion of his own agitation. On the whole, I think my own vision was the more interesting of the two. He beheld but the transcient, irresponsible spectre: I beheld the human subject, hot from the spectral presence. Nevertheless, I soon recovered my wits sufficiently to feel the necessity of guarding my friend's health against the evil results of excitement and exposure. It was tacitly established that, for the night, he was not to return to his room; and I soon made him fairly comfortable in his place by the fire. Wishing especially to obviate a chill, I removed my bedding and wrapped him about with multitudinous blankets and counterpanes. I had no nerves either for writing or sleep; so I put out my lights, renewed the fire, and sat down on the opposite side of the hearth. I found a kind of solemn entertainment in watching my friend. Silent, swathed and muffled to his chin, he sat rigid and erect with the dignity of his great adventure. For the most part his eyes were closed; though from time to time he would open them with a vast, steady expansion and gaze unblinking into the firelight, as if he again beheld without terror, the image of that blighted maid. . . . The night passed wholly without speech. Towards its close I slept for half an hour. When I awoke the awakened birds had begun to twitter. Searle sat unperturbed, staring at me. We exchanged a long look; I felt with a pang that his glittering eyes had tasted their last of natural sleep. "How is it? are you comfortable?" I asked.

He gazed for some time without replying. Then he spoke with a strange, innocent grandiloquence, and with pauses between his words, as if an inner voice were slowly prompting him. "You asked me, when you first knew me, what I was. 'Nothing,' I said, 'nothing.' Nothing I have always deemed myself. But I have wronged myself. I'm a personage! I'm rare among men! I'm a haunted man!"

Sleep had passed out of his eyes: I felt with a deeper pang that perfect sanity had passed out of his voice. From this moment I prepared myself for the worst. There was in my friend, however, such an essential gentleness and conservative patience, that to persons surrounding him the worst was likely to come without hurry or violence. He had so confirmed a habit of good manners that, at the core of reason, the process of disorder might have been long at work without finding an issue. As morning began fully to dawn upon us, I brought our grotesque vigil to an end. Searle appeared so weak that I gave him my hands to help him to rise from his chair; he retained them for some moments after rising to his feet, from an apparent inability to keep his balance. "Well," he said, "I've seen one ghost, but I doubt of my living to see another. I shall soon be myself as brave a ghost as the best of them. I shall haunt Mr. Searle! It can only mean one thing,—my near, dear death."

On my proposing breakfast, "This shall be my breakfast!" he said; and he drew from his travelling-sack a phial of morphine. He took a strong dose and went to bed. At noon I found him on foot again, dressed, shaved, and apparently refreshed. "Poor fellow!" he said, " you have got more than you bargained for—a ghost-encumbered comrade. But it won't be for long." It immediately became a question, of course, whither we should now direct our steps.

"As I have so little time," said Searle, "I should like to see the best, the best alone." I answered that, either for time or eternity, I had imagined Oxford to be the best thing in England; and for Oxford in the course of an hour we accordingly departed.

Of Oxford I feel small vocation to speak in detail. It must long remain for an American one of the supreme gratifications of travel. The impression it produces, the emotions it stirs, in an American mind, are too large and various to be compassed by words. It seems to embody with undreamed completeness a kind of dim and sacred ideal of the Western intellect,—a scholastic city, an appointed home of contemplation. No other spot in Europe, I imagine, extorts from our barbarous hearts so passionate an admiration. A finer pen than mine must enumerate the splendid devices by which it performs this great office; I can bear testimony only to the dominant tone of its effect. Passing through the various streets in which the obverse longitude of the hoary college walls seems to maintain an antique stillness, you feel this to be the most dignified of towns. Over all, through all, the great corporate fact of the University prevails and penetrates, like some steady bass in a symphony of lighter chords, like the mediæval and mystical presence of the Empire in the linked dispersion of lesser states. The plain Gothic of the long street-fronts of the colleges—blessed seraglios of culture and leisure—irritate the fancy like the blank harem-walls of Eastern towns. Within their arching portals, however, you perceive more sacred and sunless courts, and the dark verdure grateful and restful to bookish eyes. The gray-green quadrangles stand forever open with a noble and trustful hospitality. The seat of the humanities is stronger in the admonitory shadow of her great name than in a marshalled host of wardens and beadles. Directly after our arrival my friend and I strolled eagerly forth in the luminous early dusk. We reached the bridge which passes beneath the walls of Magdalen and saw the eight-spired tower, embossed with its slender shaftings, rise in temperate beauty—the perfect prose of Gothic—wooing the eyes to the sky, as it was slowly drained of day. We entered the little monkish doorway and stood in that dim, fantastic outer court, made narrow by the dominant presence of the great tower, in which the heart beats faster, and the swallows niche more lovingly in the tangled ivy, I fancied, than elsewhere in Oxford. We passed thence into the great cloister, and studied the little sculptured monsters along the entablature of the arcade. I was pleased to see that Searle became extremely interested; but I very soon began to fear that the influence of the place would prove too potent for his unbalanced imagination. I may say that from this time forward, with my unhappy friend, I found it hard to distinguish between the play of fancy and the labor of thought, and to fix the balance between perception and illusion. He had already taken a fancy to confound his

identity with that of the earlier Clement Searle; he began
to speak almost wholly as from the imagined consciousness
of his old-time kinsman.

"This was my college, you know," he said, "the noblest
in all Oxford. How often I have paced this gentle cloister,
side by side with a friend of the hour! My friends are all
dead, but many a young fellow as we meet him, dark or
fair, tall or short, reminds me of them. Even Oxford, they
say, feels about its massive base the murmurs of the tide of
time; there are things eliminated, things insinuated! Mine
was ancient Oxford—the fine old haunt of rank abuses, of
precedent and privilege. What cared I, who was a perfect gentleman, with my pockets full of money? I had an
allowance of two thousand a year."

It became evident to me, on the following day, that his
strength had begun to ebb, and that he was unequal to the
labor of regular sight-seeing. He read my apprehension in
my eyes, and took pains to assure me that I was right. "I
am going down-hill. Thank heavens it's an easy slope,
coated with English turf and with an English churchyard
at the foot." The almost hysterical emotion produced by
our adventure at Lockley Park had given place to a broad,
calm satisfaction, in which the scene around us was reflected as in the depths of a lucid lake. We took an afternoon walk through Christ-Church Meadow, and at the river-
bank procured a boat, which I pulled up the stream to Iffley
and to the slanting woods of Nuneham,—the sweetest, flat-
test, reediest stream-side landscape that the heart need de-
mand. Here, of course, we encountered in hundreds the
mighty lads of England, clad in white flannel and blue, immense, fair-haired, magnificent in their youth, lounging
down the current in their idle punts, in friendly couples or in
solitude possibly portentous of scholastic honors; or pulling
in straining crews and hoarsely exhorted from the near
bank. When, in conjunction with all this magnificent sport,
you think of the verdant quietude and the silvery sanctities
of the college gardens, you cannot but consider that the youth
of England have their porridge well salted. As my companion found himself less and less able to walk, we repaired

on three successive days to these scholastic domains, and
spent long hours sitting in their greenest places. They
seemed to us the fairest things in England and the ripest
and sweetest fruits of the English system. Locked in their
antique verdure, guarded (as in the case of New College)
by gentle battlements of silver-gray, outshouldering the
matted leafage of centenary vines, filled with perfumes and
privacy and memories, with students lounging bookishly on
the turf (as if tenderly to spare it the pressure of their
boot-heels), and with the great conservative presence of the
college front appealing gravely from the restless outer world,
they seem to lie down on the grass in forever, in the happy
faith that life is all a vast old English garden, and time an
endless English afternoon. This charmed seclusion was
especially grateful to my friend, and his sense of it reached
its climax, I remember, on the last afternoon of our three,
as we sat dreaming in the spacious garden of St. John's.
The long college façade here, perhaps, broods over the lawn
with a more effective air of property than elsewhere. Searle
fell into unceasing talk and exhaled his swarming impressions with a tender felicity, compounded of the oddest mixture of wisdom and folly. Every student who passed us
was the subject of an extemporized romance, and every
feature of the place the theme of a lyric rhapsody.

"Isn't it all," he demanded, "a delightful lie? Mightn't
one fancy this the very central point of the world's heart,
where all the echoes of the world's life arrive only to falter
and die? Listen! The air is thick with arrested voices.
It is well there should be such places, shaped in the interest
of factitious needs; framed to minister to the book-begotten
longing for a medium in which one may dream unwaked,
and believe unconfuted; to foster the sweet illusion that all
is well in this weary world, all perfect and rounded, mellow
and complete in this sphere of the pitiful unachieved and
the dreadful uncommenced. The world's made! Work's
over! Now for leisure! England's safe! Now for
Theocritus and Horace, for lawn and sky! What a sense
it all gives one of the composite life of England, and how
essential a factor of the educated, British consciousness one

omits in not thinking of Oxford! Thank heaven they had the wit to send me here in the other time. I'm not much with it, perhaps; but what should I have been without it? The misty spires and towers of Oxford seen far off on the level have been all these years one of the constant things of memory. Seriously, what does Oxford do for these people? Are they wiser, gentler, richer, deeper? At moments when its massive influence surges into my mind like a tidal wave, I take it as a sort of affront to my dignity. My soul reverts to the naked background of our own education, the dead white wall before which we played our parts. I assent to it all with a sort of desperate calmness; I bow to it with a dogged pride. We are nursed at the opposite pole. Naked come we into a naked world. There is a certain grandeur in the absence of a *mise en scène,* a certain heroic strain in those young imaginations of the West, which find nothing made to their hands, which have to concoct their own mysteries, and raise high into our morning air, with a ringing hammer ' and nails, the castles in which they dwell. *Noblesse oblige:* Oxford obliges. What a horrible thing not to respond to such obligations. If you pay the pious debt to the last farthing of interest, you may go through life with her blessing; but if you let it stand unhonored, you are a worse barbarian than we! But for better or worse, in a myriad private hearts, think how she must be loved! How the youthful sentiment of mankind seems visibly to brood upon her! Think of the young lives now taking color in her corridors and cloisters. Think of the centuries' tale of dead lads—dead alike with the close of the young days to which these haunts were a present world and the ending of the larger lives which a sterner mother-scene has gathered into her massive history! What are those two young fellows kicking their heels over on the grass there? One of them has the *Saturday Review;* the other—upon my soul— the other has Artemus Ward! Where do they live, how do they live, to what end do they live? Miserable boys! How can they read Artemus Ward under these windows of Elizabeth? What do you think loveliest in all Oxford? The poetry of certain windows. Do you see that one yonder,

the second of those lesser bays, with the broken mullion and
open casement? That used to be the window of my *fidus
Achates,* a hundred years ago. Remind me to tell you the
story of that broken mullion. Don't tell me it's not a common thing to have one's *fidus Achates* at another college.
Pray, was I pledged to common things? He was a charming fellow. By the way, he was a good deal like you. Of
course his cocked hat, his long hair in a black ribbon, his
cinnamon velvet suit, and his flowered waistcoat made a
difference! We gentlemen used to wear swords."

There was something surprising and impressive in my
friend's gushing magniloquence. . . . He was becoming
more and more a disembodied observer and critic; the shell
of sense, growing daily thinner and more transparent,
transmitted the tremor of his quickened spirit. He revealed an unexpected faculty for becoming acquainted with
the lounging gownsmen whom we met in our vague peregrinations. If I left him for ten minutes, I was sure to find
him, on my return, in earnest conversation with some affable
wandering scholar. Several young men with whom he had
thus established relations invited him to their rooms and
entertained him, as I gathered, with boisterous hospitality.
For myself, I chose not to be present on these occasions; I
shrunk partly from being held in any degree responsible for
his vagaries, and partly from witnessing that painful ag-
gravation of them which I feared might be induced by
champagne and youthful society. He reported these adventures with less eloquence than I had fancied he might
use; but, on the whole, I suspect that a certain method in
his madness, a certain firmness in his most melting *bonhomie,*
had insured him perfect respect. Two things, however, became evident—that he drank more champagne than was
good for him, and that the boyish grossness of his enter-
tainers tended rather, on reflection, to disturb in his mind
the pure image of Oxford. At the same time it completed
his knowledge of the place. Making the acquaintance of
several tutors and fellows, he dined in Hall in half a dozen
colleges, and alluded afterwards to these banquets with a
sort of religious unction. One evening, at the close of one

of these entertainments, he came back to the hotel in a cab, accompanied by a friendly student and a physician, looking deadly pale. He had swooned away on leaving table, and had remained so stubbornly unconscious as to excite great alarm among his companions. The following twenty-four hours, of course, he spent in bed; but on the third day he declared himself strong enough to go out. On reaching the street his strength again forsook him, and I insisted upon his returning to his room. He besought me with tears in his eyes not to shut him up. "It's my last chance," he said. "I want to go back for an hour to that garden of St. John's. Let me look and feel; to-morrow I die." It seemed to me possible that with a Bath-chair the expedition might be accomplished. The hotel, it appeared, possessed such a convenience: it was immediately produced. It became necessary hereupon that we should have a person to propel the chair. As there was no one available on the spot, I prepared to perform the office; but just as Searle had got seated and wrapped (he had come to suffer acutely from cold), an elderly man emerged from a lurking-place near the door, and, with a formal salute, offered to wait upon the gentleman. We assented, and he proceeded solemnly to trundle the chair before him. I recognized him as an individual whom I had seen lounging shyly about the hotel doors, at intervals during our stay, with a depressed air of wanting employment and a hopeless doubt of finding any. . . . He was, I suppose, some fifty years of age; but his pale, haggard, unwholesome visage, his plaintive, drooping carriage, and the irremediable decay of his apparel, seemed to add to the burden of his days and experience. His eyes were bloodshot and weak-looking, his handsome nose had turned to purple, and his sandy beard, largely streaked with gray, bristled with a month's desperate indifference to the razor. In all this rusty forlornness there lurked a visible assurance of our friend's having known better days. Obviously, he was the victim of some fatal depreciation in the market value of pure gentility. There had been something terribly pathetic in the way he fiercely merged the attempt to touch the greasy rim of his antiquated hat into a rounded and sweeping bow, as from jaunty equal to equal. Exchanging a few words with him as we went along, I was struck with the refinement of his tone.

"Take me by some long roundabout way," said Searle, "so that I may see as many college walls as possible."

"You can wander without losing you way?" I asked of our attendant.

"I ought to be able to, sir," he said, after a moment, with pregnant gravity. And as we were passing Wadham College, "That's my college, sir," he added.

At these words, Searle commanded him to stop and come and stand in front of him. "You say that is *your* college?" he demanded.

"Wadham might deny me, sir; but Heaven forbid I should deny Wadham. If you'll allow me to take you into the quad, I'll show you my windows, thirty years ago!"

Searle sat staring, with his huge, pale eyes, which now had come to usurp the greatest place in his wasted visage, filled with wonder and pity. "If you'll be so kind," he said, with immense politeness. But just as this degenerate son of Wadham was about to propel him across the threshold of the court, he turned about, disengaged his hands, with his own hand, from the back of the chair, drew him alongside of him and turned to me. "While we are here, my dear fellow," he said, "be so good as to perform this service. You understand?" I smiled sufferance at our companion, and we resumed our way. The latter showed us his window of thirty years ago, where now a rosy youth in a scarlet smoking-fez was puffing a cigarette in the open lattice. Thence we proceeded into the little garden, the smallest, I believe, and certainly the sweetest of all the bosky resorts in Oxford. I pushed the chair along to a bench on the lawn, wheeled it about toward the façade of the college, and sat down on the grass. Our attendant shifted himself mournfully from one foot to the other. Searle eyed him open-mouthed. At length he broke out: "God bless my soul, sir, you don't suppose that I expect you to stand! There's an empty bench."

"Thank you," said our friend, bending his joints to sit.

"You English," said Searle, "are really fabulous! I don't know whether I most admire you or despise you! Now tell me: Who are you? What are you? What brought you to this?"

The poor fellow blushed up to his eyes, took off his hat, and wiped his forehead with a ragged handkerchief. "My name is Rawson, sir. Beyond that, it's a long story."

"I ask out of sympathy," said Searle. "I have a fellow-feeling! You're a poor devil; I'm a poor devil too."

"I'm the poorest devil of the two," said the stranger, with a little emphatic nod of the head.

"Possibly. I suppose an English poor devil is the poorest of all poor devils. And then, you have fallen from a height. From Wadham College as a gentleman commoner (is that what they called you?) to Wadham College as a Bath-chair man! Good heavens, man, the fall's enough to kill you!"

"I didn't take it all at once, sir. I dropped a bit one time and a bit another."

"That's me, that's me!" cried Searle, clapping his hands.

"And now," said our friend, "I believe I can't drop further."

"My dear fellow," and Searle clasped his hand and shook it, "there's a perfect similarity in our lot."

·   ·   ·   ·   ·

Fearing that the conversation had taken a turn which might seem to cast a rather fantastic light upon Mr. Rawson's troubles, I took the liberty of asking him with great gravity how he made a living.

"I don't make a living," he answered, with tearful eyes, "I can't make a living. I have a wife and three children, starving, sir. You wouldn't believe what I have come to. I sent my wife to her mother's, who can ill afford to keep her, and came to Oxford a week ago, thinking I might pick up a few half-crowns by showing people about the colleges. But it's no use. I haven't the assurance. I don't look decent. They want a nice little old man with black gloves, and a clean shirt, and a silver-headed stick. What do I look as if I knew about Oxford, sir?"

"Dear me," cried Searle, "why didn't you speak to us before?"

"I wanted to; half a dozen times I have been on the point of it. I knew you were Americans."

"And Americans are rich!" cried Searle, laughing. "My dear Mr. Rawson, American as I am, I'm living on charity."

"And I'm not, sir! There it is. I'm dying for the want of charity. You say you're a pauper; it takes an American pauper to go bowling about in a Bath-chair. America's an easy country."

"Ah me!" groaned Searle. "Have I come to Wadham gardens to hear the praise of America?"

"Wadham gardens are very well!" said Mr. Rawson; "but one may sit here hungry and shabby, so long as one isn't too shabby, as well as elsewhere. . . . Shabby as I sit here, I have a brother with his five thousand a year. Being a couple of years my senior, he gorges while I starve. There's England for you! A very pretty place for *him!*"

"Poor England!" said Searle, softly.

"Has your brother never helped you?" I asked.

"A twenty-pound note now and then! I don't say that there have not been times when I have sorely tried his generosity. I have not been what I should. I married dreadfully amiss. But the devil of it is that he started fair and I started foul; with the tastes, the desires, the needs, the sensibilities of a gentleman—and nothing else! I can't afford to live in England."

"This poor gentleman," said I, "fancied a couple of months ago that he couldn't afford to live in America."

"I'd change chances with him!" And Mr. Rawson gave a passionate slap to his knee.

Searle reclined in his chair with his eyes closed and his face twitching with violent emotion. Suddenly he opened his eyes with a look of awful gravity. "My friend," he said, "you're a failure! Be judged! Don't talk about chances. Don't talk about fair starts and foul starts. I'm at that point myself that I have a right to speak. It lies neither in one's chance nor one's start to make one a success; nor in anything one's brother can do or can undo. It lies in one's will! You and I, sir, have had none; that's very plain! We have been weak, sir; as weak as water. Here we are, sitting staring in each other's faces and reading our weakness in each other's eyes. We are of no account!"

Mr. Rawson received this address with a countenance in which heartfelt conviction was oddly mingled with a vague suspicion that a proper self-respect required him to resent its unflattering candor. In the course of a minute a proper self-respect yielded to the warm, comfortable sense of his being understood, even to his light dishonor. "Go on, sir, go on," he said. "It's wholesome truth." And he wiped his eyes with his dingy handkerchief.

"Dear me!" cried Searle. "I've made you cry. Well! we speak as from man to man. I should be glad to think that you had felt for a moment the side-light of that great un-darkening of the spirit which precedes—which precedes the grand illumination of death."

Mr. Rawson sat silent for a moment, with his eyes fixed on the ground and his well-cut nose more deeply tinged by the force of emotion. Then at last, looking up: "You're a very good-natured man, sir; and you'll not persuade me that you don't come of a good-natured race. Say what you please about a chance; when a man's fifty—degraded, penni-less, a husband and father—a chance to get on his legs again is not to be despised. Something tells me that my chance is in your country—that great home of chances. I can starve here, of course; but I don't want to starve. Hang it, sir, I want to live. I see thirty years of life before me yet. If only, by God's help, I could spend them there! It's a fixed idea of mine. I've had it for the last ten years. It's not that I'm a radical. I've no ideas! Old England's good enough for me, but I'm not good enough for old England. I'm a shabby man that wants to get out of a room full of staring gentlefolks. I'm forever put to the blush. It's a perfect agony of spirit. Everything reminds me of my younger and better self. O, for a cooling, cleansing plunge into the unknowing and the unknown! I lie awake thinking of it."

Searle closed his eyes and shivered with a long-drawn

tremor which I hardly knew whether to take for an expression of physical or of mental pain. In a moment I perceived it was neither. "O my country, my country, my country!" he murmured in a broken voice; and then sat for some time abstracted and depressed. I intimated to our companion that it was time we should bring our *séance* to a close, and he, without hesitating, possessed himself of the little handrail of the Bath-chair and pushed it before him. We had got half-way home before Searle spoke or moved. Suddenly in the High Street, as we were passing in front of a chop-house, from whose open doors there proceeded a potent suggestion of juicy joints and suet puddings, he motioned to us to halt. "This is my last five pounds," he said drawing a note from his pocket-book. "Do me the favor, Mr. Rawson, to accept it. Go in there and order a colossal dinner. Order a bottle of Burgundy and drink it to my immortal health!" Mr. Rawson stiffened himself up and received the gift with momentarily irresponsive fingers. But Mr. Rawson had the nerves of a gentleman. I saw the titillation of his pointed finger-tips as they closed upon the crisp paper; I noted the fine tremor in his empurpled nostril as it became more deeply conscious of the succulent flavor of the spot. He crushed the crackling note in his palm with a convulsive pressure.

"It shall be Chambertin!" he said, jerking a spasmodic bow. The next moment the door swung behind him.

Searle relapsed into his feeble stupor, and on reaching the hotel I helped him to get to bed. For the rest of the day he lay in a half-somnolent state, without motion or speech. The doctor, whom I had constantly in attendance, declared that his end was near. He expressed great surprise that he should have lasted so long; he must have been living for a month on a cruelly extorted strength. Toward evening, as I sat by his bedside in the deepening dusk, he aroused himself with a purpose which I had vaguely felt gathering beneath his quietude. "My cousin, my cousin," he said, confusedly. "Is she here?" It was the first time he had spoken of Miss Searle since our exit from her brother's house. "I was to have married her," he went on.

"What a dream! That day was like a stringe of verses—
rhymed hours. But the last verse is bad measure. What's
the rhyme to 'love'? *Above!* Was she a simple person, a
sweet person? Or have I dreamed it? She had the heal-
ing gift; her touch would have cured my madness. I want
you to do something. Write three lines, three words: 'Good
by; remember me; be happy.'" And then, after a long
pause: "It's strange a man in my condition should have a
wish. Need a man eat his breakfast before his hanging?
What a creature is man! what a farce is life! Here I lie,
worn down to a mere throbbing fever-point; I breath and
nothing more, and yet I *desire!* My desire lives. If I could
see her! Help me out with it and let me die."

Half an hour later, at a venture, I despatched at note to
Miss Searle: "Your cousin is rapidly dying. He asks to
see you." I was conscious of a certain unkindness in doing
so. It would bring a great trouble, and no power to face
the trouble. But out of her distress I fondly hoped a sufficient energy might be born. On the following day my
friend's exhaustion had become so total that I began to fear
that his intelligence was altogether gone. But towards evening he rallied awhile, and talked in a maundering way
about many things, confounding in a ghastly jumble the
memories of the past weeks and those of bygone years. "By
the way," he said suddenly, "I have made no will. I haven't
much to bequeath. Yet I've something." He had been
playing listlessly with a large signet-ring on his left hand,
which he now tried to draw off. "I leave you this," working it round and round vainly, "if you can get it off. What
mighty knuckles! There must be such knuckles in the
mummies of the Pharaohs. Well, when I'm gone! Nay, I
leave you something more precious than gold—the sense of
a great kindness. But I have a little gold left. Bring me
those trinkets." I placed on the bed before him several
articles of jewelry, relics of early elegance: his watch and
chain, of great value, a locket and seal, some shirt-buttons
and scarf-pins. He trifled with them feebly for some moments, murmuring various names and dates associated with

them. At last, looking up with a sudden energy, "What's become of Mr. Rawson?"

"You want to see him?"

"How much are these things worth?" he asked, without heeding me. "How much would they bring?" And he held them up in his weak hands. "They have a great weight. Two hundred pounds? I am richer than I thought! Rawson—Rawson—you want to get out of this awful England."

I stepped to the door and requested the servant, whom I kept in constant attendance in the adjoining sitting-room, to send and ascertain if Mr. Rawson was on the premises. He returned in a few moments, introducing our shabby friend. Mr. Rawson was pale, even to his nose, and, with his suppressed agitation, had an air of great distinction. I led him up to the bed. In Searle's eyes, as they fell on him, there shone for a moment the light of a high fraternal greeting.

"Gread God!" said Mr. Rawson fervently.

"My friend," said Searle, "there is to be one American the less. Let there be one the more. At the worst, you'll be as good a one as I. Foolish me! Take these trinkets; let them help you on your way. They are gifts and memories, but this is a better use. Heaven speed you! May America be kind to you. Be kind, at the last, to your own country!"

. . . .

From the collapse into which this beneficent interview had plunged him, Searle gave few signs of being likely to emerge. He breathed, as he had said, and nothing more. The twilight deepened: I lit the night-lamp. The doctor sat silent and official at the foot of the bed; I resumed my constant place near the head. Suddenly Searle opened his eyes widely. "She'll not come," he murmured. "Amen! she's an English sister." Five minutes passed. He started forward. "She has come, she is here!" he whispered. His words conveyed to my mind so absolute an assurance, that I lightly rose and passed into the sitting-room. At the same moment, through the opposite door, the servant introduced a lady. A lady, I say; for an instant she was simply such—tall, pale, dressed in deep mourning. The next moment I had uttered her name—"Miss Searle!" She looked ten years older.

She met me, with both hands extended, and an immense question in her face. "He has just spoken your name," I said. And then, with a fuller consciousness of the change in her dress and countenance: "What has happened?"

"O death, death!" said Miss Searle. "You and I are left."

There came to me with her words a sort of sickening shock, the sense of poetic justice having been grimly shuffled away. "Your brother?" I demanded.

She laid her hand on my arm, and I felt its pressure deepen as she spoke. "He was thrown from his horse in the park. He died on the spot. Six days have passed, six months."

She took my arm. A moment later we had entered the room and approached the bedside. The doctor withdrew. Searle opened his eyes and looked at her from head to foot. Suddenly he seemed to perceive her mourning. "Already!" he cried audibly; with a smile, as I believe, of pleasure.

She dropped on her knees and took his hand. "Not for you, cousin," she whispered. "For my poor brother."

He started in all his deathly longitude as with a galvanic shock. "Dead! *he* dead! Life itself!" And then, after a moment, with a slight rising inflection: "You are free?"

"Free, cousin. Sadly free. And now—*now*—with what use for freedom?"

He looked steadily a moment into her eyes, dark in the heavy shadow of her musty mourning veil. "For me," he said, "wear colors!"

In a moment more death had come, the doctor had silently attested it, and Miss Searle had burst into sobs.

We buried him in the little churchyard in which he had expressed the wish to lie; beneath one of the mightiest of English yews and the little tower than which none in all England has a softer and hoarier gray. A year has passed. Miss Searle, I believe, has begun to wear colors.

MLLE. OLYMPE ZABRISKI *

By T. B. Aldrich

I

WE are accustomed to speak with a certain light irony
of the tendency which women have to gossip, as if
the sin itself, if it is a sin, were of the gentler sex,
and could by no chance be a masculine peccadillo. So far
as my observation goes, men are as much given to small talk
as women, and it is undeniable that we have produced the
highest type of gossiper extant. Where will you find, in or
out of literature, such another droll, delightful, chatty busy-
body as Samuel Pepys, Esq., Secretary to the Admiralty in
the reigns of those fortunate gentlemen, Charles II and
James II of England? He is the king of tattlers, as Shakespeare is the king of poets.

If it came to a matter of pure gossip, I would back Our
Club against the Sorosis or any women's club in existence.
Whenever you see in our drawing-room four or five young
fellows lounging in easy-chairs, cigar in hand, and now
and then bringing their heads together over the small round
Japanese table which is always the pivot of these social
circles, you may be sure they are discussing Tom's engagement, or Dick's extravagance, or Harry's hopeless passion
for the younger Miss Fleurdelys. It is here that old Tipple-
ton gets execrated for that everlasting *bon mot* of his which
was quite a success at dinner-parties forty years ago; it is
here the belle of the season passes under the scalpels of
merciless young surgeons; it is here B's financial condition
is handled in a way that would make B's hair stand on end;
it is here, in short, that everything is canvassed—everything

---

* By permission of, and by special arrangement with, Houghton
Mifflin Company, the authorized publishers; and by permission of
Mrs. T. B. Aldrich.

that happens in our set, I mean—much that never happens, and a great deal that could not possibly happen. It was at Our Club that I learned the particulars of the Van Twiller affair.

It was great entertainment to Our Club, the Van Twiller affair, though it was rather a joyless thing, I fancy, for Van Twiller. To understand the case fully it should be understood that Ralph Van Twiller is one of the proudest and most sensitive men living. He is a lineal descendant of Wouter Van Twiller, the famous old Dutch governor of New York, —Nieuw Amsterdam, as it was then; his ancestors have always been burgomasters or admirals or generals, and his mother is the Mrs. Vanrensselaer Vanzandt Van Twiller whose magnificent place will be pointed out to you on the right bank of the Hudson, as you pass up the historic river towards Idlewild. Ralph is about twenty-five years old. Birth made him a gentleman, and the rise of real estate— some of it in the family since the old governor's time—made him a millionaire. It was a kindly fairy that stepped in and made him a good fellow also. Fortune, I take it, was in her most jocund mood when she heaped her gifts in this fashion on Van Twiller, who was, and will be again, when this cloud blows over, the flower of Our Club.

About a year ago there came a whisper—if the word "whisper" is not too harsh a term to apply to what seemed a mere breath floating gently through the atmosphere of the billiard-room—imparting the intelligence that Van Twiller was in some kind of trouble. Just as everybody suddenly takes to wearing square-toed boots, or to drawing his neck-scarf through a ring, so it became all at once the fashion, without any preconcerted agreement, for everybody to speak of Van Twiller as a man in some way under a cloud. But what the cloud was, and how he got under it, and why he did not get away from it, were points that lifted themselves into the realm of pure conjecture. There was no man in the club with strong enough wing to his imagination to soar to the supposition that Van Twiller was embarrassed in money matters. Was he in love? That appeared nearly as improbable; for if he had been in love all the world—that is, perhaps a hundred first families—would have known all about it instantly.

"He has the symptoms," said Delaney, laughing. "I remember once when Jack Flemming—"

"Ned!" cried Flemming, "I protest against any allusion to that business."

This was one night when Van Twiller had wandered into the club, turned over the magazines absently in the reading-room, and wandered out again without speaking ten words. The most careless eye would have remarked the great change that had come over Van Twiller. Now and then he would play a game of billiards with Bret Harte or John Hay, or stop to chat a moment in the vestibule with Whitelaw Reid; but he was an altered man. When at the club he was usually to be found in the small smoking-room up-stairs, seated on a fauteuil fast asleep, with the last number of *The Nation* in his hand. Once if you went to two or three places of an evening, you were certain to meet Van Twiller at them all. You seldom met him in society now.

By and by came whisper number two, a whisper more emphatic than number one, but still untraceable to any tangible mouth-piece. This time the whisper said Van Twiller *was* in love. But with whom? The list of possible Mrs. Van Twillers was carefully examined by experienced hands, and a check placed against a fine old Knickerbocker name here and there, but nothing satisfactory arrived at. Then that same still small voice of rumor, but now with an easily detected staccato sharpness to it, said that Van Twiller was in love—with an actress! Van Twiller, whom it had taken all these years and all this waste of raw material in the way of ancestors to bring to perfection,—Ralph Van Twiller, the net result and flower of his race, the descendant of Wouter, the son of Mrs. Vanrensselaer Vanzandt Van Twiller—in love with an actress! That was too ridiculous to be believed—and so everybody believed it.

Six or seven members of the club abruptly discovered in themselves an unsuspected latent passion for the histrionic art. In squads of two or three they stormed successively all the theatres in town—Booth's, Wallack's, Daly's Fifth

Avenue (not burnt down then), and the Grand Opera House.
Even the shabby home of the drama over in the Bowery,
where the Germanic Thespis has not taken out his naturali-
zation papers, underwent rigid exploration. But no clew
was found to Van Twiller's mysterious attachment. The
opéra bouffe, which promised the widest field for investigation, produced absolutely nothing, not even a crop of sus-
picions. One night, after several weeks of this, Delaney and
I fancied we caught a glimpse of Van Twiller in the private
box of an up-town theatre, where some thrilling trapeze
performance was going on which we did not care to sit
through; but we concluded afterwards it was only somebody that looked like him. Delaney, by the way, was
unusually active in this search. I dare say he never quite
forgave Van Twiller for calling him Muslin Delaney. Ned
is fond of ladies' society and that's a fact.

The Cimmerian darkness which surrounded Van Twiller's
inamorata left us free to indulge in the wildest conjectures.
Whether she was black-tressed Melpomene, with bowl and
dagger, or Thalia, with the fair hair and the laughing face,
was only to be guessed at. It was popularly conceded, however, that Van Twiller was on the point of forming a dreadful *mésalliance.*

Up to this period he had visited the club regularly. Suddenly he ceased to appear. He was not seen on Broadway,
or in the Central Park, or at the houses he generally frequented. His chambers—and mighty comfortable ones they
were—on Thirty-fourth Street were deserted. He had
dropped out of the world, shot like a bright particular star
from his orbit in the heaven of best society.

"Where's Van Twiller?"

"Who's seen Van Twiller?"

"What has become of Van Twiller?"

Delaney picked up the *Evening Post,* and read, with a
solemnity that betrayed young Firkins into exclaiming, "By
Jove, now!"

"Married, on the 10th instant, by the Rev. Friar Laurence,
at the residence of the bride's uncle, Montague Capulet,

Esq., Miss Adrienne Le Couvreur to Mr. Ralph Van Twiller, both of this city. No cards."

"It strikes me," said Frank Livingstone, who had been ruffling the leaves of a magazine at the other end of the table, "that you fellows are in a great fever about Van Twiller."

"So we are."

"Well, he has simply gone out of town."

"Where?"

"Up to the old homestead on the Hudson."

"It's an odd time of year for a fellow to go into the country."

"He has gone to visit his mother," said Livingstone.

"In February?"

"I didn't know, Delaney, there was any statute in force prohibiting a man from visiting his mother in February if he wants to."

Delaney made some light remark about the pleasure of communing with Nature with a cold in her head, and the topic was dropped.

Livingstone was hand in glove with Van Twiller, and if any man shared his confidence it was Livingstone. He was aware of the gossip and speculation that had been rife in the club, but he either was not at liberty or did not think it worth while to relieve our curiosity. In the course of a week or two it was reported that Van Twiller was going to Europe; and go he did. A dozen of us went down to the Scotia to see him off. It was refreshing to have something as positive as the fact that Van Twiller had sailed.

II

Shortly after Van Twiller's departure the whole thing came out. Whether Livingstone found the secret too heavy a burden, or whether it transpired through some indiscretion on the part of Mrs. Vanrensselaer Vanzandt Van Twiller, I cannot say; but one evening the entire story was in the possession of the club.

Van Twiller had actually been very deeply interested—

not in an actress, for the legitimate drama was not her humble walk in life, but—in Mademoiselle Olympe Zabriski, whose really perilous feats on the trapeze had astonished New York the year before, though they had failed to attract Delaney and me the night we wandered into the up-town theatre on the trail of Van Twiller's mystery.

That a man like Van Twiller should be fascinated for an instant by a common circus-girl seems incredible; but it is always the incredible thing that happens. Besides, Mademoiselle Olympe was not a common circus-girl; she was a most daring and startling gymnaste, with a beauty and a grace of movement that gave to her audacious performance almost an air of prudery. Watching her wondrous dexterity and pliant strength, both exercised without apparent effort, it seemed the most natural proceeding in the world that she should do those unpardonable things. She had a way of melting from one graceful posture into another, like the dissolving figures thrown from a stereopticon. She was a lithe, radiant shape out of the Grecian mythology, now poised up there above the gas-lights, and now gleaming through the air like a slender gilt arrow.

I am describing Mademoiselle Olympe as she appeared to Van Twiller on the first occasion when he strolled into the theatre where she was performing. To me she was a girl of eighteen or twenty years of age (maybe she was much older, for pearl-powder and distance keep these people perpetually young), slightly but exquisitely built, with sinews of silver wire; rather pretty, perhaps, after a manner, but showing plainly the effects of the exhaustive drafts she was making on her physical vitality. Now, Van Twiller was an enthusiast on the subject of calisthenics. "If I had a daughter," Van Twiller used to say, "I wouldn't send her to a boarding-school, or a nunnery; I'd send her to a gymnasium for the first five years. Our American women have no physique. They are lilies, pallid, pretty,—and perishable. You marry an American woman, and what do you marry? A headache. Look at the English girls. They are at least roses, and last the season through."

Walking home from the theatre that first night, it flitted through Van Twiller's mind that if he could give this girl's set of nerves and muscles to any one of the two hundred high-bred women he knew, he would marry her on the spot and worship her forever.

The following evening he went to see Mademoiselle Olympe again. "Olympe Zabriski," he thought, as he sauntered through the lobby, "what a queer name! Olympe is French, and Zabriski is Polish. It is her *nom de guerre,* of course; her real name is probably Sarah Jones. What kind of creature can she be in private life, I wonder? I wonder if she wears that costume all the time, and if she springs to her meals from a horizontal bar. Of course she rocks the baby to sleep on the trapeze." And Van Twiller went on making comical domestic tableaux of Mademoiselle Zabriski, like the clever, satirical dog he was, until the curtain rose.

This was on a Friday. There was a matinée the next day, and he attended that, though he had secured a seat for the usual evening entertainment. Then it became a habit of Van Twiller's to drop into the theatre for half an hour or so every night, to assist at the interlude, in which she appeared. He cared only for her part of the programme, and timed his visits accordingly. It was a surprise to himself when he reflected, one morning, that he had not missed a single performance of Mademoiselle Olympe for two weeks.

"This will never do," said Van Twiller. "Olympe"—he called her Olympe, as if she were an old acquaintance, and so she might have been considered by that time—"is a wonderful creature; but this will never do. Van, my boy, you must reform this altogether."

But half-past nine that night saw him in his accustomed orchestra chair, and so on for another week. A habit leads a man so gently in the beginning that he does not perceive he is led—with what silken threads and down what pleasant avenues it leads him! By and by the soft silk threads become iron chains, and the pleasant avenues Avernus!

Quite a new element had lately entered into Van Twiller's

enjoyment of Mademoiselle Olympe's ingenious feats—a vaguely born apprehension that she might slip from that swinging bar, that one of the thin cords supporting it might snap, and let her go headlong from the dizzy height. Now and then, for a terrible instant, he would imagine her lying a glittering, palpitating heap at the foot-lights, with no color in her lips! Sometimes it seemed as if the girl were tempting this kind of fate. It was a hard, bitter life, and nothing but poverty and sordid misery at home could have driven her to it. What if she should end it all some night, by just unclasping that little hand? It looked so small and white from where Van Twiller sat!

This frightful idea fascinated while it chilled him, and helped to make it nearly impossible for him to keep away from the theatre. In the beginning his attendance had not interfered with his social duties or pleasures; but now he came to find it distasteful after dinner to do anything but read, or walk the streets aimlessly, until it was time to go to the play. When that was over, he was in no mood to go anywhere but to his rooms. So he dropped away by insensible degrees from his habitual haunts, was missed, and began to be talked about at the club. Catching some intimation of this, he ventured no more in the orchestra stalls, but shrouded himself behind the draperies of the private box in which Delaney and I thought we saw him on one occasion.

Now, I find it very perplexing to explain what Van Twiller was wholly unable to explain to himself. He was not in love with Mademoiselle Olympe. He had no wish to speak to her, or to hear her speak. Nothing could have been easier, and nothing further from his desire, than to know her personally. A Van Twiller personally acquainted with a strolling female acrobat! Good heavens! That was something possible only with the discovery of perpetual motion. Taken from her theatrical setting, from her lofty perch, so to say, on the trapeze-bar, Olympe Zabriski would have shocked every aristrocratic fibre in Van Twiller's body. He was simply fascinated by her marvellous grace and *élan*, and the magnetic recklessness of the girl. It was very young in him and very weak, and no member of the Sorosis, or all the Sorosisters together, could have been more severe on Van Twiller than he himself. To be weak, and to know it, is something of a punishment for a proud man. Van Twiller took his punishment, and went to the theatre, regularly.

"When her engagement comes to an end," he meditated, "that will finish the business."

Mademoiselle Olympe's engagement finally did come to an end, and she departed. But her engagement had been highly beneficial to the treasury-chest of the up-town theatre, and before Van Twiller could get over missing her she had returned from a short Western tour, and her immediate reappearance was underlined on the play-bills.

On a dead wall opposite the windows of Van Twiller's sleeping-room there appeared, as if by necromancy, an aggressive poster with *Mademoiselle Olympe Zabriski* on it in letters at least a foot high. This thing stared him in the face when he woke up, one morning. It gave him a sensation as if she had called on him overnight, and left her card.

From time to time through the day he regarded that poster with a sardonic eye. He had pitilessly resolved not to repeat the folly of the previous month. To say that this moral victory cost him nothing would be to deprive it of merit. It cost him many internal struggles. It is a fine thing to see a man seizing his temptation by the throat, and wrestling with it, and trampling it under foot like St. Anthony. This was the spectacle Van Twiller was exhibiting to the angels.

The evening Mademoiselle Olympe was to make her reappearance, Van Twiller, having dined at the club and feeling more like himself than he had felt for weeks, returned to his chamber, and putting on dressing-gown and slippers, piled up the greater portion of his library about him, and fell to reading assiduously. There is nothing like a quiet evening at home with some slight intellectual occupation, after one's feathers have been stroked the wrong way.

When the lively French clock on the mantel-piece,—a base of malachite surmounted by a flying bronze Mercury with its arms spread gracefully on the air, and not remotely suggestive of Mademoiselle Olympe in the act of executing her grand flight from the trapeze—when the clock, I repeat, struck nine, Van Twiller paid no attention to it. That was certainly a triumph. I am anxious to render Van Twiller all the justice I can at this point of the narrative, inasmuch as when the half-hour sounded musically, like a crystal ball dropping into a silver bowl, he rose from the chair automatically, thrust his feet into his walking shoes, threw his overcoat across his arm, and strode out of the room.

To be weak and scorn your weakness, and not be able to conquer it, is, as has been said, a hard thing; and I suspect it was not with unalloyed satisfaction that Van Twiller found himself taking his seat in the back part of the private box night after night during the second engagement of Mademoiselle Olympe. It was so easy not to stay away!

In this second edition of Van Twiller's fatuity, his case was even worse than before. He not only thought of Olympe quite a number of times between breakfast and dinner, he not only attended the interlude regularly, but he began, in spite of himself, to occupy his leisure hours at night by dreaming of her. This was too much of a good thing, and Van Twiller regarded it so. Besides, the dream was always the same—a harrowing dream, a dream singularly adapted to shattering the nerves of a man like Van Twiller. He would imagine himself seated at the theatre (with all the members of Our Club in the parquette), watching Mademoiselle Olympe as usual, when suddenly that young lady would launch herself desperately from the trapeze, and come flying through the air like a firebrand hurled at his private box. Then the unfortunate man would wake up with cold drops standing on his forehead.

There is one redeeming feature in this infatuation of Van Twiller's which the sober moralist will love to look upon,— the serene unconsciousness of the person who caused it. She went through her role with admirable aplomb, drew her salary, it may be assumed, punctually, and appears from first to last to have been ignorant that there was a miserable slave wearing her chains nightly in the left-hand proscenium-box.

That Van Twiller, haunting the theatre with the persistency of an ex-actor, conducted himself so discreetly as not to draw the fire of Mademoiselle Olympe's blue eyes shows that Van Twiller, however deeply under a spell, was not in love. I say this, though I think if Van Twiller had not been Van Twiller, if he had been a man of no family and no position and no money, if New York had been Paris, and Thirty-fourth Street a street in the Latin Quarter—but it is useless to speculate on what migh have happened. What did happen is sufficient.

It happened, then, in the second week of Queen Olympe's second unconscious reign, that an appalling Whisper floated up the Hudson, effected a landing at a point between Spuyten Duyvil Creek and Cold Spring, and sought out a stately mansion of Dutch architecture standing on the bank of the river. The Whisper straightway informed the lady dwelling in this mansion that all was not well with the last of the Van Twillers, that he was gradually estranging himself from his peers, and wasting his nights in a play-house watching a misguided young woman turning unmaidenly somersaults on a piece of wood attached to two ropes.

Mrs. Vanrensselaer Vanzandt Van Twiller came down to town by the next train to look into this little matter.

She found the flower of the family taking an early breakfast, at 11 A. M., in his cosey apartments on Thirty-fourth Street. With the least possible circumlocution she confronted him with what rumor had reported of his pursuits, and was pleased, but not too much pleased, when he gave her an exact account of his relations with Mademoiselle Zabriski, neither concealing nor qualifying anything. As a confession, it was unique, and might have been a great deal less entertaining. Two or three times, in the course of the narrative, the matron had some difficulty in preserving the gravity of her countenance. After meditating a few minutes, she tapped Van Twiller softly on the arm with the tip of her parasol, and invited him to return with her the next day up the Hudson and make a brief visit at the home of his ancestors. He accepted the invitation with outward alacrity and inward disgust.

When this was settled, and the worthy lady had withdrawn, Van Twiller went directly to the establishment of Messrs. Ball, Black, and Company and selected, with unerring taste, the finest diamond bracelet procurable. For his mother? Dear me, no! She had the family jewels.

I would not like to state the enormous sum Van Twiller paid for this bracelet. It was such a clasp of diamonds as would have hastened the pulsation of a patrician wrist. It was such a bracelet as Prince Camaralzaman might have sent to the Princess Badoura, and the Princess Badoura— might have been very glad to get.

In the fragrant Levant morocco case, where these happy jewels lived when they were at home, Van Twiller thoughtfully placed his card, on the back of which he had written a line begging Mademoiselle Olympe Zabriski to accept the accompanying trifle from one who had witnessed her graceful performances with interest and pleasure. This was not done inconsiderately. "Of course I must enclose my card, as I would to any lady," Van Twiller had said to himself; "a Van Twiller can neither write an anonymous letter nor make an anonymous present." Blood entails its duties as well as its privileges.

The casket despatched to its destination, Van Twiller felt easier in his mind. He was under obligations to the girl for many an agreeable hour that might otherwise have passed heavily. He had paid the debt, and he had paid it *en prince*, as became a Van Twiller. He spent the rest of the day in looking at some pictures at Goupil's, and at the club, and in making a few purchases for his trip up the Hudson. A consciousness that this trip up the Hudson was a disorderly retreat came over him unpleasantly at intervals.

When he returned to his rooms late at night, he found a note lying on the writing-table. He started as his eye caught the words "———Theatre" stamped in carmine letters on one corner of the envelope. Van Twiller broke the seal with trembling fingers.

Now, this note sometime afterwards fell into the hands of Livingstone, who showed it to Stuyvesant, who showed it to Delaney, who showed it to me, and I copied it as a literary curiosity. The note ran as follows:—

MR VAN TWILLER DEAR SIR — i am verry greatfull to you for that Bracelett. it come just in the nic of time for me. The Mademoiselle Zabriski dodg is about plaid out. My beard is getting to much for me. i shall have to grow a mustash and take to some other line of busyness, i dont no what now, but will let you no. You wont feel bad if i sell that Bracelett. i have seen Abrahams Moss and he says he will do the square thing. Pleas accep my thanks for youre Beautifull and Unexpected present.

Youre respectfull servent,
CHARLES MONTMORENCI WALTERS.

The next day Van Twiller neither expressed nor felt any unwillingness to spend a few weeks with his mother at the old homestead.

And then he went abroad.

A PRODIGAL IN TAHITI *

By CHARLES WARREN STODDARD

L ET this confession be topped with a vignette done in broad, shadowless lines and few of them—something like this:

A little flyblown room, smelling of garlic; I cooling my elbows on the oily slab of a table (breakfast for one) and looking through a window at a glaring whitewashed fence high enough to shut out the universe from my point of sight. Yet it hid not all, since it brought into relief a panting cock (with one leg in a string) which had so strained to compress itself into a doubtful inch of shade that its suspended claw clutched the air in real agony.

Having dazzled my eyes with this prospect, I turned gratefully to the vanities of life that may be had for two francs in Tahiti. *Vide* bill of fare. One fried egg, like the eye of some gigantic Albino; potatoes hollowed out bombshell fashion, primed with liver-sausage, very ingenious and palatable. The naked corpse of a fowl that cared not to live longer, from appearances, yet looked not happy in death.

Item: Wonder if there *is* a more ghastly spectacle than a chicken cooked in the French style; its knees drawn up on its breast like an Indian mummy, while its blue-black, parboiled, and melancholy visage tearfully surveys its own unshrouded remains. After a brief season of meditation I said, and I trust I meant it, "I thank the Lord for all these blessings." Then I gave the corpse of the chicken Christian burial under a fold of the window-curtain, disposed of the fried eye of the Albino, and transformed myself into a mortar for the time being, taking potato-bombshells according to my calibre.

* By special arrangement.

There was claret all the while and plenty of butterless roll, a shaving of cheese, a banana, black coffee and cognac, when I turned again to dazzle myself with the white fence, and saw with infinite pity,—a sentiment perhaps not unmixed with a suspicion of cognac or some other temporary humanizing element—I saw for a fact that the poor cock had wilted and lay flat in the sun like a last year's duster. That was too much for me. I wheeled towards the door where gleamed the bay with its lovely ridges of light; canoes drifting over it drew the eye after them irresistibly; I heard the ship-calkers on the beach making their monotonous clatter, and the drone of the bareheaded fruit-sellers squatted in rows chatting indolently with their eyes half shut. I could think of nothing but bees humming over their own sweet wares.

About this time a young fellow at the next table, who had scarcely a mouthful of English at his command, implored me to take beer with him; implying that we might, if desirable, become as tight as two bricks. I declined, much to his admiration, he regarding my refusal as a clear case of moral courage, whereas it arose simply and solely from my utter inability to see his treat and go him one better.

A grown person in Tahiti has an eating hour allotted to him twice a day, at 10 A. M. and 5 P. M. My time being up I returned to the store in an indifferent frame of mind, and upon entering the presence of my employer, who had arrived a moment before me, I was immediately covered with the deep humiliation of servitude and withdrew to an obscure corner, while Monsieur and some naval guests took absinthe unblushingly, which was, of course, proper enough in them. Call it by what name you will, you cannot sweeten servility to my taste. Then why was I there and in bondage? The spirit of adventure that keeps life in us, yet comes near to worrying it out of us now and then, lured me with my handful of dollars to the Garden of the Pacific. "You can easily get work," said some one who had been there and didn't want it. If work I must, why not better there than here, thought I; and the less money I take with me the surer am I to seek that which might not attract me under other circumstances. A few letters which proved almost valueless; an abiding trust in Providence, afterward somewhat shaken, I am sorry to state, which convinces me that I can no longer hope to travel as a shorn lamb; considerable confidence in the good feeling of my fellowmen; together with the few dollars above referred to, comprised my all when I set foot on the leaf-strewn and shady beach of Papute.

Before the day was over I saw my case was almost hopeless; I was one too many in a very meagre congregation of foreigners. In a week I was desperate, with poverty and disgrace brooding like evil spirits on either hand. Every ten minutes some one suggested something which was almost immediately suppressed by the next man I met, to whom I applied for further information. Teach, said one—there wasn't a pupil to be had in the dominion. Clerkships were out of the question likewise. I might keep store, if I could get anything to put in it; or go farther, as some one suggested, if I had money enough to get there. I thought it wiser to endure the ills I had than fly to others that I knew not of. In this state I perambulated to the green lanes of Papute, conscious that I was drawing down tons of immaterial sympathy from hearts of various nationalities, beating to the music of regular salaries in hard cash, and the inevitable ringing of their daily dinner-bell; and I continued to perambulate under the same depressing avalanches for a fortnight or more, a warning to the generation of the inexperienced that persists in sowing itself broadcast upon the edges of the earth, and learns too late how hard a thing it is to take root under the circumstances.

One gloomy day I was seized in the market-place and led before a French gentleman who offered me a bed and board for such manual compensation as I might be able to give him in his office during the usual business hours, namely, from daybreak to some time in the afternoon, unless it rained, when business was suspended, and I was dropped until fair weather should set that little world wagging again.

I was invited to enter into the bosom of his family, in fact, to be one of them, and no single man could ask to be more;

to sit at his table and hope for better days, in which diversion he proposed to join me with all his soul.

With an emotion of gratitude and a pang at being thus early a subject of charity, I began business in Papute, and learned within the hour how sharper than most sharps it is to know only your own mother-tongue when you're away from home.

Nightly I walked two hot and dusty miles through groves of bread-fruit and colonnades of palms to my new master's. I skirted, with loitering steps, a placid sea whose crystalline depths sheltered lcagucs and leagues of sun-painted corals, where a myriad fish, dyed like the rainbow, sported unceasingly. Springs gushed from the mountain, singing their song of joy; the winds sang in the dark locks of the sycamore, while the palm boughs clashed like cymbals in rhythmical accompaniment; glad children chanted their choruses, and I alone couldn't sing, nor hum, nor whistle, because it doesn't pay to work for your board and pay for little necessities out of your own pocket, in any latitude that I ever heard of.

We lived in a grove of ten thousand cocoa-palms crowning a hill-slope to the west. How all-sufficient it sounds as I write it now, but how little I cared then, for many reasons! My cottage had prior tenants, who disputed possession with me, winged tenants who sought admission at every cranny, and frequently obtained it in spite of me—these were not angels, but hens. My cottage had been a granary until it got too poor a receptacle for grains, and a better shelter left it open to the barn-fowls until I arrived. They hated me, these hungry chickens; they used to sit in rows on the window-sill and stare me out of countenance. A wide bedstead, corded with thongs, did its best to furnish my apartment. A narrow, a very narrow and thin ship's mattress, that had been a bed of torture for many a sea-sick soul before it descended to me; a flat pillow like a pancake, a condemned horse-blanket contributed by a good-natured Kanack who raked it from a heap of refuse in the yard, together with two sacks of rice, the despair of those hens in the window, were all I could boast of. With this inventory I strove (by particular request) to be one of those who were comfortable enough in the chateau adjoining. Summoned peremptorily to dinner, I entered a little latticed saloon connected with the chateau by a covered walk, discovered Monsieur seated at table and already served with soup and claret; the remainder of the company served themselves as they best could—and I saw plainly enough that the family bosom was so crowded already, that I might seek in vain to wedge myself into any corner of it, at least until some vacancy occurred.

After dinner, sat on a sack of rice in my room while it grew dark and Monsieur received calls. Wandered down to the beach at the foot of the hill and lay a long time on a bed of leaves, while the tide was out and the crabs clattered along shore and were very sociable. Natives began to kindle their evening fires of cocoanut husks; smoke, sweet as incense, climed up to the plumes of the palm-trees and was lost among the stars. Morsels of fish and bread-fruit were offered me by the untutored savage, who welcomed me to his frugal meal and desired that I should at least taste before he broke his fast. Canoes shot out from dense, shadowy points; fishers standing in the bows with a poised spear in one hand, a blazing palm-branch held aloft in the other shed a warm glow of light over their superb nakedness. Bathed by the sea in a fresh, cool spring, and returned to my little coop, which was illuminated by the glare of fifty floating beacons; looking back from the door I could see the dark outlines of the torch-bearers and hear their signal calls above the low growl of the reef a half-mile farther out from shore. It was a blessing to lie awake in my little room and watch the flicker of those fires; to think how Tahiti must look on a cloudless night from some heavenly altitude. The ocean still as death, the procession of fishermen sweeping from point to point within the reef, till the island, flooded with starlight and torchlight, lies like a green sea-garden in a girdle of flame.

A shrill bell called me from my bed at dawn. I was not unwilling to rise, for half the night I lay like a saint on the tough thongs, having turned over in sleep, thereby missing the mattress entirely. Made my toilet at a spring on the way into town; saw a glorious sunrise that was as good as breakfast, and found the whole earth and sea and all that in them is singing again while I listened and gave thanks for that privilege. At 10 A. M. I went to breakfast in the small restaurant where I have sketched myself at the top of this chronicle, and whither we may return and begin over again if it please you.

I was about to remark that probably most melancholy and homesickness may be cured or alleviated by a wholesome meal of victuals; but I think I won't, for, on referring to my note-book, I find that within an hour after my return to the store I was as heart-sick as ever and wasn't afraid to say so. It is scarcely to be wondered at; the sky was dark; aboard a schooner some sailors were making that doleful whine peculiar to them, as they hauled in to shore and tied up to a tree in a sifting rain. Then everything was ominously still as though something disagreeable were about to happen; thereupon I doubled myself over the counter like a half-shut jack-knife, and burying my face in my hands said to myself, "O, to be alone with Nature! her silence is religion and her sounds sweet music." After which the rain blew over, and I was sent with a hand-cart and one underfed Kanack to a wharf half a mile away to drag back several loads of potatoes. We two hungry creatures struggled heroically to do our duty. Starting with a multitude of sacks it was quite impossible to proceed with, we grew weaker the farther we went, so that the load had to be reduced from time to time, and I believe the amount of potatoes deposited by the way considerably exceeded the amount we subsequently arrived at the store with. Finding life a burden, and seeing the legs of the young fellow in harness with me bend under him in his frantic efforts to get our cart out of a rut without emptying it entirely, I resolved to hire a substitute at my own expense, and save my remaining strength for a new line of business. Thus I was enabled to sit on the wharf the rest of the afternoon and enjoy myself devising new means of subsistence and watching the natives swim.

Some one before me found a modicum of sweets in his cup of bitterness, and in a complacent hour set the good against the evil in single entry, summing up the same to his advantage. I concluded to do it myself, and did it, thus:

Evil	Good
I find myself in a foreign land with no one to love and none to love me.	But I may do as I please in consequence, and it is nobody's business save my own.
I am working for my board and lodging (no extras), and find it very unprofitable.	But I may quit as soon as I feel like it, and shall have no occasion to dun my employer for back salary so long as I stop with him.
My clothes are in rags. I shall soon be without a stitch to my back.	But the weather is mild and the fig-tree flourisheth. Moreover many a good savage has gone naked before me.
I get hungry before breakfast and feel faint after dinner. What are two meals a day to a man of my appetite?	But fasting is saintly. Day by day I grow more spiritual, and shall shortly be a fit subject for translation to that better world which is doubtless the envy of all those who have lost it by overeating and drinking.

Nothing can exceed the satisfaction with which I read and reread this philosophical summary, but I had relapses every few minutes so long as I lived in Tahiti. I remember one Sunday morning, a day I had all to myself, when I cried out of the depths and felt better after it. It was a real Sunday. The fowls confessed it by the indifference with which they picked up a grain of rice now and then as though they weren't hungry. The family were moving about in an unnatural way—some people are never themselves on the Lord's day. The canoes lay asleep off upon the water, evidently conscious of the long hours of rest they were sure of having. To sum it all, it seemed as though the cover had been taken off from the earth, and the angels were sitting in big circles looking at us. Our clock had run down, and I found myself half an hour too early at mass. Some diminutive native children talked together with infinite gesticulation, like little old men. At every lag in the conversation, two or three of them would steal away to the fence that surrounded the church and begin diligently counting the pickets thereof.

They were evidently amazed at what they considered a singular coincidence, namely, that the number of pickets, beginning at the front gate and counting to the right, tallied exactly with the do. do. beginning at the do. do. and counting to the left; while they were making repeated efforts to get at the heart of this mystery, the priest rode up on horseback, dismounted in our midst, and we all followed him into chapel to mass.

A young Frenchman offered me holy-water on the tips of his fingers, and I immediately decided to confide in him to an unlimited extent if he gave me the opportunity. It was a serious disappointment when I found later that we didn't know six words in any common tongue. Concluded to be independent, and walked off by myself. Got very lonesome immediately. Tried to be meditative, philosophical, botanical, conchological, and in less than an hour gave it up—homesick again, by Jove!

Strolled to the beach and sat a long time on a bit of wreck partly imbedded in the sand; consoled by the surpassing radiance of sunset, wondered how I could ever have repined, but proceeded to do it again as soon as it grew dark. Some natives drew near, greeting me kindly. They were evidently lovers; talked in low tones, deeply interested in the most trivial things, such as a leaf falling into the sea at our feet and floating stem up, like a bowsprit; he probably made some poetic allusion to it, may have proposed braving the seas with her in a shallop as fairy-like, for both fell a dreaming and were silent for some time, he worshipping her with fascinated eyes, while she, woman-like, pretended to be all unconscious of his admiration.

Silently we sat looking over the sea at Morea, just visible in the light of the young moon like a spirit brooding upon the waters, till I broke the spell by saying "Good night," which was repeated in a chorus as I withdrew to my coop and found my feathered guests had beaten in the temporary barricade erected in the broken window, entered and made themselves at home during my absence—a fact that scarcely endeared the spot to me. Next morning I was unusually merry; couldn't tell why, but tried to sing as I made my toilet at the spring; laughed nearly all the way into town, saying my prayers and blessing God, when I came suddenly upon a horseshoe in the middle of the road.   Took it as an omen and a keepsake; horseshoes aren't shed everywhere nor for everybody.   I thought it the prophecy of a change, and at once cancelled my engagement with my employer without having set foot into his house farther than the dining-room, or made any apparent impression upon the adamantine bosom of his family.

After formally expressing my gratitude to Monsieur for his renewed offers of hospitality, I turned myself into the street and was once more adrift in the world.   For the space of three minutes I was wild with joy at the thought of my perfect liberty.   Then I grew nervous, began to feel unhappy, nay, even guilty, as though I had thrown up a good thing.   Concluded it was rash of me to leave a situation where I got two meals and a mattress, with the privilege of washing at my own expense.   Am not sure that it wasn't unwise, for I had no dinner that afternoon; and having no bed either, I crept into the veranda of a house to let and dozed till daybreak.

There was but one thing to live for now, namely, to see as much of Tahiti as possible, and at my earliest convenience return like the prodigal son to that father who would doubtless feel like killing something appropriate as soon as he saw me coming.   I said as much to a couple of brothers who are living a dream-life over yonder, and whose wildest species of dissipation for the last seven years has been to rise at intervals from their settees in the arbor, go deliberately to the farther end of the garden and eat several mangoes in cold blood.

To comprehend Tahiti, a man must lose himself in forests whose resinous boughs are knotted with ribbons of sea-grass; there, overcome by the music of sibilant waters sifting through the antlers of the coral, he is supposed to sink upon drifts of orange-blossoms only to be resuscitated by the spray of an approaching shower crashing through the green solitudes like an army with chariots,—so those brothers told, with a mango poised in each hand; and they added that I

should have an official document addressed to the best blood
in the kingdom, namely, Forty, chief of Tahiti, who would
undoubtedly entertain me with true barbarian hospitality,
better the world knows not. There was a delay for some
reason; I, rather impatient, and scarcely hoping to receive so
graceful a compliment from head-quarters, trudged on alone
with a light purse and an infinitesimal bundle of necessities,
caring nothing for the weather nor the number of miles
cleared per day, since I laid no plans save the one, to see as
much as I might with the best grace possible, keeping an eye
on the road for horseshoes. Through leagues of verdure I
wandered, feasting my five senses and finding life a holiday
at last. There were numberless streams to be crossed, where
I loafed for hours on the bridges, satisfying myself with sunshine. Not a savage in the land was freer than I. No man
could say to me, "Why stand ye here idle?" for I could continue to stand as long as I liked and as idly as it pleased me,
in spite of him! There were bridgeless streams to be forded,
but the Tahitian is a nomad continually wandering from one
edge of his faithful world to the other. Moreover, he is the
soul of peace towards men of good-will; I was invariably
picked up by some bare-backed Hercules, who volunteered to
take me over the water on his brawny brown shoulders, and
could have easily taken two like me. It was good to be up
there while he strode through the swift current, for I felt that
he was perfectly able to carry me to the ends of the earth
without stopping, and that sense of reliance helped to reas-
sure my faith in humanity.

As I wandered, from most native houses came the invitation to enter and eat. Night after night I found my bed in
the corner of some dwelling whither I had been led by the
master of it, with unaffected grace. It wasn't simply showing me to a spare room, but rather unrolling the best mat and
turning everything to my account so long as it pleased me to
tarry. Sometimes the sea talked in its sleep not a rod from
the house; frequently the mosquitoes accepted me as a delicacy and did their best to dispose of me. Once I awoke
with a headache, the air was so dense with the odor of orange-
blossoms.

There was frequently a strip of blue bay that ebbed and flowed languidly and had to be launched with; or a very deep and melodious spring, asking for an interview, and, I may add, it always got it. I remember one miniature castle built in the midst of a grassy Venice by the shore. Its moats, shining with gold-fish, were spanned with slender bridges; toy fences of bamboo enclosed the rarer clumps of foliage, and there was such an air of tranquillity pervading it I thought I must belong there. Something seemed to say, "Come in." I went in, but left very soon—the place was so fairy-like, I felt as though I were liable to step through it and come out on some other side, and I wasn't anxious for such a change.

I ate when I got hungry, a very good sort of a meal, consisting usually of a tiny piglet cooked in the native fashion, swathed in succulent leaves and laid between hot stones till ready for eating; bread-fruit, like mashed potato, but a great deal better; orange-tea and cocoa-milk, surely enough for two or three francs. Took a sleep whenever sleep came along, resting always till the clouds or a shadow from the mountain covered me so as to keep cool and comfortable. Natives passed me with salutations. A white man now and then went by barely nodding, or more frequently eyeing me with suspicion and giving me as much of his dust as he found convenient. In the wider fellowship of nature, I foreswore all blood relations and blushed for the representatives of my own color as I footed it right royally. Therefore, I was enabled to scorn the fellow who scorned me while he flashed the steel hoofs of his charger in my face and dashed on to the village we were both approaching with the dusk.

What a spot it was! A long lane as green as a spring meadow, lying between wall-like masses of foliage whose deep arcades were frescoed with blossoms and festooned with vines. It seemed a pathway leading to infinity, for the blood-red bars of sunset glared at its farther end as though Providence had placed them there to keep out the unregenerated. Not a house visible all this time, nor a human, though I was in the heart of the hamlet. Passing up the turf cushioned road on either hand, I beheld, through a screen of leaves, a log spanning a rivulet that was softly singing its monody. At the end of each log the summer-house of some Tahitian, who sat in his door smoking complacently. It was a picture of still life with a suggestion of possible motion; a village to put into a green-house, water, and keep fresh forever. Let me picture it once more—one mossy street between two babbling brooks, and every house thereof set each in its own moated wilderness. This was Papeali.

Like rows of cages full of chirping birds those bamboo huts were distributed up and down the street. As I walked I knew something would cause me to turn at the right time and find a new friend ready to receive me, for it always does. So I walked slowly and without hesitation or impatience until I turned and met him coming out of his cage, crossing the rill by his log and holding out his hand to me in welcome. Back we went together, and I ate and slept there as though it had been arranged a thousand years ago— perhaps it was! There was a racket up at the farther end of the lane, by the chief's house. Songs and nose-flutings upon the night air; moreover, a bonfire and doubtless much nectar; too much, as usual, for I heard such cheers as the soul gives when it is careless of consequences, and caught a glimpse of the joys of barbarism such as even we poor Christians cannot wholly withstand, but turning our backs think we are safe enough. Commend me to him who has known temptation and not shunned it, but actually withstood it!

It was the dance, as ever it is the dance where all the aspirations of the soul find expression in the body; those bodies that are incarnate souls or those souls that are spiritualized bodies, inseparable, whatever they are, for the time being. The fire glowed fervently; bananas hung out their tattered banners like decorations; palms rustled their silver plumes aloft in the moonlight; the sea panted upon its sandy bed in heavy sleep; the night-blooming cereus opened its waxen chambers and gave forth its treasured sweets. Circle after circle of swart savage faces were turned upon the flame-lit arena where the dancers posed for a moment with their light drapery gathered about them and held carelessly in one hand. Anon the music chimed forth; a reiteration of chords caught from the birds' treble and the wind's bass. Full and resounding syllables, richly poetical, telling of orgies and of the mysteries of the forbidden revels in the charmed valleys of the gods, hearing which it were impossible not to be wrought to madness, and the dancers thereat went mad, dancing with infinite gesticulation, dancing to whirlwinds of applause till the undulation of their bodies was serpentine, and at last in frenzy they shrieked with joy, threw off their garments, and were naked as the moon. So much for a vision that kept me awake till morning, when I plodded on in the damp grass and tried to forget it, but couldn't exactly and never have to this hour. Went on and on over more bridges spanning still-flowing streams of silver, past springs that lay like great crystals framed in moss under dripping fern-clad cliffs that the sun never reaches. Came at last to a shining white-washed fort on an eminence that commands the isthmus connecting the two hemispheres of Tahiti, where down I dropped into a narrow valley full of wind and discord and a kind of dreary neglect that made me sick for any other place. More refreshment for the wayfarer, but to be paid for by the dish, and therefore limited. Was obliged to hate a noisy fellow with too much bushy black beard and a freckled nose, and to like another who eyed me kindly over his absinthe, having first mixed a glass for me. A native asked me where I was going; being unable to give any satisfactory answer, he conducted me to his canoe, about a mile distant, where he cut a sapling for a mast, another for a gaff, twisted in a few moments a cord of its fibrous bark, rigged a sail of his sleeping-blanket, and we were shortly waifted onward before a light breeze between the reef and shore.

Three of us with a bull-pup in the bows dozed under the afternoon sun. He of the paddle awoke now and then to shift sail, beat the sea impetuously for a few seconds, and fall asleep again. Voices roused me occasionally, greetings from colonies of indolent Kanacks on shore, whose business it was to sit there till they got hungry, laughing weariness to scorn.

Close upon our larboard-bow lay one of the islands that had bewitched me as I paced the shore but a few days previously; under us the measureless gardens of the sea unmasked a myriad of imperishable blossoms, centuries old some of them, but as fair and fresh as though born within the hour. All that afternoon we drifted between sea and shore, and beached at sunset in a new land. Foot-sore and weary, I approached a stable from which thrice a week stages were despatched to Papute.

A modern pilgrim finds his scrip cumbersome, if he has any, and deems it more profitable to pay his coachman than his cobbler.

I climbed to my seat by the jolly French driver, who was continually chatting with three merry nuns sitting just back of us, returning to the convent in Papute after a vacation re-treat among the hills. How they enjoyed the ride as three children might, and were quite wild with delight at meeting a corpulent *père,* who smiled amiably from his saddle and offered to show them the interior of the pretty chapel at Faaa (only three *a*'s in that word)—the very one I grew melan-choly in when I was a man of business.

So they hurled themselves madly from the high seat, one after the other, scorning to touch anything so contaminating as a man's hand, though it looked suicidal, as the driver and I agreed while the three were at prayers by the altar. Whipping up over the road townward, I could almost recog-nize my own footprints left since the time I used to take the dust in my face three mornings a week from the wheels of that very vehicle as I footed it in to business. Passing the spring, my toilet of other days, drawing to the edge of the town, we stopped being jolly and were as proper as befitted travellers. We looked over the wall of the convent garden as we drove up to the gate, and saw the mother-superior hurrying down to us with a cumbersome chair for the relief of the nuns, but before she reached us they had cast them-selves to earth again in the face of destiny, and there was kissing, crying, and commotion as they withdrew under the gateway like so many doves seeking shelter. When the gate closed after them, I heard them all *cooing* at once, but the world knows nothing further.

Where would I be dropped? asked the driver. In the

middle of the street, please you, and take half my little whole for your ride, sir! He took it, dropped me where we stood, and drove away, I pretending to be very much at my ease. God help me and all poor hypocrites!

I sought a place of shelter, or rather retirement, for the air is balm in that country. There was an old house in the middle of a grassy lawn on a by-street. Two of its rooms were furnished with a few papers and books, and certain gentlemen who contribute to its support lounge in when they have leisure for reading or a chat. I grew to know the place familiarly. I stole a night's lodging on its veranda in the shadow of a passion-vine, but, for fear of embarrassing some early student in pursuit of knowledge, I passed the second night on the floor of the dilapidated cook-house, where the ants covered me. I endured the tortures of one who bares his body to an unceasing shower of sparks; but I survived.

There was, in this very cook-house, a sink six feet in length and as wide as a coffin; the third night I lay like a galvanized corpse with his lid off till a rat sought to devour me, when I took to the streets and walked till morning. By this time the president of the club, whose acquaintance I had the honor of, tendered me the free use of any portion of the premises that might not be otherwise engaged. With a gleam of hope I began my explorations. Up a narrow and winding stair I found a spacious loft. It was like a mammoth tent, a solitary centre-pole its only ornament. Creeping into it on all-fours, I found a fragment of matting, a dry crust, an empty soda-bottle—footprints on the sands of time.

"Poor soul!" I gasped, "where did *you* come from? What *did* you come for? Whither, O, whither, have you flown?"

I might have added, How did you manage to get there? But the present was so important a consideration, I had no heart to look beyond it. The next ten nights I passed in the silent and airy apartment of my anonymous predecessor. Ten nights I crossed the unswept floor that threatened at every step to precipitate me into the reading-room below. With a faint heart and hollow stomach I threw myself upon my elbow and strove to sleep. I lay till my heart stopped beating, my joints were wooden, and my four limbs corky beyond all hope of reanimation. There the mosquito revelled, and it was a promising place for centipedes.

At either end of the building an open window admitted the tip of a banana-leaf; up their green ribs the sprightly mouse careered. I broke the backbones of these banana-leaves, though they were the joy of my soul and would have adorned the choicest conservatory in the land. Day was equally unprofitable to me. My best friend said, "Why not return to California?" Every one I met invited me to leave the country at my earliest convenience. The American consul secured me a passage, to be settled for at home, and my career in that latitude was evidently at an end. In my superfluous confidence in humanity, I had announced myself as a correspondent for the press. It was quite necessary that I should give some plausible reason for making my appearance in Tahiti friendless and poor. "I am a correspondent, friendless and poor," believing that any one would see truth in the face of it, with half an eye. "Prove it," said one who knew more of the world that I. Then flashed upon me the alarming fact that I couldn't prove it, having nothing whatever in my possession referring to it in the slightest degree. It was a fatal mistake that might easily have been avoided, but was too well established to be rectified.

In my chagrin I looked to the good old bishop for consolation. Approaching the Mission House through sunlit cloisters of palms, I was greeted most tenderly. I would have gladly taken any amount of holy orders for the privilege of ending my troublous days in the sweet seclusion of the Mission House.

As it was, I received a blessing, an autograph, and a "God speed" to some other part of creation. Added to this I learned how the address to the Forty Chiefs of Tahiti in behalf of the foreign traveler, my poor self, had been despatched to me by a special courier who found me not, and doubtless the *fêtes* I heard of and was forever missing marked the march of that messenger, my proxy, in his triumphal progress. In my innocent degradation it was still necessary to nourish the inner man.

There is a market in Papute where, under one broad roof, threescore hucksters of both sexes congregate long before daylight, and, while a few candles illumine their wares, patiently await custom. A half-dozen coolies with an eye to business serve hot coffee and chocolate at a dime per cup to any who choose to ask for it. By 7 A. M. the market is so nearly sold out that only the more plentiful fruits of the country are to be obtained at any price. A prodigal cannot long survive on husks, unless he have coffee to wash them down; I took my cup of it with two spoonfuls of sugar and ants dipped out of a cigar box, and a crust of bread into the bargain, sitting on a bench in the market-place, with a coolie and a Kanack on either hand.

It was not the coffee nor the sugared ants that I gave my dime for, but rather for the privilege of sitting in the midst of men and women who were willing to accept me as a friend and helpmate, without questioning my ancestry, and any one of whom would go me halves in the most disinterested manner. Then there was sure to be some superb fellow close at hand with a sensuous lip curled under his nostril, a glimpse of which gave me a dime's worth of satisfaction and more too. Having secreted a French roll, five cents, all hot, under my coat, and gathered the bananas that would fall in the yard so seasonably, I made my day as brief and comfortable as possible by filling up with water from time to time.

The man who had passed a grimy chop-house, wherein a frowzy fellow sat at his cheap spread, without envying the frowzy fellow his cheap spread cannot truly sympathize with me.

The man who has not felt a great hollow in his stomach which he found necessary to fill at the first fountain he came to, or go over on his beam ends for lack of ballast, cannot fall upon my neck and call me brother.

At daybreak I haunted those street fountains, waiting my turn while French cooks filled almost fathomless kegs, and coolies filled potbellied jars, and Kanacks filled their hollow bamboos that seemed fully a quarter of a mile in length. There I meekly made my toilet, took my first course for breakfast, rinsed out my handkerchiefs and stockings, and went my way. The whole performance was embarrassing, because I was a novice and a dozen people watched me in curious silence. I had also a boot with a suction in the toe; there is dust in Papute; while I walked that boot loaded and discharged itself in a manner that amazed and amused a small mob of little natives who followed me in my free exhibition, advertising my shooting-boot gratuitously.

I was altogether shabby in my outward appearance, and cannot honestly upbraid any resident of the town for his neglect of me. I know that I suffered the agony of shame and the pangs of hunger, but they were nothing to the utter loneliness I felt as I wandered about with my heart on my sleeve, and never a bite from so much as a daw.

Did you ever question the possibility of a man's temporary transformation under certain mental, moral, or physical conditions? There are times when he certainly isn't what he was, yet may be more and better than he has been if you give him time enough.

I began to think I had either suffered this transformation or been maliciously misinformed as to my personality. Was I truly what I represented myself to be, or had I been a living deception all my days? No longer able to identify myself as any one in particular, it occurred to me that it would be well to address a few lines to the gentleman I had been in the habit of calling "father," asking for some particulars concerning his absent son. I immediately drew up this document ready for mailing:—

MOSQUITO HALL, CENTIPEDE AVENUE,
PAPUTE

DEAR SIR: A nondescript awaits identification at this office. Answers to the names at the foot of this page, believes himself to be your son, to have been your son, or about to be something equally near and dear to you. He can repeat several chapters of the New Testament at the shortest notice; recites most of the Catechism and Commandments; thinks he would recognize two sisters and three brothers at sight, and know his mother with his eyes shut.

He likewise confesses to the usual strawberry-mark in fast colors. If you will kindly send by return mail a few dollars, he will clothe, feed, and water himself and return immediately to those arms, which, if his memory does not belie him, have more than once sheltered his unworthy frame. I have, dear sir, the singular fortune to be the article above described.

The six months which would elapse before I could hope for an answer would probably have found me past all recognition, so I ceased crying to the compassionate bowels of Tom, Dick, and Harry, waiting with haggard patience the departure of the vessel that was to bear me home with a palpable C. O. D. tacked on to me. Those last hours were brightened by the delicate attentions of a few good souls who learned, too late, the shocking state of my case. Thanks to them, I slept well thereafter in a real bed, and was sure of dinners that wouldn't rattle in me like a withered kernel in an old nutshell.

I had but to walk to the beach, wave my lily hand, heavily tanned about that time, when lo! a boat was immediately despatched from the plump little corvette "Cheveret," where the tricolor waved triumphantly from sunrise to sunset, all the year round.

Such capital French dinners as I had there, such offers of bed and board and boundless sympathy as were made me by those dear fellows who wore the gold-lace and had a piratical-looking cabin all to themselves, were enough to wring a heart that had been nearly wrung out in its battle with life in Tahiti.

No longer I walked the streets as one smitten with the plague; or revolved in envious circles about the market-place, where I could have got my fill for a half-dollar, but had neither the one nor the other. No longer I went at daybreak to swell the procession at the water-spout, or sat on the shore the picture of despair, waiting sunrise, finding it my sole happiness to watch a canoe-load of children drifting out upon the bay, singing like a railful of larks; nor walked solitary through the night up and down the narrow streets wherein the *gendarmes* had learned to pass me unnoticed, with my hat under my arm and my heart in my throat. Those delicious moons always seduced me from my natural sleep, and. I sauntered through the cocoa-groves whose boughs glistened like row after row of crystals, whose shadows were as mosaics wrought in blocks of silver.

I used to nod at the low whitewashed "calabooses" fairly steaming in the sun, wherein Herman Melville got some chapters of *Omoo*.

Over and over again I tracked the ground of that delicious story, saying to the bread-fruit trees that had sheltered him, "Shelter me also, and whoever shall follow after so long as your branches quiver in the wind."

O, reader of *Omoo*, think of "Motoo-Otoo" actually looking warlike in these sad days, with a row of new cannons around its edge, and pyramids of balls as big as cocoanuts covering its shady centre.

Walking alone in those splendid nights I used to hear a dry, ominous coughing in the huts of the natives. I felt as though I were treading upon the brinks of half-dug graves, and I longed to bring a respite to the doomed race.

One windy afternoon we cut our stern hawser in a fair wind and sailed out of the harbor; I felt a sense of relief, and moralized for five minutes without stopping. Then I turned away from all listeners and saw those glorious green peaks growing dim in the distance; the clouds embraced them in their profound secrecy; like a lovely mirage Tahiti floated upon the bosom of the sea. Between sea and sky was swallowed up vale, garden, and water-fall; point after point crowded with palms; peak above peak in that eternal crown of beauty, and with them the nation of warriors and lovers falling like the leaf, but unlike it, with no followers in the new season.

THE OUTCASTS OF POKER FLAT *

By Francis Bret Harte

A S Mr. John Oakhurst, gambler, stepped into the main street of Poker Flat on the morning of the twenty-third of November, 1850, he was conscious of a change in its moral atmosphere since the preceding night. Two or three men, conversing earnestly together, ceased as he approached, and exchanged significant glances. There was a Sabbath lull in the air, which, in a settlement unused to Sabbath influences, looked ominous.

Mr. Oakhurst's calm, handsome face betrayed small concern of these indications. Whether he was conscious of any predisposing cause, was another question. "I reckon they're after somebody," he reflected; "likely it's me." He returned to his pocket the handkerchief with which he had been whipping away the red dust of Poker Flat from his neat boots, and quietly discharged his mind of any further conjecture.

In point of fact, Poker Flat was "after somebody." It had lately suffered the loss of several thousand dollars, two valuable horses, and a prominent citizen. It was experiencing a spasm of virtuous reaction, quite as lawless and ungovernable as any of the acts that had provoked it. A secret committee had determined to rid the town of all improper persons. This was done permanently in regard of two men who were then hanging from the boughs of a sycamore in the gulch, and temporarily in the banishment of certain other objectionable characters. I regret to say that some of these were ladies. It is but due to the sex, however, to state that their impropriety was professional, and

---

* By arrangement with Houghton Mifflin Company.

it was only in such easily established standards of evil that Poker Flat ventured to sit in judgment.

Mr. Oakhurst was right in supposing that he was included in this category. A few of the committee had urged hanging him as a possible example, and a sure method of reimbursing themselves from his pockets of the sums he had won from them. "It's agin justice," said Jim Wheeler, "to let this yer young man from Roaring Camp—an entire stranger—carry away our money." But a crude sentiment of equity residing in the breasts of those who had been fortunate enough to win from Mr. Oakhurst overruled this narrower local prejudice.

Mr. Oakhurst received his sentence with philosophic calmness, none the less coolly that he was aware of the hesitation of his judges. He was too much of a gambler not to accept Fate. With him life was at best an uncertain game, and he recognized the usual percentage in favor of the dealer.

A body of armed men accompanied the deported wickedness of Poker Flat to the outskirts of the settlement. Besides Mr. Oakhurst, who was known to be a coolly desperate man, and for those intimidation the armed escort was intended, the expatriated party consisted of a young woman familiarly known as "The Duchess"; another, who had gained the infelicitous title of "Mother Shipton"; and "Uncle Billy," a suspected sluice-robber and confirmed drunkard. The cavalcade provoked no comments from the spectators, nor was any word uttered by the escort. Only, when the gulch which marked the uttermost limit of Poker Flat was reached, the leader spoke briefly and to the point. The exiles were forbidden to return at the peril of their lives.

As the escort disappeared, their pent-up feelings found vent in a few hysterical tears from The Duchess, some bad language from Mother Shipton, and a Parthian volley of expletives from Uncle Billy. The philosophic Oakhurst alone remained silent. He listened calmly to Mother Shipton's desire to cut somebody's heart out, to the repeated statements of The Duchess that she would die in the road, and to the alarming oaths that seemed to be bumped out of Uncle Billy as he rode forward. With the easy good-humor characteristic of his class, he insisted upon exchanging his own riding-horse, Five Spot, for the sorry mule which the Duchess rode. But even this act did not draw the party into any closer sympathy. The young woman readjusted her somewhat draggled plumes with a feeble, faded coquetry; Mother Shipton eyed the possessor of Five Spot with malevolence, and Uncle Billy included the whole party in one sweeping anathema.

The road to Sandy Bar—a camp that, not having as yet experienced the regenerating influences of Poker Flat, consequently seemed to offer some invitation to the emigrants— lay over a steep mountain range. It was distant a day's severe journey. In that advanced season, the party soon passed out of the moist, temperate regions of the foot-hills into the dry, cold, bracing air of the Sierras. The trail was narrow and difficult. At noon the Duchess, rolling out of her saddle upon the ground, declared her intention of going no farther, and the party halted.

The spot was singularly wild and impressive. A wooded amphitheatre, surrounded on three sides by precipitous cliffs of naked granite, sloped gently toward the crest of another precipice that overlooked the valley. It was undoubtedly the most suitable spot for a camp, had camping been advisable. But Mr. Oakhurst knew that scarcely half the journey to Sandy Bar was accomplished, and the party were not equipped or provisioned for delay. This fact he pointed out to his companions curtly, with a philosophic commentary on the folly of "throwing up their hand before the game was played out." But they were furnished with liquor, which in this emergency stood them in place of food, fuel, rest, and prescience. In spite of his remonstrances, it was not long before they were more or less under its influence. Uncle Billy passed rapidly from a bellicose state into one of stupor, the Duchess became maudlin, and Mother Shipton snored. Mr. Oakhurst alone remained erect, leaning against a rock, calmly surveying them.

Mr. Oakhurst did not drink. It interfered with a profession which required coolness, impassiveness, and presence of mind, and, in his own language, he "couldn't afford it."

As he gazed at his recumbent fellow-exiles, the loneliness begotten of his pariah-trade, his habits of life, his very vices, for the first time seriously oppressed him. He bestirred himself in dusting his black clothes, washing his hands and face, and other acts characteristic of his studiously neat habits, and for a moment forgot his annoyance. The thought of deserting his weaker and more pitiable companions never perhaps occurred to him. Yet he could not help feeling the want of that excitement which, singularly enough, was most conducive to that calm equanimity for which he was notorious. He looked at the gloomy walls that rose a thousand feet sheer above the circling pines around him; at the sky, ominously clouded; at the valley below, already deepening into shadow. And, doing so, suddenly he heard his own name called.

A horseman slowly ascended the trail. In the fresh, open face of the new-comer Mr. Oakhurst recognized Tom Simson, otherwise known as "The Innocent" of Sandy Bar. He had met him some months before over a "little game," and had, with perfect equanimity, won the entire fortune—amounting to some forty dollars—of that guileless youth. After the game was finished, Mr. Oakhurst drew the youthful speculator behind the door and thus addressed him; "Tommy, you're a good little man, but you can't gamble worth a cent. Don't try it over again." He then handed him his money back, pushed him gently from the room, and so made a devoted slave of Tom Simson.

There was a remembrance of this in his boyish and enthusiastic greeting of Mr. Oakhurst. He had started, he said, to go to Poker Flat to seek his fortune. "Alone?" No, not exactly alone; in fact—a giggle—he had run away with Piney Woods. Didn't Mr. Oakhurst remember Piney? She that used to wait on the table at the Temperance House? They had been engaged a long time, but old Jake Woods had objected, and so they had run away, and were going to Poker Flat to be married, and here they were. And they were tired out, and how lucky it was they had found a place to camp and company. All this the Innocent delivered rapidly, while Piney—a stout, comely damsel of fifteen—

emerged from behind the pine-tree, where she had been blushing unseen, and rode to the side of her lover.

Mr. Oakhurst seldom troubled himself with sentiment, still less with propriety; but he had a vague idea that the situation was not felicitous. He retained, however, his presence of mind sufficiently to kick Uncle Billy, who was about to say something, and Uncle Billy was sober enough to recognize in Mr. Oakhurst's kick a superior power that would not bear trifling. He then endeavored to dissuade Tom Simson from delaying further, but in vain. He even pointed out the fact that there was no provision, nor means of making a camp. But, unluckily, "The Innocent" met this objection by assuring the party that he was provided with an extra mule loaded with provisions, and by the discovery of a rude attempt at a log-house near the trail. "Piney can stay with Mrs. Oakhurst," said the Innocent, pointing to the Duchess, "and I can shift for myself."

Nothing but Mr. Oakhurst's admonishing foot saved Uncle Billy from bursting into a roar of laughter. As it was, he felt compelled to retire up the canon until he could recover his gravity. There he confided the joke to the tall pine trees, with many slaps of his leg, contortions of his face, and the usual profanity. But when he returned to the party, he found them seated by a fire—for the air had grown strangely chill and the sky overcast—in apparently amicable conversation. Piney was actually talking in an impulsive, girlish fashion to the Duchess, who was listening with an interest and animation she had not shown for many days. The Innocent was holding forth, apparently with equal effect, to Mr. Oakhurst and Mother Shipton, who was actually relaxing into amiability. "Is this yer a d—d picnic?" said Uncle Billy, with inward scorn, as he surveyed the sylvan group, the glancing fire-light, and the tethered animals in the foreground. Suddenly an idea mingled with the alcholic fumes that disturbed his brain. It was apparently of a jocular nature, for he felt impelled to slap his leg again and cram his fist into his mouth.

As the shadows crept slowly up the mountain, a slight breeze rocked the tops of the pine-trees, and moaned through their long and gloomy aisles. The ruined cabin, patched and covered with pine boughs, was set apart for the ladies. As the lovers parted, they unaffectedly exchanged a kiss, so honest and sincere that it might have been heard above the swaying pines. The frail Duchess and the malevolent Mother Shipton were probably too stunned to remark upon this last evidence of simplicity, and so turned without a word to the hut. The fire was replenished, the men lay down before the door, and in a few minutes were asleep.

Mr. Oakhurst was a light sleeper. Toward morning he awoke benumbed and cold. As he stirred the dying fire, the wind, which was now blowing strongly, brought to his cheek that which caused the blood to leave it—snow!

He started to his feet with the intention of awakening the sleepers, for there was no time to lose. But turning to where Uncle Billy had been lying, he found him gone. A suspicion leaped to his brain and a curse to his lips. He ran to the spot where the mules had been tethered; they were no longer there. The tracks were already rapidly disappearing in the snow.

The momentary excitement brought Mr. Oakhurst back to the fire with his usual calm. He did not waken the sleepers. The Innocent slumbered peacefully, with a smile on his good humored, freckled face; the virgin Piney slept beside her frailer sisters as sweetly as though attended by celestial guardians, and Mr. Oakhurst, drawing his blanket over his shoulders, stroked his mustachios and waited for the dawn. It came slowly in the whirling mist of snow-flakes, that dazzled and confused the eye. What could be seen of the landscape appeared magically changed. He looked over the valley, and summed up the present and future in two words—"Snowed in!"

A careful inventory of the provisions, which, fortunately for the party, had been stored within the hut, and so escaped the felonious fingers of Uncle Billy, disclosed the fact that with care and prudence they might last ten days longer. "That is," said Mr. Oakhurst, *sotto voce* to the Innocent, "if you're willing to board us. If you ain't—and perhaps you'd better not—you can wait till Uncle Billy gets back with provisions." For some occult reason, Mr. Oakhurst could not bring himself to disclose Uncle Billy's rascality, and so offered the hypothesis that he had wandered from the camp and had accidentally stampeded the animals. He dropped a warning to the Duchess and Mother Shipton, who of course knew the facts of their associate's defection. "They'll find out the truth about us *all*, when they find out anything," he added, significantly, "and there's no good frightening them now."

Tom Simson not only put all his worldly store at the disposal of Mr. Oakhurst, but seemed to enjoy the prospect of their enforced seclusion. "We'll have a good camp for a week, and then the snow'll melt, and we'll all go back together." The cheerful gayety of the young man and Mr. Oakhurst's calm infected the others. The Innocent, with the aid of pine boughs, extemporized a thatch for the roofless cabin, and the Duchess directed Piney in the rearrangement of the interior with a taste and tact that opened the blue eyes of that provincial maiden to their fullest extent.

"I reckon now you're used to fine things at Poker Flat," said Piney. The Duchess turned away sharply to conceal something that reddened her cheek through its professional tint, and Mother Shipton requested Piney not to "chatter." But when Mr. Oakhurst returned from a weary search for the trail, he heard the sound of happy laughter echoed from the rocks. He stopped in some alarm, and his thoughts first naturally reverted to the whiskey, which he had prudently *cached*. "And yet it don't somehow sound like whiskey," said the gambler. It was not until he caught sight of the blazing fire through the still blinding storm, and the group around it, that he settled to the conviction that it was "square fun."

Whether Mr. Oakhurst had *cached* his cards with the whiskey as something debarred the free access of the community, I cannot say. It was certain that, in Mother Shipton's words, he "didn't say cards once" during the evening. Haply the time was beguiled by an accordion, produced somewhat ostentatiously by Tom Simson, from his pack. Notwithstanding some difficulties attending the manipulation of this instrument, Piney Woods managed to pluck several reluctant melodies from its keys, to an accompaniment by the Innocent on a pair of bone castinets. But the crowning festivity of the evening was reached in a rude camp-meeting hymn, which the lovers, joining hands, sang with great earnestness and vociferation. I fear that a certain defiant tone and Covenanter's swing to its chorus, rather than any devotional quality, caused it speedily to infect the others, who at last joined in the refrain:

> I'm proud to live in the service of the Lord,
> And I'm bound to die in His army.

The pines rocked, the storm eddied and whirled above the miserable group, and the flames of their altar leaped heavenward, as if in token of the vow.

At midnight the storm abated, the rolling clouds parted, and the stars glittered keenly above the sleeping camp. Mr. Oakhurst, whose professional habits had enabled him to live on the smallest possible amount of sleep, in dividing the watch with Tom Simson, somehow managed to take upon himself the greater part of that duty. He excused himself to the Innocent, by saying that he had "often been a week without sleep." "Doing what?" asked Tom. "Poker!" replied Oakhurst, sententiously, "when a man gets a streak of luck—nigger-luck—he don't get tired. The luck gives in first. Luck," continued the gambler, reflectively, "is a mighty queer thing. All you know about it for certain is that it's bound to change. And it's finding out when it's going to change that makes you. We've had a streak of bad luck since we left Poker Flat—you come along, and slap you get into it, too. If you can hold your cards right along you're all right. For," added the gambler, with cheerful irrelevance,

> "I'm proud to live in the service of the Lord,
> And I'm bound to die in His army."

The third day came, and the sun, looking through the white-curtained valley, saw the outcasts divide their slowly decreasing store of provisions for the morning meal. It was one of the peculiarities of that mountain climate that its rays diffused a kindly warmth over the wintry landscape, as if in regretful commiseration of the past. But it revealed drift on drift of snow piled high around the hut; a hopeless, uncharted, trackless sea of white lying below the rocky shores to which the castaways still clung. Through the marvellously clear air, the smoke of the pastoral village of Poker Flat rose miles away. Mother Shipton saw it, and from a remote pinnacle of her rocky fastness, hurled in that direction a final malediction. It was her last vituperative attempt, and perhaps for that reason was invested with a certain degree of sublimity. It did her good, she privately informed the Duchess. "Just to go out there and cuss, and see." She then set herself to the task of amusing "the child," as she and the Duchess were pleased to call Piney. Piney was no chicken, but it was a soothing and ingenious theory of the pair thus to account for the fact that she didn't swear and wasn't improper.

When night crept up again through the gorges, the reedy notes of the accordion rose and fell in fitful spasms and long-drawn gasps by the flickering camp-fire. But music failed to fill entirely the aching void left by insufficient food, and a new diversion was proposed by Piney—story-telling. Neither Mr. Oakhurst nor his female companions caring to relate their personal experiences, this plan would have failed, too, but for The Innocent. Some months before he had chanced upon a stray copy of Mr. Pope's ingenious translation of the Iliad. He now proposed to narrate the principal incidents of that poem—having thoroughly mastered the argument and fairly forgotten the words—in the current vernacular of Sandy Bar. And so for the rest of that night the Homeric demigods again walked the earth. Trojan bully and wily Greek wrestled in the winds, and the great pines in the canon seemed to bow to the wrath of the son of Peleus. Mr. Oakhurst listened with quiet satisfaction. Most especially was he interested in the fate of "Ash-heels," as the Innocent persisted in denominating the "swift-footed Achilles."

So with small food and much of Homer and the accordion, a week passed over the heads of the outcasts. The sun again forsook them, and again from leaden skies the snow-flakes were sifted over the land. Day by day closer around them drew the snowy circle, until at last they looked from their prison over drifted walls of dazzling white, that towered twenty feet above their heads. It became more and more difficult to replenish their fires, even from the fallen trees beside them, now half-hidden in the drifts. And yet no one complained. The lovers turned from the dreary prospect and looked into each other's eyes, and were happy. Mr. Oakhurst settled himself coolly to the losing game before him. The Duchess, more cheerful than she had been, assumed the care of Piney. Only Mother Shipton—once the strongest of the party—seemed to sicken and fade. At midnight on the tenth day she called Oakhurst to her side. "I'm going," she said, in a voice of querulous weakness, "but don't say anything about it. Don't waken the kids. Take the bundle from under my head and open it." Mr. Oakhurst did so. It contained Mother Shipton's rations for the last week, untouched. "Give 'em to the child," she said, pointing to the sleeping Piney. "You've starved yourself," said the gambler. "That's what they call it," said the woman, querulously, as she lay down again, and, turning her face to the wall, passed quietly away.

The accordion and the bones were put aside that day, and Homer was forgotten. When the body of Mother Shipton had been committed to the snow, Mr. Oakhurst took The Innocent aside, and showed him a pair of snow-shoes, which he had fashioned from the old pack-saddle. "There's one chance in a hundred to save her yet," he said, pointing to Piney; "but it's there," he added, pointing toward Poker Flat. "If you can reach there in two days she's safe." "And you?" asked Tom Simson. "I'll stay here," was the curt reply.

The lovers parted with a long embrace. "You are not going, too?" said the Duchess, as she saw Mr. Oakhurst apparently waiting to accompany him. "As far as the canon," he replied. He turned suddenly, and kissed the Duchess, leaving her pallid face aflame, and her trembling limbs rigid with amazement.

Night came, but not Mr. Oakhurst. It brought the storm again and the whirling snow. Then the Duchess, feeding the fire, found that some one had quietly piled beside the hut enough fuel to last a few days longer. The tears rose to her eyes, but she hid them from Piney.

The women slept but little. In the morning, looking into each other's faces, they read their fate. Neither spoke; but Piney, accepting the position of the stronger, drew near and placed her arm around the Duchess's waist. They kept this attitude for the rest of the day. That night the storm reached its greatest fury, and, rending asunder the protecting pines, invaded the very hut.

Toward morning they found themselves unable to feed the fire, which gradually died away. As the embers slowly blackened, the Duchess crept closer to Piney, and broke the silence of many hours: "Piney, can you pray?" "No, dear," said Piney, simply. The Duchess, without knowing exactly why, felt relieved, and, putting her head upon Piney's shoulder, spoke no more. And so reclining, the younger and purer pillowing the head of her soiled sister upon her virgin breast, they fell asleep.

The wind lulled as if it feared to waken them. Feathery drifts of snow, shaken from the long pine boughs, flew like white-winged birds, and settled about them as they slept. The moon through the rifted clouds looked down upon what had been the camp. But all human stain, all trace of earthly travail, was hidden beneath the spotless mantle mercifully flung from above.

They slept all that day and the next, nor did they waken when voices and footsteps broke the silence of the camp. And when pitying fingers brushed the snow from their wan faces, you could scarcely have told from the equal peace that dwelt upon them, which was she that had sinned. Even the Law of Poker Flat recognized this, and turned away, leaving them still locked in each other's arms.

But at the head of the gulch, on one of the largest pine trees, they found the deuce of clubs pinned to the bark with a bowie knife. It bore the following, written in pencil, in a firm hand:

†

BENEATH THIS TREE
LIES THE BODY
OF
JOHN OAKHURST,
WHO STRUCK A STREAK OF BAD LUCK
ON THE 23D OF NOVEMBER, 1850,
AND
HANDED IN HIS CHECKS
ON THE 7TH OF DECEMBER, 1850.

✠

And pulseless and cold, with a Derringer by his side and a bullet in his heart, though still calm as in life, beneath the snow lay he who was at once the strongest and yet the weakest of the outcasts of Poker Flat.

THE CHRISTMAS WRECK *

BY FRANK STOCKTON

W ELL, sir," said old Silas, as he gave a preliminary
puff to the pipe he had just lighted, and so satisfied himself that the draught was all right, "the
wind's a-comin', an' so's Christmas. But it's no use bein'
in a hurry fur either of 'em, fur sometimes they come afore
you want 'em, anyway."

Silas was sitting in the stern of a small sailing-boat which
he owned, and in which he sometimes took the Sandport
visitors out for a sail; and at other times applied to its more
legitimate, but less profitable use, that of fishing. That
afternoon he had taken young Mr. Nugent for a brief excursion on that portion of the Atlantic Ocean which sends
its breakers up on the beach of Sandport. But he had found
it difficult, nay, impossible just now, to bring him back, for
the wind had gradually died away until there was not a
breath of it left. Mr. Nugent, to whom nautical experiences
were as new as the very nautical suit of blue flannel which
he wore, rather liked the calm; it was such a relief to the
monotony of rolling waves. He took out a cigar and lighted
it, and then he remarked:

"I can easily imagine how a wind might come before you
sailors might want it, but I don't see how Christmas could
come too soon."

"It come wunst on me when things couldn't 'a' looked more
onready fur it," said Silas.

"How was that?" asked Mr. Nugent, settling himself a
little more comfortably on the hard thwart. "If it's a story,
let's have it. This is a good time to spin a yarn."

---

* From "The Christmas Wreck and Other Stories," copyright, 1886,
by Charles Scribner's Sons. By permission of the publishers.

155

"Very well," said old Silas. "I'll spin her."

The bare-legged boy, whose duty it was to stay forward and mind the jib, came aft as soon as he smelt a story, and took a nautical position which was duly studied by Mr. Nugent, on a bag of ballast in the bottom of the boat.

"It's nigh on to fifteen year ago," said Silas, "that I was on the bark, *Mary Auguster,* bound for Sydney, New South Wales, with a cargo of canned goods. We was somewhere about longitood a hundred an' seventy, latitood nothin', an' it was the twenty-second o' December, when we was ketched by a reg'lar typhoon which blew straight along, end on, fur a day an' a half. It blew away the storm sails; it blew away every yard, spar, shroud, an' every strand o' riggin', an' snapped the masts off, close to the deck; it blew away all the boats; it blew away the cook's caboose, an' everything else on deck; it blew off the hatches, an' sent 'em spinnin' in the air, about a mile to leeward; an' afore it got through, it washed away the cap'n an' all the crew 'cept me an' two others. These was Tom Simmons, the second mate, an' Andy Boyle, a chap from the Andirondack Mountins, who'd never been to sea afore. As he was a landsman he ought, by rights, to 'a' been swep' off by the wind an' water, consid'rin' that the cap'n an' sixteen good seamen had gone a'ready. But he had hands eleven inches long, an' that give him a grip which no typhoon could git the better of. Andy had let out that his father was a miller up there in York State, an' a story had got round among the crew that his gran'father an' great gran'father was millers too; an' the way the fam'ly got such big hands come from their habit of scoopin' up a extry quart or two of meal or flour for themselves when they was levelin' off their customers' measures. He was a good-natered feller, though, an' never got riled when I'd tell him to clap his flour-scoops onter a halyard.

"We was all soaked, an' washed, an' beat, an' battered. We held on some way or other till the wind blowed itself out, an' then we got on our legs an' began to look about us to see how things stood. The sea had washed into the open hatches till the vessel was more'n half full of water, an' that had sunk her so deep that she must 'a looked like a canal boat loaded with gravel. We hadn't had a thing to eat or drink durin' that whole blow, an' we was pretty ravenous. We found a keg of water which was all right, and a box of biscuit, which was what you might call soft tack, for they was soaked through and through with sea-water. We eat a lot of them so, fur we couldn't wait, an' the rest we spread on the deck to dry, fur the sun was now shinin' hot enough to bake bread. We couldn't go below much, fur there was a pretty good swell on the sea, and things was floatin' about so's to make it dangerous. But we fished out a piece of canvas, which we rigged up agin the stump of the mainmast so that we could have somethin' that we could sit down an' grumble under. What struck us all the hardest was that the bark was loaded with a whole cargo of jolly things to eat, which was just as good as ever they was, fur the water couldn't git through the tin cans in which they was all put up; an' here we was with nothin' to live on but them salted biscuit. There was no way of gittin' at any of the ship's stores, or any of the fancy prog, fur everythin' was stowed away tight under six or seven feet of water, an' pretty nigh all the room that was left between decks was filled up with extry spars, lumber boxes, an' other floatin' stuff. All was shiftin', an' bumpin', an' bangin' every time the vessel rolled.

"As I said afore, Tom was second mate, an' I was bo's'n. Says I to Tom, 'the thing we've got to do is to put up some kind of a spar with a rag on it for a distress flag, so that we'll lose no time bein' took off.' 'There's no use a-slavin' at anythin' like that,' says Tom, 'fur we've been blowed off the track of traders, an' the more we work the hungrier we'll git, an' the sooner will them biscuit be gone.'

"Now when I heerd Tom say this I sot still, and began to consider. Being second mate, Tom was, by rights, in command of this craft; but it was easy enough to see that if he commanded there'd never be nothin' for Andy an' me to do. All the grit he had in him he'd used up in holdin' on durin' that typhoon. What he wanted to do now was to make himself comfortable till the time come for him to go to Davy Jones's Locker; an' thinkin', most likely, that Davy couldn't make it any hotter fur him than it was on that deck, still in latitood nothin' at all, fur we'd been blowed along the line pretty nigh due west. So I calls to Andy, who was busy turnin' over the biscuits on the deck. 'Andy,' says I, when he had got under the canvas, 'we's goin' to have a 'lection fur skipper. Tom here is about played out. He's one candydate, an' I'm another. Now, who do you vote fur? An', mind yer eye, youngster, that you don't make no mistake.' 'I vote fur you,' says Andy. 'Carried unanermous!' says I. 'An' I want you to take notice that I'm cap'n of what's left of the *Mary Auguster,* an' you two has got to keep your minds on that, an' obey orders.' If Davy Jones was to do all that Tom Simmons said when he heard this, the old chap would be kept busier than he ever was yit. But I let him growl his growl out, knowin' he'd come round all right, fur there wasn't no help fur it, consid'rin' Andy an' me was two to his one. Pretty soon we all went to work, an' got up a spar from below which we rigged to the stump of the foremast, with Andy's shirt atop of it.

"Them sea-soaked, sun-dried biscuit was pretty mean prog, as you might think, but we eat so many of 'em that afternoon an' 'cordingly drank so much water that I was obliged to put us all on short rations the next day. 'This is the day before Christmas,' says Andy Boyle, 'an' to-night will be Christmas Eve, an' it's pretty tough fur us to be sittin' here with not even so much hard tack as we want, an' all the time thinkin' that the hold of this ship is packed full of the gayest kind of good things to eat.' 'Shut up about Christmas!' says Tom Simmons. 'Them two youngsters of mine, up in Bangor, is havin' their toes and noses pretty nigh froze, I 'spect, but they'll hang up their stockin's all the same to-night, never thinkin' that their dad's bein' cooked alive on an empty stomach.' 'Of course they wouldn't hang 'em up,' says I, 'if they knowed what a fix you was in, but they don't know it, an' what's the use of grumblin' at 'em for bein' a little jolly?' 'Well,' says Andy, 'they couldn't be more jollier than I'd be if I could git at some of them fancy fixin's down in the hold. I worked well on to a week at 'Frisco puttin' in them boxes, an' the names of the things was on the outside of most of 'em, an' I tell you what it is, mates, it made my mouth water, even then, to read 'em, an' I wasn't hungry nuther, havin' plenty to eat three times a day. There was roast beef, an' roast mutton, an' duck, an' chicken, an' soup, an' peas, an' beans, an' termaters, an' plum-puddin', an' mince-pie—' 'Shut up with your mince-pie!' sung out Tom Simmons. 'Isn't it enough to have to gnaw on these salt chips, without hearin' about mince-pie?' 'An' more'n that,' says Andy, 'there was canned peaches, an' pears, an' plums, an' cherries.'

"Now these things did sound so cool an' good to me on that broilin' deck, that I couldn't stand it, an' I leans over to Andy, an' I says: 'Now look-a here, if you don't shut up talkin' about them things what's stowed below, an' what we ᴄan't git at, nohow, overboard you go!' 'That would make you short-handed.' says Andy, with a grin. 'Which is more'n you could say,' says I, 'if you'd chuck Tom an' me over'—alludin' to his eleven-inch grip. Andy didn't say no more then, but after a while he comes to me as I was lookin' round to see if anything was in sight, an' says he, 'I s'pose you ain't got nuthin' to say again my divin' into the hold just aft of the foremast, where there seems to be a bit of pretty clear water, an' see if I can't git up something?' 'You kin do it, if you like,' says I, 'but it's at your own risk. You can't take out no insurance at this office.' 'All right then,' says Andy, 'an' if I git stove in by floatin' boxes, you an' Tom'll have to eat the rest of them salt crackers.' 'Now, boy,' says I—an' he wasn't much more, bein' only nineteen year old—'you'd better keep out o' that hold. You'll just git yourself smashed. An' as to movin' any of them there heavy boxes, which must be swelled up as tight as if they was part of the ship, you might as well try to pull out one of the *Mary Auguster's* ribs.' 'I'll try it,' says Andy, 'fur to-morrer is Christmas, an' if I kin help it I ain't goin' to be floatin' atop of a Christmas dinner without eatin' any on it.' I let him go, fur he was a good swimmer and diver, an' I did hope he might root out somethin' or other, fur Christmas is about the worst day in the year fur men to be starvin' on, and that's what we was a-comin' to.

"Well, fur about two hours Andy swum, an' dove, an' come up blubberin', an' dodged all sorts of floatin' an' pitchin' stuff, fur the swell was still on; but he couldn't even be so much as sartain that he'd found the canned vittles. To dive down through hatchways, an' among broken bulk-heads, to hunt fur any partiklar kind o' boxes under seven feet of sea-water, ain't no easy job; an' though Andy says he got hold of the end of a box that felt to him like the big 'uns he'd noticed as havin' the meat pies in, he couldn't move it no more'n if it had been the stump of the foremast. If we could have pumped the water out of the hold we could have got at any part of the cargo we wanted, but as it was, we couldn't even reach the ship's stores, which, of course, must have been mostly spiled anyway; whereas the canned vittles was just as good as new. The pumps was all smashed, or stopped up, for we tried 'em, but if they hadn't a-been we three couldn't never have pumped out that ship on three biscuit a day, and only about two days' rations at that.

"So Andy he come up, so fagged out that it was as much as he could do to get his clothes on, though they wasn't much, an' then he stretched himself out under the canvas an' went to sleep, an' it wasn't long afore he was talking about roast turkey an' cranberry sass, an' punkin pie, an' sech stuff, most of which we knowed was under our feet that present minute. Tom Simmons he just b'iled over, an' sung out: 'Roll him out in the sun and let him cook! I can't stand no more of this!' But I wasn't goin' to have Andy treated no sech way as that, fur if it hadn't been fur Tom Simmons' wife an' young uns, Andy'd been worth two of him to anybody who was consid'rin' savin' life. But I give the boy a good punch in the ribs to stop his dreamin', fur I was as hungry as Tom was, and couldn't stand no nonsense about Christmas dinners.

"It was a little arter noon when Andy woke up, an' he went outside to stretch himself. In about a minute he give a yell that made Tom and me jump. 'A sail!' he hollered, 'a sail!' An' you may bet your life, young man, that 'twasn't more'n half a second before us two had scuffled out from under that canvas, an' was standin' by Andy. 'There she

is!' he shouted, 'not a mile to win'ard.' I give one look,
an' then I sings out: 'Tain't a sail! It's a flag of distress!
Can't you see, you land-lubber, that that's the Stars and
Stripes upside down?' 'Why, so it is,' said Andy, with a
couple of reefs in the joyfulness of his voice. An' Tom, he
began to growl as if somebody had cheated him out of half
a year's wages.

"The flag that we saw was on the hull of a steamer that
had been driftin' down on us while we was sittin' under our
canvas. It was plain to see she'd been caught in the typhoon
too, fur there wasn't a mast or a smoke stack on her; but her
hull was high enough out of the water to catch what wind
there was, while we was so low-sunk that we didn't make no
way at all. There was people aboard, and they saw us, an'
waved their hats an' arms, an' Andy an' me waved ours, but
all we could do was to wait till they drifted nearer, fur we
hadn't no boats to go to 'em if we'd 'a' wanted to.

" 'I'd like to know what good that old hulk is to us,' said
Tom Simmons. 'She can't take us off.' It did look to me
somethin' like the blind leadin' the blind; but Andy sings
out: 'We'd be better off aboard of her, fur she ain't water-
logged, an,' more'n that, I don't s'pose her stores are all
soaked up in salt water.' There was some sense in that, and
when the steamer had got to within half a mile of us, we was
glad to see a boat put out from her with three men in it.
It was a queer boat, very low, an' flat, an' not like any ship's
boat I ever see. But the two fellers at the oars pulled stiddy,
an' pretty soon the boat was 'longside of us, an' the three
men on our deck. One of 'em was the first mate of the other
wreck, an' when he found out what was the matter with us,
he spun his yarn, which was a longer one than ours. His
vessel was the *Water Crescent,* nine hundred tons, from
'Frisco to Melbourne, and they had sailed about six weeks
afore we did. They was about two weeks out when some of
their machinery broke down, an' when they got it patched
up it broke agin' worse than afore, so that they couldn't do
nothin' with it. They kep' along under sail for about a
month, makin' mighty poor headway till the typhoon struck
'em, an' that cleaned their decks off about as slick as it did

ours, but their hatches wasn't blowed off, an' they didn't ship no water wuth mentionin', an' the crew havin' kep' below, none on 'em was lost. But now they was clean out of provisions and water, havin' been short when the break-down happened, fur they had sold all the stores they could spare to a French brig in distress that they overhauled when about a week out. When they sighted us they felt pretty sure they'd git some provisions out of us. But when I told the mate what a fix we was in his jaw dropped till his face was as long as one of Andy's hands. Howsomdever he said he'd send the boat back fur as many men as it could bring over, and see if they couldn't get up some of our stores. Even if they was soaked with salt water, they'd be better than nothin'. Part of the cargo of the *Water Crescent* was tools an' things fur some railway contractors out in Australier, an' the mate told the men to bring over some of them irons that might be used to fish out the stores. All their ship's boats had been blowed away, an' the one they had was a kind of shore boat for fresh water, that had been shipped as part of the cargo, an' stowed below. It couldn't stand no kind of a sea, but there wasn't nothin' but a swell on; an' when it came back it had the cap'n in it, an' five men, besides a lot of chains an' tools.

"Them fellers an' us worked pretty nigh the rest of the day, an' we got out a couple of bar'ls of water, which was all right, havin' been tight bunged; an' a lot of sea biscuit, all soaked an' sloppy, but we only got a half bar'l of meat, though three or four of the men stripped an' dove for more'n an hour. We cut up some of the meat, an' eat it raw, an' the cap'n sent some over to the other wreck, which had drifted past us to leeward, an' would have gone clean away from us if the cap'n hadn't had a line got out an' made us fast to it while we was workin' at the stores.

"That night the cap'n took us three, as well as the provisions we'd got out, on board his hull, where the 'commodations was consid'able better than they was on the half-sunk 'Mary Auguster.' An' afore we turned in he took me aft, an' had a talk with me as commandin' off'cer of my vessel. 'That wreck o' yourn,' says he, 'has got a vallyble cargo in it, which

isn't spiled by bein' under water. Now, if you could get
that cargo into port it would put a lot of money in your
pocket, fur the owners couldn't git out of payin' you fur
takin' charge of it, an' havin' it brung in. Now I'll tell you
what I'll do. I'll lie by you, an' I've got carpenters aboard
that'll put your pumps in order, an' I'll set my men to work
to pump out your vessel. An' then, when she's afloat all
right, I'll go to work agin at my vessel, which I didn't s'pose
there was any use o' doin'; but whilst I was huntin' round
amongst our cargo to-day I found that some of the machinery we carried might be worked up so's to take the place
of what is broke in our engin'. We've got a forge aboard an'
I believe we can make these pieces of machinery fit, an' git
goin' agin. Then I'll tow you into Sydney, an' we'll divide
the salvage money. I won't git nothin' for savin' my vessel,
coz that's my bizness; but you wasn't cap'n o' yourn, an'
took charge of her a purpose to save her, which is another
thing.'

"I wasn't at all sure that I didn't take charge of the
'Mary Auguster' to save myself an' not the vessel, but I didn't
mention that, an' asked the cap'n how he expected to live all
this time. 'Oh, we kin git at your stores easy enough,' says
he, 'when the water's pumped out.' 'They'll be mostly spiled,'
says I. 'That don't matter,' says he, 'men'll eat anythin',
when they can't git nothin' else.' An' with that he left me
to think it over.

"I must say, young man, an' you kin b'lieve me if you
know anythin' about sech things, that the idee of a pile of
money was mighty temptin' to a feller like me, who had a girl
at home ready to marry him, and who would like nothin'
better'n to have a little house of his own, an' a little vessel of
his own, an' give up the other side of the world altogether.
But while I was goin' over all this in my mind, an' wonderin' if the cap'n ever could git us into port, along comes
Andy Boyle, and sits down beside me. 'It drives me pretty
nigh crazy,' says he, 'to think that to-morrer's Christmas, an'
we've got to feed on that sloppy stuff we fished out of our
stores, an' not much of it nuther, while there's all that roast
turkey, an' plum-puddin', an' mince-pie, a-floatin' out there

just before our eyes, an' we can't have none of it.' 'You hadn't oughter think so much about eatin', Andy!' says I, 'but if I was talkin' about them things I wouldn't leave out canned peaches. By George! Of a hot Christmas like this is goin' to be, I'd be the jolliest Jack on the ocean if I could git at that canned fruit.' 'Well, there's a way,' says Andy, 'that we might git some of 'em. A part of the cargo of this ship is stuff for blastin' rocks; catridges, 'lectric bat'ries, an' that sort of thing; an' there's a man aboard who's goin' out to take charge of 'em. I've been talkin' to this bat'ry man, an' I've made up my mind it'll be easy enough to lower a little catridge down among our cargo, an' blow out a part of it.' 'What ud be the good of it,' says I, 'blowed into chips?' 'It might smash some,' he said, 'but others would be only loosened, an' they'd float up to the top, where we could get 'em, 'specially them as was packed with pies, which must be pretty light.' 'Git out, Andy,' says I, 'with all that stuff!' An' he got out.

"But the idees he'd put into my head didn't git out, an' as I laid on my back on the deck, lookin' up at the stars, they sometimes seemed to put themselves into the shape of little houses, with a little woman cookin' at the kitchen fire, an' a little schooner layin' at anchor just off shore; an' then agin they'd hump themselves up till they looked like a lot of new tin cans with their tops off, an' all kinds of good things to eat inside, specially canned peaches—the big white kind—soft an' cool, each one split in half, with a holler in the middle filled with juice. By George, sir, the very thought of a tin can like that made me beat my heels agin the deck. I'd been mighty hungry, an' had eat a lot of salt pork, wet an' raw, an' now the very idee of it, even cooked, turned my stomach. I looked up to the stars agin, an' the little house an' the little schooner was clean gone, an' the whole sky was filled with nothin' but bright new tin cans.

"In the mornin', Andy, he come to me agin. 'Have you made up your mind,' says he, 'about gittin' some of them good things for Christmas dinner?' 'Confound you!' says I, 'you talk as if all we had to do was to go an' git 'em.' 'An' that's what I b'lieve we kin do,' says he, 'with the help of that bat'ry man.' 'Yes,' says I, 'an' blow a lot of the cargo into flinders, an' damage the "Mary Auguster" so's she couldn't never be took into port.' An' then I told him what the cap'n had said to me, an' what I was goin' to do with the money. 'A little catridge,' says Andy, 'would do all we want, an' wouldn't hurt the vessel nuther. Besides that, I don't b'lieve what this cap'n says about tinkerin' up his engin'. Tain't likely he'll ever git her runnin' agin, nor pump out the "Mary Auguster" nuther. If I was you I'd a durned sight ruther have a Christmas dinner in hand than a house an' wife in the bush.' 'I ain't thinkin' o' marryin' a girl in Australier,' says I. An' Andy he grinned, an' said I wouldn't marry nobody if I had to live on spiled vittles till I got her.

"A little after that I went to the cap'n, an' I told him about Andy's idea, but he was down on it. 'It's your vessel, an' not mine,' says he, 'an' if you want to try to git a dinner out of her I'll not stand in your way. But it's my 'pinion you'll just damage the ship, an' do nothin'.' Howsomdever I talked to the bat'ry man about it, an' he thought it could be done, an' not hurt the ship nuther. The men was all in favor of it, for none of 'em had forgot it was Christmas day. But Tom Simmons, he was agin it strong, for he was thinkin' he'd git some of the money if we got the 'Mary Auguster' into port. He was a selfish-minded man, was Tom, but it was his nater, an' I s'pose he couldn't help it.

"Well, it wasn't long before I began to feel pretty empty, an' mean, an' if I'd a wanted any of the prog we got out the day afore, I couldn't have found much, for the men had eat it up nearly all in the night. An' so, I just made up my mind without any more foolin', an' me, and Andy Boyle, an' the bat'ry man, with some catridges an' a coil of wire, got into the little shore boat, and pulled over to the 'Mary Auguster.' There we lowered a small catridge down the main hatch-way, an' let it rest down among the cargo. Then we rowed back to the steamer, uncoilin' the wire as we went. The bat'ry man clumb up on deck, an' fixed his wire to a 'lectric machine, which he'd got all ready afore we started. Andy and me didn't git out of the boat; we had too much sense for that, with all them hungry fellers waitin' to jump in her; but we just pushed a little off, an' sot waitin', with our mouths a waterin', for him to touch her off. He seemed to be a long time about it, but at last he did it, an' that instant there was a bang on board the 'Mary Auguster' that made my heart jump. Andy an' me pulled fur her like mad, the others a-hollerin' after us, an' we was on deck in no time. The deck was all covered with the water that had been throwed up; but I tell you, sir, that we poked an' fished about, an' Andy stripped an' went down, an' swum all round, an' we couldn't find one floatin' box of canned goods. There was a lot of splinters, but where they come from we didn't know. By this time my dander was up, an' I just pitched around savage. That little catridge wasn't no good, an' I didn't intend to stand any more foolin'. We just rowed back to the other wreck, an' I called to the bat'ry man to come down, an' bring some bigger catridges with him, fur if we was goin' to do anythin' we might as well do it right. So he got down with a package of bigger ones, an' jumped into the boat. The cap'n he called out to us to be keerful, an' Tom Simmons leaned over the rail, an' swored, but I didn't pay no 'tension to nuther of 'em, an' we pulled away.

"When I got aboard the *Mary Auguster* I says to the bat'ry man: 'We don't want no nonsense this time, an' I want you to put in enough catridges to heave up somethin' that'll do fur a Christmas dinner. I don't know how the cargo is stored, but you kin put one big catridge 'midship, another for'ard, an' another aft, an' one or nuther of 'em oughter fetch up somethin'.' Well, we got the three catridges into place. They was a good deal bigger than the one we first used, an' we j'ined 'em all to one wire, an' then we rowed back, carryin' the long wire with us. When we reached the steamer, me an' Andy was a goin' to stay in the boat as we did afore, but the cap'n sung out that he wouldn't allow the bat'ry to be touched off till we come aboard. 'Ther's got to be fair play,' says he. 'It's your vittles, but it's my side that's doin' the work. After we've blasted her this time you two can go in the boat, an' see what there is to get hold of, but two of my men must go along.' So me an' Andy had to go on deck, an' two big fellers was detailed to go with us in the little boat when the time come; an' then the bat'ry man, he teched her off.

"Well, sir, the pop that followed that tech was somethin' to remember. It shuck the water, it shuck the air, an' it shuck the hull we was on. A reg'lar cloud of smoke, an' flyin' bits of things rose up out of the *Mary Auguster*. An' when that smoke cleared away, an' the water was all bilin' with the splash of various sized hunks that come rainin' down from the sky, what was left of the *Mary Auguster* was sprinkled over the sea like a wooden carpet for water birds to walk on.

"Some of the men sung out one thing, an' some another, an' I could hear Tom Simmons swear, but Andy an' me said never a word, but scuttled down into the boat, follered close by the two men who was to go with us. Then we rowed like devils for the lot of stuff that was bobbin' about on the water, out where the *Mary Auguster* had been. In we went, among the floatin' spars and ship's timbers, I keepin' the things off with an oar, the two men rowin', an' Andy in the bow.

"Suddenly Andy give a yell, an' then he reached himself for'ard with sech a bounce that I thought he'd go overboard. But up he come in a minnit, his two 'leven-inch hands gripped round a box. He sot down in the bottom of the boat with the box on his lap, an' his eyes screwed on some letters that was stamped on one end. 'Pidjin pies!' he sings out. 'Tain't turkeys, nor 'tain't cranberries. But, by the Lord Harry, it's Christmas pies all the same!' After that Andy didn't do no more work but sot holdin' that box as if it had been his fust baby. But we kep' pushin' on to see what else there was. It's my 'pinion that the biggest part of that bark's cargo was blown into mince meat, an' the most of the rest of it was so heavy that it sunk. But it wasn't all busted up, an' it didn't all sink. There was a big piece of wreck with a lot of boxes stove into the timbers, and some of these had in 'em beef ready biled an' packed into cans, an' there was other kinds of meat, an' dif'rent sorts of vegetables, an' one box of turtle soup. I look at every one of 'em as we took 'em in, an' when we got the little boat pretty well loaded I wanted to still keep on searchin', but the men, they said that shore boat ud sink if we took in any more cargo, an' so we put back, I feelin' glummer'n I oughter felt, fur I had begun to be afeared that canned fruit, such as peaches, was heavy, an' li'ble to sink.

"As soon as we had got our boxes aboard, four fresh men put out in the boat, an' after awhile they come back with another load; an' I was mighty keerful to read the names on all the boxes. Some was meat pies, an' some was salmon, an' some was potted herrin's an' some was lobsters. But nary a thing could I see that ever had growed on a tree.

"Well, sir, there was three loads brought in, altogether, an' the Christmas dinner we had on the for'ard deck of that steamer's hull was about the jolliest one that was ever seen of a hot day aboard of a wreck in the Pacific Ocean. The cap'n kept good order, an' when all was ready the tops was jerked off the boxes, and each man grabbed a can an' opened it with his knife. When he had cleaned it out, he tuk another without doin' much questionin' as to the bill of fare. Whether anybody got pidjin pie 'cept Andy, I can't say, but the way we piled in Delmoniker prog would 'a' made people open their eyes as was eatin' their Christmas dinners on shore that day. Some of the things would 'a' been better, cooked a little more, or het up, but we was too fearful hungry to wait for that, an' they was tip-top as they was.

"The cap'n went out afterwards, an' towed in a couple of bar'ls of flour that was only part soaked through, an' he got some other plain prog that would do fur futur use; but none of us give our minds to stuff like this arter the glorious Christmas dinner that we'd quarried out of the 'Mary Auguster.' Every man that wasn't on duty went below, and turned in for a snooze. All 'cept me, an' I didn't feel just altogether satisfied. To be sure I'd had an A 1 dinner, an' though a little mixed, I'd never eat a jollier one on any Christmas that I kin look back at. But, fur all that, there was a hanker inside o' me. I hadn't got all I'd laid out to git, when we teched off the *Mary Auguster*. The day was blazin' hot, an' a lot of the things I'd eat was pretty peppery. 'Now,' thinks I, 'if there had a-been just one can o' peaches sech as

I see shinin' in the stars last night,' an' just then, as I was
walkin' aft, all by myself, I seed lodged on the stump of the
mizzenmast, a box with one corner druv down among the
splinters. It was half split open, an' I could see the tin cans
shinin' through the crack. I give one jump at it, an'
wrenched the side off. On the top of the first can I seed was
a picture of a big white peach with green leaves. That box
had been blowed up so high that if it had come down anywhere 'cept among them splinters it would a smashed itself
to flinders, or killed somebody. So fur as I know, it was the
only thing that fell nigh us, an' by George, sir, I got it!
Then we went aft, an' eat some more. 'Well,' says Andy, as
we was a-eatin', 'how d'ye feel now about blowin' up your
wife, an' your house, an' that little schooner you was goin'
to own?'

" 'Andy,' says I, 'this is the joyfulest Christmas I've had
yit, an' if I was to live till twenty hundred I don't b'lieve
I'd have no joyfuller, with things comin' in so pat, so don't
you throw no shadders.'

" 'Shadders,' says Andy, 'that ain't me. I leave that sort
of thing fur Tom Simmons.'

" 'Shadders is cool,' says I, 'an' I kin go to sleep under
all he throws.'

"Well, sir," continued old Silas, putting his hand on the
tiller and turning his face seaward, "if Tom Simmons had
kept command of that wreck, we all would 'a' laid there an'
waited an' waited till some of us was starved, an' the others
got nothin' fur it, fur the cap'n never mended his engin', an'
it was more'n a week afore we was took off, an' then it was
by a sailin' vessel, which left the hull of the *Water Crescent*
behind her, just as she would 'a' had to leave the *Mary
Auguster* if that jolly old Christmas wreck had a-been there.

"An' now sir," said Silas, "d'ye see that stretch o' little
ripples over yander, lookin' as if it was a lot o' herrin' turnin'
over to dry their sides? Do you know what that is? That's
the supper wind. That means coffee, an' hot cakes, an' a
bit of br'iled fish, an' pertaters, an' p'raps—if the old woman
feels in a partiklar good humor—some canned peaches, big
white uns, cut in half, with a holler place in the middle filled
with cool, sweet juice."

a very weak story.
Clever, however.

THE MISSION OF JANE *

By Edith Wharton

I

LETHBURY, surveying his wife across the dinner table,
found his transient glance arrested by an indefinable
change in her appearance.

"How smart you look! Is that a new gown?" he asked.

Her answering look seemed to deprecate his charging her
with the extravagance of wasting a new gown on him, and
he now perceived that the change lay deeper than any accident of dress. At the same time, he noticed that she betrayed her consciousness of it by a delicate, almost frightened
blush. It was one of the compensations of Mrs. Lethbury's
protracted childishness that she still blushed as prettily as
at eighteen. Her body had been privileged not to outstrip
her mind, and the two, as it seemed to Lethbury, were destined to travel together through an eternity of girlishness.

"I don't know what you mean," she said.

Since she never did, he always wondered at her bringing this out as a fresh grievance against him; but his wonder
was unresentful, and he said good-humoredly: "You sparkle
so that I thought you had on your diamonds."

She sighed and blushed again.

"It must be," he continued, "that you've been to a dressmaker's opening. You're absolutely brimming with illicit
enjoyment."

She stared again, this time at the adjective. His adjec-
tives always embarrassed her: their unintelligibleness sav-
oured of impropriety.

"In short," he summed up, "you've been doing something that you're thoroughly ashamed of."

To his surprise she retorted: "I don't see why I should be ashamed of it!"

Lethbury leaned back with a smile of enjoyment. When there was nothing better going he always liked to listen to her explanations.

"Well—?" he said.

She was becoming breathless and ejaculatory. "Of course you'll laugh—you laugh at everything!"

"That rather blunts the point of my derision, doesn't it?" he interjected; but she pushed on without noticing:

"It's so easy to laugh at things."

"Ah," murmured Lethbury with relish, "that's Aunt Sophronia's, isn't it?"

Most of his wife's opinions were heirlooms, and he took a quaint pleasure in tracing their descent. She was proud of their age, and saw no reason for discarding them while they were still serviceable. Some, of course, were so fine that she kept them for state occasions, like her great-grandmother's Crown Derby; but from the lady known as Aunt Sophronia she had inherited a stout set of every-day prejudices that were practically as good as new; whereas her husband's, as she noticed, were always having to be replaced. In the early days she had fancied there might be a certain satisfaction in taxing him with the fact; but she had long since been silenced by the reply: "My dear, I'm not a rich man, but I never use an opinion twice if I can help it."

She was reduced, therefore, to dwelling on his moral deficiencies; and one of the most obvious of these was his refusal to take things seriously. On this occasion, however, some ulterior purpose kept her from taking up his taunt.

"I'm not in the least ashamed!" she repeated, with the air of shaking a banner to the wind; but the domestic atmosphere being calm, the banner drooped unheroically.

"That," said Lethbury judicially, "encourages me to infer that you ought to be, and that, consequently, you've been giving yourself the unusual pleasure of doing something I shouldn't approve of."

She met this with an almost solemn directness. "No," she said. "You won't approve of it. I've allowed for that."

"Ah," he exclaimed, setting down his liqueur-glass. "You've worked out the whole problem, eh?"

"I believe so."

"That's uncommonly interesting. And what is it?"

She looked at him quietly. "A baby."

If it was seldom given her to surprise him, she had attained the distinction for once.

"A baby?"

"Yes."

"A—human baby?"

"Of course!" she cried, with the virtuous resentment of the woman who has never allowed dogs in the house.

Lethbury's puzzled stare broke into a fresh smile. "A baby I shan't approve of? Well, in the abstract I don't think much of them, I admit. Is this an abstract baby?"

Again she frowned at the adjective; but she had reached a pitch of exaltation at which such obstacles could not deter her.

"It's the loveliest baby—" she murmured.

"Ah, then it's concrete. It exists. In this harsh world it draws its breath in pain—"

"It's the healthiest child I ever saw!" she indignantly corrected.

"You've seen it, then?"

Again the accusing blush suffused her. "Yes—I've seen it."

"And to whom does the paragon belong?"

And here indeed she confounded him. "To me—I hope," she declared.

He pushed his chair back with an articulate murmur. "To *you*—?"

"To *us*," she corrected.

"Good Lord!" he said. If there had been the least hint of hallucination in her transparent gaze—but no; it was as clear, as shallow, as easily fathomable as when he had first suffered the sharp surprise of striking bottom in it.

It occurred to him that perhaps she was trying to be funny:

he knew that there is nothing more cryptic than the humor of the unhumorous.

"Is it a joke?" he faltered.

"Oh, I hope not. I want it so much to be a reality—"

He paused to smile at the limitations of a world in which jokes were not realities, and continued gently: "But since it is one already—"

"To us, I mean: to you and me. I want—" her voice wavered, and her eyes with it. "I have always wanted so dreadfully . . . it has been such a disappointment . . . not to . . ."

"I see," said Lethbury slowly.

But he had not seen before. It seemed curious now that he had never thought of her taking it in that way, had never surmised any hidden depths beneath her outspread obviousness. He felt as though he had touched a secret spring in her mind.

There was a moment's silence, moist and tremulous on her part, awkward and slightly irritated on his.

"You've been lonely, I suppose?" he began. It was odd, having suddenly to reckon with the stranger who gazed at him out of her trivial eyes.

"At times," she said.

"I'm sorry."

"It was not your fault. A man has so many occupations; and women who are clever—or very handsome—I suppose that's an occupation too. Sometimes I've felt that when dinner was ordered I had nothing to do till the next day."

"Oh," he groaned.

"It wasn't your fault," she insisted. "I never told you— but when I chose that rose-bud paper for the front-room upstairs, I always thought—"

"Well—?"

"It would be such a pretty paper—for a baby—to wake up in. That was years ago, of course; but it was rather an expensive paper . . . and it hasn't faded in the least . . ." she broke off incoherently.

"It hasn't faded?"

"No—and so I thought . . . as we don't use the room

for anything . . . now that Aunt Sophronia is dead . . . I thought I might . . . you might . . . oh, Julian, if you could only have seen it just waking up in its crib!"

"Seen what—where? You haven't got a baby upstairs?"

"Oh, no—not yet," she said, with her rare laugh—the girlish bubbling of merriment that had seemed one of her chief graces in the early days. It occurred to him that he had not given her enough things to laugh about lately. But then she needed such very elementary things: she was as difficult to amuse as a savage. He concluded that he was not sufficiently simple.

"Alice," he said almost solemnly, "what *do* you mean?"

She hesitated a moment: he saw her gather her courage for a supreme effort. Then she said slowly, gravely, as though she were pronouncing a sacramental phrase:

"I'm so lonely without a little child—and I thought perhaps you'd let me adopt one . . . It's at the hospital . . . its mother is dead . . . and I could . . . pet it, and dress it, and do things for it . . . and it's such a good baby . . . you can ask any of the nurses . . . it would never, never bother you by crying . . ."

II

Lethbury accompanied his wife to the hospital in a mood of chastened wonder. It did not occur to him to oppose her wish. He knew, of course, that he would have to bear the brunt of the situation: the jokes at the club, the enquiries, the explanations. He saw himself in the comic role of the adopted father and welcomed it as an expiation. For in his rapid reconstruction of the past he found himself cutting a shabbier figure than he cared to admit. He had always been intolerant of stupid people, and it was his punishment to be convicted of stupidity. As his mind traversed the years between his marriage and this unexpected assumption of paternity, he saw, in the light of an overheated imagination, many signs of unwonted crassness. It was not that he had ceased to think his wife stupid: she *was* stupid, limited, inflexible; but there was a pathos in the struggles of her swaddled mind, in its blind reachings toward the primal emotions. He had always thought she would have been happier with a child; but he had thought it mechanically, because it had so often been thought before, because it was in the nature of things to think it of every woman, because his wife was so eminently one of a species that she fitted into all the generalizations of the sex. But he had regarded this generalization as merely typical of the triumph of tradition over experience. Maternity was no doubt the supreme function of primitive woman, the one end to which her whole organism tended; but the law of increasing complexity had operated in both sexes, and he had not seriously supposed that, outside the world of Christmas fiction and anecdotic art, such truisms had any special hold on the feminine imagination. Now he saw that the arts in question were kept alive by the vitality of the sentiments they appealed to.

Lethbury was in fact going through a rapid process of readjustment. His marriage had been a failure, but he had preserved toward his wife the exact fidelity of act that is sometimes supposed to excuse any divagation of feeling; so that, for years, the tie between them had consisted mainly in his abstaining from making love to other women. The abstention had not always been easy, for the world is surprisingly well-stocked with the kind of woman one ought to have married but did not; and Lethbury had not escaped the solicitation of such alternatives. His immunity had been purchased at the cost of taking refuge in the somewhat rarefied atmosphere of his perceptions; and his world being thus limited, he had given unusual care to its details, compensating himself for the narrowness of his horizon by the minute finish of his foreground. It was a world of fine shadings and the nicest proportions, where impulse seldom set a blundering foot, and the feast of reason was undisturbed by an intemperate flow of soul. To such a banquet his wife naturally remained uninvited. The diet would have disagreed with her, and she would probably have objected to the other guests. But Lethbury, miscalculating her needs, had hitherto supposed that he had made ample provision for them, and was consequently at liberty to enjoy his own fare without any reproach of mendicancy at his gates. Now he beheld her pressing a starved face against the windows of his life, and in his imaginative reaction he invested her with a pathos borrowed from the sense of his own shortcomings.

In the hospital the imaginative process continued with increasing force. He looked at his wife with new eyes. Formerly she had been to him a mere bundle of negations, a labyrinth of dead walls and bolted doors. There was nothing behind the walls, and the doors led no whither: he had sounded and listened often enough to be sure of that. Now he felt like a traveler who, exploring some ancient ruin, comes on an inner cell, intact amid the general dilapidation, and painted with images which reveal the forgotten uses of the building.

His wife stood by a white crib in one of the wards. In the crib lay a child, a year old, the nurse affirmed, but to Lethbury's eye a mere dateless fragment of humanity projected against a background of conjecture. Over this anonymous particle of life Mrs. Lethbury leaned, such ecstasy reflected in her face as strikes up, in Correggio's *Night-piece,* from the child's body to the mother's countenance. It was a light that irradiated and dazzled her. She looked up at an enquiry of Lethbury's, but as their glances met he perceived that she no longer saw him, that he had become as invisible to her as she had long been to him. He had to transfer his question to the nurse.

"What is the child's name?" he asked.

"We call her Jane," said the nurse.

III

Lethbury, at first, had resisted the idea of a legal adoption; but when he found that his wife could not be brought to regard the child as hers till it had been made so by process of law, he promptly withdrew his objection. On one point only he remained inflexible; and that was the changing of the waif's name. Mrs. Lethbury, almost at once, had expressed a wish to rechristen it: she fluctuated between Muriel and Gladys, deferring the moment of decision like a lady wavering between two bonnets. But Lethbury was unyielding. In the general surrender of his prejudices this one alone held out.

"But Jane is so dreadful," Mrs. Lethbury protested.

"Well, we don't know that *she* won't be dreadful. She may grow up a Jane."

His wife exclaimed reproachfully. "The nurse says she's the loveliest—"

"Don't they always say that?" asked Lethbury patiently. He was prepared to be inexhaustibly patient now that he had reached a firm foothold of opposition.

"It's cruel to call her Jane," Mrs. Lethbury pleaded.

"It's ridiculous to call her Muriel."

"The nurse is *sure* she must be a lady's child."

Lethbury winced: he had tried, all along, to keep his mind off the question of antecedents.

"Well, let her prove it," he said, with a rising sense of exasperation. He wondered how he could ever have allowed himself to be drawn into such a ridiculous business; for the first time he felt the fully irony of it. He had visions of coming home in the afternoon to a house smelling of linseed and paregoric, and of being greeted by a chronic howl as he went up-stairs to dress for dinner. He had never been a club-man, but he saw himself becoming one now.

The worst of his anticipations were unfulfilled. The baby was surprisingly well and surprisingly quiet. Such infantile remedies as she absorbed were not potent enough to be perceived beyond the nursery; and when Lethbury could be induced to enter that sanctuary, there was nothing to jar his nerves in the mild pink presence of his adopted daughter. Jars there were, indeed: they were probably inevitable in the disturbed routine of the household; but they occurred between Mrs. Lethbury and the nurses, and Jane contributed to them only a placid stare which might have served as a rebuke to the combatants.

In the reaction from his first impulse of atonement, Lethbury noted with sharpened perceptions the effect of the change on his wife's character. He saw already the error of supposing that it could work any transformation in her. It simply magnified her existing qualities. She was like a dried sponge put in water: she expanded, but she did not change her shape. From the stand-point of scientific observation it was curious to see how her stored instincts responded to the pseudo-maternal call. She overflowed with the petty maxims of the occasion. One felt in her the epitome, the consummation, of centuries of animal maternity, so that this little woman, who screamed at a mouse and was nervous about burglars, came to typify the cave-mother rending her prey for her young.

It was less easy to regard philosophically the practical effects of her borrowed motherhood. Lethbury found with surprise that she was becoming assertive and definite. She no longer represented the negative side of his life; she showed, indeed, a tendency to inconvenient affirmations. She had gradually expanded her assumption of motherhood till it included his own share in the relation, and he suddenly found himself regarded as the father of Jane. This was a contingency he had not forseen, and it took all his philosophy to accept it; but there were moments of compensation. For Mrs. Lethbury was undoubtedly happy for the first time in years; and the thought that he had tardily contributed to this end reconciled him to the irony of the means.

At first he was inclined to reproach himself for still viewing the situation from the outside, for remaining a spectator instead of a participant. He had been allured, for a moment, by the vision of several hands meeting over a cradle, as the whole body of domestic fiction bears witness to their doing; and the fact that no such conjunction took place he could explain only on the ground that it was a borrowed cradle. He did not dislike the little girl. She still remained to him a hypothetical presence, a query rather than a fact; but her nearness was not unpleasant, and there were moments when her tentative utterances, her groping steps, seemed to loosen the dry accretions enveloping his inner self. But even at such moments—moments which he invited and caressed—she did not bring him nearer to his wife. He now perceived that he had made a certain place in his life for Mrs. Lethbury, and that she no longer fitted into it. It was too late to enlarge the space, and so she overflowed and encroached. Lethbury struggled against the sense of submergence. He let down barrier after barrier, yielding privacy after privacy; but his wife's personality continued to dilate. She was no longer herself alone: she was herself and Jane. Gradually, in a monstrous fusion of identity, she became herself, himself and Jane; and instead of trying to adapt her to a spare crevice of his character, he found himself carelessly squeezed into the smallest compartment of the domestic economy.

IV

He continued to tell himself that he was satisfied if his wife was happy; and it was not till the child's tenth year that he felt a doubt of her happiness.

Jane had been a preternaturally good child. During the eight years of her adoption she had caused her foster-parents no anxiety beyond those connected with the usual succession of youthful diseases. But her unknown progenitors had given her a robust constitution, and she passed unperturbed through measles, chicken-pox and whooping-cough. If there was any suffering it was endured vicariously by Mrs. Lethbury, whose temperature rose and fell with the patient's, and who could not hear Jane sneeze without visions of a marble angel weeping over a broken column. But though Jane's prompt recoveries continued to belie such premonitions, though her existence continued to move forward on an even keel of good health and good conduct, Mrs. Lethbury's satisfaction showed no corresponding advance. Lethbury, at first, was disposed to add her disappointment to the long list of feminine inconsistencies with which the sententious observer of life builds up his favorable induction; but circumstances presently led him to take a kindlier view of the case.

Hitherto his wife had regarded him as a negligible factor in Jane's evolution. Beyond providing for his adopted daughter, and effacing himself before her, he was not expected to contribute to her well-being. But as time passed he appeared to his wife in a new light. It was he who was to educate Jane. In matters of the intellect, Mrs. Lethbury was the first to declare her deficiencies—to proclaim them, even, with a certain virtuous superiority. She said she did not pretend to be clever, and there was no denying the truth of the assertion. Now, however, she seemed less ready, not to own her limitations, but to glory in them. Confronted with the problem of Jane's instruction she stood in awe of the child.

"I have always been stupid, you know," she said to Lethbury with a new humility, "and I'm afraid I shan't know what is best for Jane. I'm sure she has a wonderfully good mind, and I should reproach myself if I didn't give her every opportunity." She looked at him helplessly. "You must tell me what ought to be done."

Lethbury was not unwilling to oblige her. Somewhere in his mental lumber-room there rusted a theory of education such as usually lingers among the impedimenta of the childless. He brought this out, refurbished it, and applied it to Jane. At first he thought his wife had not overrated the quality of the child's mind. Jane seemed extraordinarily intelligent. Her precocious definiteness of mind was encouraging to her inexperienced preceptor. She had no difficulty in fixing her attention, and he felt that every fact he imparted was being etched in metal. He helped his wife to engage the best teachers, and for a while continued to take an ex-official interest in his adopted daughter's studies. But gradually his interest waned. Jane's ideas did not increase with her acquisitions. Her young mind remained a mere receptacle for facts: a kind of cold-storage from which anything which had been put there could be taken out at a moment's notice, intact but congealed. She developed, moreover, an inordinate pride in the capacity of her mental storehouse, and a tendency to pelt her public with its contents. She was overheard to jeer at her nurse for not knowing when the Saxon Heptarchy had fallen, and she alternately dazzled and depressed Mrs. Lethbury by the wealth of her chronological allusions. She showed no interest in the significance of the facts she amassed: she simply collected dates as another child might have collected stamps or marbles. To her foster-mother she seemed a prodigy of wisdom; but Lethbury saw, with a secret movement of sympathy, how the aptitudes in which Mrs. Lethbury gloried were slowly estranging her from her child.

"She is getting too clever for me," his wife said to him, after one of Jane's historical flights, "but I am so glad that she will be a companion to you."

Lethbury groaned in spirit. He did not look forward to Jane's companionship. She was still a good little girl; but there was something automatic and formal in her goodness, as though it were a kind of moral calisthenics which she went through for the sake of showing her agility. An early consciousness of virtue had moreover constituted her the natural guardian and adviser of her elders. Before she was fifteen she had set about reforming the household. She took Mrs. Lethbury in hand first; then she extended her efforts to the servants, with consequences more disastrous to the domestic harmony; and lastly she applied herself to Lethbury. She proved to him by statistics that he smoked too much, and that it was injurious to the optic nerve to read in bed. She took him to task for not going to church more regularly, and pointed out to him the evils of desultory reading. She suggested that a regular course of study encourages mental concentration, and hinted that inconsecutiveness of thought is a sign of approaching age.

To her adopted mother her suggestions were equally pertinent. She instructed Mrs. Lethbury in an improved way of making beef stock, and called her attention to the unhygienic qualities of carpets. She poured out distracting facts about bacilli and vegetable mould, and demonstrated that curtains and picture-frames are a hot-bed of animal organisms. She learned by heart the nutritive ingredients of the principal articles of diet, and revolutionized the cuisine by an attempt to establish a scientific average between starch and phosphates. Four cooks left during this experiment, and Lethbury fell into the habit of dining at his club.

Once or twice, at the outset, he had tried to check Jane's ardor; but his efforts resulted only in hurting his wife's feelings. Jane remained impervious, and Mrs. Lethbury resented any attempt to protect her from her daughter. Lethbury saw that she was consoled for the sense of her own inferiority by the thought of what Jane's intellectual companionship must be to him; and he tried to keep up the illusion by enduring with what grace he might the blighting edification of Jane's discourse.

V

As Jane grew up he sometimes avenged himself by wondering if his wife was still sorry that they had not called her Muriel. Jane was not ugly; she developed, indeed, a kind of categorical prettiness which might have been a projection of her mind. She had a creditable collection of features, but one had to take an inventory of them to find out that she was good-looking. The fusing grace had been omitted.

Mrs. Lethbury took a touching pride in her daughter's first steps in the world. She expected Jane to take by her complexion those whom she did not capture by her learning. But Jane's rosy freshness did not work any perceptible ravages. Whether the young men guessed the axioms on her lips and detected the encyclopædia in her eye, or whether they simply found no intrinsic interest in these features, certain it is, that, in spite of her mother's heroic efforts, and of incessant calls on Lethbury's purse, Jane, at the end of her first season, had dropped hopelessly out of the running. A few duller girls found her interesting, and one or two young men came to the house with the object of meeting other young women; but she was rapidly becoming one of the social supernumeraries who are asked out only because they are on people's lists.

The blow was bitter to Mrs. Lethbury; but she consoled herself with the idea that Jane had failed because she was too clever. Jane probably shared this conviction; at all events she betrayed no consciousness of failure. She had developed a pronounced taste for society, and went out, unweariedly and obstinately, winter after winter, while Mrs. Lethbury toiled in her wake, showering attentions on oblivious hostesses. To Lethbury there was something at once tragic and exasperating in the sight of their two figures, the one conciliatory, the other dogged, both pursuing with unabated zeal the elusive prize of popularity. He even began to feel a personal stake in the pursuit, not as it concerned Jane but as it affected his wife. He saw that the latter was the victim of Jane's disappointment: that Jane was not above the crude satisfaction of "taking it out" of her mother. Experience checked the impulse to come to his wife's defence; and when his resentment was at its height, Jane disarmed him by giving up the struggle.

Nothing was said to mark her capitulation; but Lethbury noticed that the visiting ceased and that the dressmaker's bills diminished. At the same time Mrs. Lethbury made it known that Jane had taken up charities; and before long Jane's conversation confirmed this announcement. At first Lethbury congratulated himself on the change; but Jane's domesticity soon began to weigh on him. During the day she was sometimes absent on errands of mercy; but in the evening she was always there. At first she and Mrs. Lethbury sat in the drawing-room together, and Lethbury smoked in the library; but presently Jane formed the habit of joining him there, and he began to suspect that he was included among the objects of her philanthropy.

Mrs. Lethbury confirmed the suspicion. "Jane has grown very serious-minded lately," she said. "She imagines that she used to neglect you and she is trying to make up for it. Don't discourage her," she added innocently.

Such a plea delivered Lethbury helpless to his daughter's ministrations; and he found himself measuring the hours he spent with her by the amount of relief they must be affording her mother. There were even moments when he read a furtive gratitude in Mrs. Lethbury's eye.

But Lethbury was no hero, and he had nearly reached the limit of vicarious endurance when something wonderful happened. They never quite knew afterward how it had come about, or who first perceived it; but Mrs. Lethbury one day gave tremulous voice to their discovery.

"Of course," she said, "he comes here because of Elise."

The young lady in question, a friend of Jane's, was possessed of attractions which had already been found to explain the presence of masculine visitors.

Lethbury risked a denial. "I don't thing he does," he declared.

"But Elise is thought very pretty," Mrs. Lethbury insisted.

"I can't help that," said Lethbury doggedly.

He saw a faint light in his wife's eyes, but she remarked carelessly: "Mr. Budd would be a very good match for Elise."

Lethbury could hardly repress a chuckle: he was so exquisitely aware that she was trying to propitiate the gods.

For a few weeks neither said a word; then Mrs. Lethbury once more reverted to the subject.

"It is a month since Elise went abroad," she said.

"Is it?"

"And Mr. Budd seems to come here just as often—"

"Ah," said Lethbury with heroic indifference; and his wife hastily changed the subject.

Mr. Winstanley Budd was a young man who suffered from an excess of manner. Politeness gushed from him in the driest season. He was always performing feats of drawing-room chivalry, and the approach of the most unobtrusive female threw him into attitudes which endangered the furniture. His features, being of the cherubic order, did not lend themselves to this role; but there were moments when he appeared to dominate them, to force them into compliance with an aquiline ideal. The range of Mr. Budd's social benevolence made its object hard to distinguish. He spread his cloak so indiscriminately that one could not always interpret the gesture, and Jane's impassive manner had the effect of increasing his demonstrations: she threw him into paroxysms of politeness.

At first he filled the house with his amenities; but gradually it became apparent that his most dazzling effects were directed exclusively to Jane. Lethbury and his wife held their breath and looked away from each other. They pretended not to notice the frequency of Mr. Budd's visits, they struggled against an imprudent inclination to leave the young people too much alone. Their conclusions were the result of indirect observation, for neither of them dared to be caught watching Mr. Budd: they behaved like naturalists on the trail of a rare butterfly.

In his efforts not to notice Mr. Budd, Lethbury centred his attentions on Jane; and Jane, at this crucial moment, wrung from him a reluctant admiration. While her parents went about dissembling their emotions, she seemed to have none to conceal. She betrayed neither eagerness nor surprise; so complete was her unconcern that there were moments when Lethbury feared it was obtuseness, when he could hardly help whispering to her that now was the moment to lower the net.

Meanwhile the velocity of Mr. Budd's gyrations increased with the ardor of courtship; his politeness became incandescent, and Jane found herself the centre of a pyrotechnical display culminating in the "set piece" of an offer of marriage.

Mrs. Lethbury imparted the news to her husband one evening after their daughter had gone to bed. The announcement was made and received with an air of detachment, as though both feared to be betrayed into unseemly exultation; but Lethbury, as his wife ended, could not repress the inquiry, "Have they decided on a day?"

Mrs. Lethbury's superior command of her features enabled her to look shocked. "What can you be thinking of? He only offered himself at five!"

"Of course—of course—" stammered Lethbury—"but nowadays people marry after such short engagements—"

"Engagement!" said his wife solemnly. "There is no engagement."

Lethbury dropped his cigar. "What on earth do you mean?"

"Jane is thinking it over."

"*Thinking it over?*"

"She has asked for a month before deciding."

Lethbury sank back with a gasp. Was it genius or was it madness? He felt incompetent to decide; and Mrs. Lethbury's next words showed that she shared his difficulty.

"Of course I don't want to hurry Jane—"

"Of course not," he acquiesced.

"But I pointed out to her that a young man of Mr. Budd's impulsive temperament might—might be easily discouraged—"

"Yes; and what did she say?"

"She said that if she was worth winning she was worth waiting for."

VI

The period of Mr. Budd's probation could scarcely have cost him as much mental anguish as it caused his would-be parents-in-law.

Mrs. Lethbury, by various ruses, tried to shorten the ordeal, but Jane remained inexorable; and each morning Lethbury came down to breakfast with the certainty of finding a letter of withdrawal from her discouraged suitor.

When at length the decisive day came, and Mrs. Lethbury, at its close, stole into the library with an air of chastened joy, they stood for a moment without speaking; then Mrs. Lethbury paid a fitting tribute to the proprieties by faltering out: "It will be dreadful to have to give her up—"

Lethbury could not repress a warning gesture; but even as it escaped him he realized that his wife's grief was genuine.

"Of course, of course," he said, vainly sounding his own emotional shallows for an answering regret. And yet it was his wife who had suffered most from Jane!

He had fancied that these sufferings would be effaced by the milder atmosphere of their last weeks together; but felicity did not soften Jane. Not for a moment did she relax her dominion: she simply widened it to include a new subject. Mr. Budd found himself under orders with the others; and a new fear assailed Lethbury as he saw Jane assume prenuptial control of her betrothed. Lethbury had never felt any strong personal interest in Mr. Budd; but as Jane's prospective husband the young man excited his sympathy. To his surprise he found that Mrs. Lethbury shared the feeling.

"I'm afraid he may find Jane a little exacting," she said,

after an evening dedicated to a stormy discussion of the wedding arrangements. "She really ought to make some concessions. If he *wants* to be married in a black frock-coat instead of a dark gray one—" She paused and looked doubtfully at Lethbury.

"What can I do about it?" he said.

"You might explain to him—tell him that Jane isn't always—"

Lethbury made an impatient gesture. "What are you afraid of? His finding her out or his not finding her out?"

Mrs. Lethbury flushed. "You put it so dreadfully!"

Her husband mused for a moment; then he said with an air of cheerful hypocrisy: "After all, Budd is old enough to take care of himself."

But the next day Mrs. Lethbury surprised him. Late in the afternoon she entered the library, so breathless and inarticulate that he scented a catastrophe.

"I've done it!" she cried.

"Done what?"

"Told him." She nodded toward the door. "He's just gone. Jane is out, and I had a chance to talk to him alone."

Lethbury pushed a chair forward and she sank into it.

"What did you tell him? That she is *not* always—"

Mrs. Lethbury lifted a tragic eye. "No; I told him that she always *is*—"

"Always *is*—?"

"Yes."

There was a pause. Lethbury made a call on his hoarded philosophy. He saw Jane suddenly reinstated in her evening seat by the library fire; but an answering chord in him thrilled at his wife's heroism.

"Well—what did he say?"

Mrs. Lethbury's agitation deepened. It was clear that the blow had fallen.

"He . . . he said . . . that we . . . had never understood Jane . . . or appreciated her . . ." The final syllables were lost in her handkerchief, and she left him marvelling at the mechanism of woman.

After that, Lethbury faced the future with an undaunted

eye. They had done their duty—at least his wife had done hers—and they were reaping the usual harvest of ingratitude with a zest seldom accorded to such reaping. There was a marked change in Mr. Budd's manner, and his increasing coldness sent a genial glow through Lethbury's system. It was easy to bear with Jane in the light of Mr. Budd's disapproval.

There was a good deal to be borne in the last days, and the brunt of it fell on Mrs. Lethbury. Jane marked her transition to the married state by a seasonable but incongruous display of nerves. She became sentimental, hysterical and reluctant. She quarrelled with her betrothed and threatened to return the ring. Mrs. Lethbury had to intervene, and Lethbury felt the hovering sword of destiny. But the blow was suspended. Mr. Budd's chivalry was proof against all his bride's caprices and his devotion throve on her cruelty. Lethbury feared that he was too faithful, too enduring, and longed to urge him to vary his tactics. Jane presently reappeared with the ring on her finger, and consented to try on the wedding-dress; but her uncertainties, her reactions, were prolonged till the final day.

When it dawned, Lethbury was still in an ecstasy of apprehension. Feeling reasonably sure of the principal actors he had centered his fears on incidental possibilities. The clergyman might have a stroke, or the church might burn down, or there might be something wrong with the license. He did all that was humanly possible to avert such contingencies, but there remained that incalcuable factor known as the hand of God. Lethbury seemed to feel it groping for him.

At the altar it almost had him by the nape. Mr. Budd was late; and for five immeasurable minutes Lethbury and Jane faced a churchful of conjecture. Then the bridegroom appeared, flushed but chivalrous, and explaining to his father-in-law under cover of the ritual that he had torn his glove and had to go back for another.

"You'll be losing the ring next," muttered Lethbury; but Mr. Budd produced this article punctually, and a moment or two later was bearing its wearer captive down the aisle.

At the wedding-breakfast Lethbury caught his wife's eye fixed on him in mild disapproval, and understood that his hilarity was exceeding the bounds of fitness. He pulled himself together and tried to subdue his tone; but his jubilation bubbled over like a champagne-glass perpetually refilled. The deeper his draughts the higher it rose.

It was at the brim when, in the wake of the dispersing guests, Jane came down in her travelling-dress and fell on her mother's neck.

"I can't leave you!" she wailed, and Lethbury felt as suddenly sobered as a man under a douche. But if the bride was reluctant her captor was relentless. Never had Mr. Budd been more dominant, more aquiline. Lethbury's last fears were dissipated as the young man snatched Jane from her mother's bosom and bore her off to the brougham.

The brougham rolled away, the last milliner's girl forsook her post by the awning, the red carpet was folded up, and the house door closed. Lethbury stood alone in the hall with his wife. As he turned toward her, he noticed the look of tired heroism in her eyes, the deepened lines of her face. They reflected his own symptoms too accurately not to appeal to him. The nervous tension had been horrible. He went up to her, and an answering impulse made her lay a hand on his arm. He held it there a moment.

"Let us go off and have a jolly little dinner at a restaurant," he proposed.

There had been a time when such a suggestion would have surprised her to the verge of disapproval; but now she agreed to it at once.

"Oh, that would be so nice," she murmured with a great sigh of relief and assuagement.

Jane had fulfilled her mission after all: she had drawn them together at last.

THE COURTING OF SISTER WISBY *

By Sarah Orne Jewett

ALL the morning there had been an increasing temptation to take an out-door holiday, and early in the afternoon the temptation outgrew my power of resistance. A far-away pasture on the long southwestern slope of a high hill was persistently present to my mind, yet there seemed to be no particular reason why I should think of it. I was not sure that I wanted anything from the pasture, and there was no sign, except the temptation, that the pasture wanted anything of me. But I was on the farther side of as many as three fences before I stopped to think again where I was going, and why.

There is no use in trying to tell another person about that afternoon unless he distinctly remembers weather exactly like it. No number of details concerning an Arctic ice-blockade will give a single shiver to a child of the tropics. This was one of those perfect New England days in late summer, when the spirit of autumn takes a first stealthy flight, like a spy, through the ripening country-side, and, with feigned sympathy for those who droop with August heat, puts her cool cloak of bracing air about leaf and flower and human shoulders. Every living thing grows suddenly cheerful and strong; it is only when you catch sight of a horror-stricken little maple in swampy soil—a little maple that has second-sight and fore-knowledge of coming disaster to her race—only then does a distrust of autumn's friendliness dim your joyful satisfaction.

In the midwinter there is always a day when one has the first foretaste of spring; in late August there is a morn-

---

* By permission of, and by special arrangement with, Houghton Mifflin Company, the authorized publishers.

ing when the air is for the first time autumn-like. Perhaps it is a hint to the squirrels to get in their first supplies
for the winter hoards, or a reminder that summer will soon
end, and everybody had better make the most of it. We are
always looking forward to the passing and ending of winter,
but when summer is here it seems as if summer must always
last. As I went across the fields that day, I found myself
half lamenting that the world must fade again, even that
the best of her budding and bloom was only a preparation
for another springtime, for an awakening beyond the coming winter's sleep.

The sun was slightly veiled; there was a chattering group
of birds, which had gathered for a conference about their
early migration. Yet, oddly enough, I heard the voice of
a belated bobolink, and presently saw him rise from the
grass and hover leisurely, while he sang a brief tune. He
was much behind time if he were still a housekeeper; but
as for the other birds who listened, they cared only for their
own notes. An old crow went sagging by, and gave a croak
at his despised neighbor, just as a black reviewer croaked at
Keats—so hard it is to be just to one's contemporaries. The
bobolink was indeed singing out of season, and it was impossible to say whether he really belonged most to this
summer or to the next. He might have been delayed on his
northward journey; at any rate, he had a light heart now, to
judge from his song, and I wished that I could ask him a
few questions—how he liked being the last man among the
bobolinks, and where he had taken singing lessons in the
South.

Presently I left the lower fields, and took a path that led
higher, where I could look beyond the village to the northern
country mountainward. Here the sweet fern grew thick and
fragrant, and I also found myself heedlessly treading on
pennyroyal. Nearby, in a field corner, I long ago made a
most comfortable seat by putting a stray piece of board and
bit of rail across the angle of the fences. I have spent many
a delightful hour there, in the shade and shelter of a young
pitch-pine and a wild-cherry tree, with a lovely outlook
toward the village, just far enough away beyond the green

slopes and tall elms of the lower meadows. But that day I still had the feeling of being outward bound, and did not turn aside nor linger. The high pasture land grew more and more enticing.

I stopped to pick some blackberries that twinkled at me like beads among their dry vines, and two or three yellow-birds fluttered up from the leaves of a thistle and then came back again, as if they had complacently discovered that I was only an overgrown yellow-bird, in strange disguise but perfectly harmless. They made me feel as if I were an intruder, though they did not offer to peck at me, and we parted company very soon. It was good to stand at last on the great shoulder of the hill. The wind was coming in from the sea, there was a fine fragrance from the pines, and the air grew sweeter every moment. I took new pleasure in the thought that in a piece of wild pasture land like this one may get closest to Nature, and subsist upon what she gives of her own free will. There have been no drudging, heavy-shod ploughman to overturn the soil, and vex it into yielding artificial crops. Here one has to take just what Nature is pleased to give, whether one is a yellow-bird or a human being. It is very good entertainment for a summer wayfarer, and I am asking my reader now to share the winter provision which I harvested that day. Let us hope that the small birds are also faring well after their fashion, but I give them an anxious thought while the snow goes hurrying in long waves across the buried fields, this windy winter night.

I next went farther down the hill, and got a drink of fresh cool water from the brook, and pulled a tender sheaf of sweet flag beside it. The mossy old fence just beyond was the last barrier between me and the pasture which had sent an invisible messenger earlier in the day, but I saw that somebody else had come first to the rendezvous: there was a brown gingham cape-bonnet and a sprigged shoulder-shawl bobbing up and down, a little way off among the junipers. I had taken such uncommon pleasure in being alone that I instantly felt a sense of disappointment; then a warm glow of pleasant satisfaction rebuked my selfishness. This could

be no one but dear old Mrs. Goodsoe, the friend of my childhood and fond dependence of my maturer years. I had not
seen her for many weeks, but here she was, out on one of her
famous campaigns for herbs, or perhaps just returning from
a blueberrying expedition. I approached with care, so as
not to startle the gingham bonnet; but she heard the rustle
of the bushes against my dress, and looked up quickly, as
she knelt, bending over the turf. In that position she was
hardly taller than the luxuriant junipers themselves.

"I'm a-gittin' in my mulleins," she said briskly, "an' I've
been thinking o' you these twenty times since I come out o'
the house. I begun to believe you must ha' forgot me at
last."

"I have been away from home," I explained. "Why don't
you get in your pennyroyal too? There's a great plantation
of it beyond the next fence but one."

"Pennyr'yal!" repeated the dear little old woman, with an
air of compassion for inferior knowledge; " 'tain't the right
time, darlin'. Pennyr'yal's too rank now. But for mulleins
this day is prime. I've got a dreadful graspin' fit for 'em
this year; seems if I must be goin' to need 'em extry. I
feel like the squirrels must when they know a hard winter's
comin'." And Mrs. Goodsoe bent over her work again,
while I stood by and watched her carefully cut the best full-
grown leaves with a clumsy pair of scissors, which might
have served through at least half a century of herb-gather-
ing. They were fastened to her apron-strings by a long
piece of list.

"I'm going to take my jack-knife and help you," I suggested, with some fear of refusal. "I just passed a flourishing family of six or seven heads that must have been growing on purpose for you."

"Now be keerful, dear heart," was the anxious response;
"choose 'em well. There's odds in mulleins same's there is
in angels. Take a plant that's all run up to stalk, and there
ain't but little goodness in the leaves. This one I'm at now
must ha' been stepped on by some creatur and blighted of
its bloom, and the leaves is han'some! When I was small
I used to have a notion that Adam an' Eve must ha' took

mulleins fer their winter wear. Ain't they just like flannel, for all the world? I've had experience, and I know there's plenty of sickness might be saved to folks if they'd quit horse-radish and such fiery, exasperating things, and use mullein drarves in proper season. Now I shall spread these an' dry 'em nice on my spare floor in the garrit, an' come to steam 'em for use along in the winter there'll be the valley of the whole summer's goodness in 'em, sartin." And she snipped away with the dull scissors while I listened respectfully, and took great pains to have my part of the harvest present a good appearance.

"This is most too dry a head," she added presently, a little out of breath. "There! I can tell you there's win'rows o' young doctors, bilin' over with book-larnin', that is truly ignorant of what to do for the sick, or how to p'int out those paths that well people foller toward sickness. Book-fools I call 'em, them young men, an' some on 'em never'll live to know much better, if they git to be Methuselahs. In my time every middle-aged woman who had brought up a family had some proper ideas of dealin' with complaints. I won't say but there was some fools amongst *them,* but I'd rather take my chances, unless they'd forsook herbs and gone to dealin' with patent stuff. Now my mother really did sense the use of herbs and roots. I never see anybody that come up to her. She was a meek-looking woman, but very understandin' mother was."

"Then that's where you learned so much yourself, Mrs. Goodsoe," I ventured to say.

"Bless your heart, I don't hold a candle to her; 'tis but little I can recall of what she used to say. No, her larnin' died with her," said my friend, in a self-deprecating tone. "Why, there was as many as twenty kinds of roots alone that she used to keep by her, that I forgot the use of; an' I'm sure I shouldn't know where to find the most of 'em, any. There was an herb"—*airb* she called it—"an herb called Pennsylvany; and she used to think everything of noble-liver-wort, but I never could seem to get the right effects from it as she could. Though I don't know as she ever really did use masterwort where somethin' else wouldn't ha' served. She had a cousin married out in Pennsylvany that used to take pains to get it to her every year or two, and so she felt 't was important to have it. Some set more by such things as come from a distance, but I rec'lect mother always used to maintain that folks was meant to be doctored with the stuff that grew right about 'em; 'twas sufficient, an' so ordered. That was before the whole population took to livin' on wheels, the way they do now. 'Twas never my idee that we was meant to know what's goin' on all over the world to once. There's goin' to be some sort of a set-back one o' these days, with these telegraphs an' things, an' letters comin' every hand's turn, and folks leavin' their proper work to answer 'em. I may not live to see it. 'Twas allowed to be difficult for folks to git about in old times, or to git word across the country, and they stood in their lot an' place, and weren't all just alike, either, same as pine-spills."

We were kneeling side by side now, as if in penitence for the march of progress, but we laughed as we turned to look at each other.

"Do you think it did much good when everybody brewed a cracked quart mug of herb-tea?" I asked, walking away on my knees to a new mullein.

"I've always lifted my voice against the practice, far's I could," declared Mrs. Goodsoe; an' I won't deal out none o' the herbs I save for no such nonsense. There was three houses along our road—I call no names—where you couldn't go into the livin' room without findin' a mess o' herb-tea drorin' on the stove or side o' the fireplace, winter or summer, sick or well. One was thoroughwut, one would be camomile, and the other, like as not, yellow dock; but they all used to put in a little new rum to git out the goodness, or keep it from spilin'." (Mrs. Goodsoe favored me with a knowing smile.) "Land, how mother used to laugh! But, poor creatures, they had to work hard, and I guess it never done 'em a mite o' harm; they was all good herbs. I wish you could hear the quawkin' there used to be when they was indulged with a real case o' sickness. Everybody would collect from far an' near; you'd see 'em coming along the road and across the pastures then; everybody clamorin' that nothin' would do no kind o' good but her choice o' teas or drarves to the feet. I wonder there was a babe lived to grow up in the whole lower part o' the town; an' if nothin' else 'peared to ail 'em, word was passed about that 'twas likely Mis' So-and-So's last young one was goin' to be foolish. Land, how they'd gather! I know one day the doctor come to Widder Peck's and the house was crammed so't he could scercely git inside the door; and he says, just as polite, 'Do send for some of the neighbors!' as if there wa'n't a soul to turn to, right or left. You'd ought to seen 'em begin to scatter."

"But don't you think the cars and telegraphs have given people more to interest them, Mrs. Goodsoe? Don't you believe people's lives were narrower then, and more taken up with little things?" I asked, unwisely, being a product of modern times.

"Not one mite, dear," said my companion stoutly. "There was as big thoughts then as there is now; these times was born o' them. The difference is in folks themselves; but now, instead o' doin' their own housekeepin' and watchin' their own neighbors—though that was carried to excess—they git word that a niece's child is ailin' the other side o' Massachusetts, and they drop everything and git on their best clothes, and off they jiggit in the cars. 'Tis a bad sign when folks wear out their best clothes faster 'n they do their everyday ones. The other side o' Massachusetts has got to look after itself by rights. An' besides that, Sunday-keepin's all gone out o' fashion. Some lays it to one thing an' some another, but some o' them old ministers that folks are all a-sighin' for did preach a lot o' stoff that wa'n't nothin' but chaff; 'twa'n't the word o' God out o' either Old Testament or New. But everybody went to meetin' and heard it, and come home, and was set to fightin' with their next door neighbor over it. Now I'm a believer, and I try to live a Christian life, but I'd as soon hear a surveyor's book read out, figgers an' all, as try to get any simple truth out o' most sermons. It's them as is most to blame."

"What was the matter that day at Widow Peck's?" I hastened to ask, for I knew by experience that the good, clear-minded soul beside me was apt to grow unduly vexed and distressed when she contemplated the state of religious teaching.

"Why, there wa'n't nothin' the matter, only a gal o' Miss Peck's had met with a dis'pintment and had gone into screechin' fits. 'Twas a rovin creatur that had come along hayin' time, and he'd gone off an' forsook her betwixt two days; nobody ever knew what become of him. Them Pecks was 'Good Lord, anybody!' kind o' gals, and took up with whoever they could get. One of 'em married Heron, the Irishman; they lived in that little house that was burnt this summer, over on the edge o' the plains. He was a good-hearted creatur, with a laughin' eye and a clever word for everybody. He was the first Irishman that ever came this way, and we was all for gettin' a look at him, when he first used to go by. Mother's folks was what they call Scotch-Irish, though; there was an old race of 'em settled about here. They could foretell events, some on 'em, and had second sight. I know folks used to say mother's grandmother had them gifts, but mother was never free to speak about it to us. She remembered her well, too."

"I suppose that you mean old Jim Heron, who was such a famous fiddler?" I asked with great interest, for I am always delighted to know more about that rustic hero, parochial Orpheus that he must have been!

"Now, dear heart, I suppose you don't remember him, do you?" replied Mrs. Goodsoe, earnestly. "Fiddle! He'd about break your heart with them tunes of his, or else set your heels flying up the floor in a jig, though you was minister o' the First Parish and all wound up for a funeral prayer. I tell ye there win't no tunes sounds like them used to. It used to seem to me summer nights when I was comin' along the plains road, and he set by the window playin', as if there was a betwitched human creatur in that old red fiddle o' his. He could make it sound just like a woman's voice tellin' somethin' over and over, as if folks could help her out o' her sorrows if she could only make 'em understand. I've set by the stone-wall and cried as if my heart was broke, and dear knows it wa'n't in them days. How he would twirl off

them jigs and dance tunes! He used to make somethin'
han'some out of 'em in fall an' winter, playin' at huskins
and dancin' parties; but he was unstiddy by spells, as he got
along in years, and never knew what it was to be forehanded.
Everybody felt bad when he died; you couldn't help likin'
the creatur. He'd got the gift—that's all you could say
about it.

"There was a Mis' Jerry Foss, that lived over by the
brook bridge, on the plains road, that had lost her husband
early, and was left with three child'n. She set the world
by 'em, and was a real pleasant, ambitious little woman, and
was workin' on as best she could with that little farm, when
there come a rage o' scarlet fever, and her boy and two girls
was swept off and laid dead within the same week. Every
one o' the neighbors did what they could, but she'd had no
sleep since they was taken sick, and after the funeral she
set there just like a piece o' marble, and would only shake
her head when you spoke to her. They all thought her
reason would go; and 'twould certain, if she couldn't have
shed tears. An' one o' the neighbors—'twas like mother's
sense, but it might have been somebody else—spoke o' Jim
Heron. Mother an' one or two o' the women that knew her
best was in the house with her. 'T was right in the edge
o' the woods and some of us younger ones was over by the
wall on the other side of the road where there was a couple
of old willows—I remember just how the brook damp felt—
and we kept quiet's we could, and some other folks come
along down the road, and stood waitin' on the little bridge,
hopin' somebody'd come out, I suppose, and they'd git news.
Everybody was wrought up, and felt a good deal for her, you
know. By an' by Jim Heron come stealin' right out o' the
shadows an' set down on the doorstep, an' 'twas a good while
before we heard a sound; then, oh, dear me! 'twas what
the whole neighborhood felt for that mother all spoke in the
notes, an' they told me afterwards that Mis' Foss's face
changed in a minute, and she come right over an' got into
my mother's lap—she was a little woman—an' laid her
head down, and there she cried herself into a blessed sleep.
After awhile one o' the other women stole out an' told the

folks, and we all went home. He only played that one tune.

"But there!" resumed Mrs. Goodsoe, after a silence, during which my eyes were filled with tears. "His wife always complained that the fiddle made her nervous. She never 'peared to think nothin' o' poor Heron after she'd once got him."

"That's often the way," said I, with harsh cynicism, though I had no guilty person in my mind at the moment; and we went straying off, not very far apart, up through the pasture. Mrs. Goodsoe cautioned me that we must not get so far off that we could not get back the same day. The sunshine began to feel very hot on our backs, and we both turned toward the shade. We had already collected a large bundle of mullein leaves, which were carefully laid into a clean, calico apron, held together by the four corners, and proudly carried by me, though my companion regarded them with anxious eyes. We sat down together at the edge of the pine woods, and Mrs. Goodsoe proceeded to fan herself with her limp cape-bonnet.

"I declare, how hot it is! The east wind's all gone again," she said. "It felt so cool this forenoon that I overburdened myself with as thick a petticoat as any I've got. I'm despri't afeared of having a chill, now that I ain't so young as once. I hate to be housed up."

"It's only August, after all," I assured her unnecessarily, confirming my statement by taking two peaches out of my pocket, and laying them side by side on the brown pine needles between us.

"Dear sakes alive!" exclaimed the old lady, with evident pleasure. "Where did you get them, now? Doesn't anything taste twice better out-o'-doors? I ain't had such a peach for years. Do le's keep the stones, an' I'll plant 'em; it only takes four years for a peach pit to come to bearing, an' I guess I'm good for four years, 'thout I meet with some accident."

I could not help agreeing, or taking a fond look at the thin little figure, and her wrinkled brown face and kind, twinkling eyes. She looked as if she had properly dried herself, by mistake, with some of her mullein leaves, and was likely to keep her goodness, and to last the longer in consequence. There never was a truer, simple-hearted soul made out of the old-fashioned country dust than Mrs. Goodsoe. I thought, as I looked away from her across the wide country, that nobody was left in any of the farmhouses so original, so full of rural wisdom and reminiscence, so really able and dependable, as she. And nobody had made better use of her time in a world foolish enough to sometimes under-value medicinal herbs.

When we had eaten our peaches we still sat under the pines, and I was not without pride when I had poked about in the ground with a little twig, and displayed to my crony a long fine root, bright yellow to the eye, and a wholesome bitter to the taste.

"Yis, dear, goldthread," she assented indulgently. "Seems to me there's more of it than anything except grass an' hard-tack. Good for canker, but no better than two or three other things I can call to mind; but I always lay in a good wisp of it, for old times' sake. Now, I want to know why you should ha' bit it, and took away all the taste o' your nice peach? I was just thinkin' what a han'some entertainment we've had. I've got so I 'sociate certain things with certain folks, and goldthread was somethin' Lizy Wisby couldn't keep house without, no ways whatever. I believe she took so much it kind o' puckered her disposition."

"Lizy Wisby?" I repeated inquiringly.

"You knew her, if ever, by the name of Mis' Deacon Brimblecom," answered my friend, as if this were only a brief preface to further information, so I waited with respectful expectation. Mrs. Goodsoe had grown tired out in the sun, and a good story would be an excuse for sufficient rest. It was a most lovely place where we sat, half-way up the long hillside; for my part, I was perfectly contented and happy. "You've often heard of Deacon Brimblecom?" she asked, as if a great deal depended upon his being properly introduced.

"I remember him," said I. "They called him Deacon Brimfull, you know, and he used to go about with a witch-hazel branch to show people where to dig wells."

"That's the one," said Mrs. Goodsoe, laughing. "I didn't know's you could go so far back. I'm always divided between whether you can remember everything I can, or are only a babe in arms."

"I have a dim recollection of there being something strange about their marriage," I suggested, after a pause, which began to appear dangerous. I was so much afraid the subject would be changed.

"I can tell you all about it," I was quickly answered. "Deacon Brimblecom was very pious accordin' to his lights in his early years. He lived way back in the country then, and there come a rovin' preacher along, and set everybody up that way all by the ears. I've heard the old folks talk it over, but I forget most of his doctrine, except some of his followers was persuaded they could dwell among the angels while yet on airth, and this Deacon Brimfull, as you call him, felt sure he was called by the voice of a spirit bride. So he left a good, deservin' wife he had, an' four children, and built him a new house over to the other side of the land he'd had from his father. They didn't take much pains with the buildin', because they expected to be translated before long, and then the spirit brides and them folks was goin' to appear and divide up the airth amongst 'em, and the world's folks and on-believers was goin' to serve 'em or be sent to torments. They had meetin's about in the school-houses, an' all sorts o' goin's on; some on 'em went crazy, but the deacon held on to what wits he had, an' by an' by the spirit bride didn't turn out to be much of a housekeeper, an' he had always been used to good livin', so he sneaked home ag'in. One o' mother's sisters married up to Ash Hill, where it all took place; that's how I come to have the particulars."

"Then how did he come to find his Eliza Wisby?" I inquired. "Do tell me the whole story; you've got mullein leaves enough."

"There's all yisterday's at home, if I haven't," replied Mrs. Goodsoe. "The way he come a-courtin' o' Sister Wisby was this: she went a-courtin' o' him.

"There was a spell he lived to home, and then his poor

wife died, and he had a spirit bride in good earnest, an' the childr'n was placed about with his folks and hers, for they was both out o' good families; and I don't know what come over him, but he had another pious fit that looked for all the world like the real thing. He hadn't no family cares, and he lived with his brother's folks, and turned his land in with theirs. He used to travel to every meetin' an' conference that was within reach of his old sorrel hoss's feeble legs; he j'ined the Christian Baptists that was just in their early prime, and he was a great exhorter, and got to be called deacon, though I guess he wa'n't deacon, 'less it was for a spare hand when deacon times was scercer'n usual. An' one time there was a four-days' protracted meetin' to the church in the lower part of the town. 'Twas a real solemn time; somethin' more'n usual was goin' forward, an' they collected from the whole country round. Women folks liked it, an' the men too; it give 'em a change, an' they was quartered round free, same as conference folks now. Some on 'em, for a joke, sent Silas Brimblecom up to Lizy Wisby's, though she'd give out she couldn't accommodate nobody, because of expectin' her cousin's folks. Everybody knew 'twas a lie; she was amazin' close considerin' she had plenty to do with. There was a streak that wa'n't just right somewheres in Lizy's wits, I always thought. She was very kind in case o' sickness, I'll say that for her.

"You know where the house is, over there on what they call Windy Hill? There the deacon went, all unsuspectin', and 'stead o' Lizy's resentin' of him she put in her own hoss, and they come back together to evenin' meetin'. She was prominent among the sect herself, an' he bawled and talked, and she bawled and talked, an' took up more'n the time allotted in the exercises, just as if they was showin' off to each what they was able to do at expoundin'. Everybody was laughin' at 'em after the meetin' broke up, and that next day an' the next, an' all through, they was constant, and seemed to be havin' a beautiful occasion. Lizy had always give out she scorned the men, but when she got a chance at a particular one 'twas altogether different, and the deacon

seemed to please her somehow or 'nother, and—There! you
don't want to listen to this old stuff that's past an' gone?"

"Oh, yes, I do," said I.

"I run on like a clock that's onset her striking hand,"
said Mrs. Goodsoe mildly. "Sometimes my kitchen time-
piece goes on half the forenoon, and I says to myself the day
before yisterday I would let it be a warnin', and keep it in
mind for a check on my own speech. The next news that
was heard was that the deacon an' Lizy—well, opinions differed which of 'em had spoke first, but them fools settled
it before the protracted meetin' was over, and give away
their hearts before he started for home. They considered
'twould be wise, though, considerin' their short acquaintance,
to take one another on trial a spell; 'twas Lizy's notion, and
she asked him why he wouldn't come over and stop with her
till spring, and then, if both continued to like, they could
git married any time 'twas convenient. Lizy, she come and
talked it over with mother, and mother disliked to offend
her, but she spoke pretty plain; and Lizy felt hurt, an'
thought they was showin' excellent judgment, so much harm
come from hasty unions and folks comin' to a realizin' sense
of each other's failin's when 'twas too late.

"So one day our folks saw Deacon Brimfull a-ridin' by
with a gre't coopful of hens in the back o' his wagon, and
bundles o' stuff tied to top and hitched to the exes under-
neath; and he riz a hymn just as he passed the house, and
was speedin' the old sorrel with a willer switch. 'Twas most
Thanksgivin' time, an' sooner'n she expected him. New
Year's was the time she set; but he thought he'd come while
the roads was fit for wheels. They was out to meetin' together Thanksgivin' Day, an' that used to be a gre't season
for marryin'; so the young folks nudged each other, and
some on 'em ventured to speak to the couple as they come
down the aisle. Lizy carried it off real well; she wa'n't
afraid o' what nobody said or thought, and so home they
went. They'd got out her yaller sleigh and her hoss; she
never would ride after the deacon's poor old creatur, and I
believe it died long o' the winter from stiffenin' up.

"Yes," said Mrs. Goodsoe, emphatically, after we had

silently considered the situation for a short space of time, "yes, there was consider'ble talk, now I tell you! The raskil boys pestered 'em just about to death for a while. They used to collect up there an' rap on the winders, and they'd turn out all the deacon's hens 'long at nine o'clock o' night, and chase 'em all over the dingle; an' one night they even lugged the pig right out o' the sty, and shoved it into the back entry, an' run for their lives. They'd stuffed its mouth full o' somethin', so it couldn't squeal till it got there. There wa'n't a sign o' nobody to be seen when Lizy hasted out with the light, and she an' the deacon had to persuade the creatur back as best they could; 'twas a cold night, and they said it took 'em till towards mornin'. You see the deacon was just the kind of a man that a hog wouldn't budge for; it takes a masterful man to deal with a hog. Well, there was no end to the works nor the talk, but Lizy left 'em pretty much alone. She did 'pear kind of dignified about it, I must say!"

"And then, were they married in the spring?"

"I was tryin' to remember whether it was just before Fast Day or just after," responded my friend, with a careful look at the sun, which was nearer the west than either of us had noticed. "I think likely 'twas along in the last o' April, any way some of us looked out o' the window one Monday mornin' early, and says, 'For goodness' sake! Lizy's sent the deacon home again!' His old sorrel havin' passed away, he was ridin' in Ezry Welsh's hoss-cart, with his hen-coop and more bundles than he had when he come, and looked as meechin' as ever you see. Ezry was drivin', and he let a glance fly swiftly round to see if any of us was lookin' out; an' then I declare if he didn't have the malice to turn right in towards the barn, where he see my oldest brother, Joshuay, an' says he real natural, 'Joshuay, just step out with your wrench. I believe I hear my kingbolt rattlin' kind o' loose.' Brother, he went out an' took in the sitooation, an' the deacon bowed kind of stiff. Joshuay was so full o' laugh, and Ezry Welsh, that they couldn't look one another in the face. There wa'n't nothing ailed the kingbolt, you know, an' when Josh riz up he says, 'Goin' up country for a spell, Mr. Brimblecom?'

" 'I be,' says the deacon, lookin' dreadful mortified and cast down.

" 'Ain't things turned out well with you an' Sister Wisby?' says Joshuay. 'You had ought to remember that the woman is the weaker vessel.'

" 'Hang her, let her carry less sail, then!' the deacon bu'st out, and he stood right up an' shook his fist there by the hen-coop, he was so mad; an' Ezry's hoss was a young creatur, an' started up and set the deacon right over backwards into the chips. We didn't know but he'd broke his neck; but when he see the women folks runnin' out he jumped up quick as a cat, an' clim into the cart, an' off they went. Ezry said he told him that he couldn't git along with Lizy, she was so fractious in thundery weather; if there was a rumble in the daytime she must go right to bed an' screech, and 'twas night she must git right up an' go an' call him out of a sound sleep. But everybody knew he'd never gone home unless she'd sent him.

"Somehow they made it up ag'in, him an' Lizy, and she had him back. She's been countin' all along on not havin' to hire nobidy to work about the gardin' an' so on, an' she said she wa'n't goin' to let him have a whole winter's board for nothin'. So the old hens was moved back, and they was married right off fair an' square, an' I don't know but they got along well as most folks. He brought his youngest girl down to live with 'em after a while, an' she was a real treasure to Lizy; everybody spoke well o' Phœbe Brimblecom. The deacon got over his pious fit, and there was consider'ble work in him if you kept right after him. He was an amazin' cider-drinker, and he airnt the name you know him by in his latter days. Lizy never trusted him with nothin', but she kep' him well. She left everything she owned to Phœbe, when she died, 'cept somethin' to satisfy the law. There, they're all gone now; seems to me sometimes, when I get thinkin', as if I'd lived a thousand years!"

I laughed, but I found Mrs. Goodsoe's thoughts had taken a serious turn.

"There, I come by some old graves down here in the lower edge of the pasture," she said as we rose to go. "I couldn't help thinking how I should like to be laid right out in the pasture ground, when my time comes; it looked sort o' comfortable, and I have ranged these slopes so many summers. Seems as if I could see right up through the turf and tell when the weather was pleasant, and get the goodness o' the sweet fern. Now, dear, just hand me my apernful o' mulleins out o' the shade. I hope you won't come to need none this winter, but I'll dry some special for you."

"I'm going by the road," said I, "or else by the path across the meadows, so I will walk as far as the house with you. Aren't you pleased with my company?" for she demurred at my going the least bit out of the way.

So we strolled toward the little gray house, with our plunder of mullein leaves slung on a stick which we carried between us. Of course I went in to make a call, as if I had not seen my hostess before; she is the last maker of muster-gingerbread, and before I came away I was kindly measured for a pair of mittens.

"You'll be sure to come an' see them two peach-trees after I get 'em well growin'?" Mrs. Goodsoe called after me when I had said good-by, and was almost out of hearing down the road.

THE REVOLT OF MOTHER *

By Mary E. Wilkins Freeman

"F ATHER!"

"What is it?"

"What are them men diggin' over there in the field for?"

There was a sudden dropping and enlarging of the lower part of the old man's face, as if some heavy weight had settled therein; he shut his mouth tight, and went on harnessing the great bay mare. He hustled the collar on to her neck with a jerk.

"Father!"

The old man slapped the saddle upon the mare's back.

"Look here, father, I want to know what them men are diggin' over in the field for, an' I'm goin' to know."

"I wish you'd go into the house, mother, an' 'tend to your own affairs," the old man said then. He ran his words together, and his speech was almost as inarticulate as a growl.

But the woman understood; it was her most native tongue. "I ain't goin' into the house till you tell me what them men are doin' over there in the field," said she.

Then she stood waiting. She was a small woman, short and straight-waisted like a child in her brown cotton gown. Her forehead was mild and benevolent between the smooth curves of gray hair; there were meek downward lines about her nose and mouth; but her eyes, fixed upon the old man, looked as if the meekness had been the result of her own will, never of the will of another.

They were in the barn, standing before the wide open

doors. The spring air, full of the smell of growing grass and unseen blossoms, came in their faces. The deep yard in front was littered with farm wagons and piles of wood; on the edges, close to the fence and the house, the grass was a vivid green, and there were some dandelions.

The old man glanced doggedly at his wife as he tightened the last buckles on the harness. She looked as immovable to him as one of the rocks in his pasture-land, bound to the earth with generations of blackberry vines. He slapped the reins over the horse, and started forth from the barn.

"*Father!*" said she.

The old man pulled up. "What is it?"

"I want to know what them men are diggin' over there in that field for."

"They're diggin' a cellar, I s'pose, if you've got to know."

"A cellar for what?"

"A barn."

"A barn? You ain't goin' to build a barn over there where we was goin' to have a house, father?"

The old man said not another word. He hurried the horse into the farm wagon, and clattered out of the yard, jouncing as sturdily on his seat as a boy.

The woman stood a moment looking after him, then she went out of the barn across a corner of the yard to the house. The house, standing at right angles with the great barn and a long reach of sheds and out-buildings, was infinitesimal compared with them. It was scarcely as commodious for people as the little boxes under the barn eaves were for doves.

A pretty girl's face, pink and delicate as a flower, was looking out of one of the house windows. She was watching three men who were digging over in the field which bounded the yard near the road line. She turned quietly when the woman entered.

"What are they digging for, mother?" said she. "Did he tell you?"

"They're diggin' for—a cellar for a new barn."

"Oh, mother, he ain't going to build another barn?"

"That's what he says."

A boy stood before the kitchen glass combing his hair. He combed slowly and painstakingly, arranging his brown hair in a smooth hillock over his forehead. He did not seem to pay any attention to the conversation.

"Sammy, did you know father was going to build a new barn?" asked the girl.

The boy combed assiduously.

"Sammy!"

He turned, and showed a face like his father's under his smooth crest of hair. "Yes, I s'pose I did," he said, reluctantly.

"How long have you known it?" asked his mother.

" 'Bout three months, I guess."

"Why didn't you tell of it?"

"Didn't think 'twould do no good."

"I don't see what father wants another barn for," said the girl, in her sweet, slow voice. She turned again to the window, and stared out at the digging men in the field. Her tender, sweet face was full of a gentle distress. Her forehead was as bald and innocent as a baby's with the light hair strained back from it in a row of curl-papers. She was quite large, but her soft curves did not look as if they covered muscles.

Her mother looked sternly at the boy. "Is he goin' to buy more cows?"

The boy did not reply; he was tying his shoes.

"Sammy, I want you to tell me if he's goin' to buy more cows."

"I s'pose he is."

"How many?"

"Four, I guess."

His mother said nothing more. She went into the pantry, and there was a clatter of dishes. The boy got his cap from a nail behind the door, took an old arithmetic from the shelf, and started for school. He was lightly built, but clumsy. He went out of the yard with a curious spring in the hips, that made his loose home-made jacket tilt up in the rear.

The girl went to the sink, and began to wash the dishes

that were piled up there. Her mother came promptly out of the pantry, and shoved her aside. "You wipe 'em," said she, "I'll wash. There's a good many this mornin'."

The mother plunged her hands vigorously into the water, the girl wiped the plates slowly and dreamily. "Mother," said she, "don't you think it's too bad father's going to build that new barn, much as we need a decent house to live in?"

Her mother scrubbed a dish fiercely. "You ain't found out yet we're women-folks, Nanny Penn," said she. "You ain't seen enough of men-folks yet to. One of these days you'll find it out, an' then you'll know that we know only what men-folks think we do, so far as any use of it goes, an' how we'd ought to reckon men-folks in with Providence, an' not complain of what they do any more than we do of the weather."

"I don't care; I don't believe George is anything like that, anyhow," said Nanny. Her delicate faced flushed pink, her lips pouted softly, as if she were going to cry.

"You wait an' see. I guess George Eastman ain't no better than other men. You hadn't ought to judge father, though. He can't help it, 'cause he don't look at things jest the way we do. An' we've been pretty comfortable here, after all. The roof don't leak—ain't never but once —that's one thing. Father's kept it shingled right up."

"I do wish we had a parlor."

"I guess it won't hurt George Eastman any to come to see you in a nice clean kitchen. I guess a good many girls don't have as good a place as this. Nobody's ever heard me complain."

"I ain't complained either, mother."

"Well, I don't think you'd better, a good father an' a good home as you've got. S'pose your father made you go out an' work for your livin'? Lots of girls have to that ain't no stronger an' better able to than you be."

Sarah Penn washed the frying-pan with a conclusive air. She scrubbed the outside of it as faithfully as the inside. She was a masterly keeper of her box of a house. Her one living-room never seemed to have in it any of the dust which the friction of life with inanimate matter produces.

She swept, and there seemed to be no dirt to go before the broom; she cleaned, and one could see no difference. She was like an artist so perfect that he has apparently no art. To-day she got out a mixing bowl and a board, and rolled some pies, and there was no more flour upon her than upon her daughter who was doing finer work. Nanny was to be married in the fall, and she was sewing on some white cambric and embroidery. She sewed industriously while her mother cooked; her soft milk-white hands and wrists showed whiter than her delicate work.

"We must have the stove moved out in the shed before long," said Mrs. Penn. "Talk about not havin' things, it's been a real blessin' to be able to put a stove up in that shed in hot weather. Father did one good thing when he fixed that stove-pipe out there."

Sarah Penn's face as she rolled her pies had that expression of meek vigor which might have characterized one of the New Testament saints. She was making mince-pies. Her husband, Adoniram Penn, liked them better than any other kind. She baked twice a week. Andoniram often liked a piece of pie between meals. She hurried this morning. It had been later than usual when she began, and she wanted to have a pie baked for dinner. However deep a resentment she might be forced to hold against her husband, she would never fail in sedulous attention to his wants.

Nobility of character manifests itself at loop-holes when it is not provided with large doors. Sarah Penn's showed itself to-day in flaky dishes of pastry. So she made the pies faithfully, while across the table she could see, when she glanced up from her work, the sight that rankled in her patient and steadfast soul—the digging of the cellar of the new barn in the place where Adoniram forty years ago had promised her their new house should stand.

The pies were done for dinner. Adoniram and Sammy were home a few minutes after twelve o'clock. The dinner was eaten with serious haste. There was never much conversation at the table in the Penn family. Adoniram asked a blessing, and they ate promptly, then rose up and went about their work.

Sammy went back to school, taking soft sly lopes out of the yard like a rabbit. He wanted a game of marbles before school, and feared his father would give him some chores to do. Adoniram hastened to the door and called after him, but he was out of sight.

"I don't see what you let him go for, mother," said he. "I wanted him to help me unload that wood."

Adoniram went to work out in the yard unloading wood from the wagon. Sarah put away the dinner dishes, while Nanny took down her curl papers and changed her dress. She was going down to the store to buy some more embroidery and thread.

When Nanny was gone, Mrs. Penn went to the door. "Father!" she called.

"Well, what it it!"

"I want to see you jest a minute, father."

"I can't leave this wood nohow. I've got to git it unloaded an' go for a load of gravel afore two o'clock. Sammy had ought to helped me. You hadn't ought to let him go to school so early."

"I want to see you jest a minute."

"I tell ye I can't, nohow, mother."

"Father, you come here." Sarah Penn stood in the door like a queen; she held her head as if it bore a crown; there was that patience which makes authority royal in her voice. Adoniram went.

Mrs. Penn led the way into the kitchen, and pointed to a chair. "Sit down, father," said she, "I've got somethin' I want to say to you."

He sat down heavily; his face was quite stolid, but he looked at her with restive eyes. "Well, what is it, mother?"

"I want to know what you're buildin' that new barn for, father?"

"I ain't got nothin' to say about it."

"It can't be you think you need another barn?"

"I tell ye I ain't got nothin' to say about it, mother; an' I ain't goin' to say nothin'."

"Be you goin' to buy more cows?"

Adoniram did not reply; he shut his mouth tight.

"I know you be, as well as I want to. Now, father, look here"—Sarah Penn had not sat down; she stood before her husband in the humble fashion of a Scripture woman—"I'm goin' to talk real plain to you; I never have sense I married you, but I'm goin' to now. I ain't never complained, an' I ain't goin' to complain now, but I'm goin' to talk plain. You see this room here, father; you look at it well. You see there ain't no carpet on the floor, an' you see the paper is all dirty, an' droppin' off the wall. We ain't had no new paper on it for ten year, an' then I put it on myself, an' it didn't cost but ninepence a roll. You see this room, father; it's all the one I've had to work in an' eat in an' sit in sence we was married. There ain't another woman in the whole town whose husband ain't got half the means you have but what's got better. It's all the room Nanny's got to have her company in; an' there ain't one of her mates but what's got better, an' their fathers not so able as hers is. It's all the room she'll have to be married in. What would you have thought, father, if we had had our weddin' in a room no better than this? I was married in my mother's parlor, with a carpet on the floor, an' stuffed furniture, an' a mahogany card-table. An' this is all the room my daughter will have to be married in. Look here, father!"

Sarah Penn went across the room as though it were a tragic stage. She flung open a door and disclosed a tiny bed room, only large enough for a bed and bureau, with a path between. "There, father," said she—"there's all the room I've had to sleep in forty years. All my children were born there—the two that died, an' the two that's livin'. I was sick with a fever there."

She stepped to another door and opened it. It led into the small, ill-lighted pantry. "Here," said she, "is all the buttery I've got—every place I've got for my dishes, to set away my victuals in, an' to keep my milk-pans in. Father, I've been takin' care of the milk of six cows in this place, an' now you're goin' to build a new barn, an' keep more cows, an' give me more to do in it."

She threw open another door. A narrow crooked flight of stairs wound upward from it. "There, father," said she, "I want you to look at the stairs that go up to them two unfinished chambers that are all the places our son an' daughter have had to sleep in all their lives. There ain't a prettier girl in town nor a more ladylike one than Nanny, an' that's the place she has to sleep in. It ain't so good as your horse's stall; it ain't so warm an' tight."

Sarah Penn went back and stood before her husband. "Now, father," said she, "I want to know if you think you're doin' right an' accordin' to what you profess. Here, when we was married, forty year ago, you promised me faithful that we should have a new house built in that lot over in the field before the year was out. You said you had money enough, an' you wouldn't ask me to live in no such place as this. It is forty year now, an' you've been makin' more money, an' I've been savin' of it for you ever since, an you ain't built no house yet. You've built sheds an' cow-houses an' one new barn, an' now you're goin' to build another. Father, I want to know if you think it's right. You're lodgin' your dumb beasts better than you are your own flesh an' blood. I want to know if you think it's right."

"I ain't got nothin' to say."

"You can't say nothin' without ownin' it ain't right, father. An' there's another thing—I ain't complained; I've got along forty year, an' I s'pose I should forty more, if it wasn't for that—if we don't have another house. Nanny she can't live with us after she's married. She'll have to go somewhere else to live away from us, an' it don't seem as if I could have it so, noways, father. She wasn't ever strong. She's got considerable color, but there wasn't never any backbone to her. I've always took the heft of everything off her, an' she ain't fit to keep house an' do everything herself. She'll be all worn out inside of a year. Think of her doin' all the washin' an' ironin' an' bakin' with them soft white hands an' arms, an' sweepin'! I can't have it so, noways, father."

Mrs. Penn's face was burning; her mild eyes gleamed.

She had pleaded her little cause like a Webster; she had ranged from severity to pathos; but her opponent employed that obstinate silence which makes eloquence futile with mocking echoes. Adoniram arose clumsily.

"Father, ain't you got nothin' to say?" said Mrs. Penn.

"I've got to go off after that load of gravel. I can't stan' here talkin' all day."

"Father, won't you think it over, an' have a house built there instead of a barn?"

"I ain't got nothin' to say."

Adoniram shuffled out. Mrs. Penn went into her bedroom. When she came out, her eyes were red. She had a roll of unbleached cotton cloth. She spread it out on the kitchen table, and began cutting out some shirts for her husband. The men over in the field had a team to help them this afternoon; she could hear their halloos. She had a scanty pattern for the shirts; she had to plan and piece the sleeves.

Nanny came home with her embroidery, and sat down with her needlework. She had taken down her curl-papers, and there was a soft roll of fair hair like an aureole over her forehead; her face was as delicately fine and clear as porcelain. Suddenly she looked up, and the tender red flamed all over her face and neck. "Mother," said she.

"What say?"

"I've been thinking—I don't see how we're goin' to have any—wedding in this room. I'd be ashamed to have his folks come if we didn't have anybody else."

"Mebbe we can have some new paper before then; I can put it on. I guess you won't have no call to be ashamed of your belongin's."

"We might have the wedding in the new barn," said Nanny, with gentle pettishness. "Why, mother, what makes you look so?"

Mrs. Penn had started, and was staring at her with a curious expression. She turned again to her work, and spread out a pattern carefully on the cloth. "Nothin'," said she.

Presently Adoniram clattered out of the yard in his two-wheeled dump cart, standing as proudly upright as a Roman charioteer. Mrs. Penn opened the door and stood there a minute looking out; the halloos of the men sounded louder.

It seemed to her all through the spring months that she heard nothing but the halloos and the noises of saws and hammers. The new barn grew fast. It was a fine edifice for this little village. Men came on pleasant Sundays, in their meeting suits and clean shirt bosoms, and stood around it admiringly. Mrs. Penn did not speak of it, and Adoniram did not mention it to her, although sometimes, upon a return from inspecting it, he bore himself with injured dignity.

"It's a strange thing how your mother feels about the new barn," he said, confidentially, to Sammy one day.

Sammy only grunted after an odd fashion for a boy; he had learned it from his father.

The barn was all completed ready for use by the third week in July. Adoniram had planned to move his stock in on Wednesday; on Tuesday he received a letter which changed his plans. He came in with it early in the morning. "Sammy's been to the post-office," said he, "an' I've got a letter from Hiram." Hiram was Mrs. Penn's brother, who lived in Vermont.

"Well," said Mrs. Penn, "what does he say about the folks?"

"I guess they're all right. He says he thinks if I come up country right off there's a chance to buy jest the kind of a horse I want." He stared reflectively out of the window at the new barn.

Mrs. Penn was making pies. She went on clapping the rolling-pin into the crust, although she was very pale, and her heart beat loudly.

"I dun' know but what I'd better go," said Adoniram. "I hate to go off jest now, right in the midst of hayin', but the ten-acre lot's cut, an' I guess Rufus an' the others can git along without me three or four days. I can't get a horse round here to suit me, nohow, an' I've got to have another for all that wood-haulin' in the fall. I told Hiram to watch out, an' if he got wind of a good horse to let me know. I guess I'd better go."

"I'll get out your clean chirt an' collar," said Mrs. Penn calmly.

She laid out Adoniram's Sunday suit and his clean clothes on the bed in the little bedroom. She got his shaving-water and razor ready. At last she buttoned on his collar and fastened his black cravat.

Adoniram never wore his collar and cravat except on extra occasions. He held his head high, with a rasped dignity. When he was all ready, with his coat and hat brushed, and a lunch of pie and cheese in a paper bag, he hesitated on the threshold of the door. He looked at his wife, and his manner was definitely apologetic. "*If* them cows come to-day, Sammy can drive 'em into the new barn," said he; "an' when they bring the hay up, they can pitch it in there."

"Well," replied Mrs. Penn.

Adoniram set his shaven face ahead and started. When he had cleared the door-step, he turned and looked back with a kind of nervous solemnity. "I shall be back by Saturday if nothin' happens," said he.

"Do be careful, father," returned his wife.

She stood in the door with Nanny at her elbow and watched him out of sight. Her eyes had a strange, doubtful expression in them; her peaceful forehead was contracted. She went in, and about her baking again. Nanny sat sewing. Her wedding-day was drawing nearer, and she was getting pale and thin with her steady sewing. Her mother kept glancing at her.

"Have you got that pain in your side this mornin'?" she asked.

"A little."

Mrs. Penn's face, as she worked, changed, her perplexed forehead smoothed, her eyes were steady, her lips firmly set. She formed a maxim for herself, although incoherently with her unlettered thoughts. "Unsolicited opportunities are the guide-posts of the Lord to the new roads of life," she repeated in effect, and she made up her mind to her course of action.

"S'posin' I *had* wrote to Hiram," she muttered once, when she was in the pantry—"s'posin' I had wrote, an' asked him if he knew of any horse? But I didn't, an' father's goin' wan't none of my doin'. It looks like a providence." Her voice rang out quite loud at the last.

"What you talkin' about, mother?" called Nanny.

"Nothin'."

Mrs. Penn hurried her baking; at eleven o'clock it was all done. The load of hay from the west field came slowly down the cart track, and drew up at the new barn. Mrs. Penn ran out. "Stop!" she screamed, "stop!"

The men stopped and looked; Sammy upreared from the top of the load, and stared at his mother.

"Stop!" she cried out again. "Don't you put the hay in that barn; put it in the old one."

"Why, he said to put it in here," returned one of the hay-makers, wonderingly. He was a young man, a neighbor's son, whom Adoniram hired by the year to help on the farm.

"Don't you put the hay in the new barn; there's room enough in the old one, ain't there?" said Mrs. Penn.

"Room enough," returned the hired man, in his thick, rustic tones. "Didn't need the new barn, nohow, far as room's concerned. Well, I s'pose he changed his mind." He took hold of the horses' bridles.

Mrs. Penn went back to the house. Soon the kitchen windows were darkened, and a fragrance like warm honey came into the room.

Nanny laid down her work. "I thought father wanted them to put the hay into the new barn?" she said, wonderingly.

"It's all right," replied her mother.

Sammy slid down from the load of hay, and came in to see if dinner was ready.

"I ain't goin' to get a regular dinner to-day, as long as father's gone," said his mother. "I've let the fire go out. You can have some bread an' milk an' pie. I thought we could get along." She set out some bowls of milk, some bread, and a pie on the kitchen table. "You'd better eat your dinner now," said she. "You might jest as well get through with it. I want you to help me afterwards."

Nanny and Sammy stared at each other. There was

something strange in their mother's manner. Mrs. Penn did not eat anything herself. She went into the pantry, and they heard her moving dishes while they ate. Presently she came out with a pile of plates. She got the clothes-basket out of the shed, and packed them in it. Nanny and Sammy watched. She brought out cups and saucers, and put them in with the plates.

"What you goin' to do, mother?" inquired Nanny, in a timid voice. A sense of something unusual made her tremble, as if it were a ghost. Sammy rolled his eyes over his pie.

"You'll see what I'm goin' to do," replied Mrs. Penn. "If you're through, Nanny, I want you to go up-stairs an' pack up your things; an' I want you, Sammy, to help me take down the bed in the bedroom."

"Oh, mother, what for?" gasped Nanny.

"You'll see."

During the next few hours a feat was performed by this simple, pious New England mother which was equal in its way to Wolfe's storming of the Heights of Abraham. It took no more genius and audacity of bravery for Wolfe to cheer his wondering soldiers up those steep precipices, under the sleeping eyes of the enemy, than for Sarah Penn, at the head of her children, to move all their little household goods into the new barn while her husband was away.

Nanny and Sammy followed their mother's instructions without a murmur; indeed, they were overawed. There is a certain uncanny and superhuman quality about all such purely original undertakings as their mother's was to them. Nanny went back and forth with her light load, and Sammy tugged with sober energy.

At five o'clock in the afternoon the little house in which the Penns had lived for forty years had emptied itself into the new barn.

Every builder builds somewhat for unknown purposes, and is in a measure a prophet. The architect of Adoniram Penn's barn, while he designed it for the comfort of four-footed animals, had planned better than he knew for the comfort of humans. Sarah Penn saw at a glance its possibilities. Those great box-stalls, with quilts hung before them, would make better bedrooms than the one she had occupied for forty years, and there was a tight carriage-room. The harness-room, with its chimney and shelves, would make a kitchen of her dreams. The great middle space would make a parlor, by-and-by, fit for a palace. Up stairs there was as much room as down. With partitions and windows, what a house would there be! Sarah looked at the row of stanchions before the allotted space for cows, and reflected that she would have her front entry there.

At six o'clock the stove was up in the harness room, the kettle was boiling, and the table set for tea. It looked almost as home-like as the abandoned house across the yard had ever done. The young hired man milked, and Sarah directed him calmly to bring the milk to the new barn. He came gaping, dropping little blots of foam from the brimming pails on the grass. Before the next morning he had spread the story of Adoniram Penn's wife moving into the new barn all over the little village. Men assembled in the store and talked it over, women with shawls over their heads scuttled into each other's houses before their work was done. Any deviation from the ordinary course of life in this quiet town was enough to stop all progress in it. Everybody paused to look at the staid, independent figure on the side track. There was a difference of opinion with regard to her. Some held her to be insane; some, of a lawless and rebellious spirit.

Friday the minister went to see her. It was in the forenoon, and she was at the barn door shelling peas for dinner. She looked up and returned his salutation with dignity, then she went on with her work. She did not invite him in. The saintly expression of her face remained fixed, but there was an angry flush over it.

The minister stood awkwardly before her, and talked. She handled the peas as if they were bullets. At last she looked up, and her eyes showed the spirit that her meek front had covered for a lifetime.

"There ain't no use talkin', Mr. Hersey," said she. "I've thought it all over an' over, an' I believe I'm doin' what's right. I've made it the subject of prayer, an' it's betwixt me an' the Lord an' Adoniram. There ain't no call for nobody else to worry about it."

"Well, of course, if you have brought it to the Lord in prayer, and feel satisfied that you are doing right, Mrs. Penn," said the minister, helplessly. His thin gray-bearded face was pathetic. He was a sickly man; his youthful confidence had cooled; he had to scourge himself up to some of his pastoral duties as relentlessly as a Catholic ascetic, and then he was prostrated by the smart.

"I think it's right jest as much as I think it was right for our forefathers to come over from the old country 'cause they didn't have what belonged to 'em," said Mrs. Penn. She arose. The barn threshold might have been Plymouth Rock from her bearing. "I don't doubt you mean well, Mr. Hersey," said she, "but there are things people hadn't ought to interfere with. I've been a member of the church for over forty years. I've got my own mind an' my own feet, an' I'm goin' to think my own thoughts an' go my own way, an' nobody but the Lord is goin' to dictate to me unless I've a mind to have him. Won't you come in an' set down? How is Mrs. Hersey?"

"She is well, I thank you," replied the minister. He added some more perplexed apologetic remarks; then he retreated.

He could expound the intricacies of every character study in the Scriptures, he was competent to grasp the Pilgrim Fathers and all historical innovators, but Sarah Penn was beyond him. He could deal with primal cases, but parallel ones worsted him. But, after all, although it was aside from his province, he wondered more how Adoniram Penn would deal with his wife than how the Lord would. Everybody shared the wonder. When Adoniram's four new cows arrived, Sarah ordered three to be put in the old barn, the other in the house shed where the cooking-stove had stood. That added to the excitement. It was whispered that all four cows were domiciled in the house.

Towards sunset on Saturday, when Adoniram was expected home, there was a knot of men in the road near the new barn. The hired man had milked, but he still hung around the premises. Sarah Penn had supper all ready. There were brown-bread and baked beans and a custard pie; it was the supper that Adoniram loved on a Saturday night. She had on a clean calico, and she bore herself imperturbably. Nanny and Sammy kept close at her heels. Their eyes were large, and Nanny was full of nervous tremors. Still there was to them more pleasant excitement than anything else. An inborn confidence in their mother over their father asserted itself.

Sammy looked out of the harness-room window. "There he is," he announced, in an awed whisper. He and Nanny peeped around the casing. Mrs. Penn kept on about her work. The children watched Adoniram leave the new horse standing in the drive while he went to the house door. It was fastened. Then he went around to the shed. That door was seldom locked, even when the family was away. The thought how her father would be confronted by the cow flashed upon Nanny. There was a hysterical sob in her throat. Adoniram emerged from the shed and stood looking about in a dazed fashion. His lips moved; he was saying something, but they could not hear what it was. The hired man was peeping around a corner of the old barn, but nobody saw him.

Adoniram took the new horse by the bridle and led him across the yard to the new barn. Nanny and Sammy slunk close to their mother. The barn doors, rolled back, and there stood Adoniram, with the long mild face of the great Canadian farm horse looking over his shoulder.

Nanny kept behind her mother, but Sammy stepped suddenly forward, and stood in front of her.

Adoniram stared at the group. "What on airth you all down here for?" said he. "What's the matter over to the house?"

"We've come here to live, father," said Sammy. His shrill voice quavered out bravely.

"What"—Adoniram sniffed—"what is it smells like cookin'?" said he. He stepped forward and looked in the open door of the harness-room. Then he turned to his wife. His old bristling face was pale and frightened. "What on airth does this mean, mother?" he gasped.

"You come in here, father," said Sarah. She led the way into the harness-room and shut the door. "Now, father," said she, "you needn't be scared. I ain't crazy. There ain't nothin' to be upset over. But we've come here to live, an' we're goin' to live here. We've got jest as good a right here as new horses an' cows. The house wasn't fit for us to live in any longer, an' I made up my mind I wa'n't goin' to stay there. I've done my duty by you forty year, an' I'm goin' to do it now; but I'm goin' to live here. You've got to put in some windows and partitions; an you'll have to buy some furniture."

"Why, mother!" the old man gasped.

"You'd better take your coat off an' get washed—there's the wash basin—an' then we'll have supper."

"Why, mother!"

Sammy went past the window, leading the new horse to the old barn. The old man saw him, and shook his head speechlessly. He tried to take off his coat, but his arms seemed to lack the power. His wife helped him. She poured some water into the tin basin, and put in a piece of soap. She got the comb and brush, and smoothed his thin gray hair after he had washed. Then she put the beans, hot bread, and tea on the table. Sammy came in, and the family drew up. Adoniram sat looking dazedly at his plate, and they waited.

"Ain't you goin' to ask a blessin', father?" said Sarah.

And the old man bent his head and mumbled.

All through the meal he stopped eating at intervals, and stared furtively at his wife; but he ate well. The home food tasted good to him, and his old frame was too sturdily healthy to be affected by his mind. But after supper he went out, and sat down on the step of the smaller door at the right of the barn, through which he had meant his Jerseys to pass in stately file, but which Sarah designed for her front house door, and he leaned his head on his hands.

After the supper dishes were cleared away and the milk-pans washed, Sarah went out to him. The twilight was deepening. There was a clear green glow in the sky. Before them stretched the smooth level of field; in the distance was a cluster of hay-stacks like the huts of a village; the air was very cool and calm and sweet. The landscape might have been an ideal one of peace.

Sarah bent over and touched her husband on one of his thin, sinewy shoulders. "Father!"

The old man's shoulders heaved: he was weeping.

"Why, don't do so, father," said Sarah.

"I'll—put up the—partitions, an'—everything you—want, mother."

Sarah put her apron up to her face; she was overcome by her own triumph.

Adoniram was like a fortress whose walls had no active resistance, and went down the instant the right besieging tools were used. "Why, mother," he said, hoarsely, "I hadn't no idee you was so set on't as all this comes to."

TOLD IN THE POORHOUSE *

BY ALICE BROWN

L E' me see," said old Sally Flint, "was it fifty year ago, or was it on'y forty? Some'er's betwixt 1825 an' '26 it must ha' been when they were married, an' 'twas in '41 he died."

The other old women in the Poorhouse sitting-room gathered about her. Old Mrs. Forbes, who dearly loved a story, unwound a length of yarn with peculiar satisfaction, and put her worn shoe up to the fire. Everybody knew when Sally Flint was disposed to open her unwritten book of folk-tales for the public entertainment; and to-day, having tied on a fresh apron and bound a new piece of red flannel about her wrist, she was, so to speak, in fighting trim. The other members of the Poorhouse had scanty faith in that red flannel. They were aware that Sally had broken her wrist, some twenty years before, and that the bandage was consequently donned on days when her "hand felt kind o' cold," or was "burnin' like fire embers"; but there was an unspoken suspicion that it really served as token of her inability to work whenever she felt bored by the prescribed routine of knitting and sweeping. No one had dared presume on that theory, however, since the day when an untactful overseer had mentioned it, to be met by such a stream of unpleasant reminiscence concerning his immediate ancestry that he had retreated in dismay, and for a week after, had served extra pieces of pie to his justly offended charge.

"They were married in June," continued Sally. "No, 'twa'nt; 'twas the last o' May. May thirty-fust—no, May 'ain't but thirty days, has it?"

---

* By permission of, and by special arrangement with, Houghton Mifflin Company, the authorized publishers, and by permission of the author.

225

" 'Thirty days hath September,' " quoted Mrs. Giles, with importance. "That's about all I've got left o' my schoolin', Miss Flint. May's got thirty-one days, sure enough."

"Call it the thirty-fust, then. It's nigh enough, anyway. Well, Josh Marden an' Lyddy Ann Crane was married, an' for nine year they lived like two kittens. Old Sperry Dyer, that wanted to git Lyddy himself, used to call 'em cup an' sasser. 'There they be,' he'd say, when he stood outside the meetin'-house door an' they drove up, 'there comes cup an' sasser.' Lyddy was a little mite of a thing, with great black eyes; an' if Josh hadn't been as tough as tripe, he'd ha' got all wore out waitin' on her. He even washed the potaters for her, made the fires, an' lugged water. Scairt to death if she was sick! She used to have sick headaches, an' one day he stopped choppin' pine limbs near the house 'cause the noise hurt Lyddy Ann's head. Another time, I recollect, she had erysipelas in her face, an' I went in to carry some elder-blows, an' found him readin' the Bible. 'Lord!' says I, 'Josh, that's on'y Genesis! 'twon't do the erysipelas a mite o' good for you to be settin' there readin' the begats! You better turn to Revelations.' But 'twa'nt all on his side, nuther. 'Twas give an' take with them. It used to seem as if Lyddy Ann kind o' worshipped him. 'Josh' we all called him; but she used to say 'Joshuay,' an' look at him as if he was the Lord A'mighty."

"My! Sally!" said timid Mrs. Spenser, under her breath; but Sally gave no heed, and swept on in the stream of her recollections.

"Well, it went on for fifteen year, an' then 'Mandy Knowles, Josh's second cousin, come to help 'em with the work. 'Mandy was a queer creatur. I've studied a good deal over her, an' I dunno 's I've quite got to the bottom of her yit. She was one o' them sort o' slow women, with a fat face, an' she hadn't got over dressin' young, though Lyddy an' the rest of us that was over thirty was wearin' caps an' talkin' about false fronts. But she never'd had no beaux; an' when Josh begun to praise her an' say how nice 'twas to have her there, it tickled her e'en a'most to death. She'd lived alone with her mother an' two old-maid aunts, an' she didn't know nothin' about men-folks; I al'ays thought she felt they was different somehow—kind o' cherubim an' seraphim—an' you'd got to mind 'em as if you was the Childern of Isr'el an' they was Moses. Josh never meant a mite o' harm, I'll say that for him. He was jest man-like, that's all. There's lots o' different kinds—here, Mis' Niles, you know, you've buried your third—an Josh was the kind that can't see more'n one woman to a time. He looked at 'Mandy, an' he got over seein' Lyddy Ann, that's all. Things would ha' come out all right—as right as they be for most married folk—if Lyddy Ann hadn't been so high-sperited; but she set the world by Joshuay, an' there 'twas. 'Ain't it nice to have her here?' he kep' on sayin' over'n' over to Lyddy, an' she'd say 'Yes'; but byme-by, when she found he was al'ays on hand to bring a pail o' water for 'Mandy, or to throw away her suds, or even help hang out the clo'es—I see 'em hangin' out clo'es one day when I was goin' across their lot huckleberr'in', an' he did look like a great gump, an' so did she— well, then, Lyddy Ann got to seemin' kind o' worried, an' she had more sick headaches than ever. 'Twa'nt a year afore that, I'd been in one day when she had a headache, an' he says, as if he was perfessin' his faith in meetin', 'By gum! I wish I could have them headaches for her!' an' I thought o' speakin' of it, about now, when I run in to borrer some saleratus, an' he hollered into the bedroom, 'Lyddy Ann, you got another headache? If I had such a head as that, I'd cut it off!' An' all the time 'Mandy did act like the very Old Nick, jest as any old maid would that hadn't set her mind on menfolks till she was thirty-five. She bought a red-plaid bow an' pinned it on in front, an' one day I ketched her at the lookin'-glass pullin' out a gray hair.

" 'Land, 'Mandy,' says I (I spoke right up), 'do you pull 'em out as fast as they come? That's why you ain't no grayer, I s'pose. I was sayin' the other day, " 'Mandy Knowles is gittin' on, but she holds her own pretty well. I dunno how she manages it, whether she dyes or not," ' says I.

"An' afore she could stop herself, 'Mandy turned round, red as a beet, to look at Josh an' see if he heard. He stamped out into the wood-house, but Lyddy Ann never took her eyes off her work. Them little spiteful things didn't seem to make no impression on her. I've thought a good many times sence, she didn't care how handsome other women was, nor how scrawny she was herself, if she could on'y keep Josh. An' Josh he got kind o' fretful to her, an' she to him, an' 'Mandy was all honey an' cream. Nothin' would do but she must learn how to make the gingerbread he liked, an' iron his shirts; an' when Lyddy Ann found he seemed to praise things up jest as much as he had when she done 'em, she give 'em up, an' done the hard things herself, an' let 'Mandy see to Josh. She looked pretty pindlin' then, mark my words, but I never see two such eyes in anybody's head. I s'pose 'twas a change for Josh, anyway, to be with a woman like 'Mandy, that never said her soul's her own, for Lyddy'd al'ays had a quick way with her; but, land! you can't tell about men, what changes 'em or what don't. If you're tied to one, you've jest got to bear with him, an' be thankful if he don't run some kind of a rig an' make you town-talk."

There was a murmur from gentle Lucy Staples, who had been constant for fifty years to the lover who died in her youth; but no one took any notice of her, and Sally Flint went on:

"It come spring, an' somehow or nuther 'Mandy found out the last o' March was Josh's birthday, an' nothin' would do but she must make him a present. So she walked over to Sudleigh, an' bought him a great long pocket-book that you could put your bills into without foldin' 'em, an' brought it home, tickled to death because she'd been so smart. Some o' this come out at the time, an' some wa'nt known till arterwards; the hired man told some, an' a good deal the neighbors see themselves. An' I'll be whipped if 'Mandy herself didn't tell the heft on't arter 'twas all over. She wa'n't more'n half baked in a good many things. It got round somehow that the pocket-book was comin', an' when I see 'Mandy walkin' home that arternoon, I ketched up my shawl an' run in behind her, to borrer some yeast. Nobody thought anything o' birthdays in our neighborhood, an' mebbe that made it seem a good deal more'n 'twas; but when I got in there, I vow I was sorry I come. There set Josh by the kitchen table, sort o' red an' pleased, with his old pocket-book open afore him, an' he was puttin' all his bills an' papers into the new one, an' sayin', every other word,

" 'Why, 'Mandy, I never see your beat! Ain't this a nice one, Lyddy?'

"An' 'Mandy was b'ilin' over with pride, an' she stood there takin' off her cloud; she'd been in such a hurry to give it to him she hadn't even got her things off fust. Lyddy stood by the cupboard, lookin' straight at the glass spoon-holder. I thought arterwards I didn't b'lieve she see it; an' if she did, I guess she never forgot it.

" 'Yes, it's a real nice one,' says I.

"I had to say suthin', but in a minute, I was most scairt. Lyddy turned round, in a kind of a flash; her face blazed all over red, an' her eyes kind o' went through me. She stepped up to the table, an' took up the old pocket-book.

" 'You've got a new one,' says she.   'May I have this?'

" 'Course you may,' says he.

"He didn't look up to see her face, and her voice was so soft an' still, I guess he never thought nothin' of it.   Then she held the pocketbook up tight ag'inst her dress waist an' walked off into the bedroom.   I al'ays thought she never knew I was there.   An' arterwards it come out that that old pocket-book was one she'd bought for him afore they was married,—earned it bindin' shoes."

" '*Twas* kind o' hard," owned Mrs. Niles, bending forward, and, with hands clasped over her knees, peering into the coals for data regarding her own marital experiences. "But if 'twas all wore out—did you say 'twas wore?— well, then I dunno's you could expect him to set by it.   An' 'twa'n't as if he'd give it away; they'd got it between 'em."

"I dunno; it's all dark to me," owned Sally Flint.   "I guess 'twould puzzle a saint to explain men-folks, anyway, but I've al'ays thought they was sort o' numb about some things.   Anyway, Josh Marden was.   Well, things went on that way till the fust part o' the summer, an' then they come to a turnin'-p'int.   I s'pose they'd got to, some time, an' it might jest as well ha' been fust as last.   Lyddy Ann was pretty miserable, an' she'd been dosin' with thoroughwort an' what all when anybody told her to; but I al'ays thought she never cared a mite whether she lived to see another spring. The day I'm comin' to, she was standin' over the fire fryin' fish, an' 'Mandy was sort o' fiddlin' round, settin' the table, an' not doin' much of anything arter all. I dunno how she come to be so aggravatin', for she was al'ays ready to do her part, if she *had* come between husband an' wife. You know how hard it is to git a fish dinner! Well, Lyddy Ann was tired enough, anyway. An' when Josh come in, 'Mandy she took a cinnamon-rose out of her dress, an' offered it to him.

" 'Here's a flower for your button-hole,' says she, as if she wa'n't more'n sixteen. An' then she set down in a chair, an' fanned herself with a newspaper.

"Now that chair happened to be Lyddy Ann's at the table, an' she see what was bein' done. She turned right round, with the fish-platter in her hand, an' says she, in an awful kind of a voice,

" 'You git up out o' my chair! You've took my husband away, but you sha'n't take my place at the table!'

"The hired man was there, washin' his hands at the sink, an' he told it to me jest as it happened. Well, I guess they all thought they was struck by lightnin', an' Lyddy Ann most of all. Josh he come to, fust. He walked over to Lyddy Ann.

" 'You put down that platter!' says he. An' she begun to tremble, an' set it down.

"I guess they thought there was goin' to be murder done, for 'Mandy busted right out cryin' an' come runnin' over to me, an' the hired man took a step an' stood side o' Lyddy Ann. He was a little mite of a man, Cyrus was, but he wouldn't ha' stood no violence.

"Josh opened the door that went into the front entry, an' jest p'inted. 'You walk in there,' he says, 'an' you stay there. That's your half o' the house, an' this is mine. Don't you dast to darken my doors!'

"Lyddy Ann she walked through the entry an' into the fore-room, an' he shet the door."

"I wouldn't ha' done it!" snorted old Mrs. Page, who had

spent all her property in lawsuits over a right of way.
"Ketch me!"

"You would if you'd 'a' been Lyddy Ann!" said Sally
Flint, with an emphatic nod. Then she continued: "I
hadn't more'n heard 'Mandy's story afore I was over there;
but jest as I put my foot on the door-sill, Josh he come for-
'ard to meet me.

" 'What's wanted?' says he. An' I declare for't I was
so scairt I jest turned round an' cut for home. An' there set
'Mandy, wringin' her hands.

" 'What be I goin' to do?' says she, over'n' over. 'Who
ever'd ha' thought o' this?'

" 'The thing for you to do,' says I, 'is to go straight home
to your mother, an' I'll harness up an' carry you. Don't you
step your foot inside that house ag'in. Maybe ma'am will
go over an' pack up your things. You've made mischief
enough.' So we got her off that arternoon, an' that was an
end of *her.*

"I never could see what made Josh think so quick that day.
We never thought he was brighter'n common; but jest see how
in that flash o' bein' mad with Lyddy Ann he'd planned out
what would be most wormwood for her! He gi'n her the
half o' the house she'd furnished herself with hair-cloth
chairs an' a what-not, but 'twa'n't the part that was fit to be
lived in. She stayed pretty close for three or four days, an'
I guess she never had nothin' to eat. It made me kind o'
sick to think of her in there settin' on her haircloth sofy, an'
lookin' at her wax flowers an' the coral on the what-not, an'
thinkin' what end she'd made. It was of a Monday she was
sent in there, an' Tuesday night I slipped over an' put some
luncheon on the winder-sill; but 'twas there the next day, an'
Cyrus see the old crower fly up an' git it. An' that same
Tuesday mornin', Josh had a j'iner come an' begin a partition right straight through the house. It was all rough
boards, like a high fence, an' it cut the front entry in two, an'
went right through the kitchen—so 't the kitchen stove was
one side on 't, an' the sink the other. Lyddy Ann's side had
the stove. I was glad o' that, though I s'pose she 'most had
a fit every day to think o' him tryin' to cook over the air-

tight in the settin'-room. Seemed kind o' queer to go to the front door, too, for you had to open it wide an' squeeze round the partition to git into Lyddy Ann's part, an' a little mite of a crack would let you into Josh's. But they didn't have many callers. It was a good long while afore anybody dared to say a word to her; an' as for Josh, there wa'n't nobody that cared about seein' him but the tax-collector and pedlers.

"Well, the trouble Josh took to carry out that mad fit! He split wood an' laid it down at Lyddy Ann's door, an' he divided the eggs an' milk, an' shoved her half inside. He bought her a separate barrel o' flour, an' all the groceries he could think on; they said he laid money on her winder-sill. But, take it all together, he was so busy actin' like a crazed one that he never got his 'taters dug till 'most time for the frost. Lyddy Ann she never showed her head among the neighbors ag'in. When she see she'd got to stay there, she begun to cook for herself; but one day, one o' the neighbors heard her pleadin' with Josh, out in the cow-yard, while he was milkin'.

"'O Joshuay,' she kep' a-sayin' over'n' over, 'you needn't take me back, if you'll on'y let me do your work! You needn't speak to me, an' I'll live in the other part; but I shall be crazy if you don't let me do your work. O Joshuay! O Joshuay!' She cried an' cried as if her heart would break, but Josh went on milkin', and never said a word.

"I s'pose she thought he'd let her, the old hunks, for the next day she baked some pies an' set 'em on the table in his part. She reached in through the winder to do it. But that night, when Josh come home, he hove 'em all out into the back yard, an' the biddies eat 'em up. The last time I was there, I see them very pieces o' pie-plate, white an' blue-edged, under the syringa bush. Then she kind o' give up hope. I guess— But no! I'm gittin' ahead o' my story. She did try him once more. Of course his rooms got to lookin' like a hog's nest—"

"My! I guess when she see him doin' his own washin', she thought the pocket-book was a small affair," interpolated Mrs. Niles.

"She used to go round peerin' into his winders when he

wa'n't there, an' one day, arter he'd gone off to trade some steers, she jest spunked up courage an' went in an' cleaned all up. I see the bed airin', an' went over an' ketched her at it. She hadn't more'n got through an' stepped outside when Josh come home, an' what should he do but take the wheel-barrer an', beat out as he was drivin' oxen five mile, go down to the gravel-pit an' get a barrerful o' gravel. He wheeled it up to the side door, an' put a plank over the steps, an' wheeled it right in. An' then he dumped it in the middle o' his clean floor. That was the last o' her tryin' to do for him on the sly.

"I should ha' had some patience with him if 'twa'n't for one thing he done to spite her. Seemed as if he meant to shame her that way afore the whole neighborhood. He wouldn't speak to her himself, but he sent a painter by trade to tell her he was goin' to paint the house, an' to ask her what color she'd ruther have. The painter said she acted sort o' wild, she was so pleased. She told him yaller; an' Josh had him go right to work on't next day. But he had her half painted yaller, an' his a kind of a drab, I guess you'd call it. He sold a piece o' ma'sh to pay for't. Dr. Parks said you might as well kill a woman with a hatchet, as the man did down to Sudleigh, as put her through such treatment. My! ain't it growin' late? Here, let me set back by the winder. I want to see who goes by, to-day. An' I'll cut my story short.

"Well, they lived jest that way. Lyddy Ann she looked like an old woman, in a month or two. She looked every minute as old as you do, Mis' Gridley. Ain't you sixty-nine? Well, she wa'n't but thirty-six. Her hair turned gray, an' she was all stooped over. Sometimes I thought she wa'n't jest right. I used to go in to see if she'd go coltsfootin' with me, or plummin'; but she never'd make me no answer. I recollect two things she said. One day, she set rockin' back'ards an' for'ards in a straight chair, holdin' her hands round her knees, an' she says,

" 'I ain't got no pride, Sally Flint! I ain't got no pride!'

"An' once she looked up kind o' pitiful an' says, 'Ain't it queer I can't die?' But, poor creatur', I never thought she knew what she was sayin'. She'd ha' been the last one to own she wa'n't contented if she'd had any gover'ment over her words.

"Well, Josh he'd turned the hired man away because he couldn't do for him over the air-tight stove, an' he got men to help him by day's works. An' through the winter, he jest set over the fire an' sucked his claws, an' thought how smart he was. But one day 'twas awful cold, an' we'd been tryin' out lard, an' the fat ketched fire, an' everything was all up in arms, anyway. Cyrus he was goin' by Josh's, an' he didn't see no smoke from the settin'-room stove. So he jest went to the side door an' walked in, an' there set Josh in the middle o' the room. Couldn't move hand nor foot! Cyrus didn't stop for no words, but he run over to our house, hollerin', 'Josh Marden's got a stroke!' An' ma'am left the stove all over fat an' run, an' I arter her. I guess Lyddy Ann must ha' seen us comin', for we hadn't more'n got into the settin'-room afore she was there. The place was cold as a barn, an' it looked like a hurrah's nest. Josh never moved, but his eyes follered her when she went into the bedroom to spread up the bed.

"'You help me, Cyrus,' says she, kind o' twittery-like, but calm. 'We'll carry him in here. I can lift.'

"But our men-folks got there jest about as they were tryin' to plan how to take him, an' they h'isted him onto the bed. Cyrus harnessed up our horse an' went after Dr. Parks, an' by the time he come, we'd got the rooms so's to look decent. An'—if you'll b'lieve it!—Lyddy Ann was in the bedroom tryin' to warm Josh up an' make him take some hot drink; but when I begun to sweep up, an' swop towards that gravel-pile in the middle o' the floor, she come hurryin' up, all out o' breath. She ketched the broom right out o' my hand.

"'I'll sweep, bime-by,' says she. 'Don't you touch that gravel, none on ye!' An' so the gravel laid there, an' we walked round it, watchers an' all.

"She wouldn't have no watcher in his bedroom, though; she was determined to do everything but turn him an' lift him herself, but there was al'ays one or two settin' round to keep

the fires goin' an' make sure there was enough cooked up.
I swan, I never see a woman so happy round a bed o' sickness as Lyddy Ann was! She never made no fuss when
Josh was awake, but if he shet his eyes, she'd kind o' hang
over the bed an' smooth the clo'es as if they was kittens an'
once I ketched her huggin' up the sleeve of his old barn coat
that hung outside the door. If ever a woman made a fool
of herself over a man that wa'n't wuth it, 'twas Lyddy Ann
Marden!

"Well, Josh he hung on for a good while, an' we couldn't
make out whether he had his senses or not. He kep' his eyes
shet most o' the time; but when Lyddy Ann's back was
turned, he seemed to know it somehow, an' he'd open 'em
an' foller her all round the room. But he never spoke. I
asked the doctor about it.

" 'Can't he speak, doctor?' says I. 'He can move that
hand a leetle to-day. Don't you s'pose he could speak, if
he'd a mind to?'

"The doctor he squinted up his eyes—he al'ays done that
when he didn't want to answer—an' he says,

" 'I guess he's thinkin' on't over.'

"But one day, Lyddy Ann found she was all beat out, an'
she laid down in the best bedroom an' went to sleep. I set
with Josh. I was narrerin' off, but when I looked up, he was
beckonin' with his well hand. I got up, an' went to the bed.

" 'Be you dry?' says I. He made a little motion, an' then
he lifted his hand an' p'inted out into the settin'-room.

" 'Do you want Lyddy Ann?' says I. 'She's laid down.'
No, he didn't want her. I went to the settin'-room door an'
looked out, an'—I dunno how 'twas—it all come to me.

" 'Is it that gravel-heap?' says I. 'Do you want it carried
off, an' the floor swop up?' An' he made a motion to say
'Yes.' I called Cyrus, an' we made short work o' that gravel.
When I'd took up the last mite on't, I went back to the bed.

" 'Josh Marden,' says I, 'can you speak, or can't you?'
But he shet his eyes, an' wouldn't say a word.

"When Lyddy Ann come out, I told her what he'd done,
an' then she did give way a little mite. Two tears come out

o' her eyes, an' jest rolled down her cheeks, but she didn't give up to 'em.

" 'Sally,' says she, sort o' peaceful, 'I guess I'll have a cup o' tea.'

"Well, there was times when we thought Josh would git round ag'in, if he didn't have another stroke. I dunno whether he did have another or not, but one night, he seemed to be sort o' sinkin' away. Lyddy Ann she begun to turn white, an' she set down by him an' rubbed his sick hand. He looked at her—fust time he had, fair an' square—an' then he begun to wobble his lips round an' make a queer noise with 'em. She put her head down, an' then she says, 'Yes, Joshuay! yes, dear!' An' she got up an' took the pocket-book 'Mandy had gi'n him off the top o' the bureau, an' laid it down on the bed where he could git it. But he shook his head, an' said the word ag'in, an' a queer look—as if she was scairt an' pleased— flashed over Lyddy Ann's face. She run into the parlor, an' come back with that old pocket-book he'd give up to her, an' she put it into his well hand. That was what he wanted. His fingers gripped it up, an' he shet his eyes. He never spoke ag'in. He died that night."

"I guess she died, too!" said Lucy Staples, under her breath, stealthily wiping a tear from her faded cheek.

"No, she didn't, either!" retorted Sally Flint, hastily, getting up to peer from the window down the country road. "She lived a good many year, right in that very room he'd drove her out on, an' she looked as if she owned the airth. I've studied on it consid'able, an' I al'ays s'posed 'twas because she'd got him, an' that was all she cared for. There's the hearse now, an' two carriages, step an' step."

"Land! who's dead?" exclaimed Mrs. Forbes, getting up in haste, while her ball rolled unhindered to the other end of the room.

"It's Lyddy Ann Marden," returned Sally Flint, with the triumphant quiet of one first at the goal. "I see it this mornin' in the *County Democrat,* when I was doin' up my wrist, an' you was all so busy."

AN OCCURRENCE AT OWL CREEK BRIDGE *

By Ambrose Bierce

I

A MAN stood upon a railroad bridge in northern Alabama, looking down into the swift water twenty feet below. The man's hands were behind his back, the wrists bound with a cord. A rope closely encircled his neck. It was attached to a stout cross-timber above his head and the slack fell to the level of his knees. Some loose boards laid upon the sleepers supporting the metals of the railway supplied a footing for him and his executioners—two private soldiers of the Federal army, directed by a sergeant who in civil life may have been a deputy sheriff. At a short remove upon the same temporary platform was an officer in the uniform of his rank, armed. He was a captain. A sentinel at each end of the bridge stood with his rifle in the position known as "support," that is to say, vertical in front of the left shoulder, the hammer resting on the forearm thrown straight across the chest—a formal and unnatural position, enforcing an erect carriage of the body. It did not appear to be the duty of these two men to know what was occurring at the centre of the bridge; they merely blockaded the two ends of the foot planking that traversed it.

Beyond one of the sentinels nobody was in sight; the railroad ran straight away into a forest for a hundred yards, then, curving, was lost to view. Doubtless there was an outpost farther along. The other bank of the stream was open ground—a gentle acclivity topped with a stockade of vertical tree trunks, loopholed for rifles, with a single embrasure

---

* From "In the Midst of Life," published by Boni & Liveright. Copyright by The Neale Publishing Company.

through which protruded the muzzle of a brass cannon commanding the bridge. Midway of the slope between bridge and fort were the spectators—a single company of infantry in line, at "parade rest," the butts of the rifles on the ground, the barrels inclining slightly backward against the right shoulder, the hands crossed upon the stock. A lieutenant stood at the right of the line, the point of his sword upon the ground, his left hand resting upon his right. Excepting the group of four at the centre of the bridge, not a man moved. The company faced the bridge, staring stonily, motionless. The sentinels, facing the banks of the stream, might have been statues to adorn the bridge. The captain stood with folded arms, silent, observing the work of his subordinates, but making no sign. Death is a dignitary who when he comes announced is to be received with formal manifestations of respect, even by those most familiar with him. In the code of military etiquette silence and fixity are forms of deference.

The man who was engaged in being hanged was apparently about thirty-five years of age. He was a civilian, if one might judge from his habit, which was that of a planter. His features were good—a straight nose, firm mouth, broad forehead, from which his long dark hair was combed straight back, falling behind his ears to the collar of his well-fitting frock-coat. He wore a mustache and pointed beard, but no whiskers; his eyes were large and dark gray, and had a kindly expression which one would hardly have expected in one whose neck was in the hemp. Evidently this was no vulgar assassin. The liberal military code makes provision for hanging many kinds of persons, and gentlemen are not excluded.

The preparations being complete, the two private soldiers stepped aside and each drew away the plank upon which he had been standing. The sergeant turned to the captain, saluted and placed himself immediately behind that officer, who in turn moved apart one pace. These movements left the condemned man and the sergeant standing on the two ends of the same plank, which spanned three of the crossties of the bridge. The end upon which the civilian stood almost, but not quite, reached a fourth. This plank had been held in place by the weight of the captain; it was now held by that of the sergeant. At a signal from the former the latter would step aside, the plank would tilt and the condemned man go down between two ties. The arrangement commended itself to his judgment as simple and effective. His face had not been covered nor his eyes bandaged. He looked a moment at his "unsteadfast footing," then let his gaze wander to the swirling water of the stream racing madly beneath his feet. A piece of dancing driftwood caught his attention and his eyes followed it down the current. How slowly it appeared to move! What a sluggish stream!

He closed his eyes in order to fix his last thoughts upon his wife and children. The water, touched to gold by the early sun, the brooding mists under the banks at some distance down the stream, the fort, the soldiers, the piece of drift—all had distracted him. And now he became conscious of a new disturbance. Striking through the thought of his dear ones was a sound which he could neither ignore nor understand, a sharp, distinct, metallic percussion like the stroke of a blacksmith's hammer upon the anvil; it had the same ringing quality. He wondered what it was, and whether immeasurably distant or near by—it seemed both. Its recurrence was regular, but as slow as the tolling of a death knell. He awaited each stroke with impatience and—he knew not why—apprehension. The intervals of silence grew progressively longer; the delays became maddening. With their greater infrequency the sounds increased in strength and sharpness. They hurt his ear like the thrust of a knife; he feared he would shriek. What he heard was the ticking of his watch.

He unclosed his eyes and saw again the water below him. "If I could free my hands," he thought, "I might throw off the noose and spring into the stream. By diving I could evade the bullets and, swimming vigorously, reach the bank, take to the woods and get away home. My home, thank God, is as yet outside their lines; my wife and little ones are still beyond the invader's farthest advance."

As these thoughts, which have here to be set down in

words, were flashed into the doomed man's brain rather than evolved from it, the captain nodded to the sergeant. The sergeant stepped aside.

II

Peyton Farquhar was a well-to-do planter, of an old and highly respected Alabama family. Being a slave owner and, like other slave owners, a politician he was naturally an original secessionist and ardently devoted to the Southern cause. Circumstances of an imperious nature, which it is unnecessary to relate here, had prevented him from taking service with the gallant army that had fought the disastrous campaigns ending with the fall of Corinth, and he chafed under the inglorious restraint, longing for the release of his energies, the larger life of the soldier, the opportunity for distinction. That opportunity, he felt, would come, as it comes to all in war time. Meanwhile he did what he could. No service was too humble for him to perform in aid of the South, no adventure too perilous for him to undertake if consistent with the character of a civilian who was at heart a soldier, and who in good faith and without too much qualification assented to at least a part of the frankly villainous dictum that all is fair in love and war.

One evening while Farquhar and his wife were sitting on a rustic bench near the entrance to his grounds, a gray-clad soldier rode up to the gate and asked for a drink of water. Mrs. Farquhar was only too happy to serve him with her own white hands. While she was fetching the water her husband approached the dusty horseman and inquired eagerly for news from the front.

"The Yanks are repairing the railroads," said the man, "and are getting ready for another advance. They have reached the Owl Creek bridge, put it in order and built a stockade on the north bank. The commandant has issued an order, which is posted everywhere, declaring that any civilian caught interfering with the railroad, its bridges, tunnels or trains will be summarily hanged. I saw the order."

"How far it is to the Owl Creek bridge?" Farquhar asked.

"About thirty miles."

"Is there no force on this side the creek?"

"Only a picket post half a mile out, on the railroad, and a single sentinel at this end of the bridge."

"Suppose a man—a civilian and student of hanging—should elude the picket post and perhaps get the better of the sentinel," said Farquhar, smiling, "what could he accomplish?"

The soldier reflected. "I was there a month ago," he replied. "I observed that the flood of last winter had lodged a great quantity of driftwood against the wooden pier at this end of the bridge. It is now dry and would burn like tow."

The lady had now brought the water, which the soldier drank. He thanked her ceremoniously, bowed to her husband and rode away. An hour later, after nightfall, he repassed the plantation, going northward in the direction from which he had come. He was a Federal scout.

III

As Peyton Farquhar fell straight downward through the bridge he lost consciousness and was as one already dead. From this state he was awakened—ages later, it seemed to him—by the pain of a sharp pressure upon his throat, followed by a sense of suffocation. Keen, poignant agonies seemed to shoot from his neck downward through every fibre of his body and limbs. These pains appeared to flash along well-defined lines of ramification and to beat with an inconceivably rapid periodicity. They seemed like streams of pulsating fire heating him to an intolerable temperature. As to his head, he was conscious of nothing but a feeling of fulness—of congestion. These sensations were unaccompanied by thought. The intellectual part of his nature was already effaced; he had power only to feel, and feeling was torment. He was conscious of motion. Encompassed in a luminous cloud, of which he was now merely the fiery heart, without material substance, he swung through unthinkable arcs of oscillation, like a vast pendulum. Then all at once, with terrible suddenness, the light about him shot upward with the noise of a loud plash; a frightful roaring was in his ears, and all was cold and dark. The power of thought was restored; he knew that the rope had broken and he had fallen into the stream. There was no additional strangulation; the noose about his neck was already suffocating him and kept the water from his lungs. To die of hanging at the bottom of a river!—the idea seemed to him ludicrous. He opened his eyes in the darkness and saw above him a gleam of light, but how distant, how inaccessible! He was still sinking, for the light became fainter and fainter until it was a mere glimmer. Then it began to grow and brighten, and he knew that he was rising toward the surface—knew it with reluctance, for he was now very comfortable. "To be hanged and drowned," he thought, "that is not so bad; but I do not wish to be shot. No; I will not be shot; that is not fair."

He was not conscious of an effort, but a sharp pain in his wrist apprised him that he was trying to free his hands. He gave the struggle his attention, as an idler might observe the feat of a juggler, without interest in the outcome. What splendid effort! What magnificent, what superhuman strength! Ah, that was a fine endeavor! Bravo! The cord fell away; his arms parted and floated upward, the hands dimly seen on each side in the growing light. He watched them with a new interest as first one and then the other pounced upon the noose at his neck. They tore it away and thrust it fiercely aside, its undulations resembling those of a water-snake. "Put it back, put it back!" He thought he shouted these words to his hands, for the undoing of the noose had been succeeded by the direst pang that he had yet experienced. His neck ached horribly; his brain was on fire; his heart, which had been fluttering faintly, gave a great leap, trying to force itself out at his mouth. His whole body was racked and wrenched with an insupportable anguish! But his disobedient hands gave no heed to the command. They beat the water vigorously with quick, downward strokes, forcing him to the surface. He felt his head emerge; his eyes were blinded by the sunlight; his chest expanded convulsively, and with a supreme and crowning agony his lungs engulfed a great draught of air, which instantly he expelled in a shriek!

He was now in full possession of his physical senses. They were, indeed, preternaturally keen and alert. Something in the awful disturbance of his organic system had so exalted and refined them that they made record of things never before perceived. He felt the ripples upon his face and heard their separate sounds as they struck. He looked at the forest on the bank of the stream, saw the individual trees, the leaves and the veining of each leaf—saw the very insects upon them: the locusts, the brilliant-bodied flies, the gray spiders stretching their webs from twig to twig. He noted the prismatic colors in all the dewdrops upon a million blades of grass. The humming of the gnats that danced above the eddies of the stream, the beating of the dragon-flies' wings, the strokes of the water-spiders' legs, like oars which had lifted their boat—all these made audible music. A fish slid along beneath his eyes and he heard the rush of its body parting the water.

He had come to the surface facing down the stream; in a moment the visible world seemed to wheel slowly round, himself the pivotal point, and he saw the bridge, the fort, the soldiers upon the bridge, the captain, the sergeant, the two privates, his executioners. They were in silhouette against the blue sky. The shouted and gesticulated, pointing at him. The captain had drawn his pistol, but did not fire; the others were unarmed. Their movements were grotesque and horrible, their forms gigantic.

Suddenly he heard a sharp report and something struck the water smartly within a few inches of his head, spattering his face with spray. He heard a second report, and saw one of the sentinels with his rifle at his shoulder, a light cloud of blue smoke rising from the muzzle. The man in the water saw the eye of the man on the bridge gazing into his own through the sights of the rifle. He observed that it was a gray eye and remembered having read that gray eyes were keenest, and that all famous marksmen had them. Nevertheless, this one had missed.

A counter-swirl had caught Farquhar and turned him half round; he was again looking into the forest on the bank opposite the fort. The sound of a clear, high voice in a monotonous singsong now rang out behind him and came across the water with a distinctness that pierced and subdued all other sounds, even the beating of the ripples in his ears. Although no soldier, he had frequented camps enough to know the dread significance of that deliberate, drawling, aspirated chant; the lieutenant on shore was taking a part in the morning's work. How coldly and pitilessly—with what an even, calm intonation, presaging and enforcing tranquility in the men—with what accurately measured intervals fell those cruel words:

"Attention, company! . . . Shoulder arms! . . . Ready! . . . Aim! . . . Fire!"

Farquhar dived—dived as deeply as he could. The water roared in his ears like the voice of Niagara, yet he heard the dulled thunder of the volley and, rising again toward the surface, met shining bits of metal, singularly flattened, oscillating slowly downward. Some of them touched him on the face and hands, then fell away, continuing their descent. One lodged between his collar and neck; it was uncomfortably warm and he snatched it out.

As he rose to the surface, gasping for breath, he saw that he had been a long time under water; he was perceptibly farther down stream—nearer to safety. The soldiers had almost finished reloading; the metal ramrods flashed all at once in the sunshine as they were drawn from the barrels, turned in the air, and thrust into their sockets. The two sentinels fired again, independently and ineffectually.

The hunted man saw all this over his shoulder; he was now swimming vigorously with the current. His brain was as energetic as his arms and legs; he thought with the rapidity of lightning.

"The officer," he reasoned, "will not make that martinet's error a second time. It is as easy to dodge a volley as a single shot. He has probably already given the command to fire at will. God help me, I cannot dodge them all!"

An appalling plash within two yards of him was followed by a loud, rushing sound, *diminuendo,* which seemed to travel back through the air to the fort and died in an explosion which stirred the very river to its deeps! A rising sheet of water curved over him, fell down upon him, blinded him, strangled him! The cannon had taken a hand in the game. As he shook his head free from the commotion of the smitten water he heard the deflected shot humming through the air ahead, and in an instant it was cracking and smashing the branches in the forest beyond.

"They will not do that again," he thought, "the next time they will use a charge of grape. I must keep my eye upon the gun; the smoke will apprise me—the report arrives too late; it lags behind the missile. That is a good gun."

Suddenly he felt himself whirled round and round—spinning like a top. The water, the banks, the forests, the now distant bridge, fort and men—all were commingled and blurred. Objects were represented by their colors only; circular horizontal streaks of color—that was all he saw. He had been caught in the vortex and was being whirled on with a velocity of advance and gyration that made him giddy and sick. In a few moments he was flung upon the gravel at the foot of the left bank of the stream—the southern bank—and behind a projecting point which concealed him from his enemies. The sudden arrest of his motion, the abrasion of one of his hands on the gravel, restored him, and he wept with delight. He dug his fingers into the sand, threw it over himself in handfuls and audibly blessed it. It looked like diamonds, rubies, emeralds; he could think of nothing beautiful which it did not resemble. The trees upon the bank were giant garden plants; he noted a definite order in their arrangement, inhaled the fragrance of their blooms. A strange, roseate light shone through the spaces among their trunks and the wind made in their branches the music of æolian harps. He had no wish to perfect his escape—was content to remain in that enchanting spot until retaken.

A whiz and rattle of grapeshot among the branches high above his head roused him from his dream. The baffled cannoneer had fired him a random farewell. He sprang to his feet, rushed up the sloping bank, and plunged into the forest.

All that day he traveled, laying his course by the rounding sun. The forest seemed interminable; nowhere did he discover a break in it, not ever a woodman's road. He had not known that he lived in so wild a region. There was something uncanny in the revelation.

By nightfall he was fatigued, footsore, famishing. The thought of his wife and children urged him on. At last he found a road which led him in what he knew to be the right direction. It was as wide and straight as a city street, yet it seemed untraveled. No fields bordered it, no dwelling anywhere. Not so much as the barking of a dog suggested human habitation. The black bodies of the trees formed a straight wall on both sides, terminating on the horizon in a point, like a diagram in a lesson in perspective. Over head, as he looked up through this rift in the wood, shone great golden stars looking unfamiliar and grouped in strange constellations. He was sure they were arranged in some order which had a secret and malign significance. The wood on either side was full of singular noises, among which— once, twice, and again—he distinctly heard whispers in an unknown tongue.

His neck was in pain and lifting his hand to it he found it horribly swollen. He knew that it had a circle of black where the rope had bruised it. His eyes felt congested; he could no longer close them. His tongue was swollen with thirst; he relieved its fever by thrusting it forward from between his teeth into the cold air. How softly the turf had carpeted the untraveled avenue—he could no longer feel the roadway beneath his feet!

Doubtless, despite his suffering, he had fallen asleep while walking, for now he sees another scene—perhaps he has merely recovered from a delirium. He stands at the gate of his own home. All is as he left it, and all bright and beautiful in the morning sunshine. He must have traveled the entire night. As he pushes open the gate and passes up the wide white walk, he sees a flutter of female garments; his wife, looking fresh and cool and sweet, steps down from the veranda to meet him. At the bottom of the steps she stands waiting, with a smile of ineffable joy, an attitude of matchless grace and dignity. Ah, how beautiful she is! He springs forward with extended arms. As he is about to clasp her he feels a stunning blow upon the back of the neck; a blinding white light blazes all about him with a sound like the shock of a cannon—then all is darkness and silence!

Peyton Farquhar was dead; his body, with a broken neck, swung gently from side to side beneath the timbers of the Owl Creek bridge.

THE RETURN OF A PRIVATE *

By Hamlin Garland

THE nearer the train drew toward La Crosse, the soberer the little group of "vets" became. On the long way from New Orleans they had beguiled tedium with jokes and friendly chaff; or with planning with elaborate detail what they were going to do now, after the war. A long journey, slowly, irregularly, yet persistently pushing northward. When they entered on Wisconsin territory they gave a cheer, and another when they reached Madison, but after that they sank into a dumb expectancy. Comrades dropped off at one or two points beyond, until there were only four or five left who were bound for La Crosse County.

Three of them were gaunt and brown, the fourth was gaunt and pale, with signs of fever and ague upon him. One had a great scar down his temple, one limped, and they all had unnaturally large, bright eyes, showing emaciation. There were no bands greeting them at the station, no banks of gayly dressed ladies waving handkerchiefs and shouting "Bravo!" as they came in on the caboose of a freight train into the towns that had cheered and blared at them on their way to war. As they looked out or stepped upon the platform for a moment, while the train stood at the station, the loafers looked at them indifferently. Their blue coats, dusty and grimy, were too familiar now to excite notice, much less a friendly word. They were the last of the army to return, and the loafers were surfeited with such sights.

The train jogged forward so slowly that it seemed likely to be midnight before they should reach La Crosse. The

---

* By permission of the author.

248

little squad grumbled and swore, but it was no use; the train would not hurry, and, as a matter of fact, it was nearly two o'clock when the engine whistled "down brakes."

All of the group were farmers, living in districts several miles out of the town, and all were poor.

"Now, boys," said Private Smith, he of the fever and ague, "we are landed in La Crosse in the night. We've got to stay somewhere till mornin'. Now I ain't got no two dollars to waste on a hotel. I've got a wife and children, so I'm goin' to roost on a bench and take the cost of a bed out of my hide."

"Same here," put in one of the other men. "Hide'll grow on again, dollars'll come hard. It's goin' to be mighty hot skirmishin' to find a dollar these days."

"Don't think they'll be a deputation of citizens waitin' to 'scort us to a hotel, eh?" said another. His sarcasm was too obvious to require an answer.

Smith went on, "Then at daybreak we'll start for home—at least, I will."

"Well, I'll be dummed if I'll take two dollars out o' *my* hide," one of the younger men said. "I'm goin' to a hotel, ef I don't never lay up a cent."

"That'll do f'r you," said Smith; "but if you had a wife an' three young uns dependin' on yeh—"

"Which I ain't, thank the Lord! and don't intend havin' while the court knows itself."

The station was deserted, chill and dark, as they came into it at exactly a quarter to two in the morning. Lit by the oil lamps that flared a dull red light over the dingy benches, the waiting room was not an inviting place. The younger man went off to look up a hotel, while the rest remained and prepared to camp down on the floor and benches. Smith was attended to tenderly by the other men, who spread their blankets on the bench for him, and, by robbing themselves, made quite a comfortable bed, though the narrowness of the bench made his sleeping precarious.

It was chill, though August, and the two men, sitting with bowed heads, grew stiff with cold and weariness, and were forced to rise now and again and walk about to warm their stiffened limbs. It did not occur to them, probably, to contrast their coming home with their going forth, or with the coming home of the generals, colonels, or even captains—but to Private Smith, at any rate, there came a sickness at heart almost deadly as he lay there on his hard bed and went over his situation.

In the deep of the night, lying on a board in the town where he had enlisted three years ago, all elation and enthusiasm gone out of him, he faced the fact that with the joy of home-coming was already mingled the bitter juice of care. He saw himself sick, worn out, taking up the work on his half-cleared farm, the inevitable mortgage standing ready with open jaw to swallow half his earnings. He had given three years of his life for a mere pittance of pay, and now—!

Morning dawned at last, slowly, with a pale yellow dome of light rising silently above the bluffs, which stand like some huge storm-devastated castle, just east of the city. Out to the left the great river swept on its massive yet silent way to the south. Bluejays called across the water from hillside to hillside through the clear, beautiful air, and hawks began to skim the tops of the hills. The older men were astir early, but Private Smith had fallen at last into a sleep, and they went out without waking him. He lay on his knapsack, his gaunt face turned toward the ceiling, his hands clasped on his breast, with a curious pathetic effect of weakness and appeal.

An engine switching near woke him at last, and he slowly sat up and stared about. He looked out of the window and saw that the sun was lightening the hills across the river. He rose and brushed his hair as well as he could, folded his blankets up, and went out to find his companions. They stood gazing silently at the river and at the hills.

"Looks natcher'l, don't it?" they said, as he came out.

"That's what it does," he replied. "An' it looks good. D'yeh see that peak?" He pointed at a beautiful symmetrical peak, rising like a slightly truncated cone, so high that it seemed the very highest of them all. It was touched by that morning sun and it glowed like a beacon, and a light scarf of gray morning fog was rolling up its shadowed side.

"My farm's just beyond that. Now, if I can only ketch a ride, we'll be home by dinner-time."

"I'm talkin' about breakfast," said one of the others.

"I guess it's one more meal o' hardtack f'r me." said Smith.

They foraged around, and finally found a restaurant with a sleepy old German behind the counter, and procured some coffee, which they drank to wash down their hardtack.

"Time'll come," said Smith, holding up a piece by the corner, "when this'll be a curiosity."

"I hope to God it will! I bet I've chawed hardtack enough to shingle every house in the coolly. I've chawed it when my lampers was down, and when they wasn't. I've took it dry, soaked, and mashed. I've had it wormy, musty, sour, and blue-mouldy. I've had it in little bits and big bits; 'fore coffee an' after coffee. I'm ready f'r a change. I'd like t' git holt jest about now o' some of the hot biscuits my wife c'n make when she lays herself out f'r company.

"Well, if you set there gabblin', you'll never *see* yer wife."

"Come on," said Private Smith. "Wait a moment, boys; le's take suthin'. It's on me." He led them to the rusty tin dipper which hung on a nail beside the wooden water-pail, and they grinned and drank. Then shouldering their blankets and muskets, which they were "takin' home to the boys," they struck out on their last march.

"They called that coffee Jayvy," grumbled one of them, "but it never went by the road where government Jayvy resides. I reckon I know coffee from peas."

They kept together on the road along the turnpike, and up the winding road by the river, which they followed for some miles. The river was very lovely, curving down along its sandy beds, pausing now and then under broad basswood trees, or running in dark, swift, silent currents under tangles of wild grape vines, and drooping alders, and haw trees. At one of these lovely spots the three vets sat down on the thick green sward to rest, "on Smith's account." The leaves of the trees were as fresh and green as in June, the jays called cheery greetings to them, and kingfishers darted to and fro with swooping, noiseless flight.

"I tell yeh, boys, this knocks the swamps of Loueesiana into kingdom come."

"You bet. All they c'n raise down there is snakes, niggers, and p'rticler hell."

"An' fightin' men," put in the older man.

"An' fightin' men. If I had a good hook an' line I'd sneak a pick'rel out o' that pond. Say, remember that time I shot that alligator—"

"I guess we'd better be crawlin' along," interrupted Smith, rising and shouldering his knapsack, with considerable effort, which he tried to hide.

"Say, Smith, lemme give you a lift on that."

"I guess I c'n manage," said Smith grimly.

"Course. But, yo' see, I may not have a chance right off to pay yeh back for the times you've carried my gun and hull caboodle. Say, now, gimme that gun, anyway."

"All right, if yeh feel like it, Jim." Smith replied, and they trudged along doggedly in the sun, which was getting higher and hotter each half-mile.

"Ain't it queer there ain't no teams comin' along," said Smith, after a long silence.

"Well, nó, seein's it's Sunday."

"By jinks, that's a fact. It *is* Sunday. I'll git home in time f'r dinner, sure!" he exulted. "She don't hev dinner usially till about *one* on Sundays." And he fell into a muse, in which he smiled.

"Well, I'll git home jest about six o'clock, jest about when the boys are milkin' the cows," said old Jim Cranby. "I'll step into the barn, an' then I'll say, 'H*eah!* why ain't this milkin' done before this time o' day?' An' then won't they yell!" he added, slapping his thigh in great glee.

Smith went on. "I'll jest go up the path. Old Rover'll come down the road to meet me. He won't bark—he'll know me—an' he'll come down waggin' his tail an' showin' his teeth. That's his way of laughin'. An' so I'll walk up to the kitchen door, an' I'll say, '*Dinner* f'r a hungry man!' An' then she'll jump up, an'—"

He couldn't go on. His voice choked at the thought of it. Saunders, the third man, hardly uttered a word, but walked silently behind the others. He had lost his wife the first year he was in the army. She died of pneumonia, caught in the autumn rains while working in the fields in his place.

They plodded along till at last they came to a parting of the ways. To the right the road continued up the main valley; to the left it went over the big ridge.

"Well, boys," began Smith, as they grounded their muskets and looked away up the valley, "here's where we shake hands. We've marched together a good many miles, an' now I s'pose we're done."

"Yes, I don't think we'll do any more of it f'r a while. I don't want to, I know."

" I hope I'll see yeh once in a while, boys, to talk over old times."

"Of course," said Saunders, whose voice trembled a little, too. "It ain't *exactly* like dyin'." They all found it hard to look at each other.

"But we'd ought'r go home with you," said Cranby. "You'll never climb that ridge with all them things on yer back."

"Oh, I'm all right! Don't worry about me. Every step takes me nearer home, yeh see. Well, good-by, boys."

They shook hands. "Good-by. Good luck!"

"Same to you. Lemme know how you find things at home."

"Good-by."

"Good-by."

He turned once before they passed out of sight, and waved his cap, and they did the same, and all yelled. Then all marched away with their long, steady, loping, veteran step. The solitary climber in blue walked on for a time, with his mind filled with the kindness of his comrades, and musing upon the many wonderful days they had had together in camp and field.

He though of his chum, Billy Tripp. Poor Billy! A "minie" ball fell into his breast one day, fell wailing like a cat, and tore a great ragged hole in his heart. He looked forward to a sad scene with Billy's mother and sweetheart. They would want to know all about it. He tried to recall all that Billy had said, and the particulars of it, but there was little to remember, just that wild wailing sound high in the air, a dull slap, a short, quick, expulsive groan, and the boy lay with his face in the dirt in the ploughed field they were marching across.

That was all. But all the scenes he had since been through had not dimmed the horror, the terror of that moment, when his boy comrade fell, with only a breath between a laugh and a death-groan. Poor handsome Billy! Worth millions of dollars was his young life.

These sombre recollections gave way at length to more cheerful feelings as he began to approach his home coolly. The fields and houses grew familiar, and in one or two he was greeted by people seated in the doorways. But he was in no mood to talk, and pushed on steadily, though he stopped and accepted a drink of milk once at the well-side of a neighbor.

The sun was burning hot on that slope, and his step grew slower, in spite of his iron resolution. He sat down several times to rest. Slowly he crawled up the rough, reddish-brown road, which wound along the hill-side, under great trees, through dense groves of jack oaks, with tree-tops far below him on his left hand, and the hills far above him on his right. He crawled along like some minute, wingless variety of fly.

He ate some hardtack, sauced with wild berries, when he reached the summit of the ridge, and sat there for some time, looked down into his home coolly.

Sombre, pathetic figure! His wide, round, gray eyes gazing down into the beautiful valley, seeing and not seeing, the splendid cloud-shadows sweeping over the western hills and across the green and yellow wheat far below. His head dropped forward on his palm, his shoulders took on a tired stoop, his cheek-bones showed painfully. An observer might have said, "He is looking down upon his own grave."

II

Sunday comes in a Western wheat harvest with such sweet and sudden relaxation to man and beast that it would be holy for that reason, if for no other, and Sundays are usually fair in harvest-time. As one goes out into the field in the hot morning sunshine, with no sound abroad save the crickets and the indescribably pleasant silken rustling of the ripened grain, the reaper and the very sheaves in the stubble seem to be resting, dreaming.

Around the house, in the shade of the trees, the men sit, smoking, dozing, or reading the papers, while the women, never resting, move about at the housework. The men eat on Sundays about the same as on other days, and breakfast is no sooner over and out of the way than dinner begins.

But at the Smith farm there were no men dozing or reading. Mrs. Smith was alone with her three children, Mary, nine, Tommy, six, and little Ted, just past four. Her farm, rented to a neighbor, lay at the head of a coolly or narrow gully, made at some far-off post-glacial period by the vast and angry floods of water which gullied these tremendous furrows in the level prairie—furrows so deep that undisturbed portions of the original level rose like hills on either side, rose to quite considerable mountains.

The chickens wakened her as usual that Sabbath morning from dreams of her absent husband, from whom she had not heard for weeks. The shadows drifted over the hills, down the slopes, across the wheat, and up the opposite wall in leisurely way, as if, being Sunday, they could take it easy also. The fowls clustered about the housewife as she went out into the yard. Fuzzy little chickens swarmed out from the coops, where their clucking and perpetually disgruntled mothers tramped about, petulantly thrusting their heads through the spaces between the slats.

A cow called in a deep, musical bass, and a calf answered from a little pen near by, and a pig scurried guiltily out of the cabbages. Seeing all this, seeing the pig in the cabbages, the tangle of grass in the garden, the broken fence which she had mended again and again—the little woman, hardly more than a girl, sat down and cried. The bright Sabbath morning was only a mockery without him!

A few years ago they had bought this farm, paying part, mortgaging the rest in the usual way. Edward Smith was a man of terrible energy. He worked "nights and Sundays," as the saying goes, to clear the farm of its brush and of its insatiate mortgage! In the midst of his Herculean struggle came the call for volunteers, and with the grim and unselfish devotion to his country which made the Eagle Brigade able to "whip its weight in wild-cats," he threw down his scythe and grub-axe, turned his cattle loose, and became a bluecoated cog in a vast machine for killing men, and not thistles. While the millionaire sent his money to England for safe-keeping, this man, with his girl-wife and three babies, left them on a mortgaged farm, and went away to fight for an idea. It was foolish, but it was sublime for all that.

That was three years before, and the young wife, sitting on the well-curb on this bright Sabbath harvest morning, was righteously rebellious. It seemed to her that she had borne her share of the country's sorrow. Two brothers had been killed, the renter in whose hands her husband had left the farm had proved a villain; one year the farm had been without crops, and now the over-ripe grain was waiting the tardy hand of the neighbor who had rented it, and who was cutting his own grain first.

About six weeks before, she had received a letter saying, "We'll be discharged in a little while." But no other word had come from him. She had seen by the papers that his army was being discharged, and from day to day other soldiers slowly percolated in blue streams back into the state and country, but still her hero did not return.

Each week she had told the children that he was coming, and she had watched the road so long that it had become unconscious; and as she stood at the well, or by the kitchen door, her eyes were fixed unthinkingly on the road that wound down the coolly.

Nothing wears on the human soul like waiting. If the stranded mariner, searching the sun-bright seas, could once give up hope of a ship, that horrible grinding on his brain would cease. It was this waiting, hoping, on the edge of despair, that gave Emma Smith no rest.

Neighbors said, with kind intentions: "He's sick, maybe, an' can't start north just yet. He'll come along one o' these days."

"Why don't he write?" was her question, which silenced them all. This Sunday morning it seemed to her as if she could not stand it longer. The house seemed intolerably lonely. So she dressed the little ones in their best calico dresses and home-made jackets, and, closing up the house, set off down the coolly to old Mother Gray's.

"Old Widder Gray" lived at the "mouth of the coolly." She was a widow woman with a large family of stalwart boys and laughing girls. She was the visible incarnation of hospitality and optimistic poverty. With Western open-heartedness she fed every mouth that asked food of her, and worked herself to death as cheerfully as her girls danced in the neighborhood harvest dances.

She waddled down the path to meet Mrs. Smith with a broad smile on her face.

"Oh, you little dears! Come right to your granny. Gimme a kiss! Come right in, Mis' Smith. How are ~eh, anyway? Nice mornin', ain't it? Come in an' set down. Everything's in a clutter, but that won't scare you any."

She led the way into the best room, a sunny, square room, carpeted with a faded and patched rag carpet, and papered with white and green-striped wall-paper, where a few faded effigies of dead members of the family hung in variously sized oval walnut frames. The house resounded with singing, laughter, whistling, tramping of heavy boots, and riotous scufflings. Half-grown boys came to the door and crooked their fingers at the children, who ran out, and were soon heard in the midst of the fun.

"Don't s'pose you've heard from Ed?" Mrs. Smith shook her head. "He'll turn up some day, when you ain't lookin' for 'm." The good old soul had said that so many times that poor Mrs. Smith derived no comfort from it any longer.

"Liz heard from Al the other day. He's comin' some day this week. Anyhow, they expect him."

"Did he say anything of—"

"No, he didn't," Mrs. Gray admitted. "But then it was only a short letter, anyhow. Al ain't much for writin', anyhow. But come out and see my new cheese. I tell yeh, I don't believe I ever had better luck in my life. If Ed should come, I want you should take him up a piece of this cheese."

It was beyond human nature to resist the influence of that noisy, hearty, loving household, and in the midst of the singing and laughing the wife forgot her anxiety, for the time at least, and laughed and sang with the rest.

About eleven o'clock a wagon-load more drove up to the door, and Bill Gray, the widow's oldest son, and his whole family from Sand Lake Coolly piled out amid a good-natured uproar. Every one talked at once, except Bill, who sat in the wagon with his wrists on his knees, a straw in his mouth, and an amused twinkle in his blue eyes.

"Ain't heard nothin' o' Ed, I s'pose?" he asked in a kind of bellow. Mrs. Smith shook her head. Bill, with a delicacy very striking in such a great giant, rolled his quid in his mouth, and said:

"Didn't know but you had. I hear two or three of the Sand Lake boys are comin'. Left New Orleens some time this week. Didn't write nothin' about Ed, but no news is good news in such cases, mother always says."

"Well, go put out yer team," said Mrs. Gray, "an' go'n bring me in some taters, an', Sim, you go see if you c'n find some corn. Sadie, you put on the water to bile. Come now, hustle yer boots, all o' yeh. If I feed this yer crowd, we've got to have some raw materials. If y' think I'm goin' to feed yeh on pie—you're jest mightily mistaken."

The children went off into the fields, the girls put dinner on to boil, and then went to change their dresses and fix their hair. "Somebody might come," they said.

"Land sakes, *I hope* not! I don't know where in time I'd set 'em, 'less they'd eat at the second table," Mrs. Gray laughed, in pretended dismay.

The two older boys, who had served their time in the army, lay out on the grass before the house, and whittled and talked desultorily about the war and the crops, and planned buying a threshing-machine. The older girls and Mrs. Smith helped enlarge the table and put on the dishes, talking all the time in that cherry, incoherent, and meaningful way a group of such women have—a conversation to be taken for its spirit rather than for its letter, though Mrs. Gray at last got the ear of them all and dissertated at length on girls.

"Girls in love ain't no use in the whole blessed week," she said. "Sundays they're a-lookin' down the road, expectin' he'll come. Sunday afternoons they can't think o' nothin' else, 'cause he's *here*. Monday mornin's they're sleepy and kind o' dreamy and slimpsy, and good f'r nothin' on Tuesday and Wednesday. Thursday they git absent-minded, an' begin to look off toward Sunday again, an' mope aroun' and let the dishwater git cold, right under their noses. Friday they break dishes, an' go off in the best room an' snivel, an' look out o' the winder. Saturdays they have queer spurts o' workin' like all p'ssessed, an' spurts o' frizzin' their hair. An' Sunday they begin it all over again."

The girls giggled and blushed all through this tirade from their mother, their broad faces and powerful frames anything but suggestive of lackadaisical sentiment. But Mrs. Smith said:

"Now, Mrs. Gray, I hadn't ought to stay to dinner. You've got—"

"Now you set right down! If any of them girls' beaux comes, they'll have to take what's left, that's all. They ain't s'posed to have much appetite, nohow. No, you're goin' to stay if they starve, an' they ain't no danger o' that."

At one o'clock the long table was piled with boiled potatoes, cords of boiled corn on the cob, squash and pumpkin pies, hot biscuits, sweet pickles, bread and butter, and honey. Then one of the girls took down a conch-shell from a nail, and going to the door, blew a long, fine, free blast, that showed there was no weakness of lungs in her ample chest.

Then the children came out of the forest of corn, out of the creek, out of the loft of the barn, and out of the garden.

"They come to their feed f'r all the world jest like the pigs when y' holler 'poo-ee!' See 'em scoot!" laughed Mrs. Gray, every wrinkle on her face shining with delight.

The men shut up their jack-knives, and surrounded the horse-trough to souse their faces in the cold, hard water, and in a few moments the table was filled with a merry crowd, and a row of wistful-eyed youngsters circled the kitchen wall, where they stood first on one leg and then on the other, in impatient hunger.

"Now pitch in, Mrs. Smith," said Mrs. Gray, presiding over the table. "You know these men critters. They'll eat every grain of it, if yeh give 'em a chance. I swan, they're made o' India-rubber, their stomachs is, I know it."

"Haf to eat to work," said Bill, gnawing a cob with a swift, circular motion that rivalled a corn-sheller in results.

"More like workin' to eat," put in one of the girls, with a giggle. "More eat 'n work with *you*."

"You needn't say anything, Net. Any one that'll eat seven ears—"

"I didn't no such thing. You piled your cobs on my plate."

"That'll do to tell Ed Varney. It won't go down here where we know yeh."

"Good land! Eat all yeh want! They's plenty more in the fiel's, but I can't afford to give you young uns tea. The tea is for us women-folks, and 'specially f'r Mis' Smith an' Bill's wife. We're a-goin' to tell fortunes by it."

One by one the men filled up and shoved back, and one by one the children slipped into their places, and by two o'clock the women alone remained around the débris-covered table, sipping their tea and telling fortunes.

As they got well down to the grounds in the cup, they shook them with a circular motion in the hand, and then turned them bottom-side up quickly in the saucer, then twirled them three or four times one way, and three or four times the other, during a breathless pause. Then Mrs. Gray lifted the cup, and, gazing into it with profound gravity, pronounced the impending fate.

It must be admitted that, to a critical observer, she had abundant preparation for hitting close to the mark, as when she told the girls that "somebody was comin'." "It's a man," she went on gravely. "He is cross-eyed—"

"Oh, you hush!" cried Nettie.

"He has red hair, and is death on b'iled corn and hot biscuit."

The others shrieked with delight.

"But he's goin' to get the mitten, that red-headed feller is, for I see another feller comin' up behind him."

"Oh, lemme see, lemme see!" cried Nettie.

"Keep off," said the priestess, with a lofty gesture. "His hair is black. He don't eat so much, and he works more."

The girls exploded in a shriek of laughter, and pounded their sister on the back.

At last came Mrs. Smith's turn, and she was trembling with excitement as Mrs. Gray again composed her jolly face to what she considered a proper solemnity of expression.

"Somebody is comin' to *you*," she said, after a long pause. "He's got a musket on his back. He's a soldier. He's almost here. See?"

She pointed at two little tea-stems, which really formed a faint suggestion of a man with a musket on his back. He had climbed nearly to the edge of the cup. Mrs. Smith grew pale with excitement. She trembled so she could hardly hold the cup in her hand as she gazed into it.

"It's Ed," cried the old woman. "He's on the way home. Heavens an' earth! There he is now!" She turned and waved her hand out toward the road. They rushed to the door to look where she pointed.

A man in a blue coat, with a musket on his back, was toiling slowly up the hill on the sun-bright, dusty road, toiling slowly, with bent head half hidden by a heavy knapsack. So tired it seemed that walking was indeed a process of falling. So eager to get home he would not stop, would not look aside, but plodded on, amid the cries of the locusts, the welcome of the crickets, and the rustle of the yellow wheat. Getting back to God's country, and his wife and babies!

Laughing, crying, trying to call him and the children at the same time, the little wife, almost hysterical, snatched her hat and ran out into the yard. But the soldier had disappeared over the hill into the hollow beyond, and, by the time she had found the children, he was too far away for her voice to reach him. And, besides, she was not sure it was her husband, for he had not turned his head at their shouts. This seemed so strange. Why didn't he stop to rest at his old neighbor's house? Tortured by hope and doubt, she hurried up the coolly as fast as she could push the baby wagon, the blue-coated figure just ahead pushing steadily, silently forward up the coolly.

When the excited, panting little group came in sight of the gate they saw the blue-coated figure standing, leaning upon the rough rail fence, his chin on his palms, gazing at the empty house. His knapsack, canteen, blankets, and musket lay upon the dusty grass at his feet.

He was like a man lost in a dream. His wide, hungry eyes devoured the scene. The rough lawn, the little unpainted house, the field of clear yellow wheat behind it, down across which streamed the sun, now almost ready to touch the high hill to the west, the crickets crying merrily, a cat on the fence near by, dreaming, unmindful of the stranger in blue—

How peaceful it all was. O God! How far removed from all camps, hospitals, battle lines. A little cabin in a Wisconsin coolly, but it was majestic in its peace. How did he ever leave it for those years of tramping, thirsting, killing?

Trembling, weak with emotion, her eyes on the silent figure, Mrs. Smith hurried up to the fence. Her feet made no noise in the dust and grass, and they were close upon him before he knew of them. The oldest boy ran a little ahead. He will never forget that figure, that face. It will always remain as something epic, that return of the private. He fixed his eyes on the pale face covered with a ragged beard.

"Who *are* you, sir?" asked the wife, or, rather, started to ask, for he turned, stood a moment, and then cried:

"Emma!"

"Edward!"

The children stood in a curious row to see their mother kiss this bearded, strange man, the elder girl sobbing sympathetically with her mother. Illness had left the soldier partly deaf, and this added to the strangeness of his manner.

But the youngest child stood away, even after the girl had recognized her father and kissed him. The man turned then to the baby, and said in a curiously unpaternal tone:

"Come here, my little man; don't you know me?" But the baby backed away under the fence and stood peering at him critically.

"My little man!" What meaning in those words! This baby seemed like some other woman's child, and not the infant he had left in his wife's arms. The war had come between him and his baby—he was only a strange man to him, with big eyes; a soldier, with mother hanging to his arm, and talking in a loud voice.

"And this is Tom," the private said, drawing the oldest boy to him. *"He'll* come and see me. *He* knows his poor old pap when he comes home from the war."

The mother heard the pain and reproach in his voice and hastened to apologize.

"You've changed so, Ed. He can't know yeh. This is papa, Teddy; come and kiss him—Tom and Mary do. Come, won't you?" But Teddy still peered through the fence with solemn eyes, well out of reach. He resembled a half-wild kitten that hesitates, studying the tones of one's voice.

"I'll fix him," said the soldier, and sat down to undo his knapsack, out of which he drew three enormous and very red apples. After giving one to each of the older children, he said:

"Now I guess he'll come. Eh, my little man? Now come see your pap."

Teddy crept slowly under the fence, assisted by the over-zealous Tommy, and a moment later was kicking and squalling in his father's arms. Then they entered the house, into the sitting room, poor, bare, art-forsaken little room, too, with its rag carpet, its square clock, and its two or three chromos and pictures from *Harper's Weekly* pinned about.

"Emma, I'm all tired out," said Private Smith, as he flung himself down on the carpet as he used to do, while his wife brought a pillow to put under his head, and the children stood about munching their apples.

"Tommy, you run and get me a pan of chips, and Mary, you get the tea-kettle on, and I'll go and make some biscuit."

And the soldier talked. Question after question he poured forth about the crops, the cattle, the renter, the neighbor. He slipped his heavy government brogan shoes off his poor, tired, blistered feet, and lay out with utter, sweet relaxation. He was a free man again, no longer a soldier under command. At supper he stopped once, listened and smiled. "That's old Spot. I know her voice. I s'pose that's her calf out there in the pen. I can't milk her to-night, though. I'm too tired. But I tell you, I'd like a drink o' her milk. What's become of old Rove?"

"He died last winter. Poisoned, I guess." There was a moment of sadness for them all. It was some time before the husband spoke again, in a voice that trembled a little.

"Poor old feller! He'd 'a' known me half a mile away. I expected him to come down the hill to meet me. It 'ud 'a' been more like comin' home if I could 'a' seen him comin' down the road an' waggin' his tail, an' laughin' that way he had. I tell yeh, it kind o' took hold o' me to see the blinds down an' the house shut up."

"But, yeh see, we—we expected you'd write again 'fore you started. And then we thought we'd see you if you *did* come," she hastened to explain.

"Well, I ain't worth a cent on writin'. Besides, it's just as well yeh didn't know when I was comin'. I tell you, it sounds good to hear them chickens out there, an' turkeys, an' the crickets. Do you know they don't have just the same kind o' crickets down South? Who's Sam hired t' help cut yer grain?"

"The Ramsey boys."

"Looks like a good crop; but I'm afraid I won't do much gettin' it cut. This cussed fever an' ague has got me down pretty low. I don't know when I'll get rid of it. I'll bet I've took twenty-five pounds of quinine if I've taken a bit. Gimme another biscuit. I tell yeh, they taste good, Emma. I ain't had anything like it—say, if you'd 'a' hear'd me braggin' to th' boys about your butter 'n' biscuits I'll bet your ears 'ud 'a' burnt."

The private's wife colored with pleasure. "Oh, you're always a-braggin' about your things. Everybody makes good butter."

"Yes; old lady Snyder, for instance."

"Oh, well, she ain't to be mentioned. She's Dutch."

"Or old Mis' Snively. One more cup o' tea, Mary. That's my girl! I'm feeling better already. I just b'lieve the matter with me is, I'm *starved*."

This was a delicious hour, one long to be remembered. They were like lovers again. But their tenderness, like that of a typical American family, found utterance in tones, rather than in words. He was praising her when praising her biscuit, and she knew it. They grew soberer when he showed where he had been struck, one ball burning the back of his hand, one cutting away a lock of hair from his temple, and one passing through the calf of his leg. The wife shuddered to think how near she had come to being a soldier's widow. Her waiting no longer seemed hard. This sweet, glorious hour effaced it all.

Then they rose, and all went out into the garden and down to the barn. He stood beside her while she milked old Spot. They began to plan fields and crops for next year.

His farm was weedy and encumbered, a rascally renter had run away with his machinery (departing between two days), his children needed clothing, the years were coming upon him, he was sick and emaciated, but his heroic soul did not quail. With the same courage with which he had faced his Southern march he entered upon a still more hazardous future.

Oh, that mystic hour! The pale man with big eyes standing there by the well, with his young wife by his side. The vast moon swinging above the eastern peaks, the cattle winding down the pasture slopes with jangling bells, the crickets singing, the stars blooming out sweet and far and serene;

the katydids rhythmically calling, the little turkeys crying querulously, as they settled to roost in the poplar tree near the open gate. The voices at the well drop lower, the little ones nestle in their father's arms at last, and Teddy falls asleep there.

The common soldier of the American volunteer army had returned. His war with the South was over, and his fight, his daily running fight with nature and against the injustice of his fellow-men, was begun again.

STRIKING AN AVERAGE *

By Henry B. Fuller

I

"SO FAR, so good," said Michael A. Brannigan, leading his young charge away from the sloppy bar.
"But you don't want to stop here. It ain't enough
to drink with the boys; you ought to dance now with some
of the girls."

"All right," returned Jameson Bates with great readi-
ness. He was "mixing," and it was neither time nor place
for anything like half-measures.

The air of the hall was hazy with dust and smoke. Now
and then came a whiff from across a beer-sodden area of
sawdust. The band, up in a dingy corner of the gallery,
was just beginning on *Casey Would Dance with the Straw-
berry Blonde.*

"You've got it in you," said Brannigan, eying the toe that
Jameson was beating upon the battered floor.

"Never waltzed before in my life!" returned Jameson with
a grimace.

"You didn't?" queried his guide with a note of disappointment.

"But I'm going to now," finished Jameson.

"Can you?" asked the other doubtfully.

"I guess so. It's always looked easy. For the matter of
that, never ran for alderman before. Ain't finding that very
hard, either."

"You'll get through all right," said Brannigan, grinning
in the young fellow's smooth, fair face.

"Sure thing," returned Jameson.

---

* By permission of the author and Curtis Publishing Company.

The Sons and Daughters of the Golden Signet were just taking the floor again.

"Let me introduce you to a girl or two," said Brannigan.

"Let me introduce meself," returned Jameson.

Edgar Jameson Bates was twenty-five years old. He was six feet tall, weighed one hundred and seventy pounds, was sound as a nut and strong as an ox. He had been centre rush at Yale, had hunted the Rocky Mountain sheep up beyond Calgary, and for the past year and a half had been more or less engaged in the practice of law. But Jameson was never meant to quibble and squabble; nor had he ever felt drawn, like his elder brother, into the "business"—into the great concern that their father had originated and developed and had made a household word the country through. Something more, something different was needed to give outlet to his superabundant energies. His nibble at the law had brought him within range of the City Voters' League and the Property Owners' Protective Association, and other organizations that were working toward the amelioration of local conditions. Presently came the day when Jameson felt the sudden impulse to put his young strength to the wheel and to help lift the municipal coach from the mire. "I'll join the Board of Aldermen," he said.

Michael Aloysius Brannigan welcomed the new recruit gladly; at last the ward might be got out of the hands of the condemned Republicans. What Michael Brannigan said was likely to go. He was the captain of his ward and an important wheel in the general municipal machinery. He was a city boiler inspector. He drew the salary, and the work was done by somebody else—or by nobody. He himself did not know a flue from a flange and made but a pretense of keeping a record of inspections. Now and then a steam laundry blew up and made a page for the papers. But if Michael did not give satisfaction in this cramped field, he succeeded admirably in a wider one; he was never so happy as when managing for the general body of citizens those concerns which the general body of citizens should have managed for themselves. Michael, in short, was one of the muddy ditches through which the ardent young patriot must flounder as best he may if he desires to enter the fair field of public service that lies beyond.

Jameson was too robust to be fastidious; he saw, moreover, that the game must be played with the men actually on the board. He applied to Michael Aloysius. The great man's first response was non-committal. However, he invited the neophyte to mingle with the Sons and Daughters. If he turned out a good "mixer" he might do.

"That girl in red is the one for me," declared Jameson.

Brannigan had looked at the girl in red first—involuntarily. Jameson had seen him do so. Brannigan was not aware of this.

"Yes, the one in red," repeated Jameson. "She's a beaut. Watch me."

Jameson had caught the tone of the assembly quite miraculously. After that, to catch the step of the dance was but a trifle. He walked over briskly to the girl in red and made known his modest ambition. She seemed a vigorous, positive creature, and could pull him through, as he felt with relief, if anybody could. As they stepped out to take the floor another young man, with heavy shoulders, a superabundant mustache and a careful brown scallop on his forehead, turned away forestalled and thwarted.

"No previous claim?" smiled Jameson, gathering her fingers in his big, smooth hand. These were smooth, too—as well-cared-for and ladylike as one might wish.

"First come," replied the girl, lifting her black eyebrows with quite an air. Perhaps, after all, she entertained a slight grudge against the other for his heavy, lumbering tardiness.

"Time counts," said Jameson sententiously, as he took an opening step.

"Well, let's keep it," she replied briefly. The first false start rectified, she carefully laid her face—a face framed in a wide flange of jet-black hair—against his shoulder; clearly she was meaning to abandon herself completely to the melting rhythm of the cornet, the trombone, the two fiddles and the flute. Jameson accommodated himself as well as he could to the creakle and swish of her satin skirt trimmed liberally yet inexpensively with wide-meshed black lace, and kept his feet out of tangle with more or less success. Everybody in Harmony Hall was watching him; not a soul there but knew who he was and what he was after. He himself had never before seen a single one of the lot, save Brannigan —and him but once. "Are they for me, or ag'in me?" wondered Jameson as he looked out over the top of the girl's hair.

He kept it up fearlessly. He had a natural sense of rhythm and had always been light on his feet. But the deuce seemed in it—he was barely holding his own. There was a titter from a girl whom he might have asked first, but hadn't, and a single derisive note of laughter from the muscular young man with the scalloped hair. "So it goes," muttered Jameson; "if I were doing well, they'd like it still less."

His partner suddenly lifted her flaring frame of hair from his shoulder and looked across that wide ridge with angry eyes. She was not to be balked in her triumph; if the performance called for the aid of a second mind, that mind was here. She set her straight lips firmly and took command. Respect, reluctant yet complete, ruled once more through the place.

"Well, you're a wonder," said Jameson as they toppled suddenly into a pair of rough chairs set against the wall. "You pulled me through in great shape."

"I came here to *dance*," she returned.

Her tone might have implied either reproach or determination.

"And haven't you?" he asked. "You could dance on a cinder-pile. You could dance with a clothes-horse. What is your name?"

"Well, *that's* a question! What difference does it make?"

"What difference? The name of the first young lady I ever danced with in my life?"

She stared at him.

"Well, you *have* got the nerve!"

"I need it in this business. What kind of an office do you work in?"

Such flattery was irresistible.

"My name is Marguerite Ryan," she answered with a toss of the head.

" 'Marguerite!' " he replied, throwing up his own. "Nonsense! Never in the world!"

"My name is Marguerite Ryan," she reiterated. "What do you mean by telling me it isn't?"

"Come, now," insinuated Jameson very quietly; "your mother calls you Maggie; you know she does. And your little brother calls you Mag."

The girl's eyes sparkled angrily. 'You leave my mother out. My name," she repeated, "is Marguerite—"

"Your name," interrupted Jameson in a calm, gentle tone, "is Margaret. It's a very beautiful one, and one that becomes you. Don't let anybody change it; don't let anybody tinker with it. Margaret Ryan," he repeated, looking out with seeming abstraction upon the clearing floor in front of them; "what could be better? What sweeter? What more musical?"

The girl gave a gasp. He had ruffled her with one hand, it seemed, to smooth her with the other. He had threatened to humble her, yet had raised her higher than she stood before. Taking it all around, he had let her off rather easily.

"Margaret Ryan, if you say so," she acquiesced presently. "What's yours?"

Jameson smiled as he answered. Everybody in the hall knew his name, this girl included; everybody in the city knew it. The entire community recognized in his father, Granger Bates, the head and front of one of the great industrial concerns of the West, the employer of thousands of hands and a prime mover in manufacture and transportation. Not one whit behind was his wife, a social light par excellence; she was the president of the Woman's National League; she was the "Susan Lathrop Bates" whose name stood carved in imperishable stone among the gables and gargoyles that shut in the campus of the University; and on more than one memorable occasion she had led, with a stateliness and magnificence that had intimidated her son himself, the grand march at the Charity Ball. As for his own deeds of prowess, were they not written in—

"'Jameson!'" cried the girl mockingly. "Nonsense! Never in the world!"

"My name," he reiterated, in her own solemn tone of expostulation, "is Edgar Jameson Bates——"

"Not a bit of it!" she retorted quickly. "Your father calls you Jim, you know he does. And your mother calls you Jimmy!"

"Guessed it the first shot!" cried Jameson, delighted. "You're a winner—no mistake!"

"What is she like?"

"Mother?" Jameson shrugged his shoulders; this girl knew all about his mother. The great lady's picture was in the public prints once a month throughout the year, and daily paragraphs were made of her simplest doings. "Oh," he replied, humoring the other's fantasy, "she's a solid, husky person like me—no nonsense about her."

"Well, I'd let somebody else say it."

"What! can't I speak a good word for my own mother?"

"And two for yourself."

"And two hundred for you."

"I haven't heard them yet."

"You're going to."

"What for? To bring my uncle 'round?"

"Your uncle? Who's he?"

"Didn't I see him send you over to me?"

"What! Is Michael Brannigan your uncle? I never knew it—I swear I didn't. I came of my own accord. 'There's some one girl here,' thought I, 'who ought to be taken out first, and who expects to be, and who deserves to be; one who's prettier than any of the others, and more spirited, and more stylish—'"

"That will do to say!" interrupted Margaret, waving aside a superfluous finish.

"That's why I say it. Well, what kind of an office *do* you work in?"

"What makes you think I work in any kind?" asked the girl, now almost wishing that she didn't.

"Why, you don't suppose I thought you worked in a department store, do you?"

This appreciation charmed her. "Well, if you want to know, I'm in the County Building—in the Recorder's department."

"I understand," said Jameson. "You write all day in those big books."

"And what do you do?"

"I'm a lawyer—sort o'. Perhaps you copy some of *my* things now and then. I'm death on deeds."

"And on words, too, eh?"

"I'm not so shy there, either."

"Well, if you want to get this nomination it will take more than talk."

"What nomination?" asked Jameson innocently.

"Oh, you!" said the girl. "I knew about it all along!" she added.

"Oh, me!" replied Jameson. "I knew all along you did!"

"Well, then, get up and hustle."

"What am I doing now? Do you mean it's time for another washout at the bar?"

"No, I don't. That sort of thing isn't so very necessary, I don't believe. Nor so very nice, either. Do you see that girl over in that far-away corner?"

"I do."

"Not very pretty, eh?"

"Not very."

"A good deal of a dowdy, besides?"

"I should say so."

"Well, you've got *me* on the string all right, so go over and dance with her. She's got a kind of a pull, too—at least her father has."

"Dance?" objected Jameson. "You know what my dancing is. Besides, I want to stay where I am."

"Do you think I'm going to sit here much longer? Go; you'll find the poor thing glad enough to take the will for the deed. If her father and my uncle agree—"

"Well, you know best," said Jameson, rising dejectedly. "if I could have another waltz with you, afterward—"

"Not on your life," said Margaret emphatically. "As I told you before, I came here to *dance*."

"Good-by, then."

"Good-by."

"Till we meet again."

"That will never be. By to-morrow my name might be Kate or Sally or Dorothy Jane, for all you'll be able to remember."

"It will be Margaret, just the same."

"Well, don't forget that 'Ryan' follows it—and that 'Miss' comes before."

"I hope I know how to address a—a letter to a lady," said Jameson solemnly. "What is the rest of the superscription?"

"I'm in the directory, like all the public employees. But you needn't look there."

"I shall, though."

"I forbid you."

"Then what street-car line do I take?"

"Well, for cold cheek—!"

"So you won't see me again?—not even for a quadrille?" asked Jameson, lingering.

"Well, I might consider *that*," returned the girl guardedly.

II

"He'll do," said Brannigan. "And he's the only one who can pull the old Third over on the right side of the line."

"That's what we need," observed His Honor sententiously.

"But how about Callahan?" asked the city clerk. Callahan was the stout young man with the scalloped hair. He was secretary of the Steamfitters' Union and had a following of his own. His following, as it immediately developed, included the thirty-seven precinct captains of the ward, and they had united in indorsing him for alderman.

Brannigan swore loudly on hearing of this unauthorized action, and scattered a long train of minor oaths through the dim and dirty corridors of the municipal edifice as he ploughed his way out toward his own bailiwick. He had the thirty-seven hailed before him, and asked them who was running this campaign, anyway?

"Bates is the man," he emitted amongst various sulph... ous breathings, "and I'm going to have him nominated."

The thirty-seven acquiesced. They attended the ward convention in force and applauded their leader all through his nominating address, as he spread out his big, fat hands to show how clean they were, and rolled up his eyes to the ceiling to evidence the purity of his aims, his motives, his ambitions. They applauded Jameson Bates, too, whose speech of acceptance was stuffed with reckless promises for the general good (each of which he kept, or tried to), but whose every word and gesture bore an ironical implication that he saw through them and they through him, and that they were all a pack of humbugging rascals together. Yes, Jameson quite carried them away; clearly he was not half so good as they had feared.

Jameson dined at a flashy restaurant of doubtful repute, along with six or eight of the precinct captains. As he was lying at the end of the showcase, near the droplight. Almost instinctively his hand sought the volume and began frilling over its leaves in search of the final pages of the R's. "I'm half way there," he thought; "so why shouldn't I do the decent thing and go and thank her?" He pressed another handful of cigars upon his followers and swung aboard a passing car.

Poplar Avenue turned out to be a ramshackle street set higgledy-piggledy with various ugly little edifices, brick and frame. The sidewalks were full of sudden rises, falls and dislocations, and far below, in the midst of the mud, were certain indications that pointed to the possibility of a rotting wooden pavement. No. 783 rose high above its humbler neighbors with a certain pert tinnishness of cornice and bay-window about its front of red brick and white limestone, but Jameson soon saw that each of its four floors was a separate flat. "H'm," he said, considering the whole bare, ugly prospect, "after this I shall never take elms and asphalt for granted."

The door of the third flat was opened by a plain, substantial woman who wore a serviceable black dress and who had her hair drawn smoothly across her temples. "Mother, sure enough," said Jameson. "She's all right." Mother announced that "Maggie" would be in "right away." She put Jameson on a sofa upholstered in a kind of pink and silver brocade and adorned with certain superfluous hangings, danglings and festoonings. Then, with the delicacy of her class, she retired and was seen no more.

Jameson poked at the sofa with an incredulous finger.

"Well, I've seen them often enough in the windows of the instalment stores, and now I'm actually sitting on one! Fancy!" Sheraton and Chippendale seemed a long way off. "Never mind that, though," he added.

After some little time—by no means "right away"— Margaret came in. She wore a dress of electric blue, made with a variety of liberal revers, wings, flounces and the like, and trimmed with an abundance of wide braid. She seemed to feel that the effect of her costume was very quiet, refined, ladylike. She herself, however, was just a bit flushed and breathless. Such a call was an event. So was such a dress.

"Well, here I am," said Jameson, rising with cordial abruptness. "You can't keep me down, you see."

"Who *wants* to keep a good man down, I should like to know?"

"I'm glad you think I'm good."

"I never had any doubts about it. I felt it the first time I saw you."

"Oh, come," protested Jameson. "Not too good?"

"No better than you ought to be. Just good enough. Sit down again."

She set him an example by sinking into a big, pudgy easy-chair. She carefully deployed her slim, well-kept fingers over one arm of it.

"Well, didn't I guess right about *you?*" he asked, eyeing the fingers.

"How do you mean?"

"About the office. Of course I knew you never weighed out nails."

"I should say not. Well, you got through all right?"

"Slick as a whistle. Poor Callahan, though—cut out again."

"Don't mention Callahan. He doesn't interest me."

"He did—up to the time of that quadrille."

"Well, maybe; but that's over. I knew it was a go for you," she added.

"You did? How soon?"

"As soon as you came over and asked me to dance. 'A man who can handle things like that,' thought I—What made you ask me first, anyway?"

"Because you're so dark, I expect. I'm so light myself, you see. I made one mistake, though."

"What was that? Thinking you could waltz by inspiration?"

"No. I thought at first your eyes were black. They're blue."

"Of course they are. Did you want them black?"

"Not on your life! What!—when the pupils are a blue that almost *is* black, and big enough to crowd the iris almost out of sight? And when your eyebrows *are* black, and your eyelashes, too, and your—I don't know what to call them, but I mean that little fringe on the under edge of—"

"Dear me, you'll know my eyes next time you see them!"

"Certain sure. Tell me truly, are you Irish?"

"Of course I am. Not red Irish, though; black. I got my eyes and my hair from Spain."

"I know; the Dons of the Armada. Tell me: were your forefathers kings?"

"My great-great-great—"

"Keep it up," said Jameson.

"—great-grandfather *was* king of—oh, laugh, if you want to!"

"I don't. Go ahead."

"And my mother is a lady—even if we *do* live on the wrong side of the tracks."

"So is mine. Don't you suppose I know a lady when I see one?"

"And my father is an honest man—even if he *does* work in the Special Assessment department. It's his principle that's kept him back."

"And is *my* father a scamp? Not much! What if he *has*

got five millions?—he made every dollar of them honestly. He may not be one of your hidalgos, but he is one of Nature's noblemen, all the same. Say, are those five millions going to hurt my prospects?"

"Not if you show yourself to the voters."

"I'm going to begin to-morrow. Glad hand all around, and three or four speeches every day for the next month. Don't you think I can do the heart-to-heart act?"

"I should say yes. You can jolly to beat the band."

"Come and hear me."

"I'm going to. Who is it you get it from? Your father?"

"No. Just a gift from Heaven, I guess. Father doesn't talk much. He acts."

"How did he begin?"

"He was a machinist. And my grandfather, my mother's father, was a carpenter. My mother herself—"

"Yes, do tell me about her."

"—was a washerwoman."

"Never in the world!"

"So she says. And I'll bet a cent that if she had a little back shed with a bench and a washtub in it—"

"Look here," cried the girl with a face expressive of limitless admiration and sympathy, "I'm just beginning to understand you."

"Poof!" said Jameson, tossing his head nonchalantly, "I understood *you* from the word go. At the same time," he went on, "she's a queen, just like your great-great-great—"

"Oh, stop, do," cried Margaret in distress.

"—a 'society' queen, I mean, and a grand old girl any way you put it."

"I'm sure she is. I'd give anything to know her."

"Easy thing, that. She'll call."

"Would she?"

"Sure. I'm her favorite son. My elder brother, Billy—Will-yum, I mean—has turned out something of a prig."

"Would she, truly? But not—not—not because it's politics?"

"Oh, cut politics. You're worth something in yourself, ain't you?"

"I've always hoped so."

"Well, don't call it a hope. Call it a certainty. That would be nearer right."

The girl smiled modestly, deprecatingly, almost appealingly. The amazon of Harmony Hall, no longer under the necessity of enforcing respect in a rough public gathering, was now completely obscured; even the character of a middle-class maiden earnestly parrying the advances of a half-known young millionaire was finally as good as laid aside. "She's a lady, after all—that's what she is," murmured Jameson with conviction; "and I've been about ten times too gay."

Margaret fingered the deplorable trappings of her chair with a fine effect of conscious pensiveness. Jameson studied a crayon portrait overhead, a mild, middle-aged face with a goat's beard—doubtless the just man in the Special Assessment department.

"People might think our talk rather personal," she presently observed.

"Or that we had about talked ourselves out," he rejoined, coming back from the brief silence.

"Have we?"

"Not a bit; we've hardly begun yet. Well, why shouldn't we be personal? Why shouldn't we talk about what interests us? I'm sure you interest me. And I thought I was interesting you. If I'm not—" He made a pretense of search for his hat.

"Don't ask *me* where it is," she said. "Do you know," she resumed presently, "that I copied one of your deeds day before yesterday?—one you signed yourself as somebody's attorney."

"Oh, that quit-claim?"

"Volume 6937, page 231. Document number one million eight hundred and thirty-six thousand nine hun—"

"You must have taken your own time with it. I've been sending to the Recorder's for the original for the past week."

"I did. You filled out the body yourself, too, didn't you? You write a very good hand for a lawyer."

"Call me that, if you like."

"Till I can call you alderman."

"You have a very good hand yourself," ventured Jameson. "Now, as a fact, I am an expert palm—"

"You sha'n't read *mine!*" she retorted, drawing her hand back. "I don't encourage any such—"

"You're quite right," he replied gravely. "I beg your pardon."

"Society!" she commented witheringly.

"Well, does that hurt?"

"Talk as you did at first. Oh, well, take it, if you want to."

"I don't need to. I think I know about what's likely to happen to you."

"Tell me."

"Not yet."

"Too dreadful?"

"That will be for you to say."

"My future rests with myself, then?"

"That's pretty close to it—"

There was a clumsy scuffling along the corridor. "Where's Mag?" asked a sharp little voice.

"'Mag'! There! what did I tell you—Margaret?"

"I won't allow you to—"

The cause of the disturbance appeared between the stuffy portières—a boy of ten, all legs, awkwardness, curiosity and freckles.

"Go away, Jimmy," said his sister.

"Come in, Jimmy," said his sister's caller.

Jimmy came in and looked at Jameson and grinned. Jameson gave him a dazzling smile and tousled his red hair. "Me own name, exactly," he said, and Jimmy grinned all the wider. Peter Callahan had once tried to tousle Jimmy's hair and had had his shins kicked for his pains. No, Peter could never be a successful candidate; he seemed doomed to defeat all around.

Jimmy went out as soon as Jameson left. The light was fled, the savor departed. He cast a careless glance at sister Margaret, now in reverie on the sofa, and shuffled back down the corridor.

Margaret continued to dream. They all began by tousling Jimmy's head. Could this last tousler be a serious one? And what might be expected to follow? Jimmy, always quick to detect a fraud, was thoroughly satisfied and convinced. Heigh-ho! One thing was clear, however: she should have her fill of oratory during the coming fortnight.

III

"It's the easiest proposition going," Jameson explained to his mother, as he deftly struck the tip off his egg. "Nine-tenths of it is in temperament, and the other tenth is in conforming—or in seeming to conform—to the general average of thought and manners. In other words, be a man first and a gentleman afterward. And a jollier always."

"But our standard of——" his mother began.

"Democracy has no use for a standard. The 'standard' is replaced by the 'average.' "

His mother looked doubtfully at his red eyes and listened with solicitude to his raucous tones.

"I see what you are thinking of, ma. But I'm not a drinker, as you very well know; while as for this talking the plaster off of ceilings, it will be over in a week more."

"But these awful creatures that keep coming to the house. Do you really have to 'jolly' them, as you call it?"

"Oh, there are plenty that are worse. Yes, I do. And it's a lucky thing that I can. And it's a still luckier thing that I can do it with sincerity—they're mighty quick to catch the false tone. Why, mother, we were pretty plain folks ourselves, once."

"Yes, I know we were. We can be yet, should occasion require. And do you have to drink with them all day long?"

"I'm not so sure on that point. But there was no time for a preliminary study of the situation, so I fell in with existing arrangements."

"And that explains, too, your Mr. Branni—Branni—"

"Brannigan? Yes."

"If you had only begun by having a petition circulated among our friends and neighbors—"

"Oh, come, mother, how is it when you go to the theatre? You don't scramble in any old way; you go in past the regular doorkeeper."

"Is that man the regular doorkeeper? Who made him such, I should like to know? What business has he to stand there?"

"Can't say. But there he is, and it's simpler to recognize the fact. Filson, give us another round of the toast. I get your vote, I suppose?"

"Yes, sir," said the man respectfully. "You get every vote in the house. You'd get fifty, sir, instead of five, if we had them."

Susan Bates stirred her coffee thoughtfully. "And there are those odious pictures in the papers. For years they've been calling upon our young men of wealth and position to come forward, and now when one does come—"

"Mother, dear, you wouldn't have them ignore me altogether?"

"I know. But those squibs, those caricatures, those 'pink tea' cartoons—"

"A little more of 'pink tea' would mean a good deal less of 'pink eye'!"

"And those insulting interruptions at your meetings; those silly, malapropos questions and comments—"

"Have I ever failed to return as good as was sent? Or better?"

"I don't think I'm overfastidious, Jimmy, but that last meeting of yours seemed to me to be very cheap and nasty."

"Dear ma, the world itself is rather cheap and nasty. Haven't you found that out yet?"

"No, my boy; and I don't like to hear you say that *you* have."

"I don't quite mean that, of course. But if a man's going to help it along a bit—"

"That's just what your father and I want you to do."

"—he must do it, sometimes, in its own cheap way and on its own cheap terms."

His mother looked at him soberly. "If you get in, I shall want you to become yourself again—right away, too."

"I shall; never fear. By the way, if you want to do a little—a little electioneering for me—"

"Well?" For a surprising self-consciousness had suddenly developed in his tone and air.

"I'm *not* in yet, you know, and every little helps. If you feel inclined, you might make a bit of a call on some 'constits' of mine over beyond the tracks. They have 'influence,' and—"

"H'm," said his mother.

"I really wish you would," said her son.

"I hadn't quite expected—"

"It's all right, mother. Should I ask it of you if I had the slightest doubt about the propriety of it? They're ladies, both of them."

"Very well, if you wish," she said, much in the dark.

"I wuddent go in no car-r'age, nayther," he counseled. "I'd hoof it—or ilse take the sthrate car. And make it some Saturday afternoon, if you can."

"Why, Jameson Bates!" exclaimed the good woman. "Still, if it's politics—"

Jameson flushed. "Pure politics," he said. Then: "Filson, if Katie has got that slippery elm boiled down, you may bring me the bottle and I'll put it in my pocket now."

Mrs. Bates made her trip to the other side of the ward the next Saturday afternoon, and found both the Ryan ladies at home.

"But where were the 'poplars'?" she asked Jameson.

"Where was the 'avenue'?" he returned. Then he said he hoped she had made a good impression. "For the husband and father is a big power in the ward," he declared.

"Was that his picture over the sofa?" asked his mother, plainly skeptical as to Ryan's "power."

"Well, what did you think of his wife?"

Susan Bates had come to immediate terms with Cornelia Ryan. She had found her a woman of tact, good feeling and sensibility—regardless of her being on the wrong side of the tracks. "She is not only one of your 'constits,' but a very devoted one, I should judge."

"Oh, yes," returned Jameson easily. On two or three

subsequent calls he had coaxed Cornelia Ryan from her retirement and had frankly given her a taste of his quality.
"The girl is rather a bright one, too," he added carelessly.

"Is she?" said her mother. "I found her a little prim and
sedate—formal, as well, I might say."

"Heavens!" thought Jameson. "Has Margaret been trying to be 'genteel'!"

"Still, she seemed to be intelligent enough—at least she
was pretty familiar with some of your speeches."

"Yes," said Jameson with the vastest indifference; "I've
noticed her in the audience once or twice. Queer taste of
hers—politics. Take her all 'round, she's the most singular
girl I know; as different from—"

"Jameson Bates, why did you have me go there? Tell me
the truth!"

"You'll know pretty soon. Hark! there's another voter
at the 'phone. I can't keep him waiting." And Jameson
hurried away.

IV

A week later, whiskey and slippery elm were alike of the
past, and Edgar Jameson Bates was an alderman-elect.
"My boy, you've turned the trick," said Michael Aloysius
Brannigan, in a state of extreme elation.

On the Monday evening following Jameson took his seat
along with the other new members of the Council and par-
ticipated in his first session. Every desk in the wide semi-
circle was banked with flowers; wives, mothers, sweethearts,
in early spring finery, shared the desks and helped crowd
the aisles. It was the first Council with a fair majority of
honest men that the town had known in twenty years. If
the golden age had returned, why not welcome it with floral
offering and festive apparel?

Susan Bates shared her son's desk and passed the floral
"tributes" in review.

"Whose is that?" she asked, motioning toward a green
harp compact of smilax and marguerites that towered just behind her.

"That's for Gilroy, of the Seventh."

"Whom is that for?"—pointing to a six-foot warrior done, tomahawk and all, in red carnations.

"That's from Casey's 'Indians,' in the Twenty-eighth."

She came back to her son's own desk. "Who sent you this horseshoe in calla lilies?"

"The Lincoln Republicans of my own ward. Their votes helped to put me here. How's that for an indorsement of your reviled son?"

"And this?—this?" pursued his mother.

"H'm," said Jameson. "This" was a sort of twofold arrangement in white carnations, crossed by a diagonal line of purple immortelles—the whole suggestive of an open book, with a pen laid upon it. It seemed to refer at once to his own legal studies and to the activities of some fair copyist.

His mother caught at the card. "Miss Margaret Ryan," she read. "*Your* Miss Ryan?"

"My Miss Ryan," he replied, as the mayor, rising from his empowered desk, let fall his gavel and opened the proceedings.

Susan Bates followed the course of business to the best of her ability as it went along under the stir and stimulus of novel conditions. She gave her closest heed to the halting manœuvres of new members and to the zigzag rhetoric of old ones. She studied intently the language and physiognomy of each speaker as he arose from out the floral jungle. "Such foreheads! Such grammar!" she said to her son in a terrified whisper.

"Pooh, mother!" he rejoined; "this is the best Council in years."

"A—ah!" she sighed with a world of meaning, and returned to the study of Margaret Ryan's tribute.

Jameson kept his ears open for the roll-calls that followed one another with striking frequency, and his eyes open for the giver of the floral book. When his mother looked down, he looked up. When she looked to the right he took occasion to glance off toward the left. Presently he discovered the object of his search hidden behind a miniature arch of triumph three desks away. Susan was thoughtfully studying the open book; Margaret, with a face full of strained intensity, was studying Susan; and Jameson, partly sheltered by his calla lilies, studied Margaret. Presently he moved out from his shelter and caught her eye and smiled and drew down one corner of his mouth—"All's well," it said. The girl's strained look broke into a smile of response; then she flushed and her eyes dropped, and she retired again behind her arch of triumph. Susan pondered over the book, and the appalling syntax of Alderman Ziegler flowed along unheeded.

As the session broke up Jameson signaled to the girl to meet him and his mother at the exit. Margaret timed herself accordingly, and joined them, along with her cousin, a well-to-do plumber, who at once showed himself—on this public ground, at least— as a man and a brother. Jameson looked anxiously at his mother, whom on many an occasion he had seen terrifyingly gracious, as he said:

"You remember Miss Ryan, ma? It's she who has pulled me through the campaign." And Susan greeted the girl with a plain, homely good will—the best way and the only.

"Let me thank you on my Jimmy's account," she said.

"There! 'Jimmy'!" murmured the girl.

"And do not forget to return my call," Susan Bates added, as she moved away by her son's side.

Two or three evenings later Jameson was again in Poplar Avenut, sitting on the florid dumpy sofa and reading Margaret Ryan's palm.

"It's all as plain as day," he declared, bending over her hand. "You are about to resume your royal state, to be a society queen—on the other side of the tracks. Come, make a stagger at it. Why, you can do it without turning a hair. Not one in a hundred is half so well fitted for the part—"

"Your mother?" hesitated the girl.

"Well, what of her? Isn't she your sort?"

"Yes; but—"

"And you're hers. Never fear about that. Come, let's pool our issues—we'll make a pretty even thing of it. You put in a bookkeeper and a plumber, and we put in a machinist and a carpenter. We both contribute a certain amount of royalty and a fair degree of gentility. Take it all around, we hit off the same average and stack up about the same size. To add to that, we're both in politics. And we ought to stay in—together." He bent over her hand again. "You have helped me to my place, and now you are to share its honors and responsibilities."

"You read all that there?"

"Yes, and a good deal more."

"How long will it take you to read the rest?"

"A lifetime."

"You are sure she likes me?"

"Society" as a remote abstraction might be joked at lightly; but to live, perhaps, under the same roof with it—!

"You are sure you like *me?*"

"Yes."

"Then I guarantee the rest. Come; to tell the truth, I need you in my business. You pulled me through that waltz; you pulled me through the campaign. You must be consistent now, and promise to pull me through life."

"Poor boy! I'm sorry for you! I will. I do."

EFFIE WHITTLESY *

By George Ade

MRS. Wallace assisted her husband to remove his overcoat and put her warm palms against his red and wind-beaten cheeks.

"I have good news," said she.

"Another bargain sale?"

"Pshaw, no! A new girl, and I really believe she's a jewel. She isn't young or good-looking, and when I asked her if she wanted any nights off she said she wouldn't go out after dark for anything in the world. What do you think of that?"

"That's too good to be true."

"No, it isn't. Wait and see her. She came here from the intelligence office about two o'clock and said she was willing to 'lick right in.' You wouldn't know the kitchen. She has it as clean as a pin."

"What nationality?"

"None—that is, she's a home product. She's from the country—and *green!* But she's a good soul, I'm sure. As soon as I looked at her, I just felt sure that we could trust her."

"Well, I hope so. If she is all that you say, why, for goodness sake give her any pay she wants—put lace curtains in her room and subscribe for all the story papers on the market."

"Bless you, I don't believe she'd read them. Every time I've looked into the kitchen she's been working like a Trojan and singing 'Beulah Land.'"

"Oh, she sings, does she? I knew there'd be some drawback."

---

* By permission of the author.

"You won't mind that. We can keep the doors closed."

The dinner-table was set in tempting cleanliness. Mrs. Wallace surveyed the arrangement of glass and silver and gave a nod of approval and relief. Then she touched the bell and in a moment the new servant entered.

She was a tall woman who had said her last farewell to girlhood.

Then a very strange thing happened.

Mr. Wallace turned to look at the new girl and his eyes enlarged. He gazed at her as if fascinated either by cap or freckles. An expression of wonderment came to his face and he said, "Well, by George!"

The girl had come very near the table when she took the first overt glance at him. Why did the tureen sway in her hands? She smiled in a frightened way and hurriedly set the tureen on the table.

Mr. Wallace was not long undecided, but during that moment of hesitancy the panorama of his life was rolled backward. He had been reared in the democracy of a small community, and the democratic spirit came uppermost.

"This isn't Effie Whittlesy?" said he.

"For the land's sake!" she exclaimed, backing away, and this was a virtual confession.

"You don't know me."

"Well, if it ain't Ed Wallace!"

Would that words were ample to tell how Mrs. Wallace settled back in her chair blinking first at her husband and then at the new girl, vainly trying to understand what it meant.

She saw Mr. Wallace reach awkwardly across the table and shake hands with the new girl and then she found voice to gasp, "Of all things!"

Mr. Wallace was confused and without a policy. He was wavering between his formal duty as an employer and his natural regard for an old friend. Anyway, it occurred to him that an explanation would be timely.

"This is Effie Whittlesy from Brainerd," said he. "I used to go to school with her. She's been at our house often. I haven't seen her for—I didn't know you were in Chicago," turning to Effie.

"Well, Ed Wallace, you could knock me down with a feather," said Effie, who still stood in a flustered attitude a few paces back from the table. "I had no more idee when I heard the name Wallace that it'd be you, though knowin', of course, you was up here. Wallace is such a common name I never give it a second thought. But the minute I seen you— law! I knew who it was, well enough."

"I thought you were still at Brainerd," said Mr. Wallace, after a pause.

"I left there a year ago November, and come to visit Mort's people. I s'pose you know that Mort has a position with the street-car company. He's doin' *so* well. I didn't want to be no burden on him, so I started out on my own hook, seein' that there was no use of goin' back to Brainerd to slave for two dollars a week. I had a good place with Mr. Sanders, the railroad man on the north side, but I left becuz they wanted me to serve liquor. I'd about as soon handle a toad as a bottle of beer. Liquor was the ruination of Jesse. He's gone to the dogs—been off with a circus somewheres for two years."

"The family's all broken up, eh!" asked Mr. Wallace.

"Gone to the four winds since mother died. Of course you know that Lora married Huntford Thomas and is livin' on the old Murphy place. They're doin' about as well as you could expect, with Huntford as lazy as he is."

"Yes? That's good," said Mr. Wallace.

Was this an old settlers' reunion or a quiet family dinner? The soup had been waiting.

Mrs. Wallace came into the breach.

"That will be all for the present, Effie," said she.

Effie gave a startled "Oh!" and vanished into the kitchen.

"It means," said Mr. Wallace, "that we were children together, made mud pies in the same puddle and sat next to each other in the old school-house at Brainerd. She is a Whittlesy. Everybody in Brainerd knew the Whittlesys. Large family, all poor as church mice, but sociable—and freckled. Effie's a good girl."

"Effie! *Effie!* And she called you Ed!"

"My dear, there are no misters in Brainerd. Why shouldn't she call me Ed! She never heard me called anything else."

"She'll have to call you something else here. You tell her so."

"Now, don't ask me to put on any airs with one of the Whittlesys, because they know me from away back. Effie has seen me licked at school. She has been at our house, almost like one of the family, when mother was sick and needed another girl. If my memory serves me right, I've taken her to singing-school and exhibitions. So I'm in no position to lord it over, and I wouldn't do it any way. I'd hate to have her go back to Brainerd and report that she met me here in Chicago and I was too stuck up to remember old times and requested her to address me as 'Mister Wallace.' Now, you never lived in a small town."

"No, I never enjoyed that privilege," said Mrs. Wallace, dryly.

"Well, it is a privilege in some respects, but it carries certain penalties with it, too. It's a very poor schooling for a fellow who wants to be a snob."

"I would call it snobbishness to correct a servant who addresses me by my first name. 'Ed' indeed! Why, I never dared to call you that."

"No, you never lived in Brainerd."

"And you say you used to take her to singing-school?"

"Yes, ma'am—twenty years ago, in Brainerd. You're not surprised, are you? You knew when you married me that I was a child of the soil, who worked his way through college and came to the city in a suit of store clothes. I'll admit that my past does not exactly qualify me for the Four Hundred, but it will be great if I ever get into politics."

"I don't object to your having a past, but I was just thinking how pleasant it will be when we give a dinner-party to have her come in and address you as 'Ed.'"

Mr. Wallace patted the table-cloth cheerily with both hands and laughed.

"I really don't believe you'd care," said Mrs. Wallace.

"Effie isn't going to demoralize the household," he said,

consolingly. "Down in Brainerd we may be a little slack on the by-laws of etiquette, but we can learn in time."

Mrs. Wallace touched the bell and Effie returned.

As she brought in the second course, Mr. Wallace deliberately encouraged her by an amiable smile, and she asked, "Do you get the Brainerd papers?"

"Yes—every week."

"There's been a good deal of sickness down there this winter. Lora wrote to me that your uncle Joe had been kind o' poorly."

"I think he's up and around again."

"That's good."

And she edged back to the kitchen.

With the change for dessert she ventured to say: "Mort was wonderin' about you the other day. He said he hadn't saw you for a long time. My! You've got a nice house here."

After dinner Mrs. Wallace published her edict. Effie would have to go. Mr. Wallace positively forbade the "strong talking-to" which his wife advocated. He said it was better that Effie should go, but she must be sent away gently and diplomatically.

Effie was "doing up" the dishes when Mr. Wallace lounged into the kitchen and began a roundabout talk. His wife, seated in the front room, heard the prolonged murmur. Ed and Effie were going over the familiy histories of Brainerd and recalling incidents that may have related to mud pies or school exhibitions.

Mrs. Wallace had been a Twombley, of Baltimore, and no Twombley, with relatives in Virginia, could humiliate herself into rivalry with a kitchen girl, or dream of such a thing, so why should Mrs. Wallace be uneasy and constantly wonder what Ed and Effie were talking about?

Mrs. Wallace was faint from loss of pride. The night before they had dined with the Gages. Mr. Wallace, a picture of distinction in his evening clothes, had shown himself the bright light of the seven who sat at the table. She had been proud of him. Twenty-four hours later a servant emerges from the kitchen and hails him as "Ed"!

The low talk in the kitchen continued. Mrs. Wallace had a feverish longing to tiptoe down that way and listen, or else go into the kitchen, sweepingly, and with a few succinct commands, set Miss Whittlesy back into her menial station. But she knew that Mr. Wallace would misinterpret any such move and probably taunt her with joking references to her "jealousy," so she forbore.

Mr. Wallace, with an unlighted cigar in his mouth (Effie had forbidden him to smoke in the kitchen), leaned in the doorway and waited to give the conversation a turn.

At last he said: "Effie, why don't you go down and visit Lora for a month or so? She'd be glad to see you."

"I know, Ed, but I ain't a Rockefeller to lay off work a month at a time an' go around visitin' my relations. I'd like to well enough—but—"

"O pshaw! I can get you a ticket to Brainerd to-morrow and it won't cost you anything down there."

"No, it ain't Chicago, that's a fact. A dollar goes a good ways down there. But what'll your wife do? She told me to-day she'd had an awful time gettin' any help."

"Well—to tell you the truth, Effie, you see—you're an old friend of mine and I don't like the idea of your being here in my house as a—well, as a hired girl."

"No, I guess I'm a servant now. I used to be a hired girl when I worked for your ma, but now I'm a servant. I don't see as it makes any difference what you call me, as long as the work's the same."

"You understand what I mean, don't you? Any time you come here to my house I want you to come as an old acquaintance—a visitor, not a servant."

"Ed Wallace, don't be foolish. I'd as soon work for you as any one, and a good deal sooner."

"I know, but I wouldn't like to see my wife giving orders to an old friend, as you are. You understand, don't you?"

"I don't know. I'll quit if you say so."

"Tut! tut! I'll get you that ticket and you can start for Brainerd to-morrow. Promise me, now."

"I'll go, and tickled enough, if that's the way you look at it."

"And if you come back, I can get you a dozen places to work."

Next evening Effie departed by carriage, although protesting against the luxury.

"Ed Wallace," said she, pausing in the hallway, "they never will believe me when I tell it in Brainerd."

"Give them my best and tell them I'm about the same as ever."

"I'll do that. Good-bye."

"Good-bye."

Mrs. Wallace, watching from the window, saw Effie disappear into the carriage.

"Thank goodness," said she.

"Yes," said Mr. Wallace, to whom the whole episode had been like a cheering beverage, "I've invited her to call when she comes back."

"To call—here?"

"Most assuredly. I told her you'd be delighted to see her at any time."

"The idea! Did you invite her, really?"

"Of course I did! And I'm reasonably certain that she'll come."

"What shall I do?"

" I think you can manage it, even if you never did live in Brainerd."

Then the revulsion came and Mrs. Wallace, with a return of pride in her husband, said she would try.

THE LOST PHŒBE *

BY THEODORE DREISER

THEY lived together in a part of the country which was not so prosperous as it had once been, about three miles from one of those small towns that, instead of increasing in population, is steadily decreasing. The territory was not very thickly settled; perhaps a house every other mile or so, with large areas of corn- and wheat-land and fallow fields that at odd seasons had been sown to timothy and clover. Their particular house was part log and part frame, the log portion being the old original home of Henry's grandfather. The new portion, of now rain-beaten, time-worn slabs, through which the wind squeaked in the chinks at times, and which several overshadowing elms and a butternut-tree made picturesque and reminiscently pathetic, but a little damp, was erected by Henry when he was twenty-one and just married.

That was forty-eight years before. The furniture inside, like the house outside, was old and mildewy and reminiscent of an earlier day. You have seen the what-not of cherry wood, perhaps, with spiral legs and fluted top. It was there. The old-fashioned four-poster bed, with its ball-like protuberances and deep curving incisions, was there also, a sadly alienated descendant of an early Jacobean ancestor. The bureau of cherry was also high and wide and solidly built, but faded-looking, and with a musty odor. The rag carpet that underlay all these sturdy examples of enduring furniture was a weak, faded, lead-and-pink-colored affair woven by Phœbe Ann's own hands, when she was fifteen years younger than she was when she died. The creaky wooden loom on which it had been done now stood like a dusty, bony skeleton, along with a broken rocking-chair, a worm-eaten clothes-press—Heaven knows how old—a lime-stained bench that had once been used to keep flowers on outside the door, and other decrepit factors of household utility, in an east room that was a lean-to against this so-called main portion. All sorts of other broken-down furniture were about this place; an antiquated clothes-horse, cracked in two of its ribs; a broken mirror in an old cherry frame, which had fallen from a nail and cracked itself three days before their youngest son, Jerry, died; an extension hat-rack, which once had had porcelain knobs on the ends of its pegs; and a sewing-machine, long since outdone in its clumsy mechanism by rivals of a newer generation.

The orchard to the east of the house was full of gnarled old apple-trees, worm-eaten as to trunks and branches, and fully ornamented with green and white lichens, so that it had a sad, greenish-white, silvery effect in moonlight. The low outhouses, which had once housed chickens, a horse or two, a cow, and several pigs, were covered with patches of moss as to their roof, and the sides had been free of paint for so long that they were blackish gray as to color, and a little spongy. The picket-fence in front, with its gate squeaky and askew, and the side fences of the stake-and-rider type were in an equally run-down condition. As a matter of fact, they had aged synchronously with the persons who lived here, old Henry Reifsneider and his wife Phœbe Ann.

They had lived here, these two, ever since their marriage, forty-eight years before, and Henry had lived here before that from his childhood up. His father and mother, well along in years when he was a boy, had invited him to bring his wife here when he had first fallen in love and decided to marry; and he had done so. His father and mother were the companions of himself and his wife for ten years after they were married, when both died; and then Henry and Phœbe were left with their five children growing lustily apace. But all sorts of things had happened since then. Of the seven children, all told, that had been born to them, three had died; one girl had gone to Kansas; one boy had gone to Sioux Falls, never even to be heard of after; another boy had gone to Washington; and the last girl lived five counties away in the same State, but was so burdened with cares of her own that she rarely gave them a thought. Time and a common-place home life that had never been attractive had weaned them thoroughly, so that, wherever they were, they gave little thought as to how it might be with their father and mother.

Old Henry Reifsneider and his wife Phœbe were a loving couple. You perhaps know how it is with simple natures that fasten themselves like lichens on the stones of circumstance and weather their days to a crumbling conclusion. The great world sounds widely, but it has no call for them. They have no soaring intellect. The orchard, the meadow, the corn-field, the pig-pen, and the chicken-lot measure the range of their human activities. When the wheat is headed it is reaped and threshed; when the corn is browned and frosted it is cut and shocked; when the timothy is in full head it is cut, and the hay-cock erected. After that comes winter, with the hauling of grain to market, the sawing and splitting of wood, the simple chores of fire-building, meal-getting, occasional repairing, and visiting. Beyond these and the changes of weather—the snows, the rains, and the fair days—there are no immediate, significant things. All the rest of life is a far-off, clamorous phantasmagoria, flickering like Northern lights in the night, and sounding as faintly as cow-bells tinkling in the distance.

Old Henry and his wife Phœbe were as fond of each other as it is possible for two old people to be who have nothing else in this life to be fond of. He was a thin old man, seventy when she died, a queer, crotchety person with coarse gray-black hair and beard, quite straggly and unkempt. He looked at you out of dull, fishy, watery eyes that had deep-brown crow's-feet at the sides. His clothes, like the clothes of many farmers, were aged and angular and baggy, stand-ing out at the pockets, not fitting about the neck, pro-tuberant and worn at elbow and knee. Phœbe Ann was thin and shapeless, a very umbrella of a woman, clad in shabby black, and with a black bonnet for her best wear. As time had passed, and they had only themselves to look after, their movements had become slower and slower, their activities fewer and fewer. The annual keep of pigs had been reduced from five to one grunting porker, and the single horse which Henry now retained was a sleepy animal, not over-nourished and not very clean. The chickens, of which formerly there was a large flock, had almost disappeared, owing to ferrets, foxes, and the lack of proper care, which produces disease. The former healthy garden was now a straggling memory of itself, and the vines and flower-beds that formerly ornamented the windows and dooryard had now become choking thickets. A will had been made which divided the small tax-eaten property equally among the remaining four, so that it was really of no interest to any of them. Yet these two lived together in peace and sympathy, only that now and then old Henry would become unduly cranky, complaining almost invariably that something had been neglected or mislaid which was of no importance at all.

"Phœbe, where's my corn-knife? You ain't never minded to let my things alone no more."

"Now you hush, Henry," his wife would caution him in a cracked and squeaky voice. "If you don't, I'll leave yuh. I'll git up and walk out of here some day, and then where would y' be? Y' ain't got anybody but me to look after yuh, so yuh just behave yourself. Your corn knife's on the mantel where it's allus been unless you've gone an' put it summers else."

Old Henry, who knew his wife would never leave him under any circumstances, used to speculate at times as to what he would do if she were to die. That was the one leaving that he really feared. As he climbed on the chair at night to wind the old, long-pendulumed, double-weighted clock, or went finally to the front and the back door to see that they were safely shut in, it was a comfort to know that Phœbe was there, properly esconced on her side of the bed, and that if he stirred restlessly in the night, she would be there to ask what he wanted.

"Now, Henry, do lie still! You're as restless as a chicken."

"Well, I can't sleep, Phœbe."

"Well, yuh needn't roll so, anyhow. Yuh kin let me sleep."
This usually reduced him to a state of somnolent ease.
If she wanted a pail of water, it was a grumbling pleasure
for him to get it; and if she did rise first to build the fires,
he saw that the wood was cut and placed within easy reach.
They divided this simple world nicely between them.

As the years had gone on, however, fewer and fewer people
had called. They were well-known for a distance of as
much as ten square miles as old Mr. and Mrs. Reifsneider,
honest, moderately Christian, but too old to be really interesting any longer. The writing of letters had become an
almost impossible burden too difficult to continue or even
negotiate via others, although an occasional letter still did
arrive from the daughter in Pemberton County. Now and
then some old friend stopped with a pie or cake or a roasted
chicken or duck, or merely to see that they were well; but
even these kindly minded visits were no longer frequent.

One day in the early spring of her sixty-fourth year Mrs.
Reifsneider took sick, and from a low fever passed into some
indefinable ailment which, because of her age, was no longer
curable. Old Henry drove to Swinnerton, the neighboring
town, and procured a doctor. Some friends called, and the
immediate care of her was taken off his hands. Then one
chill spring night she died, and old Henry, in a fog of sorrow
and uncertainty, followed her body to the nearest graveyard,
an unattractive space with a few pines growing in it. Although he might have gone to the daughter in Pemberton
or sent for her, it was really too much trouble and he was
too weary and fixed. It was suggested to him at once by
one friend and another that he come to stay with them
awhile, but he did not see fit. He was so old and so fixed in
his notions and so accustomed to the exact surroundings
he had known all his days, that he could not think of leaving. He wanted to remain near where they had put his
Phœbe; and the fact that he would have to live alone did
not trouble him in the least. The living children were
notified and the care of him offered if he would leave, but
he would not.

"I kin make a shift for myself," he continually announced to old Dr. Morrow, who had attended his wife in this case. "I kin cook a little, and, besides, it don't take much more'n coffee an' bread in the mornin's to satisfy me. I'll get along now well enough. Yuh just let me be." And after many pleadings and proffers of advice, with supplies of coffee and bacon and baked bread duly offered and accepted, he was left to himself. For a while he sat idly outside his door brooding in the spring sun. He tried to revive his interest in farming, and to keep himself busy and free from thought by looking after the fields, which of late had been much neglected. It was a gloomy thing to come in of an evening, however, or in the afternoon, and find no shadow of Phœbe where everything suggested her. By degrees he put a few of her things away. At night he sat beside his lamp and read in the papers that were left him occasionally or in a Bible that he had neglected for years, but he could get little solace from these things. Mostly he held his hand over his mouth and looked at the floor as he sat and thought of what had become of her, and how soon he himself would die. He made a great business of making his coffee in the morning and frying himself a little bacon at night; but his appetite was gone. The shell in which he had been housed so long seemed vacant, and its shadows were suggestive of immedicable griefs. So he lived quite dolefully for five long months, and then a change began.

It was one night, after he had looked after the front and the back door, wound the clock, blown out the light, and gone through all the selfsame motions that he had indulged in for years, that he went to bed not so much to sleep as to think. It was a moonlight night. The green-lichen-covered orchard just outside and to be seen from his bed where he now lay was a silvery affair, sweetly spectral. The moon shone through the east windows, throwing the pattern of the panes on the wooden floor, and making the old furniture, to which he was accustomed, stand out dimly in the room. As usual he had been thinking of Phœbe and the years when they had been young together, and of the children who had gone, and the poor shift he was making of his present days. The

would perhaps be with him much of the time, in the night, anyhow; and that would make him less lonely, this state more endurable.

In age and with the feeble it is not such a far cry from the subtleties of illusion to actual hallucination, and in due time this transition was made for Henry. Night after night he waited, expecting her return. Once in his weird mood he thought he saw a pale light moving about the room, and another time he thought he saw her walking in the orchard after dark. It was one morning when the details of his lonely state were virtually unendurable that he woke with the thought that she was not dead. How he had arrived at this conclusion it is hard to say. His mind had gone. In its place was a fixed illusion. He and Phœbe had had a senseless quarrel. He had reproached her for not leaving his pipe where he was accustomed to find it, and she had left. It was an aberrated fulfillment of her old jesting threat that if he did not behave himself she would leave him.

"I guess I could find yuh ag'in," he had always said. But her cackling threat had always been:

"Yuh'll not find me if I ever leave yuh. I guess I kin git some place where yuh can't find me."

This morning when he arose he did not think to build the fire in the customary way or to grind his coffee and cut his bread, as was his wont, but solely to meditate as to where he should search for her and how he should induce her to come back. Recently the one horse had been dispensed with because he found it cumbersome and beyond his needs. He took down his soft crush hat after he had dressed himself, a new glint of interest and determination in his eye, and taking his black crook cane from behind the door, where he had always placed it, started out briskly to look for her among the nearest neighbors. His old shoes clumped soundly in the dust as he walked, and his gray-black locks, now grown rather long, straggled out in a dramatic fringe or halo from under his hat. His short coat stirred busily as he walked, and his hands and face were peaked and pale.

"Why, hello, Henry! Where're yuh goin' this mornin'?" inquired Farmer Dodge, who, hauling a load of wheat to market, encountered him on the public road. He had not seen the aged farmer in months, not since his wife's death, and he wondered now, seeing him looking so spry.

"Yuh ain't seen Phœbe, have yuh?" inquired the old man, looking up quizzically.

"Phœbe who?" inquired Farmer Dodge, not for the moment connecting the name with Henry's dead wife.

"Why, my wife Phœbe, o' course. Who do yuh s'pose I mean?" He stared up with a pathetic sharpness of glance from under his shaggy, gray eyebrows.

"Wall, I'll swan, Henry, yuh ain't jokin', are yuh?" said the solid Dodge, a pursy man, with a smooth, hard, red face. "It can't be your wife yuh're talkin' about. She's dead."

"Dead! Shucks!" retorted the demented Reifsneider. "She left me early this mornin', while I was sleepin'. She allus got up to build the fire, but she's gone now. We had a little spat last night, an' I guess that's the reason. But I guess I kin find her. She's gone over to Matilda Race's, that's where she's gone."

He started briskly up the road, leaving the amazed Dodge to stare in wonder after him.

"Well, I'll be switched!" he said aloud to himself. "He's clean out'n his head. That poor old feller's been livin' down there till he's gone outen his mind. I'll have to notify the authorities." And he flicked his whip with great enthusiasm. "Geddap!" he said, and was off.

Reifsneider met no one else in this poorly populated region until he reached the whitewashed fence of Matilda Race and her husband three miles away. He had passed several other houses en route, but these not being within the range of his illusion were not considered. His wife, who had known Matilda well, must be here. He opened the picket-gate which guarded the walk, and stamped briskly up to the door.

"Why, Mr. Reifsneider," exclaimed old Matilda herself, a stout woman, looking out of the door in answer to his knock, "what brings yuh here this mornin'?"

"Is Phœbe here?" he demanded eagerly.

"Phœbe who? What Phœbe?" replied Mrs. Race, curious as to this sudden development of energy on his part.

"Why, my Phœbe, o' course. My wife Phœbe. Who do yuh s'pose? Ain't she here now?"

"Lawsy me!" exclaimed Mrs. Race, opening her mouth. "Yuh pore man! So you're clean out'n your mind now. Yuh come right in and sit down. I'll git yuh a cup o' coffee. O' course your wife ain't here; but yuh come in an' sit down. I'll find her fer yuh after a while. I know where she is."

The old farmer's eyes softened, and he entered. He was so thin and pale a specimen, pantalooned and patriarchal, that he aroused Mrs. Race's extremest sympathy as he took off his hat and laid it on his knees quite softly and mildly.

"We had a quarrel last night, an' she left me," he volunteered.

"Laws! laws!" sighed Mrs. Race, there being no one present with whom to share her astonishment as she went to her kitchen. "The pore man! Now somebody's just got to look after him. He can't be allowed to run around the country this way lookin' for his dead wife. It's turrible."

She boiled him a pot of coffee and brought in some of her new-baked bread and fresh butter. She set out some of her best jam and put a couple of eggs to boil, lying whole-heartedly the while.

"Now yuh stay right there, Uncle Henry, till Jake comes in, an' I'll send him to look for Phœbe. I think it's more'n likely she's over to Swinnerton with some o' her friends. Anyhow, we'll find out. Now yuh just drink this coffee an' eat this bread. Yuh must be tired. Yuh've had a long walk this mornin'." Her idea was to take counsel with Jake, "her man," and perhaps have him notify the authorities.

She bustled about, meditating on the uncertainties of life, while old Reifsneider thrummed on the rim of his hat with his pale fingers and later ate abstractedly of what she offered. His mind was on his wife, however, and since she was not here, or did not appear, it wandered vaguely away to a family by the name of Murray, miles away in another direction. He decided after a time that he would not wait for Jack Race to hunt his wife but would seek her for himself. He must be on, and urge her to come back.

"Well, I'll be goin'," he said, getting up and looking strangely about him. "I guess she didn't come here after all. She went over to the Murrays, I guess. I'll not wait any longer, Mis' Race. There's a lot to do over to the house to-day." And out he marched in the face of her protests taking to the dusty road again in the warm spring sun, his cane striking the earth as he went.

It was two hours later that this pale figure of a man appeared in the Murrays' doorway, dusty, perspiring, eager. He had tramped all of five miles, and it was noon. An amazed husband and wife of sixty heard his strange query, and realized also that he was mad. They begged him to stay to dinner, intending to notify the authorities later and see what could be done; but though he stayed to partake of a little something, he did not stay long, and was off again to another distant farmhouse, his idea of many things to do and his need of Phœbe impelling him. So it went for that day and the next and the next, the circle of his inquiry ever widening.

The process by which a character assumes the significance of being peculiar, his antics weird, yet harmless, in such a community is often involute and pathetic. This day, as has been said, saw Reifsneider at other doors, eagerly asking his unnatural question, and leaving a trail of amazement, sympathy, and pity in his wake. Although the authorities were informed—the county sheriff, no less—it was not deemed advisable to take him into custody; for when those who knew old Henry, and had for so long, reflected on the condition of the county insane asylum, a place which, because of the poverty of the district, was of staggering aberration and sickening environment, it was decided to let him remain at large; for, strange to relate, it was found on investigation that at night he returned peaceably enough to his lonesome domicile there to discover whether his wife had returned, and to brood in loneliness until the morning. Who would lock up a thin, eager, seeking old man with iron-gray hair and an attitude of kindly, innocent inquiry, particularly when he was well known for a past of only kindly servitude and reliability? Those who had known him best rather agreed that he should be allowed to roam at large. He could do no harm. There were many who were willing to help him as to food, old clothes, the odds and ends of his daily life—at least at first. His figure after a time became not so much a common-place as an accepted curiosity, and the replies, "Why, no, Henry; I ain't see her," or "No, Henry; she ain't been here to-day," more customary.

For several years thereafter then he was an odd figure in the sun and rain, on dusty roads and muddy ones, encountered occasionally in strange and unexpected places, pursuing his endless search. Undernourishment, after a time, although the neighbors and those who knew his history gladly contributed from their store, affected his body; for he walked much and ate little. The longer he roamed the public highway in this manner, the deeper became his strange hallucination; and finding it harder and harder to return from his more and more distant pilgrimages, he finally began taking a few utensils with him from his home, making a small package of them, in order that he might not be compelled to return. In an old tin coffee-pot of large size he placed a small tin cup, a knife, fork, and spoon, some salt and pepper, and to the outside of it, by a string forced through a pierced hole, he fastened a plate, which could be released, and which was his woodland table. It was no trouble for him to secure the little food that he needed, and with a strange, almost religious dignity, he had no hesitation in asking for that much. By degrees his hair became longer and longer, his once black hat became an earthen brown, and his clothes threadbare and dusty.

For all of three years he walked, and none knew how wide were his perambulations, nor how he survived the storms and cold. They could not see him, with homely rural understanding and forethought, sheltering himself in haycocks, or by the sides of cattle, whose warm bodies protected him from the cold, and whose dull understandings were not opposed to his harmless presence. Overhanging rocks and trees kept him at times from the rain, and a friendly hay-loft or corn-crib was not above his humble consideration.

The involute progression of hallucination is strange.

From asking at doors and being constantly rebuffed or de-
nied, he finally came to the conclusion that although his
Phœbe might not be in any of the houses at the doors of
which he inquired, she might nevertheless be within the sound
of his voice. And so, from patient inquiry, he began to call
sad, occasional cries, that ever and anon waked the quiet
landscapes and ragged hill regions, and set to echoing his
thin "O-o-o Phœbe! O-o-o Phœbe!" It had a pathetic,
albeit insane, ring, and many a farmer or plowboy came to
know it even from afar and say, "There goes old Reifsneider."

Another thing that puzzled him greatly after a time and
after many hundreds of inquiries was, when he no longer
had any particular dooryard in view and no special inquiry
to make, which way to go. These cross-roads, which occasionally led in four or even six directions, came after a time
to puzzle him. But to solve this knotty problem, which became more and more of a puzzle, there came to his aid another
hallucination. Phœbe's spirit or some power of the air or
wind or nature would tell him. If he stood at the centre of
the parting of the ways, closed his eyes, turned thrice about,
and called "O-o-o Phœbe!" twice, and then threw his cane
straight before him, that would surely indicate which way to
go, for Phœbe, or one of these mystic powers would surely
govern its direction and fall! In whichever direction it
went, even though, as was not infrequently the case, it took
him back along the path he had already come, or across
fields, he was not so far gone in his mind but that he gave
himself ample time to search before he called again. Also
the hallucination seemed to persist that at some time he
would surely find her. There were hours when his feet were
sore, and his limbs weary, when he would stop in the heat to
wipe his seamed brow, or in the cold to beat his arms. Sometimes, after throwing away his cane, and finding it indicat-
ing the direction from which he had just come, he would
shake his head wearily and philosophically, as if contemp-
lating the unbelievable or an untoward fate, and then start
briskly off. His strange figure came finally to be known in

the farthest reaches of three or four counties. Old Reifsneider was a pathetic character. His fame was wide.

Near a little town called Watersville, in Green County,
perhaps four miles from that minor centre of human activity,
there was a place or precipice locally known as the Red
Cliff, a sheer wall of red sandstone, perhaps a hundred feet
high, which raised its sharp face for half a mile or more
above the fruitful cornfields and orchards that lay beneath,
and which was surmounted by a thick grove of trees. The
slope that slowly led up to it from the opposite side was
covered by a rank growth of beech, hickory, and ash, through
which threaded a number of wagon-tracks crossing at various angles. In fair weather it had become old Reifsneider's
habit, so inured was he by now to the open, to make his bed
in some such patch of trees as this, to fry his bacon or boil
his eggs at the foot of some tree, before laying himself down
for the night. Occasionally, so light and inconsequential
was his sleep, he would walk at night. More often, the
moonlight or some sudden wind stirring in the trees or a
reconnoitering animal arousing him, he would sit up and
think, or pursue his quest in the moonlight or the dark, a
strange, unnatural, half wild, half savage-looking but utterly
harmless creature, calling at lonely road crossings, staring at
dark and shuttered houses, and wondering where, where
Phœbe could really be.

That particular lull that comes in the systole-diastole of
this earthly ball at two o'clock in the morning invariably
aroused him, and though he might not go any farther he
would sit up and contemplate the darkness or the stars, wondering. Sometimes in the strange processes of his mind
he would fancy that he saw moving among the trees the figure
of his lost wife, and then he would get up to follow, taking
his utensils, always on a string, and his cane. If she seemed
to evade him too easily he would run, or plead, or, or, suddenly losing track of the fancied figure, stand awed or disappointed, grieving for the moment over the almost insur-
mountable difficulties of his search.

It was in the seventh year of these hopeless peregrinations,
in the dawn of a similar springtime to that in which his wife

had died, that he came at last one night to the vicinity of this self-same patch that crowned the rise to the Red Cliff. His far-flung cane, used as a divining-rod at the last cross-roads, had brought him hither. He had walked many, many miles. It was after ten o'clock at night, and he was very weary. Long wandering and little eating had left him but a shadow of his former self. It was a question now not so much of physical strength but of spiritual endurance which kept him up. He had scarcely eaten this day, and now, exhausted, he set himself down in the dark to rest and possibly to sleep.

Curiously on this occasion a strange suggestion of the presence of his wife surrounded him. It would not be long now, he counseled with himself, although the long months had brought him nothing, until he should see her, talk to her. He fell asleep after a time, his head on his knees. At midnight the moon began to rise, and at two in the morning, his wakeful hour, was a large silver disk shining through the trees to the east. He opened his eyes when the radiance became strong, making a silver pattern at his feet and lighting the woods with strange lusters and silvery, shadowy forms. As usual, his old notion that his wife must be near occurred to him on this occasion, and he looked about him with a speculative, anticipatory eye. What was it that moved in the distant shadows along the path by which he had entered —a pale, flickering will-o'-the-wisp that bobbed gracefully among the trees and riveted his expectant gaze? Moonlight and shadows combined to give it a strange form and a stranger reality, this fluttering of bog-fire or dancing of wandering fire-flies. Was it truly his lost Phœbe? By a circuitous route it passed about him, and in his fevered state he fancied that he could see the very eyes of her, not as she was when he last saw her in the black dress and shawl, but now a strangely younger Phœbe, gayer, sweeter, the one whom he had known years before as a girl. Old Reifsneider got up. He had been expecting and dreaming of this hour all these years, and now as he saw the feeble light dancing lightly before him he peered at it questioningly, one thin hand in his gray hair.

Of a sudden there came to him now for the first time in many years the full charm of her girlish figure as he had known it in boyhood, the pleasing, sympathetic smile, the brown hair, the blue sash she had once worn about her waist at a picnic, her gray, graceful movements. He walked around the base of the tree, straining with his eyes, forgetting for once his cane and utensils, and following eagerly after. On she moved before him, a will-o'-the-wisp of the spring, a little flame above her head, and it seemed as though among the small saplings of ash and beech and the thick trunks of hickory and elm that she signaled with a young, a lightsome hand.

"O Phœbe! Phœbe!" he called. "Have yuh really come? Have yuh really answered me?" And hurrying faster, he fell once, scrambling lamely to his feet, only to see the light in the distance dancing illusively on. On and on he hurried until he was fairly running, brushing his ragged arms against the trees, striking his hands and face against impeding twigs. His hat was gone, his lungs were breathless, his reason quite astray, when coming to the edge of the cliff he saw her below among a silvery bed of apple-trees now blooming in the spring.

"O Phœbe!" he called. "O Phœbe! Oh, no, don't leave me!" And feeling the lure of a world where love was young and Phœbe, as this vision presented her, a delightful epitome of their quondam youth, he gave a gay cry of "Oh, wait, Phœbe!" and leaped.

Some farmer-boys, reconnoitering this region of bounty and prospect some few days afterward, found first the tin utensils tied together under the tree where he had left them, and then later at the foot of the cliff, pale, broken, but elate, a molded smile of peace and delight upon his lips, his body. His old hat was discovered lying under some low-growing saplings, the twigs of which had held it back. No one of all the simple population knew how eagerly and joyously he had found his lost mate.

A FAILURE *

By Edith Wyatt

THROUGH the rooms and halls of a high building on Wabash Avenue there sound all day, and sometimes far into the night, the note and phrase and rhythm of beating music. Scales and chords, throbbing violin tones, clear piano arpeggios, and soaring voices quiver in the air; and almost at the same moment one may hear wavering through the open doors of studios and practice-rooms endeavor at the technique of art, and its result swelling through the transoms of music and concert-halls.

In one of the rooms of this building toiled like a galley-slave Professor Alberto Wright, a violin master. He was a tall, thin, brown gentleman, of Italian-American parentage, dressed always in Prince Albert coat, tapering gray trousers, and a puffing white satin tie. In the winter he wore an overcoat with a deep chinchilla collar, and it was in this he had his photograph taken to give to the pupils at Christmas-time, with "From your loving teacher, Alberto C. Wright," written in a swashing, black hand across the corner.

Far from being a loving teacher, Professor Alberto was as cross and tyrannical a master as possible. Still his pupils all liked him, and the more sensible stoutly admired him, for his work was done with honesty and enthusiasm; and his crossness arose from a native inability to understand why any moral and intelligent person should do otherwise than devote his whole time and energies to learning the violin. A few of his pupils really were inspired by him to such a devotion; the rest were chiefly without talent or ear, inadequately diligent, and horribly berated; but among the inade-

---

* By permission of, and arrangement with, Doubleday, Page & Company, and the author.

312

quately diligent was one pupil who had a very fine musical
talent.

This was a Southern girl, a Miss Hallie Patterson, gifted
with a quick ear, an instinctive musical understanding, and
a talent for sympathetic expression on the violin. She had
played it ever since she was four years old, when she had
picked it up from her father's Negro-man, Poley.

Miss Hallie was extremely pretty, with brown curls and
lazy, drifting eyes; she dressed outrageously, almost always
wearing her brother's round felt hat; and she was so indolent that Professor Alberto often nearly wept at her slov-
enly runs and double thirds. She lived with her father, Dr.
Patterson, her semi-invalid mother, Mrs. Patterson, her sister, Linda, her young brother, Clement, and Poley, in a
large frame house, out on the West Side. When the doctor
had moved into this house, twelve years before, he had had
the ceilings frescoed, velvet carpets put on the floors, and
small statuettes of Italian marble placed at the windows;
and the house had received almost no attention since. Mrs.
Patterson cared not a pin for the place. The doctor, after
his one week's brilliant dash into housekeeping, was soon absorbed in his business again; and Hallie and Linda managed
the house and brought themselves up, with Poley's assistance.

They certainly managed the house very ill. It was bare
and dingy and almost always so cold that one had to wear a
shawl. Hallie, Linda, and Mrs. Patterson always wore
shawls; Clement grumbled frightfully about the cold, and in
the wintriest weather kept his coat-collar ostentatiously
turned up, and wore a bicycle-cap during dinner, while
Professor Alberto, young Mr. Waters, Claudie Dawson, and
other youthful admirers of Miss Hallie and Miss Linda,
often sat through the meal at the doctor's with teeth positively chattering. Hallie and Linda had left school when
they were about twelve years old, and they spent all their
time in taking drives in a shambling cast-off phaeton of the
doctor's with an old family-horse, in talking to a pet rac-
coon in the back yard, and in receiving calls. They were
both pretty, both entirely amiable and indolent and devoted
to easy, unambitious pleasures; and they both exercised a

remarkable fascination over men and boys of all kinds, so that when Miss Hallie was not driving in the phaeton or feeding the coon, her attention was always occupied with some affair.

She simply had no conception of work, and when Professor Alberto would ask, crossly, "Miss Hallie, might I ask in what valuable way you spend your time that not one scrap is left for practice?" she would merely glance non-committally around the room, smiling sweetly.

"Will you do me the goodness to tell me that, Miss Hallie?"

"Why, Mistah Wright, the reason I coulden practice yestahday was, I jus' ran out to Austin with Mistah Watahs and Sist' Linda and a friend to get a few wild-flowahs."

Professor Alberto nearly choked with rage at these moments. In his early acquaintance with Miss Hallie he had visited the Pattersons in the hope of inducing Mrs. Patterson to spur her daughter to practice—a hope soon dashed.

"Ah wish Hallie *would* practice a little," she said, plaintively, in reply to Professor Alberto's remarks, "though Ah'd rathah she took the piano instead of the fiddle, it seems so much moah lady-like. A'hm passionat'ly fond of music mahself, Mistah Wright. Ah think every lady *ought* to know a little something about it—an' that's why Ah wanted to have daughtah take it up."

Mr. Wright twisted slightly in his chair.

"Do you play *Juanita*, Mistah Wright? It's right pretty—Clemmie, deah, please don't do that. It looks so rude—"

Clement was carelessly chinning himself at the parlor transom.

"Don't you think so, Professor?" Mr. Wright glanced discreetly at the floor. "The' do get on my nerves sometimes, Mistah Wright, racketing around the way the' do. Ah jus' can't do anything with them. The' don't pay any attention to mah advice. Daughtah Linda sometimes she almost weahs me to the bone. Now theah was Mistah Roy Pottah, a lovely fellow. Ah've almost nevah been so taken with any of the guhls' company as Ah was with Mistah Roy Pottah." She lowered her voice. "And *de*tuhmined to marry daughtah Linda. *Well.* He took it very well. As Ah say, he was a lovely fellow; and *so* sweet with Clemmie. He gave him moah lovely books, *Willie's Trial* and *His One Fault.*"

"Darned old stiff," muttered Clement.

"And now he is engaged to a lovely guhl in Kans' City. Someone, *Ah hope,* who can appreciate him," she raised her voice a little with didactic intent to strike the ear of Miss Linda, passing at the moment in teaching the five-step to Claudie Dawson.

The next morning at breakfast Mrs. Patterson observed plaintively to Hallie:

"Daughtah, Ah think you ought to try to practice moah foah Mistah Wright. He is a chawming gentleman, and Ah can see he is jus' wrapped up in his music."

"Well, mother, I will. But Clem hid my violin yesterday."

"Yes, sir. You bet I did; an' the next time you borrow my rub' boots without telling me, an' I look for 'em for an hour, I'll hide it again."

"Hush, Clemmie! Daughtah, Ah wish you wouldn't borrow Clemmie's things so much. Ah hate to see you in his hats the whole time; and Ah don't like to see you wearing that black lace scarf around your neck every day, Hallie. It *is* handsome, Ah will allow, *an'* becoming—but so odd. Othah young ladies weah linen collahs."

"Well, I asked Poley to get me some collars downtown."

"Miss Hallie, clean fergit tell you. Dee all out of youah size. Dee get it in to-day.

This was the manner of Miss Hallie's spurring to work. However, one spring, after a winter of blame and despair with Mr. Wright, she was suddenly inspired with an intention to do better. After all, she liked music better than anything else; and the long effort of Mr. Wright and the popularity and success of a celebrated violinist visiting the city touched her with a wish to endeavor to succeed in her art and with an impatience of her technical faults.

She practiced for a month diligently and with good results, and when, late in May, Mr. Wright determined to give a chamber concert, a pupils' recital, and bestow on her the most important numbers, she was more than ever stirred.

For while Mr. Wright with one hand depressed this concert to the level of a simple, almost domestic occasion, with the other he raised it to the rank of an important musical event.

Hallie thought very little about it at first; but as time went on she became more and more painfully aware that she must keep up to the mark—a feeling she extremely disliked.

Mr. Wright, meanwhile, sometimes pretended that the concert was of no moment, and at others represented to Miss Hallie that it was the beginning of her musical career and if she failed in it she would be little better than damned. He kept inviting more and more musicians, musical critics, and friends of musical art to come to the chamber concert; he had one pupil he particularly wished they should hear. He thought she had a career before her since she certainly had a brilliant musical talent.

On the day of the concert Mr. Wright was so nervous that he even communicated his nervousness to Miss Hallie. He told her several times that she must not forget that someone would carry in her violin-stand and put it up for her. At the same time she must forget the audience and put all her energies into her work. But remember to stand facing the house; and not to keep looking at the piano when it was time for it to come in, in the concerto—that gave a very awkward appearance. She ought to have flowers. Everything counted in the beginning of a career. He tore out at the last moment and bought her some—no one else, he was sure, could do it so quickly—and handed them to her furiously.

Looking out from the side of the concert-stage, poor Miss Hallie could see that the chamber was crowded, and with a critical, musical audience; though in the front row sat a comfortable group of Dr. Patterson, Clement, Linda, Claudie Dawson, and several of the youthful admirers. Poley was wandering restlessly near the entrance. He was almost as nervous as Professor Alberto.

The concert opened with two colorless trilling numbers

by frightened pupils; and then Miss Hallie came out on the platform with her violin. She looked very youthful and a little pale and scared in Mrs. Patterson's best black grenadine dress and a little bonnet. Her hand was quivering and she was unable to lift her eyes to the audience. She settled her violin under her chin, tightened a string with a desperate sense that now, *now* was actually the moment she had thought about so long, and began the introduction of the *Norwegian Dance* of Mr. Wright's selection.

Once the first familiar notes had sounded she was at ease in her performance. She played with her native perception and fire and more than her ordinary power and mastery. She completely filled her hearers' sense and her own with the splendid rhythm of the fierce Norwegian music, until, absorbed in her rendition, she glanced up carelessly, and, at the sight of all the faces and eyes about her, panic possessed her.

Her hand faltered. Grieg's music vanished from her mind as though it had been swept off with a sponge. She turned white and giddy, the room began to reel before her; and then it seemed she plunged down a bottomless abyss.

The next thing she knew was that she was lying on a couch in Professor Alberto's studio, with her father standing beside her and Poley, Clement, and Linda looking in at her from the door.

"Lie still, daughter, lie still," said her father, gently. He poured a little wine for her, and after she had drunk it Miss Hallie sat up on the couch and began to cry. She could hear the music of the next number sounding dimly through the transom. "Oh, how terribly Mistah Wright will feel," she said. "I don't know what was the matter with me. Heavens! I nevah will go on that platform again. I want you to tell Professor that I nevah will go neah that platform. I simply can't stand it."

The doctor gazed on her in distress and softly closed the door on Linda, Clement, and Poley. He soothed Miss Hallie as well as he could, gave her a little wine, took off her unaccustomed bonnet, and clumsily smoothed her hair, with anxiety and tenderness written on his lank, kind face.

"And, besides, I can't stand it to see Mistah Wright again, befoh we go home."

The recollection of Mr. Wright's uncontrolled gloom arose before the doctor. "Perhaps that would be as well," he assented.

"My daughter," he continued, gravely. "I know you feel now that life is closed to you. At your age that is natural. I thought many times when I was a young man that I could not possibly continue in the medical careah." He looked down at the floor. "And I never can have the success I once expected. But my work has been very much to me. You know we sometimes get more ourselves from our work than anyone else could give us." Miss Hallie was an honest girl. "But, fathah," she said, quakingly, "I nevah took my music like that. I don't really care to practise much, though I'm awfully fond of music. I like it about as much as anything I know of."

"Well, that is a relief, in some ways," said the doctor. "But so much seemed to be made of this."

"No, that was all Mistah Wright. He sort of worked me up, I reckon. He always said I hadn't any application or any ambition, an' I guess it's true, I haven't." The tears began to fall over her face.

"Don't, daughter, don't," said the doctor, hastily, "it's bad for your eyes, my dear."

"Well, fathah, I guess if I had ambition I'd cry lots harder. Dear! How disappointed Poley will be," she began to laugh a little, and the doctor smiled, too, more from a good-hearted pleasure at seeing her rally than from any humerous perception of Poley's attitude. When Miss Hallie was safely started for home in the carriage with Poley, the doctor waited till after the concert was over and the sympathetic musical friends had dispersed, and talked long with Mr. Wright, who found him far more satisfactory than any other of the Pattersons.

"You have taught my daughter nobly, sir," he said, "Nobly. I appreciate your work with her, but for many reasons—temperamental and othah reasons—she could nevah have a musical careah. In my profession, and all

professional work, sir, I have learned to appreciate the
necessity of not yielding to a sudden mood, and ah—application—"

Professor Alberto nearly fell on the doctor's neck.

That evening, while the doctor was sitting in his office,
he heard Hallie's violin quivering and singing through the
frescoed parlors. Mrs. Patterson, in complainant confi-
dences, was murmuring to young Mr. Waters at one end of
the room, and Clement, Linda, and some of the youthful
admirers were sitting out on the front steps, all rather silent,
and a little tired from the exhausting day. Linda had nearly
fallen asleep once or twice.

The fragrance of Professor Alberto's roses wafted through
the empty rooms on the cool spring wind through the open
windows. The tones of Hallie's violin rose and fell on the
still air in the *Suwanee River* and *Dixie,* and in their
wild lilting melody there sounded to the girl all the joys of
her regained ease and liberty. "And I wish I was in Dixie,
Away! Away! In Dixie's land I'll take my stand, to live
and die in Dixie Land"; here for no reason but that of
countless vague associations there sounded to her fancy a
hundred happy days of waltzing and dancing in her father's
parlors, of hours in the barn with Poley and long drives with
Linda in the old phaeton, of innumerable worthless moments
radiant with careless joy and freedom.

The lamp-light from the street fell in dusky and purple-
flecked lights and shadows on the floor, and an overwhelming
tenderness for the familiar house and its kind, funny ways
swept her. At the moment everything in her whole life, its
every circumstance, seemed to her suffused and radiant with
the warmest loveliness. She played on and on, her heart
beating high with happiness. Perhaps she really was getting more from her work than anyone else would have given
her.

THE YELLOW WALL-PAPER *

By Charlotte Perkins Stetson Gilman

IT is very seldom that mere ordinary people like John and myself secure ancestral halls for the summer.

A colonial mansion, a hereditary estate, I would say a haunted house, and reach the height of romantic felicity—but that would be asking too much of fate!

Still I will proudly declare that there is something queer about it.

Else, why should it be let so cheaply? And why have stood so long untenanted?

John laughs at me, of course, but one expects that in John is practical in the extreme. He has no patience with faith, an intense horror of superstition, and he scoffs openly at any talk of things not to be felt and seen and put down in figures.

John is a physician, and *perhaps*—(I would not say it to a living soul, of course, but this is dead paper and a great relief to my mind)—*perhaps* that is one reason I do not get well faster.

You see he does not believe I am sick! And what can one do?

If a physician of high standing, and one's own husband, assures friends and relatives that there is really nothing the matter with one but temporary nervous depression—a slight hysterical tendency—what is one to do?

My brother is also a physician, and also of high standing, and he says the same thing.

So I take phosphates or phosphites—whichever it is—and tonics, and journeys, and air, and exercise, and am absolutely forbidden to "work" until I am well again.

Personally, I disagree with their ideas.

---

* By permission of the author.

Personally, I believe that congenial work, with excitement and change, would do me good.

But what is one to do?

I did write for a while in spite of them; but it *does* exhaust me a good deal—having to be so sly about it, or else meet with heavy opposition.

I sometimes fancy that in my condition if I had less opposition and more society and stimulus—but John says the very worst thing I can do is to think about my condition, and I confess it always makes me feel bad.

So I will let it alone and talk about the house.

The most beautiful place! It is quite alone, standing well back from the road, quite three miles from the village. It makes me think of English places that you read about, for there are hedges and walls and gates that lock, and lots of separate little houses for the gardeners and people.

There is a *delicious* garden! I never saw such a garden —large and shady, full of box-bordered paths, and lined with long grape-covered arbors with seats under them.

There were greenhouses, too, but they are all broken now.

There was some legal trouble, I believe, something about the heirs and co-heirs; anyhow, the place has been empty for years.

That spoils my ghostliness, I am afraid, but I don't care —there is something strange about the house—I can feel it.

I even said so to John one moonlight evening, but he said what I felt was a draught, and shut the window.

I get unreasonably angry with John sometimes. I'm sure I never used to be so sensitive. I think it is due to this nervous condition.

But John says if I feel so I shall neglect proper self-control; so I take pains to control myself—before him, at least, and that makes me very tired.

I don't like our room a bit. I wanted one downstairs that opened on the piazza and had roses all over the window, and such pretty old-fashioned chintz hangings! But John would not hear of it.

He said there was only one window and not room for two beds, and no near room for him if he took another.

He is very careful and loving, and hardly lets me stir without special direction.

I have a schedule prescription for each hour in the day; he takes all care from me, and so I feel basely ungrateful not to value it more.

He said we came here solely on my account, that I was to have perfect rest and all the air I could get. "Your exercise depends on your strength, my dear," said he, "and your food somewhat on your appetite; but air you can absorb all the time." So we took the nursery at the top of the house.

It is a big, airy room, the whole floor nearly, with windows that look all ways, and air and sunshine galore. It was nursery first and then playroom and gymnasium, I should judge; for the windows are barred for little children, and there are rings and things in the walls.

The paint and paper look as if a boys' school had used it. It is stripped off—the paper—in great patches all around the head of my bed, about as far as I can reach, and in a great place on the other side of the room low down. I never saw a worse paper in my life.

One of those sprawling flamboyant patterns committing every artistic sin.

It is dull enough to confuse the eye in following, pronounced enough constantly to irritate and provoke study, and when you follow the lame uncertain curves for a little distance they suddenly commit suicide—plunge off at outrageous angles, destroy themselves in unheard of contradictions.

The color is repellant, almost revolting; a smouldering unclean yellow, strangely faded by the slow-turning sunlight.

It is a dull yet lurid orange in some places, a sickly sulphur tint in others.

No wonder the children hated it! I should hate it myself if I had to live in this room long.

There comes John, and I must put this away—he hates to have me write a word.

*   *   *   *   *   *   *   *

We have been here two weeks, and I haven't felt like writing before, since that first day.

I am sitting by the window now, up in this atrocious nursery, and there is nothing to hinder my writing as much as I please, save lack of strength.

John is away all day, and even some nights when his cases are serious.

I am glad my case is not serious!

But these nervous troubles are dreadfully depressing.

John does not know how much I really suffer. He knows there is no *reason* to suffer, and that satisfies him.

Of course it is only nervousness. It does weigh on me so not to do my duty in any way!

I meant to be such a help to John, such a real rest and comfort, and here I am a comparative burden already!

Nobody would believe what an effort it is to do what little I am able—to dress and entertain, and order things.

It is fortunate Mary is so good with the baby. Such a dear baby!

And yet I *cannot* be with him, it makes me so nervous.

I suppose John never was nervous in his life. He laughs at me so about this wall-paper!

At first he meant to repaper the room, but afterwards he said that I was letting it get the better of me, and that nothing was worse for a nervous patient that to give way to such fancies.

He said that after the wall-paper was changed it would be the heavy bedstead, and then the barred windows, and then that gate at the head of the stairs, and so on.

"You know the place is doing you good," he said, "and really, dear, I don't care to renovate the house just for a three months' rental."

"Then do let us go downstairs," I said, "there are such pretty rooms there."

Then he took me in his arms and called me a blessed little goose, and said he would go down cellar, if I wished, and have it whitewashed into the bargain.

But he is right enough about the beds and windows and things.

It is an airy and comfortable room as any one need wish, and, of course, I would not be so silly as to make him uncomfortable just for a whim.

I'm really getting quite fond of the big room, all but that horrid paper.

Out of one window I can see the garden, those mysterious deep-shaded arbors, the riotous old-fashioned flowers, and bushes and gnarly trees.

Out of another I get a lovely view of the bay and a little private wharf belonging to the estate. There is a beautiful shaded lane that runs down there from the house. I always fancy I see people walking in these numerous paths and arbors, but John has cautioned me not to give way to fancy in the least. He says that with my imaginative power and habit of story-making, a nervous weakness like mine is sure to lead to all manner of excited fancies, and that I ought to use my will and good sense to check the tendency. So I try.

I think sometimes that if I were only well enough to write a little it would relieve the press of ideas and rest me.

But I find I get pretty tired when I try.

It is so discouraging not to have any advice and companionship about my work. When I get really well, John says we will ask Cousin Henry and Julia down for a long visit; but he says he would as soon put fireworks in my pillowcase as to let me have those stimulating people about now.

I wish I could get well faster.

But I must not think about that. This paper looks to me as if it *knew* what a vicious influence it had!

There is a recurrent spot where the pattern lolls like a broken neck and two bulbous eyes stare at you upside down.

I get positively angry with the impertinence of it and the everlastingness. Up and down and sideways they crawl, and those absurd, unblinking eyes are everywhere. There is one place where two breadths didn't match, and the eyes go all up and down the line, one a little higher than the other.

I never saw so much expression in an inanimate thing before, and we all know how much expression they have! I used to lie awake as a child and get more entertainment and terror out of blank walls and plain furniture than most children could find in a toy-store.

I remember what a kindly wink the knobs of our big, old bureau used to have, and there was one chair that always seemed like a strong friend.

I used to feel that if any of the other things looked too fierce I could always hop into that chair and be safe.

The furniture in this room is no worse than inharmonious, however, for we had to bring it all from downstairs. I suppose when this was used as a playroom they had to take the nursery things out, and no wonder! I never saw such ravages as the children have made here.

The wall-paper, as I said before, is torn off in spots, and it sticketh closer than a brother—they must have had perseverance as well as hatred.

Then the floor is scratched and gouged and splintered, the plaster itself is dug out here and there, and this great heavy bed which is all we found in the room, looks as if it had been through the wars.

But I don't mind it a bit—only the paper.

There comes John's sister. Such a dear girl as she is, and so careful of me! I must not let her find me writing.

She is a perfect and enthusiastic housekeeper, and hopes for no better profession. I verily believe she thinks it is the writing which made me sick!

But I can write when she is out, and see her a long way off from these windows.

There is one that commands the road, a lovely shaded winding road, and one that just looks off over the country. A lovely country, too, full of great elms and velvet meadows.

This wall-paper has a kind of sub-pattern in a different shade, a particularly irritating one, for you can only see it in certain lights, and not clearly then.

But in the places where it isn't faded and where the sun is just so—I can see a strange, provoking, formless sort of figure, that seems to skulk about behind that silly and conspicuous front design.

There's sister on the stairs!

*   *   *   *   *   *   *   *

Well, the Fourth of July is over! The people are all gone and I am tired out. John thought it might do me good to see a little company, so we just had mother and Nellie and the children down for a week.

Of course I didn't do a thing. Jennie sees to everything now.

But it tired me all the same.

John says if I don't pick up faster he shall send me to Weir Mitchell in the fall.

But I don't want to go there at all. I had a friend who was in his hands once, and she says he is just like John and my brother, only more so!

Besides, it is such an undertaking to go so far.

I don't feel as if it was worth while to turn my hand over for anything, and I'm getting dreadfully fretful and querulous.

I cry at nothing, and cry most of the time.

Of course I don't when John is here, or anybody else, but when I am alone.

And I am alone a good deal just now. John is kept in town very often by serious cases, and Jennie is good and lets me alone when I want her to.

So I walk a little in the garden or down that lovely lane, sit on the porch under the roses, and lie down up here a good deal.

I'm getting really fond of the room in spite of the wallpaper. Perhaps *because* of the wallpaper.

It dwells in my mind so!

I lie here on this great immovable bed—it is nailed down, I believe—and follow that pattern about by the hour. It is as good as gymnastics, I assure you. I start, we'll say, at the bottom, down in the corner over there where it has not been touched, and I determine for the thousandth time that I *will* follow that pointless pattern to some sort of a conclusion.

I know a little of the principle of design, and I know this thing was not arranged on any laws of radiation, or alternation, or repetition, or symmetry, or anything else that I ever heard of.

It is repeated, of course, by the breadths, but not otherwise.

Looked at in one way each breadth stands alone, the bloated curves and flourishes—a kind of "debased Romanesque" with delirium tremens—go waddling up and down in isolated columns of fatuity.

But, on the other hand, they connect diagonally, and the sprawling outlines run off in great slanting waves of optic horror, like a lot of wallowing sea-weeds in full chase.

The whole thing goes horizontally, too, at least it seems so, and I exhaust myself trying to distinguish the order of its going in that direction.

They have used a horizontal breadth for a frieze, and that adds wonderfully to the confusion.

There is one end of the room where it is almost intact, and there, when the crosslights fade and the low sun shines directly upon it, I can almost fancy radiation after all,—the interminable grotesques seem to form around a common centre and rush off in headlong plunges of equal distraction.

It makes me tired to follow it. I will take a nap I guess.

*   *   *   *   *   *   *   *

I don't know why I should write this.

I don't want to.

I don't feel able.

And I know John would think it absurd. But I *must* say what I feel and think in some way—it is such a relief!

But the effort is getting to be greater than the relief.

Half the time now I am awfully lazy, and lie down ever so much.

John says I mustn't lose my strength, and has me take cod liver oil and lots of tonics and things, to say nothing of ale and wine and rare meat.

Dear John! He loves me very dearly, and hates to have me sick. I tried to have a real earnest reasonable talk with him the other day, and tell him how I wish he would let me go and make a visit to Cousin Henry and Julia.

But he said I wasn't able to go, nor able to stand it after I got there; and I did not make out a very good case for myself, for I was crying before I had finished.

It is getting to be a great effort for me to think straight. Just this nervous weakness I suppose.

And dear John gathered me up in his arms, and just carried me upstairs and laid me on the bed, and sat by me and read to me till it tired my head.

He said I was his darling and his comfort and all he had, and that I must take care of myself for his sake, and keep well.

He says no one but myself can help me out of it, that I must use my will and self-control and not let any silly fancies run away with me.

There's one comfort, the baby is well and happy, and does not have to occupy this nursery with the horrid wallpaper.

If we had not used it, that blessed child would have! What a fortunate escape! Why, I wouldn't have a child of mine, an impressionable little thing, live in such a room for worlds.

I never thought of it before, but it is lucky that John kept me here after all, I can stand it so much easier than a baby, you see.

Of course I never mention it to them any more—I am too wise—but I keep watch for it all the same.

There are things in that paper that nobody knows but me, or ever will.

Behind that outside pattern the dim shapes get clearer every day.

It is always the same shape, only very numerous.

And it is like a woman stooping down and creeping about behind that pattern. I don't like it a bit. I wonder—I begin to think—I wish John would take me away from here!

* * * * * * * *

It is so hard to talk with John about my case, because he is so wise, and because he loves me so.

But I tried it last night.

It was moonlight. The moon shines in all around just as the sun does.

I hate to see it sometimes, it creeps so slowly, and always comes in by one window or another.

John was asleep and I hated to waken him, so I kept still

and watched the moonlight on that undulating wallpaper till I felt creepy.

The faint figure behind seemed to shake the pattern, just as if she wanted to get out.

I got up softly and went to feel and see if the paper *did* move, and when I came back John was awake.

"What is it, little girl?" he said. "Don't go walking about like that—you'll get cold."

I thought it was a good time to talk so I told him that I really was not gaining here, and that I wished he would take me away.

"Why darling!" said he, "our lease will be up in three weeks, and I can't see how to leave before.

"The repairs are not done at home, and I cannot possibly leave town just now. Of course if you were in any danger, I could and would, but you really are better, dear, whether you can see it or not. I am a doctor, dear, and I know. You are gaining flesh and color, your appetite is better, I feel really much easier about you."

"I don't weigh a bit more," said I, "nor as much; and my appetite may be better in the evening when you are here, but it is worse in the morning when you are away!"

"Bless her little heart!" said he with a big hug, "she shall be as sick as she pleases! But now let's improve the shining hours by going to sleep, and talk about it in the morning!"

"And you won't go away?" I asked gloomily.

"Why, how can I, dear? It is only three weeks more and then we will take a nice little trip of a few days while Jennie is getting the house ready. Really, dear, you are better!"

"Better in body perhaps—" I began, and stopped short, for he sat up straight and looked at me with such a stern, reproachful look that I could not say another word.

"My darling," said he, "I beg of you, for my sake and for our child's sake, as well as for your own, that you will never for one instant let that idea enter your mind! There is nothing so dangerous, so fascinating, to a temperament like yours. It is a false and foolish fancy. Can you not trust me as a physician when I tell you so?"

So of course I said no more on that score, and we went to sleep before long. He thought I was asleep first, but I wasn't, and lay there for hours trying to decide whether that front pattern and the back pattern really did move together or separately.

* * * * * * * *

On a pattern like this, by daylight, there is a lack of sequence, a defiance of law, that is a constant irritant to a normal mind.

The color is hideous enough, and unreliable enough, and infuriating enough, but the pattern is torturing.

You think you have mastered it, but just as you get well underway in following, it turns a back-somersault and there you are. It slaps you in the face, knocks you down, and tramples upon you. It is like a bad dream.

The outside pattern is a florid arabesque, reminding one of a fungus. If you can imagine a toadstool in joints, an interminable string of toadstools, budding and sprouting in endless convolutions— why, that is something like it.

That is, sometimes!

There is one marked peculiarity about this paper, a thing nobody seems to notice but myself, and that is that it changes as the light changes.

When the sun shoots in through the east window—I always watch for that first, long, straight ray—it changes so quickly that I never can quite believe it.

That is why I watch it always.

By moonlight—the moon shines in all night when there is a moon—I wouldn't know it was the same paper.

At night in any kind of light, in twilight, candlelight, lamplight, and worst of all by moonlight, it becomes bars! The outside pattern I mean, and the woman behind it is as plain as can be.

I didn't realize for a long time what the thing was that showed behind, that dim sub-pattern, but now I am quite sure it is a woman.

By daylight she is subdued, quiet. I fancy it is the pattern that keeps her so still. It is so puzzling. It keeps me quiet by the hour.

I lie down ever so much now. John says it is good for me, and to sleep all I can.

Indeed he started the habit by making me lie down for an hour after each meal.

It is a very bad habit I am convinced, for you see I don't sleep.

And that cultivates deceit, for I don't tell them I'm awake —O, no!

The fact is I am getting a little afraid of John.

He seems very queer sometimes, and even Jennie has an inexplicable look.

It strikes me occasionally, just as a scientific hypothesis, that perhaps it is the paper!

I have watched John when he did not know I was looking, and come into the room suddenly on the most innocent excuses, and I've caught him several times *looking at the paper!* And Jennie too. I caught Jennie with her hand on it once.

She didn't know I was in the room, and when I asked her in a quiet, a very quiet voice, with the most restrained manner possible, what she was doing with the paper—she turned around as if she had been caught stealing, and looked quite angry—asked me why I should frighten her so!

Then she said that the paper stained everything it touched, that she had found yellow smooches on all my clothes and John's, and she wished we would be more careful!

Did not that sound innocent? But I know she was studying that pattern, and I am determined that nobody shall find it out but myself!

* * * * * * * *

Life is very much more exciting now than it used to be. You see I have something more to expect, to look forward to, to watch. I really do eat better, and am more quiet than I was.

John is so pleased to see me improve! He laughed a little the other day, and said I seemed to be flourishing in spite of my wallpaper.

I turned it off with a laugh. I had no intention of telling him it was *because* of the wallpaper—he would make fun of me. He might even want to take me away.

I don't want to leave now until I have found it out. There is a week more, and I think that will be enough.

* * * * * * * *

I'm feeling ever so much better! I don't sleep much at night, for it is so interesting to watch developments; but I sleep a good deal in the daytime.

In the daytime it is tiresome and perplexing.

There are always new shoots on the fungus, and new shades of yellow all over it. I cannot keep count of them, though I have tried conscientiously.

It is the strangest yellow, that wallpaper! It makes me think of all the yellow things I ever saw—not beautiful ones like buttercups, but old foul, bad yellow things.

But there is something else about that paper—the smell! I noticed it the moment we came into the room, but with so much air and sun it was not bad. Now we have had a week of fog and rain, and whether the windows are open or not, the smell is here.

It creeps all over the house.

I find it hovering in the dining-room, skulking in the parlor, hiding in the hall, lying in wait for me on the stairs.

It gets into my hair.

Even when I go to ride, if I turn my head suddenly and surprise it—there is that smell!

Such a peculiar odor, too! I have spent hours in trying to analyze it, to find what it smelled like.

It is not bad—at first, and very gentle, but quite the subtlest, most enduring odor I ever met.

In this damp weather it is awful, I wake up in the night and find it hanging over me.

It used to disturb me at first. I thought seriously of burning the house—to reach the smell.

But now I am used to it. The only thing I can think of that it is like is the *color* of the paper! A yellow smell.

There is a very funny mark on this wall, low down, near the mopboard. A streak that runs round the room. It goes behind every piece of furniture, except the bed, a long, straight, even *smooch,* as if it had been rubbed over and over.

I wonder how it was done and who did it, and what they did it for. Round and round and round—round and round and round—it makes me dizzy!

*　　*　　*　　*　　*　　*　　*　　*

I really have discovered something at last.

Through watching so much at night, when it changes so, I have finally found out.

The front pattern *does* move—and no wonder! The woman behind shakes it!

Sometimes I think there are a great many women behind, and sometimes only one, and she crawls around fast, and her crawling shakes it all over.

Then in the very bright spots she keeps still, and in the very shady spots she just takes hold of the bars and shakes them hard.

And she is all the time trying to climb through. But nobody could climb through that pattern—it strangles so; I think that is why it has so many heads.

They get through, and then the pattern strangles them off and turns them upside down, and makes their eyes white!

If those heads were covered or taken off it would not be half so bad.

*　　*　　*　　*　　*　　*　　*　　*

I think that woman gets out in the daytime!

And I'll tell you why—privately—I've seen her!

I can see her out of every one of my windows!

It is the same woman, I know, for she is always creeping, and most women do not creep by daylight.

I see her in that long shaded lane, creeping up and down. I see her in those dark grape arbors, creeping all around the garden.

I see her on that long road under the trees, creeping along, and when a carriage comes she hides under the blackberry vines.

I don' blame her a bit. It must be very humiliating to be caught creeping by daylight!

I always lock the door when I creep by daylight. I can't do it at night, for I know John would suspect something at once.

And John is so queer now, that I don't want to irritate him. I wish he would take another room! Besides, I don't want anybody to get that woman out at night but myself.

I often wonder if I could see her out of all the windows at once.

But, turn as fast as I can, I can only see out of one at one time.

And though I always see her, she *may* be able to creep faster than I can turn!

I have watched her sometimes away off in the open country, creeping as fast as a cloud shadow in a high wind.

* * * * * * * *

If only that top pattern could be gotten off from the under one! I mean to try it, little by little.

I have found out another funny thing, but I shan't tell it this time! It does not do to trust people too much.

There are only two more days to get this paper off, and I believe John is beginning to notice. I don't like the look in his eyes.

And I heard him ask Jennie a lot of professional questions about me. She had a very good report to give.

She said I slept a good deal in the daytime.

John knows I don't sleep very well at night, for all I'm so quiet!

He asked me all sorts of questions, too, and pretended to be very loving and kind.

As if I couldn't see through him!

Still, I don't wonder he acts so, sleeping under this paper for three months.

It only interests me, but I feel sure John and Jennie are secretly affected by it.

* * * * * * * *

Hurrah! This is the last day, but it is enough. John to stay in town over night, and won't be out until this evening.

Jennie wanted to sleep with me—the sly thing! but I told her I should undoubtedly rest better for a night all alone.

That was clever, for really I wasn't alone a bit! As soon as it was moonlight and that poor thing began to crawl and shake the pattern, I got up and ran to help her.

I pulled and she shook, I shook and she pulled, and before morning we had peeled off yards of that paper.

A strip about as high as my head and half around the room.

And then when the sun came and that awful pattern began to laugh at me, I declared I would finish it to-day!

We go away to-morrow, and they are moving all my furniture down again to leave things as they were before.

Jennie looked at the wall in amazement, but I told her merrily that I did it out of pure spite at the vicious thing.

She laughed and said she wouldn't mind doing it herself, but I must not get tired.

How she betrayed herself that time!

But I am here, and no person touches this paper but Me— not *alive!*

She tried to get me out of the room— it was too patent! But I said it was so quiet and empty and clean now that I believed I would lie down again and sleep all I could; and not to wake me even for dinner—I would call when I woke.

So now she is gone, and the servants are gone, and the things are gone, and there is nothing left but that great bedstead nailed down, with the canvas mattress we found on it.

We shall sleep downstairs to-night, and take the boat home to-morrow.

I quite enjoy the room, now it is bare again.

How those children did tear about here!

This bedstead is fairly gnawed!

But I must get to work.

I have locked the door and thrown the key down into the front path.

I don't want to go out ,and I don't want to have anybody come in, till John comes.

I want to astonish him.

I've got a rope up here that even Jennis did not find. If

that woman does get out, and tries to get away, I can tie her!

But I forgot I could not reach far without anything to stand on!

This bed will *not* move!

I tried to lift and push it until I was lame, and then I got so angry I bit off a little piece at one corner—but it hurt my teeth.

Then I peeled off all the paper I could reach standing on the floor. It sticks horribly and the pattern just enjoys it! All those strangled heads and bulbous eyes and waddling fungus growths just shriek with derision!

I am getting angry enough to do something desperate. To jump out of the window would be admirable exercise, but the bars are too strong even to try.

Besides I wouldn't do it. Of course not. I know well enough that a step like that is improper and might be misconstrued.

I don't like to *look* out of the windows even—there are so many of those creeping women, and they creep so fast.

I wonder if they all come out of that wallpaper as I did?

But I am securely fastened now by my well-hidden rope— you don't get *me* out in the road there!

I suppose I shall have to get back behind the pattern when it comes night, and that is hard!

It is so pleasant to be out in this great room and creep around as I please!

I don't want to go outside. I won't, even if Jennie asks me to.

For outside you have to creep on the ground, and everything is green instead of yellow.

But here I can creep smoothly on the floor, and my shoulder just fits in that long smooch around the wall, so I cannot lose my way.

Why there's John at the door!

It is no use, young man, you can't open it!

How he does call and pound!

Now he's crying for an axe.

It would be a shame to break down that beautiful door!

"John dear!" said I in the gentlest voice, "the key is down by the front steps, under a plantain leaf!"

That silenced him for a few moments.

Then he said, very quietly indeed, "Open the door, my darling!"

"I can't," said I. "The key is down by the front door under a plantain leaf!"

And then I said it again, several times, very gently and slowly, and said it so often that he had to go and see, and he got it of course, and came in. He stopped short by the door.

"What is the matter?" he cried. "For God's sake, what are you doing!"

I kept on creeping just the same, but I looked at him over my shoulder.

"I've got out at last," said I, "in spite of you and Jane. And I've pulled off most of the paper, so you can't put me back!"

Now why should that man have fainted? But he did, and right across my path by the wall, so that I had to creep over him every time!

THE LITTLE ROOM *

By Madelene Yale Wynne

"HOW would it do for a smoking room?"

"Just the very place! Only, you know, Roger, you must not think of smoking in the house. I am almost afraid that having just a plain, common man around, let alone a smoking man, will upset Aunt Hannah. She is New England—Vermont New England—boiled down."

"You leave Aunt Hannah to me; I'll find her tender side. I'm going to ask her about the old sea-captain and the yellow calico."

"Not yellow calico—blue chintz."

"Well, yellow *shell* then."

"No, no! don't mix it up so; you won't know yourself what to expect, and that's half the fun."

"Now you tell me again exactly what to expect; to tell the truth, I didn't half hear about it the other day; I was wool-gathering. It was something queer that happened when you were a child, wasn't it?"

"Something that began to happen long before that, and kept happening, and may happen again—but I hope not."

"What was it?"

"I wonder if the other people in the car can hear us?"

"I fancy not; we don't hear them—not consecutively, at least."

"Well, mother was born in Vermont, you know; she was the only child by a second marriage. Aunt Hannah and Aunt Maria are only half-aunts to me, you know."

"I hope they are half as nice as you are."

"Roger, be still—they certainly will hear us."

---

* By special arrangement.

"Well, don't you want them to know we are married?"

"Yes, but not just married. There's all the difference in the world."

"You are afraid we look too happy!"

"No, only I want my happiness all to myself."

"Well, the little room?"

"My aunts brought mother up; they were nearly twenty years older than she. I might say Hiram and they brought her up. You see, Hiram was bound out to my grandfather when he was a boy, and when grandfather died Hiram said he 's'posed he went with the farm, 'long o' the critters,' and he has been there ever since. He was my mother's only refuge from the decorum of my aunts. They are simply workers. They make me think of the Maine woman who wanted her epitaph to be: 'She was a *hard* working woman.'"

"They must be almost beyond their working-days. How old are they?"

"Seventy, or thereabouts; but they will die standing; or, at least, on a Saturday night, after all the house-work is done up. They were rather strict with mother, and I think she had a lonely childhood. The house is almost a mile away from any neighbors, and off on top of what they call Stony Hill. It is bleak enough up there, even in summer."

"When mamma was about ten years old they sent her to cousins in Brooklyn, who had children of their own, and knew more about bringing them up. She stayed there till she was married; she didn't go to Vermont in all that time, and of course hadn't seen her sisters, for they never would leave home for a day. They couldn't even be induced to go to Brooklyn for her wedding, so she and father took their wedding trip up there."

"And that's why we are going up there on our own?"

"Don't, Roger; you have no idea how loud you speak."

"You never say so except when I am going to say that one little word."

"Well, don't say it, then, or say it very, very quietly."

"Well, what was the queer thing?"

"When they got to the house, mother wanted to take

father right off into the little room; she had been telling him about it, just as I am going to tell you, and she had said that of all the rooms, that one was the only one that seemed pleasant to her. She described the furniture and the books and paper and everything, and said it was on the north side, between the front and back room. Well, when they went to look for it, there was no little room there; there was only a shallow china-closet. She asked her sisters when the house had been altered and a closet made of the room that used to be there. They both said the house was exactly as it had been built—that they had never made any changes, except to tear down the old wood-shed and build a smaller one.

"Father and mother laughed a good deal over it, and when anything was lost they would always say it must be in the little room, and any exaggerated statement was called 'little-roomy.' When I was a child I thought that was a regular English phrase, I heard it so often.

"Well, they talked it over, and finally they concluded that my mother had been a very imaginative sort of a child, and had read in some book about such a little room, or perhaps even dreamed it, and then had 'made believe,' as children do, till she herself had really thought the room was there."

"Why, of course, that might easily happen."

"Yes, but you haven't heard the queer part yet; you wait and see if you can explain the rest as easily.

"They staid at the farm two weeks, and then went to New York to live. When I was eight years old my father was killed in the war, and mother was broken-hearted. She never was quite strong afterwards, and that summer we decided to go up to the farm for three months.

"I was a restless sort of a child, and the journey seemed very long to me; and finally, to pass the time, mamma told me the story of the little room, and how it was all in her own imagination, and how there really was only a china-closet there.

"She told it with all the particulars; and even to me, who knew beforehand that the room wasn't there, it seemed just as real as could be. She said it was on the north side, be-

tween the front and back rooms; that it was very small, and
they sometimes called it an entry. There was a door also
that opened out-of-doors, and that one was painted green,
and was cut in the middle like the old Dutch doors, so that
it could be used for a window by opening the top part only.
Directly opposite the door was a lounge or couch; it was
covered with blue chintz—India chintz—some that had
been brought over by an old Salem sea-captain as a
'venture.' He had given it to Hannah when she was a
young girl. She was sent to Salem for two years to school.
Grandfather originally came from Salem."

"I thought there wasn't any room or chintz."

"*That is just it.* They had decided that mother had
imagined it all, and yet you see how exactly everything was
painted in her mind, for she had even remembered that
Hiram had told her that Hannah could have married the
sea-captain if she had wanted to!

"The India cotton was the regular blue stamped chintz,
with the peacock figure on it. The head and body of the
bird were in profile, while the tail was full front view behind it. It had seemed to take mamma's fancy, and she drew
it for me on a piece of paper as she talked. Doesn't it
seem strange to you that she could have made all that up,
or even dreamed it?

"At the foot of the lounge were some hanging shelves with
some old books on them. All the books were leather-colored
except one; that was bright red, and was called the *Ladies'
Album*. It made a bright break between the other thicker
books.

"On the lower shelf was a beautiful pink sea-shell, lying
on a mat made of balls of red shaded worsted. This shell
was greatly coveted by mother, but she was only allowed to
play with it when she had been particularly good. Hiram
had shown her how to hold it close to her ear and hear the
roar of the sea in it.

"I know you will like Hiram, Roger; he is quite a character in his way.

"Mamma said she remembered, or *thought* she remembered,
having been sick once, and she had to lie quietly for some

days on the lounge; then was the time she had become so familiar with everything in the room, and she had been allowed to have the shell to play with all the time. She had had her toast brought to her in there, with make-believe tea. It was one of her pleasant memories of her childhood; it was the first time she had been of any importance to anybody, even herself.

"Right at the head of the lounge was a light-stand, as they called it, and on it was a very brightly polished brass candlestick and a brass tray with snuffers. That is all I remember of her describing, except that there was a braided rag rug on the floor, and on the wall was a beautiful flowered paper—roses and morning-glories in a wreath on a light blue ground. The same paper was in the front room."

"And all this never existed except in her imagination?"

"She said that when she and father went up there, there wasn't any little room at all like it anywhere in the house; there was a china-closet where she had believed the room to be."

"And your aunts said there had never been any such room."

"That is what they said."

"Wasn't there any blue chintz in the house with a peacock figure?"

"Not a scrap, and Aunt Hannah said there had never been any that she could remember; and Aunt Maria just echoed her—she always does that. You see, Aunt Hannah is an up-and-down New England woman. She looks just like herself; I mean, just like her character. Her joints move up and down or backward and forward in a plain square fashion. I don't believe she ever leaned on anything in her life, or sat in an easy-chair. But Maria is different; she is rounder and softer—she hasn't any ideas of her own, she never had any. I don't believe she would think it right or becoming to have one that differed from Aunt Hannah's, so what would be the use of having any? She is an echo, that's all.

"When mamma and I got there, of course I was all excitement to see the china-closet, and I had a sort of feeling that it would be the little room after all. So I ran ahead and threw open the door, crying, 'Come and see the little room.'

"And Roger," said Mrs. Grant, laying her hand in his, "there really was a little room there, exactly as mother had remembered it. There was the lounge, the peacock chintz, the green door, the shell, the morning-glory, and the rose paper, *everything exactly as she had described it to me.*"

"What in the world did the sisters say about it?"

"Wait a minute and I will tell you. My mother was in the front hall still talking with Aunt Hannah. She didn't hear me at first, but I ran out there and dragged her through the front room, saying, 'The room *is* here—it is all right.'

"It seemed for a minute as if my mother would faint. She clung to me in terror. I can remember now how strained her eyes looked and how pale she was.

"I called out to Aunt Hannah and asked her when they had had the closet taken away and the little room built; for in my excitement I thought that was what had been done.

" 'That little room has always been there,' said Aunt Hannah, 'ever since the house was built.'

" 'But mamma said there wasn't any little room here, only a china-closet, when she was here with papa,' said I.

" 'No, there has never been any china-closet there; it has always been just as it is now,' said Aunt Hannah.

"Then mother spoke; her voice sounded weak and far off. She said, slowly, and with an effort, 'Maria, don't you remember that you told me that there had *never been any little room here,* and Hannah said so too, and then I said I must have dreamed it?'

" 'No, I don't remember anything of the kind,' said Maria, without the slightest emotion. 'I don't remember you ever said anything about any china-closet. The house has never been altered; you used to play in this room when you were a child, don't you remember?'

" 'I know it,' said mother, in that queer slow voice that made me feel frightened. 'Hannah, don't you remember my finding the china-closet here, with the gilt-edged china on the shelves, and then you said the *china-closet* had always been here?'

" 'No,' said Hannah, pleasantly but unemotionally, 'no, I don't think you ever asked me about any china-closet, and we haven't any gilt-edged china that I know of.'

"And that was the strangest thing about it. We never could make them remember that there had ever been any question about it. You would think they could remember how surprised mother had been before, unless she had imagined the whole thing. Oh, it was so queer! They were always pleasant about it, but they didn't seem to feel any interest or curiosity. It was always this answer: 'The house is just as it was built; there have never been any changes, so far as we know.'

"And my mother was in an agony of perplexity. How cold their gray eyes looked to me! There was no reading anything in them. It just seemed to break my mother down, this queer thing. Many times that summer, in the middle of the night, I have seen her get up and take a candle and creep softly down-stairs. I could hear the steps creak under her weight. Then she would go through the front room and peer into the darkness, holding her thin hand between the candle and her eyes. She seemed to think the little room might vanish. Then she would come back to bed and toss about all night, or lie still and shiver; it used to frighten me.

"She grew pale and thin, and she had a little cough; then she did not like to be left alone. Sometimes she would make errands in order to send me to the little room for something—a book, or her fan, or her handkerchief; but she would never sit there or let me stay in there long, and sometimes she wouldn't let me go in there for days together. Oh, it was pitiful!"

"Well, don't talk any more about it, Margaret, if it makes you feel so," said Mr. Grant.

"Oh yes, I want you to know all about it, and there isn't much more—no more about the room.

"Mother never got well, and she died that autumn. She used often to sigh, and say, with a wan little laugh, 'There is one thing I am glad of, Margaret; your father knows now all about the little room.' I think she was afraid I distrusted her. Of course, in a child's way, I thought there was something queer about it, but I did not brood over it. I was too young then, and took it as a part of her illness. But, Roger, do you know, it really did affect me. I almost hate to go there after talking about it; I somehow feel as if it might, you know, be a china-closet again."

"That's an absurd idea."

"I know it; of course it can't be. I saw the room, and there isn't any china-closet there, and no gilt-edged china in the house, either."

And then she whispered: "But, Roger, you may hold my hand as you do now, if you will, when we go to look for the little room."

"And you won't mind Aunt Hannah's gray eyes?"

"I won't mind *anything*."

It was dusk when Mr. and Mrs. Grant went into the gate under the two old Lombardy poplars and walked up the narrow path to the door, where they were met by the two aunts.

Hannah gave Mrs. Grant a frigid but not unfriendly kiss; and Maria seemed for a moment to tremble on the verge of an emotion, but she glanced at Hannah, and then gave her greeting in exactly the same repressed and non-committal way.

Supper was waiting for them. On the table was the *gilt-edged* china. Mrs. Grant didn't notice it immediately, till she saw her husband smiling at her over his teacup; then she felt fidgety, and couldn't eat. She was nervous, and kept wondering what was behind her, whether it would be a little room or a closet.

After supper she offered to help about the dishes, but, mercy! she might as well have offered to help bring the seasons round; Maria and Hannah couldn't be helped.

So she and her husband went to find the little room, or closet, or whatever was to be there.

Aunt Maria followed them, carrying the lamp, which she set down, and then went back to the dish-washing.

Margaret looked at her husband. He kissed her, for she seemed troubled; and then, hand in hand, they opened the door. It opened into a *china-closet*. The shelves were neatly draped with scalloped paper; on them was the gilt-edged china, with the dishes missing that had been used at the supper, and which at that moment were being carefully washed and wiped by the two aunts.

Margaret's husband dropped her hand and looked at her. She was trembling a little, and turned to him for help, for some explanation, but in an instant she knew that something was wrong. A cloud had come between them; he was hurt, he was antagonized.

He paused for an appreciable instant, and then said, kindly enough, but in a voice that cut her deeply:

"I am glad this ridiculous thing is ended; don't let us speak of it again."

"Ended!" said she. "How ended?" And somehow her voice sounded to her as her mother's voice had when she stood there and questioned her sisters about the little room. She seemed to have to drag her words out. She spoke slowly: "It seems to me to have only begun in my case. It was just so with mother when she—"

"I really wish, Margaret, you would let it drop. I don't like to hear you speak of your mother in connection with it. It—" He hesitated, for was not this their wedding-day? "It doesn't seem quite the thing, quite delicate, you know, to use her name in the matter."

She saw it all now; *he didn't believe her.* She felt a chill sense of withering under his glance.

"Come," he added, "let us go out, or into the dining-room, somewhere, anywhere, only drop this nonsense."

He went out; he did not take her hand now—he was vexed, baffled, hurt. Had he not given her his sympathy, his attention, his belief—and his hand?—and she was fooling him. What did it mean? She so truthful, so free from morbidness—a thing he hated. He walked up and down under the poplars, trying to get into the mood to go and join her in the house.

Margaret heard him go out; then she turned and shook

the shelves; she reached her hand behind them and tried to push the boards away; she ran out of the house on to the north side and tried to find in the darkness, with her hands, a door, or some steps leading to one. She tore her dress on the old rose-trees, she fell and rose and stumbled, then she sat down on the ground and tried to think. What could she think—was she dreaming?

She went into the house and out into the kitchen, and begged Aunt Maria to tell her about the little room—what had become of it, when they had built the closet, when had they bought the gilt-edged china?

They went on washing dishes and drying them on the spotless towels with methodical exactness; and as they worked they said that there had never been any little room, so far as they knew; the china-closet had always been there, and the gilt-edged china had belonged to their mother, it had always been in the house.

"No, I don't remember that your mother ever asked about any little room," said Hannah. "She didn't seem very well that summer, but she never asked about any changes in the house; there hadn't ever been any changes."

There it was again: not a sign of interest, curiosity, or annoyance, not a spark of memory.

She went out to Hiram. He was telling Mr. Grant about the farm. She had meant to ask him about the room, but her lips were sealed before her husband.

Months afterwards, when time had lessened the sharpness of their feelings, they learned to speculate reasonably about the phenomenon, which Mr. Grant had accepted as something not to be scoffed away, not to be treated as a poor joke, but to be put aside as something inexplicable on any ordinary theory.

Margaret alone in her heart knew that her mother's words carried a deeper significance than she had dreamed of at that time. "One thing I am glad of, your father knows now," and she wondered if Roger or she would ever know.

Five years later they were going to Europe. The packing was done; the children were lying asleep, with their traveling things ready to be slipped on for an early start.

Roger had a foreign appointment. They were not to be back in America for some years. She had meant to go up to say good-by to her aunts; but a mother of three children intends to do a great many things that never get done. One thing she had done that very day, and as she paused for a moment between the writing of two notes that must be posted before she went to bed, she said:

"Roger, you remember Rita Lash? Well, she and Cousin Nan go up to the Adirondacks every autumn. They are clever girls, and I have intrusted to them something I want done very much."

"They are the girls to do it, then, every inch of them."

"I know it, and they are going to."

"Well?"

"Why, you see, Roger, that little room—"

"Oh—"

"Yes, I was a coward not to go myself, but I didn't find time, because I hadn't the courage."

"Oh! *that* was it, was it?"

"Yes, just that. They are going, and they will write us about it."

"Want to get—?"

"No; I only want to know."

Rita Lash and Cousin Nan planned to go to Vermont on their way to the Adirondacks. They found they would have three hours between trains, which would give them time to drive up to the Keys farm, and they could still get to the camp that night. But, at the last minute, Rita was prevented from going. Nan had to go to meet the Adirondack party, and she promised to telegraph Rita when she arrived at the camp. Imagine Rita's amusement when she received this message: "Safely arrived; went to Keys farm; it is a little room."

Rita was amused, because she did not in the least think Nan had been there. She thought it was a hoax; but it put it into her mind to carry the joke further by really stopping herself when she went up, as she meant to do the next week. She did stop over. She introduced herself to the two maiden ladies, who seemed familiar, as they had been described by Mrs. Grant.

They were, if not cordial, at least not disconcerted at her visit, and willingly showed her over the house. As they did not speak of any other stranger's having been to see them lately, she became confirmed in her belief that Nan had not been there.

In the north room she saw the roses and morning-glory paper on the wall, and also the door that should open into— what?

She asked if she might open it.

"Certainly," said Hannah; and Maria echoed, "Certainly."

She opened it, and found the china-closet. She experienced a certain relief; she at least was not under any spell. Mrs. Grant left it a china-closet; she found it the same. Good.

But she tried to induce the old sisters to remember that there had at various times been certain questions relating to a confusion as to whether the closet had always been a closet. It was no use; their stony eyes gave no sign.

Then she thought of the story of the sea-captain, and said, "Miss Keys, did you ever have a lounge covered with India chintz, with a figure of a peacock on it, given to you in Salem by a sea-captain, who brought it from India?"

"I dun'no as I ever did," said Hannah. That was all. She thought Maria's cheeks were a little flushed, but her eyes were like a stone wall.

She went on that night to the Adirondacks. When Nan and she were alone in their room she said: "By-the-way, Nan, what did you see at the farm-house, and how did you like Maria and Hannah?"

Nan didn't mistrust that Rita had been there, and she began excitedly to tell her all about her visit. Rita could almost have believed Nan had been there if she hadn't known it was not so. She let her go on for some time, enjoying her enthusiasm, and the impressive way in which she described her opening the door and finding the "little room." Then Rita said: "Now, Nan, that is enough fibbing. I went to the farm myself on my way up yesterday, and there is *no* little room, and there *never* has been any; it is a china-closet, just as Mrs. Grant saw it last."

She was pretending to be busy unpacking her trunk, and did not look up for a moment; but as Nan did not say anything, she glanced at her over her shoulder. Nan was actually pale, and it was hard to say whether she was most angry or frightened. There was something of both in her look. And then Rita began to explain how her telegram had put her in the spirit of going up there alone. She hadn't meant to cut Nan out. She only thought— Then Nan broke in: "It isn't that; I am sure you can't think it is that. But I went myself, and you did not go; you can't have been there, for *it is a little room*."

Oh, what a night they had! They couldn't sleep. They talked and argued, and then kept still for a while, only to break out again, it was so absurd. They both maintained that they had been there, but both sure the other one was either crazy or obstinate beyond reason. They were wretched; it was perfectly ridiculous, two friends at odds over such a thing; but there it was—"little room," "china-closet," "china-closet," "little room."

The next morning Nan was tacking up some tarlatan at a window to keep the midges out. Rita offered to help her, as she had done for the past ten years. Nan's "No, thanks," cut her to the heart.

"Nan," said she, "come right down from that step-ladder and pack your satchel. The stage leaves in just twenty minutes. We can catch the afternoon express train, and we will go together to the farm. I am either going there or going home. You had better go with me."

Nan didn't say a word. She gathered up the hammer and tacks, and was ready to start when the stage came round.

It meant for them thirty miles of staging and six hours of train, besides crossing the lake; but what of that, compared to having a lie lying round loose between them! Europe would have seemed easy to accomplish, if it would settle the question.

At the little junction in Vermont they found a farmer with a wagon full of meal-bags. They asked him if he could not take them up to the old Keys farm and bring them back in time for the return train, due in two hours.

They had planned to call it a sketching trip, so they said, "We have been there before, we are artists, and we might find some views worth taking; and we want also to make a short call upon the Misses Keys."

"Did ye calculate to paint the old *house* in the picture?"

They said it was possible they might do so. They wanted to see it, anyway.

"Waal, I guess you are too late. The *house* burnt down last night, and everything in it."

AUNT SANNA TERRY *

By LANDON R. DASHIELL

DAT ain' my true name. Miss Honey jes' call me dat. My name is Mrs. Leah Heber Jenkins an' I'se been sellin' fried chicken an' coffee, pies an' milk fuh mo'n twenty years at de depot uv dis here town where mo'n ten trains pass evvy day. I allers make ernuf ter feed me an' my good-fuh-nothin' son an' ter keep a roof over we-alls' haids, his'n an' mine, dat is, when he was little. Now dat he is done growed up he's allers up ter some devilment, drunk an' sich, an' I has a hard ole time, you jes' bet yo' sweet life I does. Dey got him in jail now, 'cause a white gent'man done tole me 'twas de bes' place fuh him to larn some sense, ef he got any. I'se tryin' it, but I'se got my doubts.

Evvy day, rain an' shine, I'se brought my waiter uv good eatin's an' my bilin' hot coffee ter dis depot an' in all dat time I ain' done payin' dem 'stallmint tickets on my house an' lot on de aidge uv town where I raises my chickens.

Dere was a time when we-all colored women folks could sell we-alls' eatin's fum de flatform, but dat done been stopped a long an' a merry ago. De railroad done bought de hotel an' dem black boys, callin' deyself waiters fum de hotel, sells fum de flatform an' we-all has ter sell fum de yuther side uv de train. Dem boys ain' nothin' but heathens an' idols an' de wuss kinder black trash, so I don' pay no 'tention ter 'em.

One drizzly mawnin' 'bout seben erclock I took my waiter full, my stool, an' my umberrell ter de depot an' sot myself down ter wait fuh Number 19, due at seben-fifteen an' allers late. I took two cat-naps 'fo' I heerd her whistle and

* By permission of the author.

pres'ny here she come, ringin' an' tootin' an snortin', jes
like she was de one an only. I sot my waiter on de stool an'
prop my umberrell over it an' watched de winders fuh hungry folks. One winder flewed up an' a pale-face' young
lady look out at me an' smile.

"Oh! Auntie," she say, "fuh goodness sake gim me two
pieces uv chicken an' a cup uv coffee. I been travelin' sence
'fo' fo' erclock dis mawnin' an' I'se jes' starvin'."

I knowed she was quality folks when I fus seen her, an'
when she talked I knowed it fuh sho. I picked de bes' fuh
her an' po'd out a cup uv my good coffee soon as I could.
She et up de chicken like smoke an' ast fuh mo', but she jes'
sip at de coffee. Den she pop her haid out uv de winder
ergin.

"Dey tells me dat dis train stops here half a hour," she
say, "so I'se goin' to git off an' talk ter you a while."

I was busy with yuther hungry folks an' I jes' say, hearty
like, "Come erlong, Honey, an' talk much as you wanter."
She look so puitty an' smile so sweet dat I couldn't keep dese
ole eyes off her.

"Do you know you has de bes' fried chicken I ever tasted
an' your pie looks jes' as good, but your coffee is vile, puf-
fickly vile!"

Jes' like dat she said it ter me an' me been makin' coffee
evvy sence 'fo' she was bornded. But she was quality an'
talk jes' as puitty, but it made me sorter mad fuh ter hear
my coffee spoke uv sich a pernickety way. I hilt myself up
wid my bes' manners an' look at her. "Some folks," I say,
"don't know dey own business when dey see it comin' down
de road."

"Well," she say, "you see I has ter drink it an' it is my
business in a way." She spoke gentle an' I knowed dat she
done been riz up as well as me ter know dat manners is a
sign uv quality. "Well ma'am," I says, "I'se sorry you
don't like it. Most folks, dem uv de quality, thinks it are
fine." I bow to her.

"Now don't be offended," she say, "I want to be your fren'
an' give you a few sirgestions." Not knowin' what dey is
I didn't said nothin'. "Perhaps, howsomever, you don't

need no help." I tole her I had a hard time fuh ter make dem two eends meet what folks is allers talkin' 'bout. Den she talked erlong so puitty dat soon I done tole her all my troubles. She stood leanin' erginst de fence wid her little short skirt showin' mo'n jes' her little feet. My! my! dat skirt was short, but it didn't seem ter make no sorter difference to her. She picked a mawnin'-glory blossom off de fence an' pulled it ter pieces while she was studyin' like.

"Now I'se goin' ter say sumpin' dat you may not like," she say, "but jes' believe dat I wants ter help you." She look at me outen de cornder uv her eye an' I knowed she wanted ter fin' out ef I was one uv dem easy 'fended folks. I call my manners ter stan' by. "You have heerd people say dat cleanliness is nex' ter godliness?" I nod my haid, but I ain' never heerd enny but preacher folks say it an' dey pay much 'tention ter it. I ain' never fin' it in de Bible, de onlies' book I got time ter read.

"Well," she say, "cleanliness is a big part uv godliness. I know you are a good woman," she kep' on, crinklin' up her eyes an' smilin' at me 'tell I felt real at home wid her. "I'se good accordin' ter my lights," says I.

"I want you ter do sumpin fuh me," she say. (I might er knowed it was comin' ter dat!) "I want you ter wear here at de depot a white cap, a large white ap'on an' white cotton gloves an' a lovely white han'kerchief folded ercross dis way," smilin' an' crossin' her little white han's over her puitty front.

"Lawd-a-mussy, Honey, I ain' got time ter truck wid all dat foolishness, an' mo'n dat I ain' go no money fuh ter git all dem things." "If you will use the things I will sen' you a supply uv 'em when I gets home ter-day," she say.

"Honey, I sho is 'bleeged ter you, but I can' wear no gloves. Dese here han's is done serve widout gloves sence I was little an' I 'spec' dey is goin' on doin' it. I don' min' de ap'on an' sich, but dem gloves goes erginst my grain." "Ah! please try it, fuh my sake," she say. "I will be back here in a week fum termorrow an' it would 'joice my heart ter see you look so enticin'."

"I don't know 'bout enticin'," I say, "but don' I look all

right?" "Not a patch on what you kin look!" she say, "Mo'somover, jes' now you had to slap dat po', hungry, yeller dog away fum yo' waiter an' dat ain' neither clean nor sannerterry." Den she pout her puitty mouth out wid all dem foolishest words she was er sayin'.

"I mos' gineral kicks dat good-fuh-nothin', bone-eatin' hound, but I'se been er slappin' er kickin' him, er one like him, fuh mo'n twenty years. I don' reckon, Miss Honey, dat you notis dat I allers puts my chicken an' my pie in paper bags when I han's 'em ter folks." "Yes, I know you do," she say, "an' we won't argue 'bout dat. If you will do as I sirgest you will double your sales in a week. Try it an' let me know. I will send de package anyway." Her train was comin' an' she smiled good-bye while I hustled ter sell what I could.

Nex' day, shonuff, de package come an' a note ter say de day she would be back. I thought I would wait tell dat day ter dress up in dem sirgestions, but what she done say 'bout double sales onsettled my min' so dat I couldn't wait. I 'member'd all her young an' foolish talkmints an' I knowed 'twon' no good comin' by mixin' cleanliness an' godliness de way she say. It did'n soun' right ter me. Dat Produgal Boy did'n had no shirt ter his back, an' John de Baptis' did'n had no gloves fuh ter eat his locusses an' wil' honey wid. Jezebel an' Sheba seem ter me to be de onlies' ones ter do all de dressin' up an' den 'twon' fuh no good puppose.

Howsomever, I went ter de depot dat ebenin', mad 'fo' I start in 'cas' some uv dem fresh brats try ter sass me, an' I wan' ter be ready fuh 'em. I had on all de sirgestions but dem gloves. I couldn' go 'em, but I 'spec' Miss Honey will bring me to 'em yit. Ef I didn't look like de Queen uv Sheba I looked like a big fat fool an' felt wuss. I hilt my haid high an' sot my stool down in de place where it berlong, an' lift my waiter off my haid and sot it on de stool. All de time I could hear what de yuthers was sayin' an' it 'pear like ter me dat I could hear sumpin' fum dat black trash on de flatform.

"Fuh Gawd sake, look at Sis' Leah Jenkins!" say Sis'

Malviny Jones, her wid de scar. "Is she done los' her min'?"

"All dat truck ter wash, too," say one uv de yuthers, "an' makin' herself dat 'spicuous. 'Tain' like Sis' Leah ter do dat way; at her aidge an' size she ought ter know better. Look like trouble wid dat boy uv hern done turn her min'."

"Look at de Queen uv de May, fuh Gawd sake!" I heered fum de flatform fum one uv dem Niggerdemusses. Dat was ernuff fer Leah! I went over de track an' step up on de flatform an' slapped de face uv de foremus one, an' he shet up. De yuthers back off an' I followed dem up an' shuck my fis' an' tole 'em dey was jes' de ve'y spittin' image of dat generation of vipers in de Bible an' hell won't hot ernuff fuh 'em. I'd fix 'em sho as I was a Christian woman. Some uv 'em look solemn an' some uv 'em laff, but dey didn' said no mo'. Dey knowed I could lay out two er three uv 'em wid my fisses. I ain' goin' ter fight enny mo'n I has ter, but de incipiency uv dese young niggers is almos' onpossible fuh a lady ter stan'. Laffin at me! de low-down trash! I'll larn 'em some sense. I made my min' up den an dere fuh ter wear all dem sirgestions, gloves an' all, dat Miss Honey done sont me ef I had ter kill some uv dem smarties on de flatform. I ain' feared uv nothin' but de Lawd.

Arter a while Number 6 come in an' folkses haids was stickin' out all de winders, hollerin' "Chicken! Pie! here!" Some uv 'em look at me an' wave dey han' an' one say, "Don' she look sweet?" Dat was de fus' kin' word I heered dat ebenin'. Well, I was busy! I never was so busy befo'. An' de money come in, too. 'Fo' de nex' train come I slip on dem gloves 'cause my han's was real dirty by dat time. Fus' I flung some bones ter dat yeller dog an' give him a kick ter 'member me by. Evvybody wanted my chicken an' ast me so many questions dat I was mos' confusticated. But dey kep' on buyin' an' dat jes' suit me down ter de groun'. I sold mo'n mo'. When de train was gone de yuthers come 'roun' me an' ast questions, tryin' ter fin' a way ter make me talk. I ain' no talker an' mo'n dat I was still mad wid 'em all fuh dey sass. I knowed some uv 'em would be tryin' ter follow my 'sperience 'fo' long.

"Sis' Leah," said Sis' Lily Langtry, she wid de flat nose. "Don' you 'Sis' Leah' me tell you larn better manners," says I, an' she shet up.

De day my Miss Honey come back was bright an' hot. I was at my place wid all dem things on, wash'd an' i'on'd overnight. I jes couldn't keep my face straight when I sawn her lookin' outen de winder as de train come ter a stop.

"My! Leah, how gran' you look!" she say, "I have half hour ter wait an' I want ter hear evvything an' eat evvything!"

When I had done my sales an' she had done et, I gave her de stool an' sot myself on a turn'd over box an' den I tole her evvything where done happen sence she went erway. Mo'n dat, I tole her how dem low-down hounds on de flat-form done gimme some uv dere sass. She laffed an' I laffed wid her an' tole her dey was all feered uv me fum dat time.

"How much has you made dis week?" she ast. "Twenty dollars, Miss Honey, "mo'n I ever is make befo' in two." "Good," she say, "you are goin' ter make mo'n mo' fum dis time on, 'cause I'se brought you a percolator fuh ter make coffee. We are goin' ter have such good coffee dat people will travel jes ter tas'e it!" She laff so loud an' look so puitty an' sweet dat I didn't said nothin' 'tall 'bout my doubts 'bout dat coffee.

"Well," I say, "I'se got so much trade now dat I has ter git a 'oman ter fry my chickens an' bake my pies an' you know I has ter pay her, Miss Honey."

"Dat don' make no difference," she say, " 'cause you'se goin' to make heap mo'."

"Honey, what is dat perambulator an' what does you do wid it?" "It takes the place uv dis horrid coffee-pot," she say. "We are not goin' ter have enny mo' biled coffee."

"Well, Honey, 'tain go be fitten fuh ter drink den. Coffee is got ter be biled er 'tis jes' slop." She laffed so hard dat I was s'prised, but was too perlite ter tell her so. I jes' laffed sof' an' lady-like.

"Does you use cream' an' what kin' uv sugar?" she ast. "I bleeged ter tell you de truf. I uses milk an' dis here granbolated sugar. I don' never use dem lumps 'cause de octangurality uv dat sugar spile de frugality uv de coffee. I don' use it fuh nothin'," I say, an' she jes' laffed sof', an' crinkle up her eyes at me.

Den she set ter work ter show me how ter use dat perambulator. She open her suit-case dat one ov dem young blacks fotch fum de flatform an' took out de whole perambulator. She lit de little tin can where came wid it an' sot it under a qua't can in a rack fuh ter git hot water, an' Gawd knows ennybody kin do dat. Den she scoiled out de perambulator, and took an' fill a little cup wid holes in it dat belongs inside de perambulator, wid some good-smellin' coffee an' I notis it took a lot ter fill it. Den she put de contraption back in de perambulator an' tuk an' po'd in 'bout two pints uv bilin' water, when evvybody know you ought ter put in cold water de fus'. Arter dat she sot de pot on de little rack an' soon de water commence ter bubble an' squirt up thu a pipe an' dreen back thu de coffee. When it had done bubble an' skuirt fuh 'bout fifteen minits she say de coffee was ready an' sont me ter de hotel for a pot uv cream. Cream indeed! I could see my twenty dollars a week wid all dis sweet nonsense would soon go up ter de spout. Den where would Leah be?

"Now, Leah, you has seen me make it an' you can do it jes' as well an' maybe better. Keep it hot an' allers serve it wid cream an' you kin go on usin' de granbolated sugar. Yo kin sell mo'n you kin make. Call it drip coffee. Good-bye!"

"Miss Honey," I say, "don' go 'tell you say whedder shonuff yu think dis is a good business fuh me. I'se po' an' I'se got ter pay dem 'stallmint tickets on my house and lot."

"You jes' try it an' I'll stan' by you, but you won't need me long." Den she wave her han' an' step on de train an' kep' on lookin' back to wave her han' ter me, ole Leah!

"Well, Leah," I says ter myself, "wid de help uv de Lawd we will try ter fotch a livin' outen dis mighty foolish-seemin' business ter me an' ter Him."

I was low in my min' uv ebenin's tell I could count my money fuh dat day an' somehow it look all right. 'Pear like my Honey Child did had some sense in her puitty little haid. I had near ernuff ter pay two 'stallmint tickets by de eend uv de business. I allers made de pies myself yearly in de mawnin'. Mo'n dat I didn't had no trouble wid dat perambulator, nor wid de coffee, only folks couldn't git ernuff. Dey kep' on callin' fuh dat drippin' coffee tell 'twan' no mo'. But I didn't part wid my ole pot uv biled coffee 'cause dere was some dat want ole biled coffee wid milk, an' dey got it.

'Twas a long mont' 'fo' I seen Miss Honey ergin. One day she trip offen de train an' come ter me. She stood quiet while I han' up ter a gent'mun at de winder two pieces uv chicken, two pieces uv pie, an' two cups uv dripping coffee, an' he was a good-lookin' man at dat.

"Leah," she says, "I jes' got a few minits. How's business?"

"I'se so glad ter see you, Miss Honey," I say. "Good-mawnin' ter you." I allers is pertickler to watch my manners 'cause sometimes de nices' folks fergits em an' comes breezin' an' blowin' ter business. "Good-mawnin', Leah," she say, wid a smile.

"May de Lawd bless you, Miss Honey, fuh comin' my way dat time you was so hungry. Your 'vice is done help me sho. Evvybody loves my fixin's an' I loves 'em now myself, eben ter de gloves. I sells out mo' waiters full den dey all put togedder an' I sho is making good money."

She jes' clap her han's fuh joy. "One think I got ter tell you, howsomever, 'bout dis perambulated coffee. 'Tain' ernuff ter saterfy dem as likes it an' I has ter charge ten cent a cup 'count uv de cream. But some uv 'em still wants de ole biled coffee wid milk, an' dey gets it fuh five cent a cup."

"Now how 'bout your son an' de 'stallmints?" she ast.

"Dis here place has done gone probation, Miss Honey, an' he can't git nothin' fuh ter git drunk on. He's got a job now hol'in' him down. I has paid all de 'stallmints but two an' next week I will git my deed. De good Lawd blessed me when He sont you my way. My trade is prestablished in de Lawd an' His mussey retches fum de horizin' ter de rosettin' uv de sun!" Den I wipe my eyes 'cause she look so kin' an' lovin' at me.

I notis a tall straight-up man watchin' my Honey Child fum de back flatform uv de train an' I ast her why dat straight-up man was lookin' at her so hard an' who was he.

"Who is he?" she say, an' laffed, "Oh! he's jes' a man." I s'picioned sumpin' an' started ter say dat he knew how ter look at folks, but I membered my manners an' didn' said nothin'. Den dat man got hisself offen de back flatform uv de train an' comes up ter we-all an' lift offen his hat. "We've got three minits, my dear," he says.

Den I look at Miss Honey an' I knowed by sumpin' dat my Honey Child had done gone an' got herself married an' I jes' thew my ole arms 'round her an' bless her an' bless him an' dey run fuh de train. No wonder he look at her so hard an' got two uv all de eatin's offen my waiter. Bless dey hearts!

Dey come out on de back flatform as de train start an' I called ter 'em, "Don' you-all want me fuh ter come an' cook fuh you all?"

Miss Honey jes' laffed an' say, "Not yet," but he standin' behime her wave a chicken leg at me an' noddin' his haid, say, "Yes!"

THE LOTUS EATERS *

By VIRGINIA TRACY

"AND leaves me to starve," said Estella, cutting off a leg of the chicken and throwing it to the nearest dog. "Leaves me to starve in the gutter and leaves Regina, his own flesh and blood—look at that child, Kate, look at her! What sort of a brute could desert a child like that? Was her mother's comfort, yes, she was!—leaves Regina without a rag to her back." She absent-mindedly put a piece of chicken into her mouth and leaned her elbows on the table.

"I really don't know what we shall do about the rent," said Mrs. Donnelly. "When he came for it this morning he told Barbara he'd be back this afternoon, and it's a hot day for anybody to be out, let alone a fat fellow like him. You can't put off the landlord himself like you can an agent, anyway. I could pay ten dollars on account next Saturday night. If he won't take that, or your alimony doesn't come, I don't know what will become of us."

"I'm sure I don't know either," said Estella. "It seems such a nuisance to move. Speak for it then." "Woof! Woof!" said Dooley, the fatter of the Scotch terriers. "I thought we were going to be so happy here, too, when we first came. He seemed such a nice, unassuming sort of man."

Tony, who was washing the household linen in the kitchen, put his head through the doorway. It was rather a lordly little black head and belonged to a young fellow of a slender middle height, motions extraordinarily light and free, and blue, humorous, inquisitive, confidential eyes. Said he: "I beg your pardon, Estella, but the big dishpan—has it gone to heaven?"

---

* By permission of the author, and the Century Company.

"It's out on the fire-escape," replied Estella, "with gasoline in it. I put all the old gloves I could find into gasoline this morning, so that if any of us should happen to get an engagement, they'd have clean gloves anyway."

Tony withdrew. He had not looked at Estella, but at Barbara, the Beauty, who sat in the window-sill and continued to look neither at him nor at Estella nor at the riot of the dogs and the chicken-bones and Regina upon the uncarpeted floor, but across the shining roof-tops to the Palisades.

The mistress of this Harlem flat was Mrs. Baker, Estella Cortelyou in stage life. Mr. Baker was divorced. He was a prosperous person and paid a considerable alimony, with which he was not always sufficiently prompt. With Mrs. Baker lived her infant daughter, Regina Rosalys, and her younger sister, Barbara Floyd. Also she had as summer boarders Mr. Anthony Regnault, a young actor who seldom happened to be out of work, Mr. Fred Donnelly, not much older, who seldom happened to be in it, and Mrs. Kate Donnelly, an elderly typist, who had married a brother Donnelly, deceased. All the boarders paid far more than their board, when they had it, and nothing at all when they had not. At the present movement, they had been some time through lunch without having as yet cleared away its remains, and Estella and Mrs. Donnelly, whose employer was away on his own vacation, had been regaling the company with accounts of the Russian coronation, which they read from the newspapers that strewed the room. Fred Donnelly, who was busy pinning the edge of his tie over a spot he had just discovered on his shirt-front, gloomily commented upon Estella's last remark: "I guess it'll be a long enough day before any of us get an engagement!"

"You forget Tony!" said his sister-in-law.

"I ain't ever let to," Fred responded with some savagery. "I—can't you stop gorging on those papers a minute? They're two months old."

"That makes 'em all the lovelier," replied Estella. "Tony threw them off the kitchen shelf this morning, and I felt so good to read it all over again. You feel sure, then, that it's all true."

"Tony's generous with his old newspapers. That's because he's signed for a job. But he don't begin till November. November—Lord! you can't believe there's ever going to be such a month."

"Oh, we may all be working by then," cried Estella in her voice of tragic fire. "You can't tell. You don't suppose we're going to go on like this, do you?"

"Not if we don't pay the rent, we ain't," said Fred. "We'll have fifteen dollars the week after next, Barbara and me, if we pose for those kinetoscope things. But we owe all that now, in little bills."

"That reminds me, Tony," Estella called, "I wish you could get both the tablecloths ironed by to-night, 'cause you can't do it to-morrow. No; they're going to shut off the gas to-night; we had a notice from 'em yesterday."

"Well, this fellow was just right," declared Mrs. Donnelly, glaring up from her newspaper; "this one that refused to kiss the Czarina's hand. It's a nasty, silly thing to do. They'll never catch me doing it."

"Nor me, I'm afraid," said Tony, reappearing with a bucket that brimmed wet tableclothes. He paused for a moment in the doorway and leaned there, exceedingly comfortable and cool. Indeed, on this midsummer afternoon, when the unshaded dining-room appeared altogether huddled and tousled and hot, there was in the look of this very competent amateur laundryman something so tranquil, so airy and sylvan, that it might have suggested a beneficient gentleman-dryad but for the absurd great pipe which was hanging out of his mouth. "I'll take these up to the roof now, Estella; I've just hung out the smaller pieces. We can't tell but that later Barbara'll help me take them down. But I do hope, Stella Cortelyou, that the next flat we appropriate will have a coal range. If we are to have no fire to iron with to-morrow, how shall we cook?"

"I suppose we'll have to go out to our meals. I've got my wedding-ring yet. He can force me to part with that,

Tommy Baker can, but he can't force me to let our child starve."

"That must be very disenchanting for Tommy," Tony answered. "But I think I'll leap out with a chair or two before it comes to our eating up your wedding-ring, Estella."

Regina Rosalys, who was at that moment recuperating from her wrestling matches with the dogs, said suddenly:

"Anny Bobs gah go ring."

"No, no, darling. Poor Auntie Barbara hasn't got any ring at all. You lost Auntie Barbara's little blue ring down the stationary washstand, don't you remember?"

"No, no, Anny Bobs gah go ring." Regina's fat little hands formed an oblong about the size of a cucumber. "Big," she persisted, nodding.

"She means that Indian bracelet," said Estella. Tony looked anxiously and a little fearfully at Barbara, and forgot to joke. At that moment the door bell rang. Tony leaned back into the kitchen and pressed the little electric button which opened the street door.

"Oh!" cried Estella, "that's the expressman with my money now." She rose and ran into the hall.

There was a waiting silence. Tony continued to lean on the doorway and look at the girl in the window-seat. She had gray eyes of a miraculous, deep clearness, but she kept these turned away in a far-off quiet, profound enough to strike cold upon a suitor's heart. Tony had to content himself with the faint bright color in the oval of her cheeks; the pale rose of her faded and shrunken cotton blouse stopped in a little drawn circle at her throat; the throat itself was very white and regal looking under the piled fairness of Barbara's brown hair. One hand dropped, motionless, against her old gray skirt, and Tony smiled to it wistfully. It was a modest smile, under a trick of audacity. Tony was three-and-twenty, and all women except Barbara had done their best to spoil him,—except Barbara, who had remained silent the summer through before his love. By the community before which so much of it had, perforce, to be carried on, the love-making was encouragingly ignored, but the community was beginning to get restless, because from the lady it re-

ceived no confidence. The summer was sunning itself away,
and still Barbara rested, whether or not to be wooed, passive, idle, enigmatic, lovely; and still prayerfully, and with
deft derision, Tony continued publicly to woo her. Now,
though he could not catch her glance, his eyes spoke declara-
tions twenty times a minute, and formally proposed to her.
They besought, commanded, laughed at her, adored her.
Suddenly, when there seemed least hope, she turned round and
looked at him. It was a very steadfast, searching look, and
Tony tingled and rejoiced to meet it. He lifted his head
happily, with a singular pride, and at the little motion the
girl put her hand sharply to her throat and turned away.

"He's a long time coming upstairs," said Fred.

At that moment Estella ran back into the hall of the flat
and closed the door with the effect of a subdued cyclone.

"It's not the expressman!" she called, in a shrieking whisper. "The top of his head looks like the milkman, and his
bill's due." Tony laughed aloud.

"Tell him to come again," suggested Kate Donnelly, still
fortified by immersion in the coronation glories.

"Told him that last time," said Fred.

"Oh, well, maybe he wasn't coming here," said Estella,
listening a moment, and continued. "Maybe it was only the
janitor, after all. Once before the alimony didn't come, and
then it turned out the expressman had brought it two or
three times, only the downstairs bell didn't ring, so to-day
I asked the janitor to ring the bell every time he went past,
so I'd feel quite easy."

The upstairs bell unkindly rang.

"Ssh!" hissed Estella; "pretend we're out."

"Is he to suppose the downstairs door was opened by a
spook?" Tony whispered.

"Well, you needn't talk. You did it." She came back into
the dining-room, and sat down with infinite non-rustling
precautions. "I'm sure I'd like to pay him as well as anybody. Indeed, nobody has the horror of debt I've got. I
tremble with it when I wake in the night. It's born in me,
I don't know why. But I can't pay what I haven't got, not
if I was to coin my blood for it." The bell rang again.

"Well, he can just tire himself out at that," Estella added. "I should think he'd know we'd have opened it before if we'd wanted him."

Tony's eyes overran with laughter. Regina threw herself into Barbara's lap, and Barbara put her face into the black mop of Regina's curls, and began to whisper a story to her.

"I wish I was out of the whole business," muttered Fred; "out of the profession, I mean. I wish I knew another durned thing to do. I had a chance to be a dentist once, but I was too good for it then. When that old aunt of mine in Ireland dies, I bet I take my share of what she leaves and buy an interest in a business. And when you're all down on your luck, you can come to me, people, and I'll help you out."

"My share in that pneumatic tire'll be worth thousands of dollars by then," said Mrs. Donnelly, refolding her newspaper. "They've got a backer for it now who's going to put it right on the market. Will Knowles says there's a fortune in it, and he's an inventor."

"I was thinking the other day it would be nice to invent something," replied Estella; "but I never get mine finished, somehow."

The enemy without gave a final knock and ring, and departed. He was pursued downstairs by the barks of the terriers and the shrieks of Regina, who at that moment rushed, all three, into each other's arms.

"Look here," said Fred; "are you sure it wasn't Mr. Bates, come for the rent? He told Barbara he'd be here at three o'clock."

"Mercy! Look out of the window, Barbara, and see who it was." Barbara leaned out and down, watching.

"Well, I vow!" said Mrs. Donnelly. "Do you know what those Gostioffs, or whatever their name is, have been doing? The Czar said everybody could make their crowns out of silver-gilt, because some of 'em are as poor as church mice, and those Gostioffs have been over to Paris and had theirs made out of solid gold!"

"Who told you?"

"It's in the paper. And he's just come of age, a while ago, and paid all his debts."

"Seems rather an excessive person," Tony commented.

Mrs. Donnelly made a little clucking noise to her newspaper: "Tsu! Tsu!—well, poor boy, he does all he can."

"Who?" demanded Fred.

"The Emperor of all the Russias," answered Tony, laughing from under his eyelashes at Kate. "Kate's very partial to him. I sometimes feel quite piqued."

"Well, I don't care. He's a very good man; he wants—"

"They say," remarked Estella dreamily, "that she's got a gold typewriter set with diamonds."

"It was the milkman," announced Barbara, drawing in her head.

Estella had picked up an illustrated weekly, and she now passed it with a tender smile to Mrs. Donnelly. "Wouldn't Barbara look sweet fixed just the way the Czarina is? Those pearl ropes—I'll bet they're yards long—they're just the sort of thing that suits Barbara."

Mrs. Donnelly gravely regarded the Czarina's likeness. "She looks very handsome," she said. "I hope she'll be happy. She's got a kind of a sad look. I knew a girl once, a nice, pretty girl as could be—she looked something like our Barbara, too, only Barbara's the handsomest of the lot—had something that same look at her wedding, and before the very first year was out he had run off to Canada with a pot of money—he was a partner in a wholesale bicycle business—and another woman, and she, poor thing, had to take in boarders."

Estella sat up, clutched her floating yellow dressing-sack about her neck, and with the other hand shoved back the toppling mass of her black hair. "Well!" she cried, "I'd like to know what you mean by that, Kate Donnelly! I didn't think I should ever be insulted at my own lunch-table by people talking as if it were a disgrace to take boarders! You ought to honor me for it, or any other honest way of making my living. I've got my fatherless child to support, and I'm proud of it, and as God is my witness, I think a woman can be a lady, no matter how little money she has. And if you mean to insinuate anything against Tom Baker, I can tell you that whatever my troubles with my husband may have been—and I think you might have had more consideration for Regina than to mention a woman —there never was a breath against his honesty, and he never quarrelled with but one of his employers in his life, that would bring men he knew home, drunk, to sleep in the office, and that diamond bracelet I gave him to get the doctor's bill on once when he was out of work, he went and got out and gave it back to me as soon as I got my divorce!"

There was a glass pitcher full of lemonade on the table. Estella helped herself to a long drink, and added: "And even so, I shouldn't call you exactly boarders, anyway."

Mrs. Donnelly arose in trembling majesty and took her hat off the mantelpiece. "I'll send you my address, Estella Baker," she said, "as soon as I get one. And you can send your bill in when you like. I wouldn't speak to a dog as you've spoken to me, and I wouldn't take it from you if you were the Queen of England. And as for calling us boarders, I should think you wouldn't, with Tony working like a black slave, and Fred putting off the butcher, and me paying regular every Saturday. I wouldn't have stayed here to have my ears deafened the way you screech, Estella Baker, for anybody but Tony, that was the sweetest child I ever saw when I used to go on as extra in the Amazon marches at his father's theatre, before that sneaking hound of a Gillespie got it away from him—though I've worked hard here to help you, and glad to do it, as you well know. I hope, when I'm gone—"

"Before you go, Kate, dear," said Tony, putting his pipe on the mantelpiece, "we'd better clear off the table, or I fear Barbara will be forced to work."

Barbara rose hurriedly, but like a creature moving in a sleep, and Mrs. Donnelly snatched up a plate with one hand, and with the other pushed the young girl back into the window-seat. "Stay where you are," said she, and strode majestically into the kitchen. Her brother-in-law, who had not bestowed so much as a glance upon the previous debate, now lifted a newspaper in his turn. "There's a cut of the

Felix house," he said. "Down below, you know, on River-
side Drive, the white stone place. Good print, isn't it? I
wish I'd gone in for photography when I had that chance
three years ago."

"I never thought I'd much care about having that house,"
said Estella. "The windows come so low down, I'd always
be afraid Regina would fall out. Still, of course, you could
put wires across them."

"Forgot the tablecloths." cried Tony, running in and
snatching up the bucket. "None of you thought of them, of
course—loafers! If I have a sunstroke on the roof, say I
died true." Tony peered into the pitcher of lemonade as he
passed it. "Oof! Little drops of lemon. Nothing more
spirited for the laborer, the poor laborer, Mrs. Tommy?"
At the hall door—"I will return to you, Barbara," he said
to the back of that young lady's head, and vanished.

"Tony's gone pok?" asked Regina.

"I wonder," said Estella, "if Tony's written those words
for Barbara to sing Sunday night."

"Anny Bobs ta Rina pok?" Regina persisted.

"No, no," said Estella, "Auntie Barbara can't take **Regina**
to the park now; it's too hot."

"Too hot?"

"Yes; too hot. Make Auntie sick. **Poor Auntie.**"

"Poo Anny; Anny Bobs ta Rina pok?"

"No; now, Regina, you're naughty."

Regina puffed out an under-lip and nodded: "Rina awn
do finey aws," she said plaintively.

"Oh, Regina, why don't you learn to talk plainer? Oo
bid dirl, ess oo is bid dirl! You mostly know what she
says, Fred."

"She said, 'Regina wants to go on the flying horses.'"

"Oh, darling, mamma hasn't any money for that—no,
indeed, Barbara, car-fare and everything! You can go on
the flying horses when mamma gets an engagement. Here—
here's a nickel. You can play with that."

Regina turned the nickel over and over in the creases of
her warm little hand, and Fred returned to his former state-

ment—"I guess it'll be a long day before any of us get an engagement."

"I'll bet you anything you like," cried Estella, "that I'll be starring in my own play before the year's out. That play's bound to succeed, because it speaks right to people's hearts. I wrote every word of it out of my own soul. There isn't a line in it without a throb, and yet the comedy interest's good, too. I think Barbara'll be quite sweet in that. She's a little tall for comedy, but then—. You know Dick Tannehill. He says it's the greatest play that's been written in America since 'The Banker's Daughter.' "

Mrs. Donnelly, who had been going to and from the kitchen with the dishes, now swept away the tablecloth, and Estella, still clutching the lemonade, and waving the butter-knife, leaned back to give her free play. She concluded, "He asked me why I didn't let Olga Nethersole have it."

"Well, dearie," said Mrs. Donnelly, "Why don't you? I'm sure you deserve a little luck."

"Well," said Estella, "I guess not. Nobody'll ever play that part but me. There's plenty of managers would be glad to take the play, and put their own old stars into it; night and day I'm afraid some one will steal my ideas. If I could only get a good part in New York and show people just once what I could do, there'd be plenty of managers ready to back me in my play afterward!"

Fred yawned. "Stella," said he, "when you do get an engagement, you quarrel with the stage-manager and come home."

Estella planted her elbows on the table. "That's because they've got such old fuss-budgets of stage managers. I guess after I've sat up all night wearing myself to pieces studying my art I'm not going to be dictated to by those ignorant things. It was mean of that old Dawkins, though, to fight with me when I'd had my pink crepe dress made for their old piece, and I hadn't even got it paid for yet. Wasn't that a sweet dress, Kate? I wore my real coral and gold belt with it, that Tommy gave me while we were married. He always said he did like me to look nice, Tommy did. I've got plenty of clothes to take an engagement, if I could only get one. I wish the dogs hadn't broken Whopper, and I'd ask her when we any of us were going to get anything."

"We always ask her that, and she always lies. We'd better ask her when the alimony's coming."

Estella looked at the pieces of the broken planchette which were scattered over the floor. "They looked so cunning breaking it up—and Tony would name her that," she added, with apparent irrelevance. "Hand me the cards, Fred, and let me see if I can see anything."

As she shuffled the pack, her mind went back to the pink crepe.

"If she likes to fix it over, I'll let Barbara wear that dress to Helen Graham's Sunday night, and I can take her blue waist; you know, Kate, that one you made out of the old pair of sleeves."

She looked cordially at Barbara, but the girl did not answer nor turn her head.

"She's dreaming," said Fred. "Love's young dream, Barbara? Estella, do you see a dark man?"

"Let her be," pleaded Mrs. Donnelly; "maybe she is really thinking about Tony."

"You make me tired, Kate!" said the fraternal Fred. "You bet Tony can do his own love-making. You bet he can look after himself. I wonder," he added in a half-voice, "if she says things to him, though, when they're alone. He keeps on so."

"You never can tell," Estella sighed.

"She might be very glad to have the chance of him!" Mrs. Donnelly almost cried aloud.

"I guess my sister doesn't need to be glad of anybody, Kate Donnelly, and he's very unsettled and extravagant; I've always heard so."

"Oh, rot!" said Fred, getting in ahead of his sister-in-law. "What of it? He's only a boy, and most of the year he's more money than he knows what to do with. I don't know why it should be worse for him to throw gold dollars around than for anybody else to do it."

"Slander loves a shining mark," said Mrs. Donnelly sententiously.

Fred laughed. "Well, there's nothing so very shining about Tony, except a first-class job with the great Engle in the fall. But, of course, he's lucky to have that, at his age; and I daresay it's his luck and his good looks and those kid ways of his starts those notions. He's really a corking fellow, Tony is, and straight, as far as I know. But if he buys a girl a pair of gloves—and I don't say he doesn't like a pretty girl—there's as much cackle as if another man had bought her Fifth Avenue. And he's too easy-tempered; he lets stories get around about him, things that matter. Look at that old gander last week at Reilly's—said it was Mrs. Rexal who got him that part with Rexal, and—you know what people say."

"Oh!" said Barbara, "it's all cowardly. It's a lie." ("Why, she's awake after all," laughed Fred.) She turned in upon them from the window, and her live voice broke into the room with its curious, little throaty richness. "I—I don't deceive myself about Tony. I daresay he's wild, I daresay he's unreliable, but we must all know that he was never—base." Her face flushed and paled, her hands clinched in her lap. "We're unsteady and extravagant ourselves, Estella, and what should we have done this summer, who would have given us any pleasure, who would have helped us, who would have worked for us, what should we have done here, without Tony? I remember all the time, even if we're only a caprice of his, even if he doesn't mean a word he says, we are his debtors a thousand, thousand times!"

The hall door opened, and they heard Tony banging the bucket and whistling "My girl's a high-born lady" as he went into his own room.

"My dear! my dear!" Estella warned her.

"That's right, Barbara," said Fred. "I tell you the truth, I didn't think you had so much sense. There's nothing the matter with Tony except a first-class appetite for being happy. Look at him all this summer—till his next season's manager puts a stop to it—goes and makes a darned jockey of himself, for ten dollars a week, riding their plug steeplechasers in a backwoods melodrama. Does anybody say a word for him about that? Why, no. You'd think they all did it! But he went to dinner at the Waldorf last night with a fellow I know that had made some money at Brighton, and a couple of girls, and I'll bet you everybody on Broadway's talking about it."

"At the Waldorf? Is that where he was?" cried Barbara. "Last night!" She leaned forward and stared at Fred intently. Something in her accent recalled to the assemblage their own last night's dinner; the little, hot, untidy diningroom, and the scramble in getting the dishes washed up, and the fact that the ice had given out. Only Estella remembered for the first time that Barbara had dressed her hair elaborately yesterday afternoon, and had tried to press out her white lace waist, and had scorched it. She remembered in the same flash that the morning before, Tony had praised the stately habit of dressing for dinner. She pushed away the cards, and in her turn looked at Barbara, as Barbara was looking at Fred.

"Was *that* where he was?" said the girl again.

"I'm sure he had every right to be!" cried Kate.

"I'm sure we should be the last to question that right," Barbara said.

" 'Feathered like a peacock, just as gay,' " sang Tony's whistle, clipped suddenly by the sound of splashing water.

"That boy's got his head under the faucet again!" exclaimed Mrs. Donnelly. "He'll give himself neuralgia."

"Why, Barbara!" Estella cried; "yesterday was—"

"Oh, yes," she moved her hands helplessly in her lap, "I was twenty yesterday."

"Oh, dearie! I'm so sorry! I never thought of it."

"Tony never knew of it," said Kate.

"Why, no," Barbara replied; "why should he?"

"Here he comes now," said Fred.

He came in as radiant with idleness as he had lately been with work, and very fresh from his encounter with the faucet, whose drops were still shining, bright and cold, in his black hair. There was what Estella called a divan at one side of the room. Tony composed himself upon its cushions with a fan and a glass of lemonade and lounged there, staring at the ceiling like a contented child. He found considerable diversion in teaching himself to drink without changing his attitude and, while he was acquiring this art, the talk tried to jerk itself past his interruption. Everybody had been a little startled by Barbara's outbreak, everybody felt that Fred would better have kept his knowledge to himself, and a little uneasy bewilderment, as at a treachery to Tony, shadowed more lively interests and quieted the loud talk. They looked rather gravely at the profile view which was once more accorded them of Barbara's head.

"What's the matter, Estella?" asked Tony, glancing at the newspapers. "Aren't there any murders?" At the continued silence he lifted his head. "Hello! What's the scandal?"

"You are!" said Estella. "The idea of you being around here, anyhow, and me with a sister that's just twenty!"

"There has to be somebody to watch Fred," said Tony.

"It's Fred's been giving you away. Oh, he didn't mean to! But he says you throw your money around."

"He wants to show you what a beautiful nature I have," said the accused. He looked lovingly at Fred, because he had black murder in his heart. He looked with anxious stealth at Barbara, but Barbara seemed not to notice.

"He says people say things about you," Estella continued.

"Slander loves a shining mark," repeated Mrs. Donnelly, with solemn emphasis.

"Nice Kate!" said Tony. He went and sat down on the floor by her chair, and stroked her hand. "Good Kate! Pretty Kate!"

"I'm sure," continued Mrs. Donnelly, pretending to push him off, "nobody could be a better boy around the house than he is. Could they, now could they? I bet you'd all want him back, fast enough, if he went away! I've known him since he was no bigger than that," measuring about the height of a footstool, "and never saw a cross word come out of his mouth, and I can tell you, if this never having a cent is hard on us, he's had more money to throw away when he was a child on a rocking-horse than would pay this miserable old rent time and again, and not a complaint out of him."

"Good Tony!" said that gentleman. He added in a tone of profound conviction, "Noble Tony!"

Estella studied him with her chin in her hand.

"Yes," she said, "you're a very sweet boy. But—you're Irish."

"I once had a father, Mrs. Baker, and he was French."

"Well, goodness, that only makes it worse!"

"Oh, dear!" said Tony drowsily, "where French and Irish meet, and make a mixture that is not discreet. That's for you, Barbara, who love the poets!" He opened his eyes and stared sadly at his hostess. "It's inelegant to display such a prejudice against the foreign, dear Estella."

"I hope you've written those new verses to Gus Nevins' song, since you're so smart; Barbara won't have time to learn them Sunday night, Tony Regnault, if you've put them off again, and she won't sing the old ones. Mr. Nevins's going to be there to hear her, Sunday, and he's going to sing himself."

"Dear me, how unnecessary of him!" said Tony. He went back to the couch where his banjo lay, and began to touch an air upon it as he spoke the lines. Certainly, he looked at Barbara.

> The sleeping princess quiet lay
> And dreamed the empty years away,
>   Her love delayed;
> And princes came and princes went,
> And mighty kings magnificent
> As they above her beauty bent
>   Were all afraid, afraid.
>
> And no man knew what word would wake,
> Nor for what fortune's golden sake,
>   Or deed of love,
> That shining princess would arise,
> Unveil the kindness of her eyes,
> And stretch the hand that he would prize
>   All worlds above, above.
>
> A beggar at the palace gate
> Had a light heart to tempt his fate
>   And entered in;
> He wished no other joy but this,
> And this for death he would not miss;
> He touched her sweet mouth with a kiss—
>   She waked for him, for him!

"Oh!" cried Mrs. Donnelly, "isn't that lovely!"

"That last line doesn't rhyme, Tony," said Estella, with severity.

"Will you sing it, Barbara?" Tony asked.

"Thank you," she said. "It's very charming. You were very kind to write it. But I don't think I shall sing it. I don't think I shall sing at all."

Said Tony: "That pink thing you have on is very becoming to you, my own."

"You musn't call Barbara that, Tony!" cried Estella. "It doesn't sound well. I can't have it."

"Not even when it isn't true?" Tony pleaded. "Not even to please Barbara? If you'll move over a little, Barbara, I'll sit by you a minute." He secured to himself a part of the window seat, and remained there, swinging his heels and playing "Daisy" on the banjo. Barbara's slim young stateliness, aided by her trailing skirts, made her look almost as tall as he, and far more resolute. She seemed to him, as he studied her out of the corner of an eye, to be very pale and very tragically sweet.

"I'm glad, Estella," he said, "that you are beginning to awaken to a sense of your responsibilities about us. We shall be almost grown up in a minute. 'These pretty babes went hand in hand!'—you remember what happened to *their* wicked guardian, Mrs. Baker, after the robin-redbreasts had covered them with leaves? I am afraid Barbara would be rather long for robin-redbreasts; she would keep them busy."

Estella smiled disdainfully. "You look like a yard of pump-water, the both of you," said she.

"The each of us, Estella. And it's still incorrect to be cross with my physique—Napoleon was once slender. Barbara's, to be sure," lifting Barbara's lovely wrist between his thumb and finger, and critically regarding it—"Barbara's, to be sure, is no great shakes."

She did not smile, she did not even withdraw her hand. Tony laid it carefully in her lap. "Cheer up, Anny Bobs!" he whispered.

At this moment the entire apartment was filled with the

roar of Regina's rage. "Mahmu a my nicky-Mahmu a my nicky."

"What?" said everyone; "what is it?"

"Mahmu a my nicky! A my nicky! Bah Mahmu!"

Fred was stooping over Regina. "Mohammed ate my nickel," he translated. Mohammed was the older terrier.

"A my nicky," assented Regina.

"Ate her nickel? Heavens, swallowed it? It'll kill him!" Estella fell on her knees and glared down the throat of Mohammed, who wagged his tail feebly. "Bah Mahmu!" cried Regina, beating the air and howling lustily. "A my nicky! Mahmu a my nicky!"

"Do you think it'll kill him?" persisted Estella; "was Stella's old boy? Did want doctor?"

"Wa my nicky!" entreated Regina.

"It seems to me extremely forehanded of him," said Tony to Regina. "You know you nearly ate it yourself."

Regina stopped crying and stared at him. She began slowly to smile and dimple, and presently extended a hand. "Nicky," said she.

Tony laid a copper on her palm. "Penny," he said; "not nicky. Nough."

Regina went over to Estella and pulled her arm. "Mahma, nicky."

Estella closed Mohammed's mouth with her fingers and kissed his nose. "Him eat nickels?" she inquired. "No, I haven't got another nickel for you, Regina, I haven't got— Oh, don't cry. Here, you can have my pearl heart. And here," reaching for a clean napkin and a blue pencil from a crowded trunk-lid at her back, "we'll make rag-dolly, shall we?"

Tony leaped upon her, and wrenched the napkin from her grasp. "I would never wish to interfere with any of your little diversions, Estella," said he, returning in triumph to his seat, "but it is I who wash the linen."

"Oh, Lord, oh, Lord, oh, Lord!" yawned Fred. "What a deadly drag it is! I wonder shall I ever work again?"

"I wonder," said Estella, "why it's always us who can't get parts? We can all act."

"Well," said Fred, "we could if we were let. But the question now is—Mr. Bates told Barbara he'd be here, after that blamed rent, at three o'clock, and it's about that now; what are we going to tell him?"

"If I could only get a backer for my play—" began Estella. "Oh, I do wish you'd stop fooling with that banjo, Tony, you put me out so!"

"Say, look here, Tony!" cried Fred, "since you've got a job coming to you—I know it isn't the proper thing, but— couldn't you get something in advance from your manage-ment?"

"Oh!" cried Mrs. Donnelly, "and start out in debt and be all the season getting even!"

Tony looked hopefully at Barbara, but Barbara positively frowned.

"Unh-unh!" said Tony, shaking his head at Fred. "Nev-er bor-row from the man-age-ment. If—you—do— you'll—never save a cent"—he struck a discreet tinkle from the banjo, and added: "In—the—mean-time, who will pay the rent?"

Without turning her head round to the company, Barbara said; "I daresay we shan't have to pay the rent at all, if I marry Mr. Bates."

They were too surprised to speak, but as they gradually recovered their breath they turned and stared at her; all but Tony, who went on touching the banjo and looked at it carefully. Estella leaned forward and knocked on the table with the handle of the butter-knife.

"What do you mean by that?" she said.

Barbara put up one hand and smoothed her back hair with deliberate fingers. "When I went into the hall this morning to see if I couldn't inveigle him to go away"—Tony lifted his head quickly and angrily, and frowned from Barbara to Estella—"as I was asked to do," Barbara continued, "he asked me if I would marry him. Or rather he asked me to think about it. He's coming back at three to—to help us think about it. He wants to speak to you, Estella."

"Well, I'm not going to have anything to do with it!" Estella cried. "And you needn't frown at me, Tony Regnault, for I was taking the curling-irons out of the gas-range that very minute, or I would have gone out to him myself. Nobody shall ever say I forced her into it. I wouldn't wreck the life of my own sister, not if he was to pay me for it in diamonds! But God knows, Tony, what's to become of her, the way things are; for even if ever she can make up her mind and marry you, you're all alike, you actors; I wouldn't trust a girl's heart to the best of you, though it's true Jim Folso did take care of his mother till the day she died—I know that myself—sent her ten dollars a week year out and in; he's had to borrow it from Tommy, many a time. No, sir, she'll have to decide it for her own self, Barbara will."

And at this moment, as though by special arrangement with a dramatic deity, there was a ring at the front door.

"It needn't be he, you know," said Estella, confronting a a circle of stricken faces.

But it was he. Fred went to the door, and ushered in a large, plump, blond gentleman in the elder middle years. He had his coat on his arm and his hat in his hand, and he was mopping his face and forehead with a huge clean handkerchief.

"Good-day, all," said he. "No, don't trouble yourself for me, ma'am," to Estella, who had risen, mute and regal, and was schooling herself to the manner of a dowager empress. He accepted a chair, however, and looked around with simple confidence upon the company. "It is hot! When you come to my time of life, you feel the stairs."

"You'll have a glass of lemonade, Mr. Bates," said Tony. He had brought a glassful and his own fan to the landlord, and the two men looked at each other as the glass changed hands.

"Thank you," said Mr. Bates, "I don't object."

An embarrassed silence followed these civilities. Tony had cuddled on to the couch again with his inevitable banjo, and the terriers had come forward and were sniffing at Mr. Bates's legs. Dooley drew back suddenly and showed his teeth; Mohammed instantly broke into a volley of shrill yelps.

"Knows I'm the landlord," tactfully remarked Mr. Bates,

setting down his glass and smiling jovially around. He snapped his fingers at Dooley, "Nice boy, good fellow." The dogs thrust their bodies back and their heads forward and continued to grumble and to growl. "Well, I guess from what Miss Barbara told me this morning, you didn't want to see me to-day."

"I'll be frank with you, Mr. Bates," said Estella. "My allowance hasn't come yet. God is my witness, I expected it the day before yesterday. Though why I should expect it from a man that forsakes his own child, and that I never would have married if I hadn't been infatuated with him—a girl's infatuation, Mr. Bates, you know what that is—I don't know. But I was so sure it would come to-day, while that lace sale was on at Siegel & Cooper's I thought of dressing to be ready right after lunch—didn't I, Barbara? But it hasn't come. I'm sure you're the last man, Mr. Bates, that would want me to take the bread out of my child's mouth."

"Must be a pretty mean man," said Mr. Bates; "won't send money to keep his own little girl. But you know, Mrs. Baker, I know people talk, especially the Irish, but owners have to make their property pay, someways."

"Oh, well," said Estella, "after all, this isn't a flat you could really expect much rent for. If I'd had my money this month, there's a lot of things I'd have spoken to you about. We haven't any awnings, for one thing, and it makes the place like a bake-oven, and it makes it look like a tenement; though, for that matter, there isn't a tenement but what has awnings. And that woman in the flat over us, you'll have to speak to her. She says insulting things about my dogs, down the airshaft. Yes, she does; she means to insult me, because I told her she ought to be ashamed to let her parrot use such language. I couldn't let Regina listen to it, Mr. Bates, indeed I couldn't. And the storeroom leaks, or a pipe's burst in it, or something, and I shan't pay my rent at all if my Saratoga trunk is damaged, for there's a lot of wardrobe in it, and things no money could replace. My white satin—I only wore it two weeks—is in there, and my husband's miniature's in that trunk. I shouldn't like to see that damaged."

"Well, well," said Mr. Bates, heartlessly putting the miniature of Mr. Baker to one side: "I guess you know it isn't altogether about the rent I came. I guess maybe Miss Barbara's told you about what I said to her this morning. No, ma'am, no, gent'men, don't go. I know it's not the usual thing, but you've always seemed sort of like a family here, and I know you'll all talk about it when I'm gone, so might's well have it now. And I'm counting that maybe you'll kind of help me out. I'm not supposing"—he turned a pair of patient eyes on Barbara, and the tame, kindly lovingness in them seemed at once to shield and to caress her—"I'm not supposing Miss Barbara's what's called in love with me. 'Twouldn't be natural. But I think she might like me if she came to know me and gave me a fair show. Especially when she knows more o' the way people get along than she does now; she'd see how different I'd treat her from the way a lot of men do that have got wives and don't know how to use 'em. I always thought this was a kind of rough world for women, and I'd like to do what's really right by one of them."

Nobody answered, but Tony lifted a long grave look to his.

"And so I thought," continued Mr. Bates, "that some of you who haven't such fancy ideas as it's natural enough she's got, would speak to her, and tell her that if—if you don't see something as pretty as you'd like, it's best to take something that's all wool."

He was greatly pleased at this flower of speech, and looked up quickly and brightly at Barbara, and Barbara smiled. She had a slow smile of infinite possibilities, and Mr. Bates looked at it a little before he proceeded: "I've got money, a couple of hundred thousand, one way and another, and more making—and I've got health and good habits, and the store I set by her, you wouldn't believe it. Well, I guess she's kind of notiony and high-spirited, and I don't seem much to her, but I'm relying you'll tell her those are things make life comfortable and worth having just the same; and I should think you, Mrs. Baker, that's had your own troubles in your time, would feel kind o' scared to have anything so pretty and so kind of high-headed and proud, around like this."

"God is my witness, Mr. Bates—" began Estella leaning forward.

"Not," hurriedly continued the suitor, "not as I've got anything to say against your profession. Those that like it—why, let 'em, I say. But it ain't the life for a woman, is it? Now, is it? Nor, I shouldn't think myself, for a man either. I don't mean any disrespect, but it does seem to me a lady like Miss Barbara's got something more coming to her than this, and what's more," he added, meditatively, "it seems like it don't pay."

Tony, who was leaning on his knees with his chin in his hands, lifted his guileless eyes, and said sweetly; "It's only fair to the profession, Mr. Bates, to tell you that we are not its most victorious exponents."

"Likely, likely," admitted Mr. Bates, a little mystified. "But we can keep a woman out of it, Mr. Reeno, and take her clean away from all this stage business."

"You don't think," inquired Tony—this was the only base advantage Tony took—"you don't think she ought to have anything to say about it, herself—the being taken clean away from all this stage business?"

"Not when she's got a man to look after her," said Mr. Bates, "and give her a comfortable home."

"Oh!" admitted Tony, and confided a twinkle to the flooring.

"Well, my dear," said Estella, "it's a very great responsibility for me, and I don't want to urge you. But if I'd married Mr. Fettercamp when he wanted me to, we'd all be rolling in our own carriages this minute. There was his sister married an Italian prince, and she wasn't a circumstance to Barbara. She's dead, now, poor girl, but she married him. But, no, I would have Tommy Baker because I loved him—indeed, I did, Barbara Floyd, I loved him madly —but there's no use marrying for love when you can't even be sure he'll send you your alimony right. And because I wrecked my life, Barbara, I'd like to see you marry somebody worthy. I'd say the same if it was Regina. Regina—

Regina Baker, don't you put that penny in your mouth. Come here—come here to mamma."

Regina advanced slowly, and Estella gathered the curls out of her warm little neck and hastily polished off her face with a handkerchief. "Don't you know Mr. Bates, darling? What do nice little girls say to gentlemen?"

Regina ducked her head, made an unintelligible sound and extended her hand.

"How-de-do, miss," said Mr. Bates, shaking the hand. "I'm sorry I didn't think to bring you some candy. Better luck next time, eh? Why, why, you mustn't begin to cry, little girl. Don't you want to be friends with me!" Regina nodded. "Don't you want to grow up and have a pony to ride, and learn the piano?"

"Awn go finey aws," said Regina.

"She wants to go on the flying horses," translated the patient Fred. "Merry-go-round, you know."

"And so she shall!" assented Mr. Bates.

Regina glowed with joy. "An Anny Bobs?"

"And Auntie Barbara?" Mr. Bates repeated after Fred, "why yes, indeed."

Regina, in a kind of vacuous triumph, smiled around the room and had an inspiration. "An Tony?"

"Why," responded Mr. Bates hesitatingly, "maybe he wouldn't want to."

A perfect torrent of joyous sounds, intended to be affirmative, burst from Regina's lips. In the vigor of her confidence she flung herself upon the legs of Mr. Bates and beat his knees. "Oh, yef! As time, as time, aw lone, Rina an Anny Bobs and Tony go finey aws, go roun an roun an roun, an Tony caw go ring!"

There was a suspicion of thickness in the voice of the translator: "Once, last time, nobody else happened to be there. Tony and Barbara rode, too, and Tony caught the gold ring; you know, with those little blunt swords."

"Why, he's a very clever young man," Mr. Bates affably replied.

Regina smote his knees and shrieked with joy. "Oh, yef!" she repeated, "an Anny Bobs gah go ring."

"You said it was Mr. Tony caught the gold ring, little girl."

"That's what she means to say," said Fred.

"No! no!" Regina passionately insisted.

"Anny Bobs *gah* go ring! Anny Bobs gah go ring *now!* Rina fine it."

"Well, well, Regina," Estella interrupted, "Mr. Bates can't talk to you all day!"

"I paid it her as a reward of merit. I assure you, I gave the man a dime for it," said Tony, softly, with a little blush.

Mr. Bates passed over the insignificance of Tony's shabby boyhood with the good temper of a potentate. "Well," said he, giving his face a final wipe, "I guess I've said what I laid out to. I didn't come here to talk soft. That part of it's just my business, and hers—if she'll have it." He got up and took his hat and went over to Barbara. "Miss Barbara," he said, "if you can make out to like me—like me well enough to have me—you'll never regret it." He held out his hand, and Barbara gave him hers with her long boyish clasp. Kate followed him to the door and let him out.

An unpleasant silence settled upon the company. Its members were suddenly set face to face with decision and responsibility; they were crowded and jostled and made to feel strange and ill at ease, here, in the dilapidated cheer of their own home, by the encroaching wisdom of other worlds. Barbara continued to sit idly in the blinding sunshine, like a person passive before the issue of events and indifferent to it. The fierce light seemed to set her apart from counsel and from tenderness and to blare aloud her beauty.

Estella, after two or three clearings of her throat, inquired with a kind of trembling pomp: "And what do you think about it yourself, my dear?"

Barbara rose and came slowly to the table. She stood stroking the edge of it with her hand, and finally she said: "I'll tell you what I think. I think that if I were married to Mr. Bates, I shouldn't have to run out into the hall to ogle landlords to cheat them out of their rent. I think I shouldn't have to pretend to be out when the milkman comes, nor wheedle the butcher, nor have the gas turned off. I shouldn't have to walk out of a hateful mess like this"—Estella gasped—"dressed as if I were going to a beauty show, because I wanted work, and into offices where I should be looked over as if I were a horse. I think I shouldn't owe every stitch I wear and everything I put into my mouth to my sister's divorced husband. That's what I think. I think I should be looked out for and taken care of and kept away from hurt, as other women are!"

Estella began: "Well, of all the—"

"And I think," continued Barbara, her voice rising to a hysteric pitch, "that my husband would be respected everywhere, and would work for me and be true and good, and not depend for his pleasure upon a friend's getting some money, and taking him out to dinner with girls—"

"Oh, oh! Barbara!" cried Fred.

"It was such a good dinner, Barbara!" said Tony. Unquestionably, his smile was coming back.

The dogs at the same moment began to quarrel over a bone and their voices rose in ear-splitting dispute. Estella cuffed one of them and the other carried the bone into the sitting-room, from whence issued ecstatic lickings and crunchings.

In the comparative pause Mrs. Donnelly's tearful indignation burst upon Barbara: "We all know what you mean by that last, Barbara Floyd," she cried. "And I guess there are other people, besides you, in this house that are sick and tired of being poor, and the fuss there is about meals, and that have spent all their money on you, and whose fathers were rich and famous, and thought nothing of living at Delmonico's, before ever you were born. If the butcher is swindled out of his meat, I don't see but you eat your share of it. If you think it's messy here, why don't you get up and clean it? Tony's scrubbed the kitchen while you've been lolling there, and you wouldn't know how to cook anything but a boiled egg and a pickle to this day if it wasn't for Tony. You're a bad, ungrateful girl, Barbara Floyd, and Tony—"

Estella pitched her voice above the voices of Mrs. Donnelly and the dogs: "Don't you try to bully my sister, Kate Donnelly, she—"

Tony struck the table sharply with his hand. "Come, Barbara," he said. "We must get the washing down now." He held the door open for her, and without looking round she went past him into the hall.

At the head of the top flight of stairs there was a door with a heavy, sliding weight, and Tony, who had run upstairs in advance, pushed it open, and with a wave of the hand, like a lavish host, welcomed Barbara to the great, shining roof. It was very wide and hot and silent, and little airs that the sidewalk never knew drifted over its cornices. Said Tony: "'To where, beyond the voices, there is peace.'"

Barbara stepped out fearlessly between the glare of the red roofs and the glare of the blue and golden sky. With a happy breath she turned her unshielded face up to the light. This stretch of gleaming tin had long been their private garden, and they had known it in many kinds of weather. "Oh, Tony!" she said, in a little soft, fluttered, laughing voice, "we needn't bother about the washing yet, need we?"

"Come," said Tony. "I've found a place where we can see the river. I found it for us this morning. Musn't tell!"

"No," she said, and put her hand out to him, like a child. "Show me."

Behind its newer and broader substitute an old chimney rose out of the roof's western bulwark, from which it parted company a few feet above the ground in an angle of crumbling brick and mortar. Tony jumped into the niche of this angle and held down a hand to Barbara. "Step up and I'll lift you," he directed. She was beside him in an instant, and found herself breast-high above the parapet, which served as an elbow rest. It was too broad to let them see straight down into the common, cluttered street, and beyond the shops and the low buildings over the way stumbled the vine-smothered huts of squatters; past a bit of leafy, broken ground the wide green of market gardens was dotted with the gold of sunflowers and the scarlet of geraniums, a single close-shorn lawn was banked with the white and the mystic blue of hydrangeas. Further yet, between the shimmer of poplars and the frown of purple hills, the river flashed and drifted.

"It's good here," said Tony.

Barbara stretched her arm across the parapet as though she stretched it into the coolness of fresh water. "There's a yacht—a white one; watch! Going down the river! Let's pretend it's going straight to sea, Tony—what fun! Across the sea."

"We're going with it, you know. Just ourselves, of course, and a telescope, maybe, and plenty of honey wrapped up in a five-pound note. All the little fishes will come and beg us for the honey, and you'll give it to them out of your hands, till I shall be jealous. It isn't nice to be jealous. I wouldn't let even a little fish suffer it, if I were you, Barbara—Why, Barbara! what foolishness you talk! And you don't even hear me!"

"I wish I could see all this from my own window," she said.

"Ah, but you can't! I had to show it to you, Barbara. It was quite easy to find, but you know you never found it." The little rosy ruffle of Barbara's sleeve lay on the rough edge of the parapet, and Tony bent his head and kissed it. "I was sure you'd like it here. Be good," he said.

The voices of some children singing ring-games on a near fire-escape rose with an accent of their own natures to the two truants on the housetop. Otherwise they seemed the only living souls in a universe made up of two expanses; below them, the wide, sparkling, burning roofs, with one distant fringe of leaves and waters, and above, the radiant, hot blue, luminous and quivering, and scarcely tinged by the white clouds which slowly sailed across it and banked themselves on the horizon into palaces and temples. Toward the west, where the sun blazed in a splendor that even the eyes of lovers dared not meet, the heavens were almost white —not in pallor, but effulgence, like light incarnate. Small, lazy breezes floated through the sunshine, and brushed, fresh and sweet, against their faces.

"Barbara," said Tony, leaning forward and catching her by both wrists, "where did Regina find my ring?"

She was startled both by the suddenness of his attack and by the strength of his hold, and straining back upon his grasp she remained alert and silent, like a deer. He waited a moment, but she continued passionately quiet, passionately studious of his face. In the pause, the voices of the children arose with a new clearness:

> And on his breast he wore a star,
> Pointing to the East and West.

"Barbara!"

"Hush!" she insisted. Her breath was fluttering on her lips, and her eyes shining into his:

> Go choose your East, go choose your West
> Go choose the one that you love best.

"You kept that ring!" he said. "You kept it—because of me!" Almost as he spoke she had leaped down and away from him, and was running across the roof.

He caught up with her on the low platform of wooden slats amid the flutter of the wet linens.

"Help me take these in," she called to him: "Estella will be angry." She was struggling with the clothes-pins, and their fingers met over a row of pillow-slips.

"They're not dry yet. Listen, I—"

"There's a breeze come up. It will dry them in a minute." She was moving further and further away.

"Why, see, my sweet, you don't know what you're saying! I want to tell you—"

"Oh," she cried, pausing oppressedly, "what does everybody tell me? That you are idle, that you are extravagant, that you—that you—that girls—"

"Barbara," he said, "though they follow me in their thousands and their ten thousands, though their dead bodies strew my pathway, I will be blind to them. I love you, Barbara."

She retreated again, making as though to reach the door, and he stood still in a sudden bitterness, with a little wound in the dignity of his love. The next instant he was startled to see her, who was so light and true of step, stumble and lose her footing on a broken slat and sink down in a heap with her hands over her face.

He ran up and bent over her without touching her. "Oh, my dear!" he asked; "what is it? Are you hurt? Or were you angry? Would you like me to go away? What is it?"

She lifted her face to his and put her arms around his neck.

"I was thinking of you," she said.

Half an hour later as they still sat on the platform the roof rang with their names, and from under their damp canopy of tablecloths and towels they perceived Estella in the doorway.

"Come on!" she called. "Why, whatever's kept you? Come on! The alimony's come, and we're all going to Coney Island for dinner!"

"Don't be so noisy, Estella!" said Tony. "We're engaged."

"Really? Really, Barbara? Well, I'm glad of it.— Yes, Regina," she called over her shoulder, "come up. Mamma's here.—Well, I'm very glad. And I'll have my white satin cleaned for her as soon as I can. How jolly we're going out to dinner! Like a party for you, Barbara."

"Splendid!" said Tony. "The alimony baked meats did coldly furnish forth the marriage tables."

He sprang up and handed Barbara to her feet. There fell to the ground something Barbara had been showing Tony—a slender ribbon, as long as a watch-chain, and, dangling from its end, a great, clumsy, ridiculous gilt ring. Regina, who came staggering through the doorway, fell upon this latter object with a shriek of joyous recognition. "Anny Bobs gah go ring!" she cried. "Rina awn go finey aws, go finey aws, go roun an roun an roun!"

JEAN-AH POQUELIN *

By G. W. Cable

IN the first decade of the present century, when the newly established American Government was the most hateful thing in Louisiana—when the Creoles were still kicking at such vile innovations as the trial by jury, American dances, anti-smuggling laws, and the printing of the Governor's proclamation in English—when the Anglo-American flood that was presently to burst in a crevasse of immigration upon the delta had thus far been felt only as slippery seepage which made the Creole tremble for his footing—there stood, a short distance above what is now Canal Street, and considerably back from the line of villas which fringed the river-bank on Tchoupitoulas Road, an old colonial plantation-house half in ruin.

It stood aloof from civilization, the tracts that had once been its indigo fields given over to their first noxious wildness, and grown up into one of the horridest marshes within a circuit of fifty miles.

The house was of heavy cypress, lifted up on pillars, grim, solid, and spiritless, its massive build a strong reminder of days still earlier, when every man had been his own peace officer and the insurrection of the blacks a daily contingency. Its dark, weather-beaten roof and sides were hoisted up above the jungly plain in a distracted way, like a gigantic ammunition-wagon stuck in the mud and abandoned by some retreating army. Around it was a dense growth of low water willows, with half a hundred sorts of thorny or fetid bushes, savage strangers alike to the "language of flowers" and to the botanist's Greek. They were hung with countless strands of discolored and prickly smilax, and the impassable mud below

---

* From "Old Creole Days," copyright, 1879, 1883, by Charles Scribner's Sons. By permission of the publishers, and the author.

bristled with *chevaux de frise* of the dwarf-palmetto. Two lone forest-trees, dead cypresses, stood in the centre of the marsh, dotted with roosting vultures. The shallow strips of water were hid by myriads of aquatic plants, under whose coarse and spiritless flowers, could one have seen it, was a harbor of reptiles, great and small, to make one shudder to the end of his days.

The house was on a slightly raised spot, the levee of a draining canal. The waters of this canal did not run; they crawled, and were full of big, ravening fish and alligators, that held it against all comers.

Such was the home of old Jean Marie Poquelin, once an opulent indigo planter, standing high in the esteem of his small, proud circle of exclusively male acquaintances in the old city; now a hermit, alike shunned by and shunning all who had ever known him. "The last of his line," said the gossips. His father lies under the floor of the St. Louis Cathedral, with the wife of his youth on one side, and the wife of his old age on the other. Old Jean visits the spot daily. His half-brother—alas! there was a mystery; no one knew what had become of the gentle, young half-brother, more than thirty years his junior, whom once he seemed so fondly to love, but who, seven years ago, had disappeared suddenly, once for all, and left no clew of his fate.

They had seemed to live so happily in each other's love. No father, mother, wife to either, no kindred upon earth. The elder a bold, frank, impetuous, chivalric adventurer; the younger a gentle, studious, book-loving recluse; they lived upon the ancestral estate like mated birds, one always on the wing, the other always in the nest.

There was no trait in Jean Marie Poquelin, said the old gossips, for which he was so well known among his few friends as his apparent fondness for his "little brother." "Jacques said this," and "Jacques said that," he "would leave this or that, or anything to Jacques," for "Jacques was a scholar," and "Jacques was good," or "wise," or "just," or "far-sighted," as the nature of the case required; and "he should ask Jacques as soon as he got home," since Jacques was never elsewhere to be seen.

It was between the roving character of the one brother, and the bookishness of the other, that the estate fell into decay. Jean Marie, generous gentleman, gambled the slaves away one by one, until none was left, man or woman, but one old African mute.

The indigo-fields and vats of Louisiana had been generally abandoned as unremunerative. Certain enterprising men had substituted the culture of sugar; but while the recluse was too apathetic to take so active a course, the other saw larger, and, at that time, equally respectable profits, first in smuggling, and later in the African slave-trade. What harm could he see in it? The whole people said it was vitally necessary, and to minister to a vital public necessity, —good enough, certainly, and so he laid up many a doubloon, that made him none the worse in the public regard.

One day old Jean Marie was about to start upon a voyage that was to be longer, much longer, than any that he had yet made. Jacques had begged him hard for many days not to go, but he laughed him off, and finally said, kissing him:

"*Adieu, 'tit frère.*"

"No," said Jacques, "I shall go with you."

They left the old hulk of a house in the sole care of the African mute, and went away to the Guinea coast together.

Two years after, old Poquelin came home without his vessel. He must have arrived at his house by night. No one saw him come. No one saw "his little brother"; rumor whispered that he, too, had returned, but he had never been seen again.

A dark suspicion fell upon the old slave-trader. No matter that the few kept the many reminded of the tenderness that had ever marked his bearing to the missing man. The many shook their heads. "You know he has a quick and fearful temper"; and "why does he cover his loss with mystery?" "Grief would out with the truth."

"But," said the charitable few, "look in his face; see that expression of true humanity." The many did look in his face, and, as he looked in theirs, he read the silent question: "Where is thy brother Abel?" The few were silenced, his former friends died off, and the name of Jean Marie Poquelin became a symbol of witchery, devilish crime, and hideous nursery fictions.

The man and his house were alike shunned. The snipe and duck hunters forsook the marsh, and the woodcutters abandoned the canal. Sometimes the hardier boys who ventured out there snake-shooting heard a slow thumping of oar-locks on the canal. They would look at each other for a moment half in consternation, half in glee, then rush from their sport in wanton haste to assail with their gibes the un-offending, withered old man who, in rusty attire, sat in the stern of a skiff rowed homeward by his white-headed African mute.

"O Jean-ah Poquelin! O Jean-ah! Jean-ah Poquelin!"

It was not necessary to utter more than that. No hint of wickedness, deformity, or any physical or moral demerit; merely the name and tone of mockery: "Oh, Jean-ah Poque-lin!" and while they tumbled one over another in their need-less haste to fly, he would rise carefully from his seat, while the aged mute, with downcast face, went on rowing, and roll-ing up his brown fist and extending it toward the urchins, would pour forth such an unholy broadside of French impre-cation and invective as would all but craze them with de-light.

Among both blacks and whites the house was the object of a thousand superstitions. Every midnight, they affirmed, the *feu follet* came out of the marsh and ran in and out of the rooms, flashing from window to window. The story of some lads, whose words in ordinary statements were worth-less, was generally credited, that the night they camped in the woods, rather than pass the place after dark, they saw, about sunset, every window blood-red, and on each of the four chimneys an owl sitting, which turned his head three times round, and moaned and laughed with a human voice. There was a bottomless well, everybody professed to know, beneath the sill of the big front door under the rotten veranda; whoever set his foot upon that threshold disappeared forever in the depth below.

What wonder the marsh grew as wild as Africa! Take all the Faubourg Ste. Marie, and half the ancient city, you would not find one graceless dare-devil reckless enough to pass within a hundred yards of the house after nightfall.

The alien races pouring into old New Orleans began to find the few streets named after the Bourbon princes too strait for them. The wheel of fortune, beginning to whirl, threw them off beyond the ancient corporation lines, and sowed civilization and even trade upon the lands of the Graviers and Girods. Fields became roads, roads streets. Everywhere the leveller was peering through his glass, rodsmen were whacking their way through willow-brakes and rose-hedges, and the sweating Irishmen tossed the blue clay up with their long-handled shovels.

"Ha! that is all very well," quoth the Jean-Baptistes, feeling the reproach of an enterprise that asked neither co-operation nor advice of them, "but wait till they come yonder to Jean Poquelin's marsh; ha! ha! ha!" The supposed predicament so delighted them, that they put on a mock terror and whirled about in an assumed stampede, then caught their clasped hands between their knees in excess of mirth, and laughed till the tears ran; for whether the street-makers mired in the marsh, or contrived to cut through old "Jean-ah's" property, either event would be joyful. Meantime a line of tiny rods, with bits of white paper in their split tops, gradually extended its way straight through the haunted ground, and across the canal diagonally.

"We shall fill that ditch," said the men in mud-boots, and brushed close along the chained and pad-locked gate of the haunted mansion. Ah, Jean-ah Poquelin, those were not Creole boys, to be stampeded with a little hard swearing.

He went to the governor. That official scanned the odd figure with no slight interest. Jean Poquelin was of short, broad frame, with a bronzed leonine face. His brow was ample and deeply furrowed. His eye, large and black, was bold and open like that of a war-horse, and his jaws shut together with the firmness of iron. He dressed in a suit of Attakapas cottonade, and his shirt, unbuttoned and thrown back from the throat and bosom, sailor-wise, showed a herculean breast, hard and grizzled. There was no fierceness or defiance in his look, no harsh ungentleness, no symptom of his unlawful life or violent temper; but rather a peaceful and peaceable fearlessness. Across the whole face, not marked in one or another feature, but, as it were, laid softly upon the countenance like an almost imperceptible veil, was the imprint of some great grief. A careless eye might easily overlook it, but, once seen, there it hung—faint, but unmistakable.

The Governor bowed.

"Parlez-vous français?" asked the figure.

"I would rather talk English, if you can do so," said the Governor.

"My name, Jean Poquelin."

"How can I serve you, Mr. Poquelin?"

"My 'ouse is yond'; *dans le marais là-bas.*"

The Governor bowed.

"Dat *marais* billong to me."

"Yes, sir."

"To me; Jean Poquelin; I hown 'im meself."

"Well, sir?"

"He don't billong to you; I get him from me father."

"That is perfectly true, Mr. Poquelin, as far as I am aware."

"You want to make strit pass yond'?"

"I do not know, sir; it is quite probable; but the city will indemnify you for any loss you may suffer—you will get paid, you understand."

"Strit can't pass dare."

"You will have to see the municipal authorities about that, Mr. Poquelin."

A bitter smile came upon the old man's face:

"Pardon, Monsieur, you is not *le Gouverneur?"*

"Yes."

"Mais, yes. You har *le Gouverneur*—yes. Veh-well. I come to you. I tell you, strit can't pass at me 'ouse."

"But you will have to see"—

"I come to you. You is *le Gouverneur.* I know not the new laws. I ham a Fr-r-rench-a-man! Fr-rench-a-man have something *aller au contraire*—he come at his *Gouverneur.* I come at you. If me not had been bought from me king like *bossals* in the hold time, ze king gof—France would-a-show *Monsieur le Gouverneur* to take care of his men to make strit in right places. *Mais,* I know; we billong to *Monsieur le Président.* I want you do somesin for me, eh?"

"What is it?" asked the patient Governor.

"I want you tell *Monsieur le Président,* strit—can't—pass —at—me—'ouse."

"Have a chair, Mr. Poquelin;" but the old man did not stir. The Governor took a quill and wrote a line to a city official, introducing Mr. Poquelin, and asking for him every possible courtesy. He handed it to him, instructing him where to present it.

"Mr. Poquelin," he said with a conciliatory smile, "tell me, is it your house that our Creole citizens tell such odd stories about?"

The old man glared sternly upon the speaker, and with immovable features said:

"You don't see me trade some Guinea nigga'?"

"Oh, no."

"You don't see me make some smugglin'?"

"No, sir; not at all."

"But, I am Jean Marie Poquelin. I mine me hown bizniss. Dat all right? Adieu."

He put his hat on and withdrew. By and by he stood, letter in hand, before the person to whom it was addressed. This person employed an interpreter.

"He says," said the interpreter to the officer, "he come to make you the fair warning how you muz not make the street pas' at his 'ouse."

The officer remarked that "such impudence was refreshing"; but the experienced interpreter translated freely.

"He says: 'Why you don't want?'" said the interpreter.

The old slave-trader answered at some length.

"He says," said the interpreter, again turning to the officer, "the marass is too unhealth' for peopl' to live."

"But we expect to drain his old marsh; it's not going to be a marsh."

"Il dit . . ." the interpreter explained in French.

The old man answered tersely.

"He says the canal is a private," said the interpreter.

"Oh! *that* old ditch; that's to be filled up. Tell the old man we're going to fix him up nicely."

Translation being duly made, the man in power was amused to see a thunder-cloud gathering on the old man's face.

"Tell him," he added, "by the time we finish, there'll not be a ghost left in his shanty."

The interpreter began to translate, but—

"*J' comprends, J' comprends,*" said the old man, with an impatient gesture, and burst forth, pouring curses upon the United States, the President, the Territory of Orleans, the Congress, the Governor and all his subordinates, striding out of the apartment as he cursed, while the object of his maledictions roared with merriment and rammed the floor with his foot.

"Why, it will make his old place worth ten dollars to one," said the official to the interpreter.

"'Tis not for de worse of de property," said the interpreter.

"I should guess not," said the other, whittling his chair, "seems to me as if some of these old Creoles would liever live in a crawfish hole than to have a neighbor."

"You know what make old Jean Poquelin make like that? I will tell you. You know—"

The interpreter was rolling a cigarette, and paused to light his tinder; then, as the smoke poured in a thick double stream from his nostrils, he said, in a solemn whisper:

"He is a witch."

"Ho, ho, ho!" laughed the other.

"You don't believe it? What you want to bet?" cried the interpreter, jerking himself half up and thrusting out one arm while he bared it of its coat-sleeve with the hand of the other. "What you want to bet?"

"How do you know?" asked the official.

"Dass what I goin' to tell you. You know, one evening I was shooting some *grosbec*. I killed three; but I had trouble to fin' them, it was becoming so dark. When I have them I start' to come home; then I got to pas' at Jean Poquelin's house."

"Ho, ho, ho!" laughed the other, throwing his leg over the arm of his chair.

"Wait," said the interpreter. "I come along slow, not making some noises; still, still—"

"And scared," said the smiling one.

"*Mais*, wait. I get all pas' the 'ouse. 'Ah!' I say, 'all right!' Then I see two thing' before! Hah! I get as cold and humide, and shake like a leaf. You think it was nothing? There I see, so plain as can be (though it was making nearly dark), I see Jean—Marie—Po-que-lin walkin' right in front, and right there beside of him was something like a man—but not a man—white like paint!—I drop' on the grass from scared—they pass'; so sure as I live 'twas the ghos' of Jacques Poquelin, his brother!"

"Pooh!" said the listener.

"I'll put my han' in the fire," said the interpreter.

"But did you never think," asked the other, "that that might be Jack Poquelin, as you call him, alive and well, and for some cause hid away by his brother?"

"But there har' no cause!" said the other, and the entrance of third parties changed the subject.

Some months passed and the street was opened. A canal was first dug through the marsh, the small one which passed so close to Jean Poquelin's house was filled, and the street. or rather a sunny road just touched a corner of the old mansion's dooryard. The morass ran dry. Its venomous denizens slipped away through the bulrushes; the cattle roaming freely upon its hardened surface trampled the superabundant undergrowth. The bellowing frogs croaked to westward. Lilies and the flower-de-luce sprang up in the place of reeds; smilax and poison-oak gave way to the purple-plumed iron-weed and pink spiderwort; the bindweeds ran everywhere, blooming as they ran, and on one of the dead cypresses a giant creeper hung its green burden of foliage and lifted its scarlet trumpets. Sparrows and red-birds flitted through the bushes, and dewberries grew ripe beneath. Over all these came a sweet, dry smell of salubrity which the place

had not known since the sediments of the Mississippi first
lifted it from the sea.

But its owner did not build. Over the willow-brakes, and
down the vista of the open street, bright new houses, some
singly, some by ranks, were prying in upon the old man's
privacy. They even settled down towards his southern side.
First a wood-cutter's hut or two, then a market gardener's
shanty, then a painted cottage, and all at once the faubourg
had flanked and half surrounded him and his dried-up marsh.

Ah! then the common people began to hate him. "The
old tyrant!" "You don't mean an old *tyrant?*" Well, then,
why don't he build when the public need demands it? What
does he live in that unneighborly way for?" "The old
pirate!" "The old kidnapper!" How easily even the most
ultra Louisianians put on the imported virtues of the North
when they could be brought to bear against the hermit.
"There he goes, with the boys after him! Ah! ha! ha!
Jean-ah Poquelin! Ah! Jean-ah! Aha! aha! Jean-ah
Marie! Jean-ah Poquelin! The old villain!" How merrily the swarming Américains echo the spirit of persecution!
"The old fraud," they say, "pretends to live in a haunted
house, does he? We'll tar and feather him some day. Guess
we can fix him."

He cannot be rowed home along the old canal now; he
walks. He has broken sadly of late, and the street urchins
are ever at his heels. It is like the days when they cried:
"Go up, thou bald-head," and the old man now and then
turns and delivers ineffectual curses.

To the Creoles—to the incoming lower class of superstitious Germans, Irish, Sicilians, and others—he became an
omen and embodiment of public and private ill-fortune.
Upon him all the vagaries of their superstitions gathered and
grew. If a house caught fire, it was imputed to his machina-
tions. Did a woman go off in a fit, he had bewitched her.
Did a child stray off for an hour, the mother shivered with
the apprehension that Jean Poquelin had offered him to
strange gods. The house was the subject of every bad boy's
invention who loved to contrive ghostly lies. "As long as
that house stands we shall have bad luck. Do you not see

our pease and beans dying, our cabbages and lettuce going to seed and our gardens turning to dust, while every day you can see it raining in the woods? The rain will never pass old Poquelin's house. He keeps a fetich. He has conjured the whole Faubourg Ste. Marie. And why, the old wretch? Simply because our playful and innocent children call after him as he passes."

A "Building and Improvement Company," which had not yet got its charter, "but was going to," and which had not, indeed, any tangible capital yet, but "was going to have some," joined the "Jean-ah Poquelin" war. The haunted property would be such a capital site for a market-house! They sent a deputation to the old mansion to ask its occupant to sell. The deputation never got beyond the chained gate and a very barren interview with the African mute. The President of the Board was then empowered (for he had studied French in Pennsylvania and was considered qualified) to call and persuade M. Poquelin to subscribe to the company's stock; but—

"Fact is, gentlemen," he said at the next meeting, "it would take us at least twelve months to make Mr. Pokaleen understand the rather original features of our system, and he wouldn't subscribe when we'd done; besides, the only way to see him is to stop him on the street."

There was a great laugh from the Board; they couldn't help it. "Better meet a bear robbed of her whelps," said one.

"You're mistaken as to that," said the President. "I did meet him, and stopped him, and found him quite polite. But I could get no satisfaction from him; the fellow wouldn't talk in French, and when I spoke in English he hoisted his old shoulders up, and gave the same answer to everything I said."

"And that was—?" asked one or two impatient of the pause.

"That it 'don't worse w'ile.'"

One of the Board said: "Mr. President, this market-house project, as I take it, is not altogether a selfish one; the community is to be benefited by it. We may feel that we are working in the public interest (the Board smiled knowingly), if we employ all possible means to oust this old nuisance from among us. You may know that at the time the street was cut through, this old Poquelann did all he could to prevent it. It was owing to a certain connection which I had with that affair that I heard a ghost story (smiles, followed by a sudden dignified check), a ghost story, which, of course, I am not going to relate; but I *may* say that my profound conviction, arising from a prolonged study of that story, is, that this old villain, John Poquelann, has his brother locked up in that old house. Now, if this is so, and we can fix it on him, I merely *suggest* that we can make the matter highly useful. I don't know," he added, beginning to sit down, "but that it is an action we owe to the community —hem!"

"How do you propose to handle the subject?" asked the President.

"I was thinking," said the speaker, "that, as a Board of Directors, it would be unadvisable for us to authorize any action involving trespass; but if you, for instance, Mr. President, should, as it were, for mere curiosity, *request* some one, as, for instance, our excellent Secretary, simply as a personal favor, to look into the matter—this is merely a suggestion."

The Secretary smiled sufficiently to be understood that, while he certainly did not consider such preposterous service a part of his duties as secretary, he might, notwithstanding, accede to the President's request; and the Board adjourned.

Little White, as the Secretary was called, was a mild, kind-hearted little man, who, nevertheless, had no fear of anything, unless it was the fear of being unkind.

"I tell you frankly," he privately said to the President, "I go into this purely for reasons of my own."

The next day, a little after nightfall, one might have descried this little man slipping along the rear fence of the Poquelin place, preparatory to vaulting over into the rank, grass-grown yard, and bearing himself altogether more after the manner of a collector of rare chickens than according to the usage of secretaries.

The picture presented to his eye was not calculated to enliven his mind. The old mansion stood out against the western sky, black and silent. One long, lurid pencil-stroke along a sky of slate was all that was left of daylight. No sign of life was apparent; no light at any window, unless it might have been on the side of the house hidden from view. No owls were on the chimneys, no dogs were in the yard.

He entered the place, and ventured up behind a small cabin which stood apart from the house. Through one of its many crannies he easily detected the African mute crouched before a flickering pine-knot, his head on his knees, fast asleep.

He concluded to enter the mansion, and, with that view, stood and scanned it. The broad rear steps of the veranda would not serve him; he might meet some one midway. He was measuring, with his eye, the proportions of one of the pillars which supported it, and estimating the practicability of climbing it, when he heard a footstep. Some one dragged a chair out toward the railing, then seemed to change his mind and began to pace the veranda, his footfalls resounding on the dry boards with singular loudness. Little White drew a step backward, got the figure between himself and the sky, and at once recognized the short, broad-shouldered form of old Jean Poquelin.

He sat down upon a billet of wood, and, to escape the stings of a whining cloud of mosquitoes, shrouded his face and neck in his handkerchief, leaving his eyes uncovered.

He had sat there but a moment when he noticed a strange, sickening odor, faint, as if coming from a distance, but loathsome and horrid.

Whence could it come? Not from the cabin; not from the marsh, for it was as dry as powder. It was not in the air; it seemed to come from the ground.

Rising up, he noticed, for the first time, a few steps before him a narrow footpath leading toward the house. He glanced down it—Ha! right there was some one coming—ghostly white!

Quick as thought, and as noiselessly, he lay down at full length against the cabin. It was bold strategy, and yet, there was no denying it, little White felt that he was frightened.

"It is not a ghost," he said to himself. "I *know* it cannot be a ghost"; but the perspiration burst out at every pore, and the air seemed to thicken with heat. "It is a living man," he said in his thoughts. "I hear his footsteps, and I hear old Poquelin's footsteps, too, separately, over on the veranda. I am not discovered; the thing has passed; there is that odor again; what a smell of death! Is it coming back? Yes. It stops at the dóor of the cabin. Is it peering in at the sleeping mute? It moves away. It is in the path again. Now it is gone." He shuddered. "Now, if I dare venture, the mystery is solved." He rose cautiously, close against the cabin, and peered along the path.

The figure of a man, a presence if not a body—but whether clad in some white stuff or naked the darkness would not allow him to determine—had turned, and now, with a seeming painful gait, moved slowly from him. "Great Heaven! can it be that the dead do walk?" He withdrew again the hands which had gone to his eyes. The dreadful object passed between two pillars and under the house. He listened. There was a faint sound as of feet upon a staircase; then all was still except the measured tread of Jean Poquelin walking on the veranda, and the heavy respirations of the mute slumbering in the cabin.

The little Secretary was about to retreat; but as he looked once more toward the haunted house a dim light appeared in the crack of a closed window, and presently old Jean Poquelin came, dragging his chair, and sat down close against the shining cranny. He spoke in a low, tender tone in the French tongue, making some inquiry. An answer came from within. Was it the voice of a human? So unnatural was it—so hollow, so discordant, so unearthly—that the stealthy listener shuddered again from head to foot, and when something stirred in some bushes near by—though it may have been nothing more than a rat—and came scuttling through the grass, the little Secretary actually turned and fled. As he left the enclosure he moved with bolder leisure through the bushes; yet now and then he spoke aloud: "Oh, oh! I see, I understand!" and shut his eyes in his hands.

How strange that henceforth little White was the champion of Jean Poquelin! In season and out of season—wherever a word was uttered against him—the Secretary, with a quiet, aggressive force that instantly arrested gossip, demanded upon what authority the statement or conjecture was made; but as he did not condescend to explain his own remarkable attitude, it was not long before the disrelish and suspicion which had followed Jean Poquelin so many years fell also upon him.

It was only the next evening but one after his adventure that he made himself a source of sullen amazement to one hundred and fifty boys, by ordering them to desist from their wanton hallooing. Old Jean Poquelin, standing and shaking his cane, rolling out his long-drawn maledictions, paused and stared, then gave the Secretary a courteous bow and started on. The boys, save one, from pure astonishment, ceased but a ruffianly little Irish lad, more daring than any had yet been, threw a big hurtling clod that struck old Poquelin between the shoulders and burst like a shell. The enraged old man wheeled with uplifted staff to give chase to the scampering vagabond, and, he may have tripped, or he may not, but he fell full length. Little White hastened to help him up, but he waved him off with a fierce imprecation and staggering to his feet resumed his way homeward. His lips were reddened with blood.

Little White was on his way to the meeting of the Board. He would have given all he dared spend to have staid away, for he felt both too fierce and too tremulous to brook the criticisms that were likely to be made.

"I can't help it, gentlemen; I can't help you to make a case against the old man, and I'm not going to."

"We did not expect this disappointment, Mr. White."

"I can't help that, sir. No, sir, you had better not appoint any more investigations. Somebody'll investigate himself into trouble. No. sir, it isn't a threat, it is only my advice, but I warn you that whoever takes the task in hand will rue it to his dying day—which may be hastened, too."

The President expressed himself "surprised."

"I don't care a rush," answered little White, wildly and foolishly. "I don't care a rush if you are, sir. No, my nerves are not disordered; my head's as clear as a bell. No, I'm *not* excited."

A Director remarked that the Secretary looked as though he had waked from a nightmare.

"Well, sir, if you want to know the fact, I have; and if you choose to cultivate old Poquelin's society you can have one, too."

"White," called a facetious member, but White did not notice. "White," he called again.

"What?" demanded White, with a scowl.

"Did you see the ghost?"

"'Yes, sir; I did," cried White, hitting the table, and handing the President a paper which brought the Board to other business.

The story got among the gossips that somebody (they were afraid to say little White) had been to the Poquelin mansion by night and beheld something appalling. The rumor was but a shadow of the truth, magnified and distorted as is the manner of shadows. He had seen skeletons walking, and had barely escaped the clutches of one by making the sign of the cross.

Some madcap boys with an appetite for the horrible plucked up courage to venture through the dried marsh by the cattle-path, and come before the house at a spectral hour when the air was full of bats. Something which they but half saw—half a sight was enough—sent them tearing back through the willow-brakes and acacia bushes to their homes, where they fairly dropped down, and cried:

"Was it white?" "No—yes—nearly so—we can't tell—but we saw it." And one could hardly doubt, to look at their ashen faces, that they had, whatever it was.

"If that old rascal lived in the country we come from," said certain Américains, "he'd have been tarred and feathered before now, wouldn't he, Sanders?"

"Well, now he just would."

"And we'd have rid him on a rail, wouldn't we?"

"That's what I allow."

"Tell you what you *could* do." They were talking to some rollicking Creoles who had assumed an absolute necessity for doing *something*. "What is it you call this thing where an old man marries a young girl, and you come out with horns and—"

"*Charivari?*" asked the Creoles.

"Yes, tha's it. Why don't you shivaree him?" Felicitous suggestion.

Little White, with his wife beside him, was sitting on their doorsteps on the sidewalk, as Creole custom had taught them, looking toward the sunset. They had moved into the lately-opened street. The view was not attractive on the score of beauty. The houses were small and scattered, and across the flat commons, spite of the lofty tangle of weeds and bushes, and spite of the thickets of acacia, they needs must see the dismal old Poquelin mansion, tilted awry and shutting out the declining sun. The moon, white and slender was hanging the tip of its horn over one of the chimneys.

"And you say," said the Secretary, "the old black man has been going by here alone? Patty, suppose old Poquelin should be concocting some mischief; he don't lack provocation; the way that clod hit him the other day was enough to have killed him. Why, Patty, he dropped as quick as *that!* No wonder you haven't seen him. I wonder if they haven't heard something about him up at the drug-store. Suppose I go and see."

"Do," said his wife.

She sat alone for half an hour, watching that sudden going out of day peculiar to the latitude.

"That moon is ghost enough for one house," she said, as her husband returned. "It has gone right down the chimney."

"Patty," said little White, "the drug-clerk says the boys are going to shivaree old Poquelin to-night. I'm going to try to stop it."

"Why, White," said his wife, "you'd better not. You'll get hurt."

"No, I'll not."

"Yes, you will."

"I'm going to sit out here until they come along. They're compelled to pass right by here."

"Why, White, it may be midnight before they start; you're not going to sit out here till then."

"Yes, I am."

"Well, you're very foolish," said Mrs. Whie in an undertone, looking anxious, and tapping one of the steps with her foot.

They sat a very long time talking over little family matters.

"What's that?" at last said Mrs. White.

"That's the nine-o'clock gun," said White, and they relapsed into a long-sustained, drowsy silence.

"Patty, you'd better go in and go to bed," said he at last.

"I'm not sleepy."

"Well, you're very foolish," quietly remarked little White, and again silence fell upon them.

"Patty, suppose I walk out to the old house and see if I can find out anything."

"Suppose," said she, "you don't do any such—listen!"

Down the street arose a great hubbub. Dogs and boys were howling and barking; men were laughing, shouting, groaning, and blowing horns, whooping, and clanking cowbells, whinnying, and howling, and rattling pots and pans.

"They are coming this way," said little White. "You had better go into the house, Patty."

"So had you."

"No. I'm going to see if I can't stop them."

"Why, White!"

"I'll be back in a minute," said White, and went toward the noise.

In a few moments the little Secretary met the mob. The pen hesitates on the word, for there is a respectable difference, measurable only on the scale of the half-century, between a mob and a *charivari*. Little White lifted his ineffectual voice. He faced the head of the disorderly column, and cast himself about as if he were made of wood and moved by the jerk of a string. He rushed to one who seemed, from the size and clatter of his tin pan, to be a leader. *"Stop these fellows, Bienvenu, stop them just a minute, till I tell them something."* Bienvenu turned and brandished his instruments of discord in an imploring way to the crowd. They slackened their pace, two or three hushed their horns and joined the prayer of little White and Bienvenu for silence. The throng halted. The hush was delicious.

"Bienvenu," said little White, "don't shivaree old Poquelin to-night; he's"—

"My fwang," said the swaying Bienvenu, "who tail you I goin' to chahivahi somebody, eh? You sink bickause I make a little playfool wiz zis tin pan zat I am *dhonk?*"

"Oh, no, Bienvenu, old fellow, you're all right. I was afraid you might not know that old Poquelin was sick, you know, but you're not going there, are you?"

"My fwang, I vay soy to tail you zat you ah dhonk as de dev'. I am *shem* of you. I ham ze servan' of ze *publique.* Zese *citoyens* goin' to wickwest Jean Poquelin to give to the Ursuline' two hondred fifty dolla'—"

"*Hé quoi!*" cried a listener, "*Cinq cent piastres, oui!*"

"*Oui!*" said Bienvenu, "and if he wiffuse we make him some lit' *musique;* ta-ra-ta!" He hoisted a merry hand and foot, then frowning, added: "Old Poquelin got no bizniz dhink s'much w'isky."

"But, gentlemen," said little White, around whom a circle had gathered, "the old man is very sick."

"My faith!" cried a tiny Creole, "we did not make him to be sick. W'en we have say we going make *le charivari,* do you want that we hall tell a lie? My faith! 'sfools!"

"But you can shivaree somebody else," said desperate little White.

"*Oui!*" cried Bienvenu, "*et chahivahi* Jean-ah Poqueliı tomo'w!"

"Let us go to Madame Schneider!" cried two or three, and amid huzzas and confused cries, among which was heard a stentorian Celtic call for drinks, the crowd again began to move.

"*Cent piastres pour l'hôpital de charité!*"

"Hurrah!"

"One hondred dolla' for Charity Hospital!"

"Hurrah!"

"Whang!" went a tin pan, the crowd yelled, and pandemonium gaped again. They were off at a right angle.

Nodding, Mrs. White looked at the mantle-clock.

"Well, if it isn't away after midnight."

The hideous noise down street was passing beyond earshot. She raised a sash and listened. For a moment there was silence. Some one came to the door.

"Is that you, White?"

"Yes." He entered. "I succeeded, Patty,"

"Did you?" said Patty, joyfully.

"Yes. They've gone down to shivaree the old Dutch-woman who married her step-daughter's sweetheart. They say she has got to pay a hundred dollars to the hospital before they stop."

The couple retired, and Mrs. White slumbered. She was awakened by her husband snapping the lid of his watch.

"What time?" she asked.

"Half-past three. Patty, I haven't slept a wink. Those fellows are out yet. Don't you hear them?"

"Why, White, they're coming this way!"

"I know they are," said White, sliding out of bed and drawing on his clothes, "and they're coming fast. You'd better go away from that window, Patty. My! what a clatter!"

"Here they are," said Mrs. White, but her husband was gone. Two or three hundred men and boys passed the place at a rapid walk straight down the broad, new street, toward the hated house of ghosts. The din was terrific. She saw little White at the head of the rabble brandishing his arms and trying in vain to make himself heard; but they only shook their heads laughing and hooting the louder, and so passed, bearing him on before them.

Swiftly they pass out from among the houses, away from the dim oil lamps of the street, out into the broad starlit commons, and enter the willowy jungles of the haunted ground. Some hearts fail and their owners lag behind and turn back, suddenly remembering how near morning it is. But the most part push on, tearing the air with their clamor.

Down ahead of them in the long, thicket-darkened way

there is—singularly enough—a faint, dancing light. It must be very near the old house; it is. It has stopped now. It is a lantern, and is under a well-known sapling which has grown up on the wayside since the canal was filled. Now it swings mysteriously to and fro. A goodly number of the more ghost-fearing give up the sport; but a full hundred move onward at a run, doubling their devlish howling and banging.

Yes; it is a lantern, and there are two persons under the tree. The crowd draws near—drops into a walk; one of the two is the old African mute; he lifts the lantern up so that it shines on the other; the crowd recoils; there is a hush of all clangor, and all at once, with a cry of mingled fright and horror from every throat, the whole throng rushes back, dropping everything, sweeping past little White and hurrying on, never stopping until the jungle is left behind, and then to find that not one in ten has seen the cause of the stampede, and not one of the tenth is certain what it was.

There is one huge fellow among them who looks capable of any villany. He finds something to mount on, and, in the Creole *patois*, calls a general halt. Bienvenu sinks down, and, vainly trying to recline gracefully, resigns the leadership. The herd gather round the speaker; he assures them that they have been outraged. Their right peaceably to traverse the public streets has been trampled upon. Shall such encroachments be endured? It is now daybreak. Let them go now by the open light of day and force a free passage of the public highway.

A scattering consent was the response, and the crowd, thinned now and drowsy, straggled quietly down toward the old house. Some drifted ahead, others sauntered behind, but every one, as he again neared the tree, came to a standstill. Little White sat upon a bank of turf on the opposite side of the way looking very stern and sad. To each newcomer he put the same question:

"Did you come here to go to old Poquelin's?"

"Yes."

"He's dead." And if the shocked hearer started away he would say: "Don't go away."

"Why not?"

"I want you to go to the funeral presently."

If some Louisianian, too loyal to dear France or Spain to understand English, looked bewildered, some one would interpret for him; and presently they went. Little White led the van, the crowd trooping after him down the middle of the way. The gate, that had never been seen before unchained, was open. Stern little White stopped a short distance from it; the rabble stopped behind him. Something was moving out from under the veranda. The many whisperers stretched upward to see. The African mute came very slowly toward the gate, leading by a cord in the nose a small brown bull, which was harnessed to a rude cart. On the flat body of the cart, under a black cloth, were seen the outlines of a long box.

"Hats off, gentlemen," said White, as the box came in view, and the crowd solemnly uncovered.

"Gentlemen," said little White, "here comes the last remains of Jean Marie Poquelin, a better man, I'm afraid, with all his sins,—yes a better, a kinder man to his blood, a man of more self-forgetful goodness—than all of you put together will ever dare to be."

There was a profund hush as the vehicle came creaking through the gate; but when it turned away from them toward the forest, those in front started suddenly. There was a backward rush, then all stood still again staring one way; for there, behind the bier, with eyes cast down and labored step, walked the living remains—all that was left—of little Jacques Poquelin, the long-hidden brother—a leper, as white as snow.

Dumb with horror, the cringing crowd gazed upon the walking death. They watched, in silent awe, the slow *cortége* creep down the long, straight road and lessen on the view, until by and by it stopped where a wild, unfrequented path branched off into the undergrowth toward the rear of the ancient city.

"They are going to the *Terre aux Lépreux*," said one in in the crowd. The rest watched them in silence.

The little bull was set free; the mute, with the strength of an ape, lifted the long box to his shoulder. For a moment more the mute and the leper stood in sight, while the former adjusted his heavy burden; then, without one backward glance upon the unkind human world, turning their faces toward the ridge in the depths of the swamp known as the Leper's Land, they stepped into the jungle, disappeared, and were never seen again.

BRER RABBIT, BRER FOX, AND THE TAR BABY

By Joel Chandler Harris

YESTERDAY the lady whom Uncle Remus calls "Miss Sally" missed her little six-year-old. Making search for him through the house, she heard the sound of voices on the back piazza, and, looking through the window, saw the child sitting by Uncle Remus. His head rested against the old man's arm, and he was gazing with an expression of the most intense interest into the rough, weather-beaten face, that beamed so kindly upon him. This is what "Miss Sally" heard:

"Bimeby, one day, arter Mr. Fox bin doin' all dat he could fer ter ketch Mr. Rabbit, an' Mr. Rabbit bin doin' all he could fer to keep 'im fum it, Mr. Fox say to hisse'f dat he'd put up a game on Mr. Rabbit, an' he hadn't mo'n got de wuds out'n his mouf twell Mr. Rabbit come a lopin' up de big road lookin' ez plump, an' ez fat, an' ez sassy ez a Morgan hoss in a barley-patch.

" 'Hol' on dar, Brer Rabbit,' sez Mr. Fox, sezee.

" 'I ain't got time, Brer Fox,' sez Mr. Rabbit, sezee, sorter mendin' his licks.

" 'But I wanter have some confab wid you, Brer Rabbit,' sezee.

" 'All right, Brer Fox, but you better holler fum whar you stan'. I'm monst'us full uv fleas dis mawnin',' sezee.

" 'I seed Brer B'ar yistiddy,' sez Mr. Fox, sezee, 'en he sorter raked me over de coals kaze you an' me didn't make frens an' live naberly, an' I tole 'im dat I'd see you.'

"Den Mr. Rabbit scratch one year wid his off hinefoot sorter jub'usly, an' den he ups an' sez, sezee:

" 'All a settin', Brer Fox. Spose'n you drap roun' ter-morrer an' take dinner wid me. We ain't got no great doin's

413

at our house, but I speck de old 'oman an' de chilluns kin sorter scramble roun' an' git up sump'n fer ter stay yo' stummuck.'

" 'I'm 'gree'ble, Brer Rabbit,' sez Mr. Fox, sezee.

" 'Den I'll 'pen' on you,' sez Mr. Rabbit, sezee.

" Nex' day, Mr. Rabbit an' Miss Rabbit got up soon, 'fo day, an' raided on a gyarden like Miss Sally's out dar, an' got some cabbage, an' some roas'n years, an' some sparrergrass, an' dey fixed up a smashin' dinner. Bimeby one er de little Rabbits, playing out in de back-yard, come runnin' in hollerin', 'Oh, ma! oh, ma! I seed Mr. Fox a comin'!' An' den Mr. Rabbit he tuck de chilluns by dere years an' made um set down, an' den him and Miss Rabbit sorter dallied roun' waitin' for Mr. Fox. An' dey kep' on waitin', but no Mr. Fox. Arter 'while Mr. Rabbit goes to de do', easy like, an' peep out, an' dar, stickin' out fum behime de cornder, wuz de tip eend uv Brer Fox's tail. Den Mr. Rabbit shot de do' an' sot down, an' put his paws behine his years an' begin for ter sing:

> " 'De place wharbouts you spill de grease,
>   Right dar youer boun' ter slide,
> An' whar you fine a bunch uv ha'r,
>   You'll sholy fine de hide."

"Nex' day, Brer Fox sont word by Mr. Mink an' skuse hisse'f kaze he wuz too sick fer ter come, an' he ax Mr. Rabbit fer to come an' eat dinner wid him, an' Mr. Rabbit say he wuz 'gree'ble.

"Bimeby, when de shadders wuz at dere shortes', Mr. Rabbit he sorter bresh up an' santer down unto Mr. Fox's house, an' when he got dar, he hear somebody groanin', an' he look in de door an' dar he see Mr. Fox settin' up in a rockin' cheer all wrapped up wid flannels, an' he look mighty weak. Mr. Rabbit look all 'roun', but he don't see no dinner De dish-pan was settin' on de table, an' close by wuz a kyarvin' knife.

" 'Look like you gwineter have chicken fer dinner, Brer Fox,' sez Mr. Rabbit, sezee.

" 'Yes, Brer Rabbit, deyer nice, an' fresh, an' tender,' sez Brer Fox, sezee.

"Den Mr. Rabbit sorter pull his mustash an' sez: 'You ain't got no calamus root, is you, Brer Fox? I got so now that I can't eat no chicken 'cept she's seasoned up wid calamus root.' An' wid dat Mr. Rabbit lipt out er de do' and dodged 'mong de bushes, an' sot dar watchin' fer Mr. Fox; an' he didn't watch long, nudder, kaze Mr. Fox flung off de flannels an' crope out er de house an' got whar he could close in on Mr. Rabbit, an' bimeby Mr. Rabbit hollered out: 'Oh, Brer Fox! I'll put yo' calamus root out here on dis stump. Better come git it while hit's fresh,' and wid dat Mr. Rabbit galloped off home. An' Mr. Fox ain't never cotch 'im yet; an' w'at's more, honey, he ain't gwineter."

"Didn't the fox *never* catch the rabbit, Uncle Remus?" asked the little boy to whom the old man delights to relate his stories.

"He come mighty nigh it, honey, sho's you bawn—Brer Fox did. One day atter Brer Rabbit fool 'im wid dat calamus root, Brer Fox went ter wuk en got 'im some tar, en mixt it wid some turkentime, en fixt up a contrapshun dat he call a Tar Baby, en he tuck dish yer Tar Baby en sot 'er in de big road, den he laid off in de bushes fer to see wat de news wuz gwine to be. En he didn't hatter wait long, nudder, case bimeby here come Brer Rabbit pacin' down de road—lippity-clippity, clippity-lippity—des ez sassy ez a hotel nigger. Brer Fox, he lay low. Brer Rabbit come prancin' 'long twell he spied de Tar Baby, en den he fotch up on his behime legs like he wuz 'stonished. De Tar Baby, he sot dar, en Brer Fox, he lay low.

" 'Mawnin'!' sez Brer Rabbit, sezee. 'Nice wedder dis mawnin',' sezee.

"Tar Baby ain't sayin' nothin', en Brer Fox, he lay low.

" 'How duz yo' sym'tums seem ter segashuate?' sez Brer Rabbit, sezee.

"Brer Fox, he wink his eye slow, en lay low, en de Tar Baby, he ain't saying nuthin'.

" 'How you come on, den? Is you deaf?' sez Brer Rabbit, sezee. 'Caze if you is, I kin holler louder,' sezee.

"Tar Baby lay quiet, en Brer Fox he lay low.

" 'Youer stuck up, dat's w'at you is,' says Brer Rabbit,

sezee, 'en I'm gwine to kyore you, dat's w'at I'm agwineter do,' sezee.

"Brer Fox he sorter chuckle in his stummuck, but Tar Baby ain't sayin' nothin'.

"'I'm gwineter larn you howter talk ter 'spectable people ef hit's de las' ack,' sez Brer Rabbit, sezee. 'Ef you don't take off dat hat en tell me howdy, I'm gwineter bus' you wide open,' sezee.

"Tar Baby stay still, en Brer Fox he lay low.

"Brer Rabbit keep on axin' 'im, en de Tar Baby keep on sayin' nothin', twell present'y Brer Rabbit drew back wid his fis', en blip he tuck him side er de head. Right dar's whar he broke his molasses jug. His fis' stuck, en he couldn't pull loose. De tar hilt 'im.

"'If you don't lemme loose, I'll hit you agin,' sez Brer Rabbit, sezee, en wid dat he fotch him a wipe wid de udder han', en dat stuck. Brer Fox he lay low.

"'Turn me loose, fo' I kick de natal stuffin' outen you,' sez Brer Rabbit, sezee; but de Tar Baby hilt on, en den Brer Rabbit lose de use un his feet in de same way. Brer Fox, he lay low. Den Brer Rabbit squalled out dat ef de Tar Baby didn't turn 'im loose he'd butt him cranksided. En he butted, en his head got fastened. Den Brer Fox, he sa'ntered fort', lookin' des ez innercent ez wunner yo' mammy's mockin' birds.

"'Howdy, Brer Rabbit,' sez Brer Fox, sezee. 'You look sorter stuck up dis mawnin',' sezee, en den he rolled on de groun' en laft en laft twell he couldn't laugh no mo'. 'I speck you'll take dinner wid me dis time, Brer Rabbit. I done laid in some calamus root, en I ain't gwinter take no skuse,' sez Brer Fox, sezee."

Here Uncle Remus paused, and drew a two-pound yam out of the ashes.

"Did the fox eat the rabbit?" asked the little boy to whom the story had been told.

"Dat's all de fur de tale goes," replied the old man. "He mout, en den again he moutent. Some say Jedge B'ar come 'long en loosed 'im—some say he didn't. I hear Miss Sally callin'. You better run 'long."

BIOGRAPHY AND BIBLIOGRAPHY

ADE, GEORGE *(1866-   )*, was born in Kentland, Indiana. He is a graduate of Purdue University, of which he became later a trustee. His first newspaper work was done in Lafayette, Indiana. In 1890 he went to Chicago, where he was a reporter and special writer for *The Chicago Daily News* until 1900. He has taken an active interest in politics and was a delegate to the Republican National Convention in 1908. He now resides on a farm in Indiana. He is unmarried. He is a member of the National Institute of Arts and Letters.

Artie, A Story of the Streets and Town (1896); Pink Marsh, A Story of the Streets and Town (1897); Doc Horne (1898); Fables in Slang (1899); More Fables (1900); Forty Modern Fables (1901); The Girl Proposition, A Bunch of He and She Fables (1902); People You Know (1903); Breaking Into Society (1903); Circus Day (1903); True Bells (1904); In Pastures New (1906); The Slim Princess (1907); Knocking the Neighbors (1912); In Babel, Stories of Chicago (1912); Ade's Fables (1914); Hand-made Fables (1920).
Operas and Plays: The Sultan of Sulu (1902); The County Chairman (1903); Peggy from Paris (1903); Sho-gun (1904); The College Widow (1904); The Bad Samaritan (1905); Just Out of College (1905); Marse Covington (1906); Mrs. Peekham's Carouse (1906); Father and the Boys (1907); The Fair Co-ed (1908); The Old Town (1909); Nettie (1914).

ALDRICH, THOMAS BAILEY *(1836-1907)*, was born in Portsmouth, New Hampshire, of colonial ancestry. He was taken to New Orleans to live until he was nine. While he was preparing for college his father died and he went to New York to work in his uncle's counting-room from 1852-1855. During this time he wrote a little verse. He secured a position as proof-reader for a publisher and later became a reader. He contributed to magazines—among them *Putnam's, The Knickerbocker,* and *The Evening Mirror.* He was on the staff of *The New York Home Journal.* During the Civil War he was a war correspondent for *The Tribune.* In 1865 he was married; his only children were two sons, twins. From 1881-1890 he was editor of *The Atlantic Monthly.* After retiring from this position he continued to live in Boston until his death.

Daisy's Necklace (1856); Out of His Head, A Romance In

Prose (1862); The Story of a Bad Boy (1870); Marjorie Daw and Other People (1873); Prudence Palfrey, a Novel (1874); The Queen of Sheba (1877); The Stillwater Tragedy (1880); From Ponkapog to Pesth (1883); Merceded (1883); Pauline Pavlovna, A Drama in One Act; An Old Town by the Sea (1893); Two Bites at a Cherry and Other Tales (1894); Judith and Holofernes, A Poem (1896); Poems, in 2 vols. (1901); Ponkapog Papers (1903); A Sea Turn and Other Matters; The Sister's Tragedy.

BIERCE, AMBROSE *(1842-?),* was born in Mieggs County, Ohio. His father was a farmer. He served throughout the Civil War and was brevetted major for distinguished service. In 1866 he edited *The News Letter,* San Francisco. He spent several years in London, where he was associated with *London Fun* and edited a paper called *The Lantern,* which was financed by the ex-Empress Eugenie of France. In 1876 he returned to California. He edited successively *The Argonaut* and *The Wasp* and contributed to *The Examiner* and *The Overland Monthly.* He made daring and bitter personal attacks in his writings. In the eighties he wrote many short stories, a great number of which were ghost stories. He lived for several years in Washington, D. C. In 1914 he went to Mexico to fight with Villa and has never been heard from since.

An edition of his collected works has been published by the Neale Publishing Co.

In the Midst of Life, Stories of Soldiers and Civilians (1891); The Monk and the Hangman's Daughter (1892); Black Beetles in Amber (Poems) (1892); Can Such Things Be? (1894); Fantastic Fables (1899); Shapes of Clay (Verse) (1903); The Cynic's Word Book (1906); The Shadow on the Dial (1909); Write it Right (1909); V. 1, Ashes of the Beacon, The Land Beyond the Blow, For the Ahkoond, John Smith, Liberator, Bits of Autobiography; V. 7, The Devil's Dictionary; V. 8, Negligible Tales; V. 9, Tangential Views; V. 10, The Opinionator, The Reviewer, The Controversialist, The Timorous Reporter, The March Hare; V. 11, Antepenultimate; V. 12, In Motley: Wings of Beasts.

BROWN, ALICE *(1857-),* was born at Hampton Falls, New Hampshire, of a family of farmers. She was educated in the little district school near her father's farm and later at a seminary in Exeter. She taught school for several years— in the country and in Boston—hating it every minute. She gave up this profession for writing, which she had always wished to do. Her first contributions were to *The Christian Register* and *The Youth's Companion.* Many of her stories have appeared in *The Atlantic* and in *Harper's*. In 1915 her play—*Children of Earth*—received the $10,000 prize offered by Winthrop Ames. Miss Brown now lives on her farm in New Hampshire.

Meadow-grass, Tales of New England Life (1895); The Rose of Hope (1896); The Day of His Youth (1897); Tiverton Tales (1899); King's End (1901); Margaret Warrener (1901); The County Road (1906); The Court of Love (1906); High Noon (1906); Life of Mercy Otis Warren (1906); Paradise (1906); The Mannerings (1906); Rose MacLeod (1908); The Story of Thyrza (1909); Country Neighbors (1910); John Winterbourne's Family (1910); The One-Footed Fairy (1911); My Love and I (1912); The Secret of the Clan (1912); Robin Hood's Barn (1913); Vanishing Points (1913); Joint Owners in Spain, A Comedy in One Act (1914); Children of Earth, A Play of New England (1915); The Prisoner (1916); Bromley Neighborhood (1917); The Road to Castaly and Later Poems (1917); The Flying Teuton and Other Stories (1918); By Oak and Thorn (English Travels); Fools of Nature; Robert Louis Stevenson (with Louise Imogen Guiney).

CABLE, GEORGE WASHINGTON *(1844-   )*, was born in New Orleans, where the scene of many of his stories is laid. He was educated in the public schools. He has received honorary degrees from Yale, Bowdoin, Washington and Lee. During the Civil War he served in a cavalry troop for the Confederacy. After the war he became a reporter on *The New Orleans Picayune* and remained with the paper until 1879. He was the founder of the Home Culture Clubs, now known as the Northampton People's Institute, designed as a means of self-education for working people. He has both lectured and written for these clubs. He is a member of the Simplified Spelling Board and the American Academy of Arts and Letters. Since 1886 he has lived at Northampton, Massachusetts. Many of his stories have been contributed to *Scribner's*.

Old Creole Days (1879); The Grandissimes (1880); Madame Delphine (1881); Social Statistics of Cities, History and Present Conditions of New Orleans and Report on the City of Austin, Texas (1881); The Creoles of Louisiana (1884); Dr. Sevier (1884); Professional Christianity (1885); The Silent South (1885); Bonaventure (1888); Strange True Stories of Louisiana (1889); The Negro Question (1890); John Marsh, Southerner (1894); Famous Adventures and Prison Escapes of the Civil War (G. W. Cable and other authors) (1896); Strong Hearts (1899); The Cavalier (1901); Bylow Hill (1902); Kincaid's Battery (1908); Posson Jone and Père Rapheal (1909); The Amateur Garden (1914); Gideon's Band (1914).

DREISER, THEODORE *(1871-   )*, was born in Terre Haute, Indiana; educated in the public schools and Indiana University. He first wrote for newspapers. Going to Chicago in 1892, he wrote for *The Chicago Daily Globe.* He was editor of *Every Month* (a literary and musical magazine) from 1895-8. Later he became a special magazine writer, contributing to *Harper's, McClure's, Century, Cosmopolitan,* and *Munsey's.* In 1905-6 he was editor of *Smith's Magazine;* in 1906-7 of *The Broadway Magazine;* 1907-10 editor-in-chief of the Butterick publications, including *The Delineator, Designer, New Idea,* and *English Delineator.*

Sister Carrie (1900); Jennie Gerhardt, A Novel (1911); The Financier, A Novel (1912); A Traveller at Forty (1913); The Titan (1914); The "Genius" (1915); Plays of the Natural and Supernatural (The Girl in the Coffin, The Blue Sphere, Laughing Gas, In the Dark, The Spring Recital, The Light in the Window, "Old Ragpicker") (1916); A Hoosier Holiday (1916); The Hand of the Potter, A Tragedy (1917); Free and Other Stories (1918); Twelve Men (1919); Hey Rub-a-Dub-Dub (1920); The Bulwark (in preparation).

FREEMAN, MARY E. WILKINS *(1862-   )*, was born at Randolph, Massachusetts. She was educated at Mt. Holyoke Seminary. When she began writing for magazines she had an immediate success. Her first stories and poems were for children. Many of her short stories have appeared first in *Harper's Magazine.* In 1902 she married Dr. Charles M. Freeman of Metuchen, N. J., and has resided there since her marriage.

A Humble Romance and Other Stories (1887); A New England Nun and Other Stories (1891); Young Lucretia (1892); Jane Field (1892); Jiles Corey (1893); Pembroke, A Novel (1894); Madelon (1896); Jerome, a Poor Man (1897); Silence (1898); Evelina's Garden (1899); The Love of Parson Lord (1900); The Heart's Highway (1900); The Portion of Labor (1901); Understudies, Short Stories (1901); Six Trees (1903); The Wind in the Rose Bush (1903); The Givers, Short Stories (1904); Doc Gordon (1906); The People of Our Neighborhood (1906); By the Light of the Soul (1907); The Shoulders of Atlas (1908); The Winning Lady (1909); The Green Door (1910); The Butterfly House (1912); Yates Pride (1912); The Copy-Cat and Other Stories (1914); The Jamesons; The Debtor; The Fair Lavinia.

FULLER, HENRY B. *(1857-   )*, was born in Chicago, of New England parents. His first two books were set in European backgrounds. His third book, *"The Cliff-dwellers,"* deals with conditions in the slums of Chicago.

The Chevalier of Pensiere-Vani (1890); The Chatelaine of La Trinité (1892); The Cliff-Dwellers (1893); With the Procession (1895); The Puppet-Booth, Twelve Plays (1896); From the Other Side: Stories of Transatlantic Travel (1898); The Last Refuge (1900); Under the Skylights (1901); Waldo Trench and Others (1908); Lines, Long and Short—Biographical Sketches in Various Rhymes (1917); On the Stairs (1918); Bertram Cope's Year (1919).

GARLAND, HAMLIN, *(1860-   ),* was born in West Salem, Wisconsin, and was educated in private schools—between school terms he worked on the farm. He lived for a time in Iowa, where the scene of his story, *"Boy Life on the Prairie,"* and other stories is laid. From time to time he taught school. He tramped through the eastern states. He took up a land claim in Dakota, but remained there only a short time, removing to Boston. He studied and taught English and American literature in the Boston School of Oratory. In 1893 he went to Chicago. He was married in 1899 and now lives in New York. He is a member of the American Academy of Arts and Letters.

Main-Travelled Roads (1890); Jason Edwards (1891); A Little Norsk (1891); A Member of the Third House (1892); Prairie Folk (1892); A Spoil of Office (1892); Crumbling Idols (1894); Prairie Songs (1894); Rose of Dutcher's Cooly (1895); Wayside Courtships (1897); The Spirit of Sweet Water (1898); Ulysses S. Grant: His Life and Character (1898); The Eagle's Heart (1900); Her Mountain Lover (1901); The Captain of the Gray Horse Troop (1902); Hesper (1903); Light of the Star (1904); The Tyranny of the Dark (1905); Boy Life on the Prairie (1907); The Long Trail (1907); Money Magic (1907); The Shadow World (1908); Cavanaugh Forest Ranger (1909); Victor Olnee's Discipline (1911); Other Main-Travelled Roads (1913); A Son of the Middle Border (1917).

HALE, EDWARD EVERETT *(1822-1909),* was born in Boston, where he always lived. He was educated in private schools and at Harvard, where he was graduated in 1839. For two years he taught school while reading theses in preparation for becoming a Congregationalist minister. After six years of work he received charge of a church in Worcester. Later he was the minister of the South Congregational (Unitarian) Church of Boston. He was active in organizing societies to broaden the scope of the church. For some time he was the editor of *The Daily Advertiser,* of which he was South American editor. In this work he became an authority on Spanish-

American history. As a boy he had learned to set type in the office of this paper, which was owned by his father, and had also been a reporter on it. Other papers of which he was editor were: *The Christian Examiner, The Sunday School Gazette, Lend a Hand,* and *Old and New.* This last paper ran for only six years after it was founded in 1869, and then merged into *Scribner's* monthly. His first published story was *"My Double and How He Undid Me,"* which appeared in *The Atlantic* in 1859.

Collected works published by Little, Brown & Company.

The Rosary (1848); Margaret Percival in America (1850); Sketches of Christian History (1850); Letters on Irish Emigration (1852); Kansas and Nebraska (1854); Ninety Days Worth of Europe (1861); The Man Without a Country (1863); The President's Words (with Rev. John Williams) (1865); If, Yes and Perhaps (1868); Puritan Politics in England and New England (1869); The Ingham Papers (1869); How To Do It (1870); His Level Best and Other Stories (1870); Daily Bread and Other Stories (1870); Ups and Downs, An Every Day Novel (1871); Sybaris, and Other Homes (1871); Christmas Eve and Christmas Day (1874); In His Name (1874); A Summer's Vacation: Four Sermons (1874); Workingmen's Homes, Essays and Stories (1874); The Good Time Coming or Our New Crusade (1875); One Hundred Years (1875); Philip Nolan's Friends (1876); Back to Back (1877); Gone to Texas, or the Wonderful Adventures of a Pullman (1877); What Career? (1878); Mrs. Merriam's Scholars (1878); The Life in Common (1879); The Bible and Its Revision (1879); The Kingdom of God (1880); Crusoe in New York (1880); Stories of War (1880); June to May (1881); Stories of the Sea (1881); Stories of Adventure (1881); Stories of Discovery (1883); Seven Spanish Cities (1883); Fortunes of Rachel (1884); Christmas in a Palace (1884); Christmas at Narragansett (1884); Stories of Invention (1885); Easter (1886); Franklin in France (1887); The Life of Washington (1887); The History of the United States; Poems; The Story of Massachusetts; If Jesus Came to Boston; James Russell Lowell and His Friends; Ralph Waldo Emerson; Historic Boston and Its Neighborhood; The Foundations of the Republic; Curtis, Whittier, and Longfellow; Tarry at Home Travels; Tom Torrey's Tariff Talks; We, the People: a Series of Papers on Topics of To-day (1903).
Contributions to: Proceedings of the American Antiquarian Society; The American Peace Society, Boston; The American Unitarian Association.

HARRIS, JOEL CHANDLER *(1848-1908),* was born in Eatonton, Georgia. When he was twelve years old he became a printer's boy. His employer, who owned a fine library, permitted him to read what he wished in it. The boy saw much of the negroes on the estate of the editor and owner of the paper, talked to them, and listened to their tales. In 1864 his employer fled from the invasion of Sherman's army, leaving Harris, sixteen years old, in charge of the paper, *The Countryman*. He, however, soon decided to move to the city; he wrote for papers in Macon and Forsyth, Georgia, in New Orleans, and in Savannah. In Savannah he was on the staff of *The Daily News* until he was made editor of *The Atlanta Constitution*, in 1876, where he remained for twenty-five years. He began writing his negro stories for that paper. Toward the end of his life he edited a magazine which he called *Uncle Remus' Home Magazine*. He was married in 1873 to Miss LaRue of Canada.

Uncle Remus: His Songs and Sayings (1880); Nights with Uncle Remus (1883); Mingo and Other Sketches in Black and White (1884); Free Jo and Other Georgian Sketches (1887); Balaam and His Master and Other Sketches and Stories (1891); Uncle Remus and His Friends (1892); Little Mr. Thimble Finger and His Queer Country (1894); Daddy Jake, the Runaway, and Short Stories Told After Dark (1896); Georgia from the Invasion of De Soto to Recent Times (1896); Stories of Georgia (1896); On the Plantation, a Story of a Georgia Boy's Adventures During the War (1897); Aaron in the Wild Woods (1897); Tales of the Home Folks in Peace and War (1898); The Chronicles of Aunt Minervy Anne (1899); Plantation Pageants (1899); The Tar Baby and Other Rhymes of Uncle Remus (1904); Told by Uncle Remus—New Stories of the Old Plantation (1906).

HARTE, FRANCIS BRET *(1839-1902)*, was born in Albany, New York. His father was a school teacher. He was educated in the public schools. When he was fifteen he went to California, where he lived in remote mountain settlements. He started a school, but it was a failure. He became a compositor at Eureka. He was a miner, and for a time an express messenger. In 1857 he went to San Francisco to work as a compositor. While engaged in this work the attention of the editor of the paper for which he worked was attracted by some of his sketches and he printed some of them. Harte was appointed secretary of the U. S. Mint in San Francisco, and while holding this position wrote stories, sketches and poems. In 1868 he was made the first editor of *The Overland Monthly*. His first contribution was *"The Luck of Roaring Camp,"* of which the other editors of the magazine staff disapproved. He insisted that it be published—immediately it attracted much attention throughout the country. In 1870 he was appointed professor of literature in the University of California, but he held the position for one year only before moving to New York. He contributed regularly to *The Atlantic Monthly*. In the early eighties he entered the consular service; he was stationed for two years in Germany, and for five years at Glasgow, Scotland.

His complete works are published by Houghton, Mifflin & Co.

Condensed Novels (1867); Poems (1870); The Luck of Roaring Camp and Other Sketches (1871); East and West Poems (1871); Poetical Works (1873); Mrs. Skagg's Husbands (1873); Echoes of the Foot Hills (1874); Tales of the Argonauts (1875); Two Men of Sandy Bar (1876); Thankful Blossom (1876); The Story of a Mine (1877); Drift from Two Shores (1878); The Twins of Table Mountain (1879); Flip, and Found at Blazing Star (1882); In the Carquinez Woods (1883); On the Frontier (1884); By Shore and Sedge (1885); Maruja, a Novel (1885); Snowbound at Eagle's (1886); A Millionaire of Rough and Ready (1887); The Queen of the Pirate Isle (1887); The Argonauts of North Liberty (1888); A Phyllis of the Sierras (1888); Cressy (1889); The Heritage of Dedlow Marsh (1889); A Waif of the Plains (1890); Condensed Novels (1902).

JAMES, HENRY *(1843-1916),* was born in New York City. His father was a well-known theological writer of the Swedenborgian sect. Henry James was educated for the most part in Europe—in Geneva, Paris, Boulogne-sur-mer. He studied law at the Harvard Law School. After 1869 he made his home in England with the exception of the years 1874-5, when he was a member of the editorial staff of *The Atlantic Monthly,* to which he contributed many of his short stories. A large number of his novels appeared first in serial form in *Harper's, The Atlantic, Cornhill Magazine* (English).

Poor Richard (1867); Gabrielle de Bergerac (1869); Watch and Ward (1871); Roderick Hudson (1871); Trans-Atlantic Sketches (1875); A Passionate Pilgrim and Other Stories (1875); The American (1878); Daisy Miller (1878); An International Episode (1878); The Europeans (1878); Pension Beaurepas (1878); French Poets and Novelists (1878); Hawthorne, in English Men of Letters Series; Confidance (1879); Washington Square (1880); A Bundle of Letters (1880); Diary of a Man of Fifty (1880); The Portrait of a Lady (1881); The Siege of London (1883); Portraits of Places (1884); A Little Tour in France (1884); Tales of Three Cities (1884); The Author of Beltraffio (1885); The Bostonians (1886); Princess Casamassima (1881); Partial Portraits (1888); The Reverberator (1888); A London Life (1889); The Tragic Muse (1890);

Theatricals—Two Comedies—Tenants Disengaged (1894); Terminations (1896); The Spoils of Poynton (1897); The Other House (1897); What Maysie Knew (1897); In the Cage (1898); The Two Magics (1898); The Awkward Age (1899); The Soft Side (1900); The Sacred Fount (1901); The Wings of a Dove (1902); The Better Sort (1903); The Question of Our Speech and the Lesson of Balzac: Two Lectures (1905); The American Scene (1906); Views and Reviews (1908); Italian Hours (1909); Julia Bride (1909); The Finer Grain (1910); The Outcry (1911); A Small Boy and Others (1913); Notes on Novelists with Some Other Notes (1914); Within the Rim and Other Essays (1914); Notes of a Son and Brother (1914); The Question of the Mind (1915); The Ivory Tower (Unfinished 1918); The Sense of the Past (Unfinished 1918); Travelling Companions (1919); A Landscape Painter (1919); The Golden Bowl.

Other short stories reprinted in collected works edited by Chas. Scribner's Sons: including The Turn of the Screw; The Madonna of the Future.

JEWETT, SARAH ORNE *(1849-1909),* was born in South Berwick, Maine, of New England ancestry. Her father was a country doctor, and in making his professional calls he frequently took his daughter with him. In that way she became acquainted with many New England types of whom she wrote.

Deephaven (1877); Country Byways (1881); A Marsh Island (1885); A White Heron and Other Stories (1886); The King of Folly Island and Other People (1888); Strangers and Wayfarers (1890); Tales of New England (1892); A Native of Wimby and Other Tales (1893); The Country of the Pointed Firs (1896); The Normans (1901); Play Days, a Book of Stories for Children (1906); Letters of Sarah Orme Jewett (edited by A. Fields) (1911).

GILMAN, CHARLOTTE PERKINS (STETSON) *(1860-),* was born in Hartford, Connecticut, a descendant of Lyman Beecher. She has been twice married, first in 1884 to C. W. Stetson, and second in 1900 to George H. Gilman of New York. In 1890 she became a lecturer on ethics, economics, and sociology and spoke throughout this country and abroad. She also contributed to magazines. She is chiefly interested in labor problems and the advance of women. In 1909 she founded *The Forerunner,* of which she was the editor until it was discontinued. She is a member of the American Academy of Political and Social Science, and the American Sociological Association.

Woman and Economics (1898); In This Our World, and

Other Poems (1898); The Yellow Wall-Paper (1899); Concerning Children (1900); The Home: Its Work and Influence (1903); Human Work (1904); The Man-Made World, or Our Androcentric Culture (1910); What Diantha Did, a Novel (1910); The Crux (1911); Moving the Mountain (1911); also pamphlets on the woman question published by the National American Woman Suffrage Association.

SPOFFORD, HARRIET PRESCOTT *(1835-)*, was born in Maine, but moved to Massachusetts when a child and went to school in Newburyport, where she lived. Her first story attracted much attention when it appeared in *The Atlantic Monthly*. It was a tale of Paris, although the young authoress had never been outside of New England. The editor suspected it of being a translation but was reassured of its genuineness by Mr. T. W. Higginson, at that time pastor of the church Miss Prescott attended. In 1865 Miss Prescott married Mr. Spofford, a prominent lawyer of Boston. She has lived in Boston since her marriage.

Sir Rohan's Ghost, a Romance (1860); New England Legends (1871); The Thief in the Night (1872); Art Decoration Applied to Furniture (1878); Azarian, an Episode (1881); A Master Spirit (1896); In Titian's Garden and Other Poems (1897); Old Madame and Other Tragedies (1900); The Children of the Valley (1901); The Great Procession (1902); Four Days of God (1905); Old Washington (1906); A Fairy Changeling (1910); The Making of a Fortune (1911); The King's Easter (1912); A Little Book of Friends (1916); The Marquis of Carabas; A Lost Jewel; Hester Stanley at St. Mark's; Hester Stanley's Friends; The Scarlet Poppy; House and Hearth; The Servant Girl Question; Ballads About Authors; The Amber Gods; A Master Spirit; An Inheritance; The Maid He Married; Priscilla's Love Story.

STOCKTON, FRANK R. *(1834-1902)*, was born in Philadelphia, Pennsylvania, and educated there in the public school and high school. He first worked as a wood-engraver, illustrating and later writing children's stories. He contributed to *The Philadelphia Post, N. Y. Hearth and Home, Scribner's,* and *St. Nicholas* and was on the staff of the last three at different times. While doing editorial work he wrote children's stories. *"The Lady or the Tiger?"* was written for a literary society, and later published. He and his wife lived in New Jersey until he bought an estate in West Virginia.

Collected works in 23 volumes, published by Chas. Scribner's Sons, N. Y.: v. 1, The Late Mrs. Null (1886); v. 2, The Squirrel Inn. The Merry Chanter (1890); v. 3, Rudder Grange (1879);

v. 4, The Hundredth Man (1887); v. 5, Ardis Claverden (1890);
v. 6, Dusky Philosophy. The Great War Syndicate. The Knife
That Killed Po Hanay. The Stories of the Three Burglars
(1889); v. 7, The House of Martha (1891); v. 8, Euphemia
Among the Pelicans. Pomona's Daughter. Pomona's Travels.
The Rudder Grangers in England (1891); v. 9, The Adventures
of Captain Horn (1895); v. 10, Mrs. Cliff's Yacht (1897); v.
11, The Great Storm of Sardes. The Watch Devil; v. 12. The
Girl of Cobhurst (1898); v. 13. The Casting Away of Mrs.
Lecks and Mrs. Aleshim. The Vizier of the Two Horned Alex-
ander; v. 14. The Associate Hermits; v. 15. The Baker of
Bambury. A Borrowed Month. Derelict. The Discourager of
Hesitancy. Every Man His Own Letter-Writer. The Lady or
the Tiger? On the Training of Parents. Our Story. The
Spectral Mortgage. That Same Old Cover. The Transformed
Ghost. The Watch-Maker's Wife; v. 16. As One Woman to
Another. Asaph. The Cloverfield's Carriage. My Bull Calf.
My Terminal Moraine. Our Fire-Screen. Plain Fishing. The
Remarkable Wreck of the "Thomas Hyke." The Story of As-
sisted Fate. A Tale of Negative Gravity. An Unhistoric Page;
v. 17. Amos Kilbright, His Adscititious Experiences. The
Banished King. The Battle of the Third Cousins. The Bee-
man of Orne. The Bishop's Ghost and the Printer's Baby.
Christmas Before Last. The Christmas Shadrach. The Clocks
of Rondaine. The Griffin and the Minor Canon. Old Pipes
and the Driad. The Philopena. The Philosophy of Relative
Existences. Prince Hassak's March. The Queen's Museum;
v. 18. Captain Eli's Best Ear. The Christmas Wreck. "His
Wife's Deceased Sister." Love Before Breakfast. The Magic
Egg. Mr. Tolmon. My Unwilling Neighbor. My Will and
What Came of It. Our Archery Club. A Piece of Red Calico.
The Staying Power of Sir Rohan. The Widow's Cruise; v. 19.
Afield and Afloat. "Come in New Year." The Ghosts in My
Tower. The Governor General. The Great Staircase at Lan-
dover Hall. The Landsman's Tale. Old Applejoy's Ghost.
The Romance of a Mule-car. A Sailor's Knot. The Skipper
and El Capitan. Struck by a Boomerang; v. 21. John Gay-
ther's Garden; v. 22. The Captain's Toll-Gate; v. 23. A Bicycle
of Cathay, Also a Bibliography and Biography.
    Stories of New Jersey (1896); Buccaneers and Pirates of Our
Coasts (1898).

STODDARD, CHARLES WARREN *(1843-1909),* was born
in Rochester, N. Y.; educated in the public schools there and
in California, and at the University of California. Ill health
prevented his graduation from the university. He later received
the degrees of L.H.D. from the Catholic University of America,
and Ph.D. from Santa Clara College, California. For seven
years he was travelling correspondent of *The San Francisco*

Chronicle. He spent five years in the South Seas. He was professor of English Literature in the University of Notre Dame, Indiana, from 1885-7. After 1889 he held the same chair in the Catholic University of America.

Poems (1867); South Sea Idyls (1873); Marshallah, a Flight Into Egypt (1881); The Lepers of Molokai (1885); A Troubled Heart (1885); Lazy Letters From Low Latitudes (1894); The Wonder Worker of Padua (1896); A Trip to Hawaii (1897); A Cruise Under the Crescent from Suez to San Marco (1898); Over the Rocky Mountains to Alaska; In the Footprints of the Padres (1902); Exits and Entrances, a Book of Essays and Sketches (1903); For the Pleasure of His Company (1903); Father Damien, a Sketch (1903); The Island of Tranquil Delights (1904); Old Mission Idyls (1906); The Confessions of a Reformed Poet (1907); The Dream Lady (1907); Poems (1907).

TRACY, VIRGINIA *(1875-   )*, was born in New York City and educated mainly at a private school in Chicago. She is a member of a stage family and herself became an actress when she was eighteen. She played with Mrs. Carter in *The Heart of Maryland,* and with Robert Mantell. She left the stage after ten years on account of ill health and wrote many short stories dealing with stage life—most of them appearing in *Collier's.*

Her only published books are: They Also Serve (Short Stories) (1908); Merely Players (Short Stories) (1909); Persons Unknown (Detective Story) (1914).

TWAIN, MARK (SAMUEL L. CLEMENS) *(1835-1910)*, was born in Florida, Missouri, whence he moved to Hannibal, where he went to school. When he was twelve years old his father died and he went to work as an apprentice in the local newspaper office and remained for three years. He then came east—to New York, Philadelphia, Cincinnati, and back to St. Louis—still doing newspaper work in all these places. He had always longed to become a pilot on a Mississippi River boat, and he now realised his ambition. He continued at this from 1857 until the Civil War, when he entered the Confederate army. His next move was to Nevada, as secretary for his brother. He also worked as a silver miner, but was unsuccessful and went back to newspaper work. Reaching San Francisco, he wrote for *The Morning Call,* took another turn at mining, and then became a lecturer. In 1867 he went to Europe with some friends, and when he returned he wrote *Innocents Abroad,* which had an immediate success. He married in 1870. He purchased *The Buffalo Express* and edited it for a short time, before de-

ciding to settle in Hartford, Connecticut, and devote his time
to writing. His works are translated into most European lan-
guages. He founded a publishing firm of his own, C. L. Webster
& Co., which was a failure and involved him in heavy losses.
His only child was a daughter who survived him.

The Jumping Frog (1867); Innocents Abroad (1869); Autobiography and First Romance (1871); The Gilded Age (with
C. D. Warner) (1873); Roughing It (1872); Sketches, Old and
New (1873); Tom Sawyer (1876); Punch Brother, Punch
(1878); A Tramp Abroad (1880); The Prince and the Pauper
(1880); The Stolen White Elephant (1882); Life on the Mis-
sissippi (1883); The Adventures of Huckleberry Finn (1885);
A Connecticut Yankee in King Arthur's Court (1889); The
American Claimant, etc. (1892); Merry Tales (1892); The
£1,000,000 Bank Note (1893); Pudd'n-head Wilson (1894); Tom
Sawyer Abroad (1894); Joan of Arc (1896); More Tramps
Abroad (1897); Following the Equator (1898); The Man That
Corrupted Hadleyburg (1900); Edmund Burke on Croker and
Tammany (1901); A Double-Barrelled Detective Story (1902);
Articles on Christian Science (1903); A Dog's Tale (1903);
Editorial Wild Oats (1905); King Leopold's Soliloquy (1905);
Eve's Diary (1905); A Horse's Tale (1906); The $30,000 Be-
quest (1906); Christian Science (1907); Extract from Captain
Stormfield's Visit to Heaven (1909); Is Shakespeare Dead?
(1909); The Curious Republic of Gondour and Other Whimsical
Sketches (1919); In Defense of Harriet Shelley and Other
Essays; What Is Man, and Other Essays; The Mysterious
Stranger; Autobiography.

WYATT, EDITH (FRANKLIN) *(1873-   )*, was born in
Tomah, Wisconsin, and educated in the Chicago public schools
and at Bryn Mawr College, which she attended for two years.
She is at present living in Chicago. Among the magazines to
which she has contributed are *The Atlantic, McClure's,* and
The North American Review.

Every One His Own Way (1901); True Love (1903); Making
Both Ends Meet: the Income and Outlay of New York Work-
ing Girls (with S. A. Clark) (1911); Great Companions (Short
Stories and Essays) (1917); The Wind in the Corn and Other
Poems (1917).

WHARTON, EDITH *(1862-   )*, was born in New York
City, a descendant of distinguished Revolutionary ancestors.
She was educated at home. From her youth she was familiar
with the literature of France, Germany, and Italy, and was
most influenced by the writings of Goethe. Among the English
novelists her taste is for George Eliot. In 1885 she married

Edward Wharton, of Boston. She has spent much of her life in Italy. During the war she was most active in relief work in France, and has been decorated by the French government for her services.

The Decoration of Houses (1897); The Greater Inclination (8 Short Stories) (1899); The Touch Stone (1900); Crucial Instances (1901); The Valley of Decision (1902); Sanctuary (1903); The Descent of Man and Other Stories (1904); Italian Villas and Their Gardens (1904); Italian Backgrounds (1905); The House of Mirth (1905); Madame de Treymes (1907); The Fruit of the Tree (1907); The Hermit and the Wild Woman and Other Stories (1908); A Motor Flight Through France (1908); Artemis to Actaeon and Other Verse (1909); Summer, A Novel (1909); The Reef (1912); The Custom of the Country (1913); Ethan Frome (1914); The Book of the Homeless (1915); Fighting France (1915); Xingu and Other Stories (1916); Tales of Men and Ghosts (1917); The Marne (1918); French Ways and Their Meaning; The Joy of Living.

WYNNE, MADELENE YALE *(1847-1913)*, was born in Newport, New York. Besides her interest in writing she devoted much time to artistic work in metals. She studied at the Boston Art Museum and at the Art Students' League in New York. She was president of the Deerfield (Mass.) Arts and Crafts Society. She lived in Chicago.

Her only published book was The Little Room and Other Stories (1895).